A Little Folly

By Jude Morgan and available from Headline Review

The King's Touch
Passion
Indiscretion
Symphony
An Accomplished Woman
The Taste of Sorrow
A Little Folly

A Little Folly

JUDE MORGAN

headline
review

First published in 2010 by HEADLINE REVIEW
An imprint of HEADLINE PUBLISHING GROUP

1

Cataloguing in Publication Data is available from the British Library

ISBN 978 0 7553 0766 1 (Hardback)
ISBN 978 0 7553 5961 5 (Trade paperback)

Typeset in Bembo by Palimpsest Book Production Ltd, Grangemouth, Stirlingshire

Printed and bound in Great Britain by
Clays Ltd, St Ives plc

Headline's policy is to use papers that are natural, renewable and recyclable products and made from wood grown in sustainable forests. The logging and manufacturing processes are expected to conform to the environmental regulations of the country of origin.

HEADLINE PUBLISHING GROUP
An Hachette UK Company
338 Euston Road
London NW1 3BH

www.headline.co.uk
www.hachette.co.uk

A Little Folly

Chapter I

Sir Clement Carnell's ruling passion, until the very last moment of his life, was his passion for ruling.

In other times and circumstances he might have made a fine king of the absolute and despotic sort, bringing troublesome provinces to order, crushing rebels under his chariot wheels, and inscribing on a giant column his exact and fearsome laws. Being, however, only a country gentleman of Devonshire, he had to make do with tyrannising his wife and children.

He had married late; not through any lack of eligibility on his own part, for he possessed a good estate, and was impressive, even handsome in looks. Marital candidates there had been, but all had exhibited some deplorable shortcoming, such as a mild independence of mind, or a wish to have their feelings occasionally considered, which had rendered them unacceptable to a man of Sir Clement's character. The bride he at last chose was much younger than he, and sufficiently impressionable to mistake the awe she felt for him as love. She liked, as she said, a man to be masterful. The best that could be said for the unhappy consequences of her choice was that she had not long to endure them. She died less than ten years after her marriage, having presented Sir Clement with two children, and having had her opinion of herself so thoroughly lowered, degraded and trampled by her husband that her dying regrets at leaving her little boy and girl were almost overcome by the conviction that they would be better off without her.

Where another man might have been given solemn pause by the prospect of bringing up two motherless children, Sir Clement, once the obligations of grief were over, rather welcomed it. His experience of matrimony had given him a disdain for feminine softness, and in taking exclusive charge of these two young lives he saw an opportunity.

He was a man of harsh, narrow and illiberal views, considering the times decayed and most men fools; – and not being afraid to say so, he had quarrelled with most of his neighbours. In his younger years he had done his duty as a Parliament-man, and there his unthinking deference to the great and powerful had been enough to secure his knighthood. Now he was done with London, which he condemned as a haunt of fashion and idleness; and was very ready to remain at his country seat of Pennacombe, isolated and self-sufficient, and there pursue a sort of experiment in authority, which would demonstrate to the world what could be achieved by a man who was determined truly to be master in his own house.

His tenants and servants knew, to their cost, the sharpness of his temper and the ferocity of Sir Clement's demands for obedience; but their subjection was as nothing to that of his children, who must live every moment under his close supervision. There, he could not only dominate but manipulate; could bend them to his will by playing upon the natural love that even so undeserving a parent must elicit; and in short, could reduce them to a continual state of fearful and self-doubting unhappiness, equal to everything his caprice and ill-nature could devise.

Education there must be, but of his choosing. Neither boy nor girl must be sent away, out of his sight and control: instead Sir Clement engaged, for Valentine and Louisa, a succession of tutors and governesses. They came and went rapidly. Partly this was the consequence of Sir Clement's infinite capacity for finding fault; but more than that, as soon as any of these teachers began to manifest an influence over their pupils, he was roused to jealousy; – and if any were unlucky enough actually to be liked by their charges, their doom was sealed at once. For while he did nothing to secure his children's affection, he could not endure to see it bestowed elsewhere; and was quick to impress on them that in doing so, they were very ungrateful and unnatural creatures.

Valentine, when the time came, was sent up to Oxford, chiefly because Sir Clement had been there; but after a single term, his father put an end to his university career. A couple of tailor's bills, a few unwontedly cheerful and spirited remarks, were enough to convince Sir Clement that his son was going rapidly to the bad. As he stood sole heir to Pennacombe, there was no necessity for Valentine to pursue a profession; but after the Oxford disaster, he did speak tentatively of studying the law, only to have the idea firmly rejected – because it was his idea, because all lawyers were fools and knaves, and because it would mean his going to London, at the furthest remove from his father's surveillance and control. No, he was to remain at Pennacombe – and remain there quite without interest or occupation; for while many men of Sir Clement's age and situation would have been glad to pass on to their grown sons some of the responsibilities of the estate, of stewardship and accounting and management of the home farm, Sir Clement kept them all under his own hand. As a result, at the age of twenty-three Valentine was just such an idle and discontented young man as Sir Clement had always sharply condemned; and he could not understand it.

As for Louisa, there his self-appointed task was simpler. He was so far from a friend to learning in females that he would have spared even the usual accomplishments of music and drawing if convention had not made them obligatory. But the sole aim and purpose of a daughter of Sir Clement Carnell must be to make a good marriage; and that he had already planned to his own satisfaction, having chosen the candidate when she was scarce sixteen. Only the sentimental degeneracy of the times, indeed, had prevented him drawing up a contract with an attorney, and binding her to it there and then. Some evidences of her own will in the matter there had been – taking the form of evasions, shifts and silences rather than mutiny – but he had no doubt of conquering it when the time came. It would never have occurred to Sir Clement that he knew his daughter very little: that his continual scrutiny had necessarily fostered in her the habit of reserve, and the art of disguise – especially when, as often happened, she undertook to shield her brother from the worst excesses of his authority. Being a woman, she was in his view not only as frail as glass but as transparent.

Alas for Sir Clement, he could not absolutely direct the lives of Valentine and Louisa once they were come to adulthood, as he could when they were children. Some concessions there must be to the forms of society, for though he did not mind being disliked, he was averse to being despised. He could not deprive them of the odd tea-visit, riding-party or even ball without injuring his own standing: the Carnells must make a figure in the social life of the neighbourhood in which he was the chief landowner. But he contented himself by making sure that they did not go about often, that their acquaintance was strictly limited, that their conduct was always rigidly regulated, and that they enjoyed themselves as little as possible.

It is not wonderful to relate that Louisa and Valentine Carnell depended greatly on each other, and were joined by a bond of exceptional affection, loyalty and mutual protectiveness. They were so sustained by it that those who came upon them expecting to find them pitiable objects were much surprised. Their aspect was rather subdued than crushed; they were not at all tongue-tied, if their father was not by; and both were so well grown, well figured and handsome – their infrequent smiles, as light springing from darkness, so entrancing – that one could only wonder what effect might be produced by a little more confidence of address, and a little less of a tendency to look over their shoulder.

What the interested observer must find the most intriguing conjecture, however, was their likely future: – if and when that single dominating influence were to be removed, and they found themselves at liberty.

One such observer was Mrs Lappage, the widow of the former rector of Pennacombe. During the rector's life, and for some time after, she had been one of the few people in the district on easy terms with the family at Pennacombe House. Having no children of her own, and being a civil, active, good-natured woman, never happier than when she was giving herself trouble about something, she became as near as she dared a friend to the motherless Carnells, with an ear for their whispered confidences, and a heart to feel always for their situation, regardless of the little power she had to ameliorate it. But even this degree of influence was ended before Louisa and Valentine were grown. She decided to marry again – she was never quite sure why: it was, she supposed, someone to talk to. Her choice, Mr Lappage, was a retired corn-factor. He was a respectable, comfortable, unassuming man, and his manners, when he was awake, were perfectly good. But Mrs Lappage had found herself immediately sunk in Sir Clement's estimation.

'He had known the times were sadly decayed: – still he was shocked, deeply shocked, to see the widow of a clergyman so blind to decorum, and so willing to throw away the good opinion of society, and lower herself by such a connection, especially at *her* time of life.' Mrs Lappage was no longer welcome at the great house, and calls at Mr Lappage's pleasant grange-house were entirely proscribed. Mrs Lappage must satisfy her curiosity and compassion – both equally lively – by such chance encounters with Louisa and Valentine as could be managed; and soothe her feelings by many reiterations that it was a shame and scandal how that odious old man carried on, and by gathering every grain of intelligence about what went on behind the high park walls of Pennacombe.

And it was from this source that came the story of Sir Clement Carnell's last hours; of how they had been marked, and even hastened, by his domineering temper. The servants and labourers in his employ were always welcome at the kitchen-door of the Grange, there to eat a slice of pie and drink a cup of Mrs Lappage's excellent table-beer, and incidentally unburden themselves of any news from Pennacombe House. When, in the late autumn of 1813, it was given out that Sir Clement Carnell had died, the account was merely 'suddenly at home, after a short illness', a theme subsequently taken up in the newspaper obituaries; but Mrs Lappage knew the facts in all their revealing detail.

Sir Clement, a devoted huntsman, had returned from the day's chase and, faithful to habit, had stayed lingering about the stables to see his horse unsaddled, and minutely direct every stage of the operation. He had begun the day in more than usually irritable mood; his face, the groom recalled, had been red as beefsteak; and then had come the moment the young man could only recollect hazily, so awful were the circumstances. He had hung a piece of riding-tackle on the wrong hook – a hook quite apt for the purpose, but not the usual one – and Sir Clement had begun violently berating him. The groom had not been long in his employ and, half flustered and half desperate, had answered that it didn't signify.

Didn't signify! At this Sir Clement burst into a passion, excessive even for him. Perhaps this simple assertion so flew in the face of everything he believed that he experienced a touch of self-doubt, of which only the extremes of fury could purge him. He roared that he would teach the idle fellow what signified, ordered him to follow him to the house, even began bodily marching him thither – whether to give him notice, or simply make a blazing example of him before the other servants, was unknown, and would for ever remain so. Halfway across the stableyard he was struck by a paroxysm that dropped him speechless to the ground.

He was carried into the house insensible, and remained so through the succeeding night, except for a brief stir of consciousness in which he was heard to mutter something that sounded like 'Doesn't signify . . . !' His physician did all he could in the way of bleeding, sighing and looking grave; but the heart-stroke was too severe, and come the morning those relentless and all-seeing eyes were finally closed.

There was matter here for the moralist; – Mrs Lappage, for one, could not resist a frequent shake of the head, and a murmur about chickens coming home to roost. Her first concern, however, was not with the dead but with the living: what must be the feelings of Louisa and Valentine – their shock, the grief that they were too natural not to feel, and their probable bewilderment at the utter transformation of their lives that must ensue?

'It is not my intention to speak ill of the departed,' she told her husband. 'That would never do. The evils of Sir Clement's character were well known in his lifetime, and I shall not allude to them now. Still, everyone must acknowledge – due respect being paid – that it is a release for his children. It would be doing violence to the truth to deny it.'

Mr Lappage showing no signs of denying it, or of doing anything at all, she went on: 'Still, it is a most perplexing situation they are placed in. I almost wonder whether that frightful old tyrant – not to speak ill of him – has so long denied them the power of thinking for themselves that now it is theirs they will hardly know how to exercise it. And you know even the most unsightly old building, when it is gone, somehow leaves a vacancy, and the eye misses it.'

'Like Phelps's barn,' Mr Lappage offered.

But Mrs Lappage was not thinking of Phelps's barn, as she reminded him with some vexation. She was thinking of Louisa and Valentine, and such was her anxiety that she almost determined to attend the burial of Sir Clement in the Carnell vault at Pennacombe church, so that she might see them. But it had not been the custom of her youth for women to attend funerals, and she could not overcome the scruple. She must content herself with her husband's promise to give her a full report of the occasion; though his powers of observation and description were not great. Some years ago at Weymouth he had come face to face with the King; but he had never been able to give any stronger idea of him to his wife's eager mind than that he had a hat on.

Mr Lappage did his best, however: counted the carriages, marked the black plumes on the horses' heads, and memorised some choice phrases of the officiating rector's. This did not satisfy.

'But Louisa and Valentine,' his wife cried, 'what of them?'

'Oh, they were there, right enough,' Mr Lappage assured her. 'The only family that I could see, in fact.'

'No surprise in that: – there are no close connections left on *his* side, for he outlived them all; and as for poor Lady Carnell's family, he quarrelled with them long ago, and would not even hear them mentioned.'

'Ah! well, there it is,' said Mr Lappage, with peaceful finality, and was about to enquire about dinner, when his wife caught him up with vehemence.

'But how did they appear? Louisa and Valentine – they will look I am sure very well in mourning, with their height and colouring – but how do they bear up? With dignity I am sure – they never lack that, though heaven knows how they maintained it under *his* rule – but, then, they are very unaccustomed to that sort of exposure, poor creatures.'

'Well, if you want the truth of it,' said Mr Lappage, seating himself and thoughtfully patting his waistcoat, 'I never saw anyone so absolutely broken up as those two today. Lord! It was as if the world had ended.'

Mrs Lappage pondered on this; and astonishment soon made room for understanding. The liveliness of her interest in the two young people quickened to an almost unbearable degree; but it was not to be easily assuaged. She had too much delicacy to call at a house where only a week ago her presence had been forbidden: it seemed a vulgar presumption – as if to say that now *he* was out of the way she could do as she liked. But to the accustomed quiet and retirement of a house in mourning there seemed, in the subsequent weeks and then months, something else added. Neither Louisa nor Valentine was much seen about: short polite notes were sent out in reply to those who had made the formalities of condolence; and from any evidence that Mrs Lappage could gather, there might have been no change at Pennacombe House – no lifting of a weight of oppressive authority – nothing to show that the estate had a new master and mistress, young, free, and with the world before them.

'I am very much afraid,' she said to herself, as she walked again by the high park walls, and in the leafless grey of February, 'that that monstrous old man – not to speak ill of him – is still in command of that house, and that his influence will never end!'

Chapter II

'Louisa,' said Valentine, as they sat together after dinner one evening, 'do you want the fire-screen?'

'No,' she replied, somewhat startled, for her brother had been sunk in deep reflection for a good half-hour. 'No, thank you, Valentine.'

'You never do want the fire-screen, do you?'

Still surprised, Louisa considered. 'Well, no: if I feel the fire too much, I generally draw back my chair.'

'Which is exactly the case with me,' Valentine said with energy; and springing up, he approached the fire-screen and examined it as if he had never seen it before. 'It is not a handsome article by any means.'

'Decidedly ugly.'

'All these – these cherubs.'

'I am not an admirer of cherubs. And one of them is doing something particularly disagreeable with an arrow.'

'I really see no reason, you know,' he said, laying hands on the fire-screen, 'why we should keep this in the drawing-room any longer, when neither of us uses it or likes it. Do you?'

It was a simple enough question; but there was a great challenge in it too, a challenge reflected in the long look, half anxious, half elated, that brother and sister exchanged, before Louisa answered in a firm voice: 'No, Valentine, I do not.'

'Very well, then.'

Briskly Valentine folded the screen and carried it out of the room. A momentary agitation assailed her, in which she nearly called out to him that he had better put it back; but she conquered it.

'Where did you put it?' she asked, when he returned, a little flushed with triumph.

'Oh, in the summer parlour for now. We can find a place for it in time. – Perhaps in one of the guest bedrooms.'

'Ah, those,' she said doubtfully; for while there were several spare bedrooms at Pennacombe House, she had never thought of them as guest bedrooms, for the cogent reason that they never had any guests.

But Valentine caught her look and, with a deeper flush, urged: 'Well, Louisa, who knows? After all, we—' He stopped pacing about, and joined her on the sofa. 'We can surely talk of this now. After all, we have begun, haven't we?'

Their glance fell in unison on the spot where the fire-screen had stood. It had been, of course, their father's fire-screen: as peculiar to him as his snuff-box, his gout-slippers, his cold, scornful laugh, and his brassy shout of command.

'What *have* we begun, I wonder?' she said.

'To live,' Valentine said, seizing her hand. 'Louisa, do you not agree that we are entitled to do so? No one could reproach us for not observing a due period of mourning. Nor – I believe – can either of us reproach ourselves for any hardness of heart. I freely confess that there were times with Father – the worst times – when secretly I almost wished him gone. You can imagine the agony of that recollection when the blow did fall. I have spent so long hating myself – feeling that I was unjust to him in life, and fearing that I fail in respect for his memory . . . Do you understand me?'

'No one could understand you better, Valentine. And I am sure we are entitled to live. – But it is so very strange. People in our position often console themselves with the thought that "He would wish us to go on with life, and be happy." And yet, try as I may, I cannot apply that comforting formula to Father.'

'No,' he said, fully; and they sat for some moments looking at each other in an intense perplexity, divided between laughter and tears.

'When you speak of beginning to live,' she said at last, 'you mean changing our way of living?'

'I mean *living*. Again, it is hard to talk of this without seeming to cast an ill reflection on Father. But if we were to enlarge our views, to be more active in the world, to make decisions – what is to say us nay?'

'Only the consideration of what Father would think.'

'Precisely. Now I am three-and-twenty. You are one-and-twenty.'

'This is easier. My arithmetic is equal to this.'

'At such an age, we may surely depend upon our own judgement. Indeed we must, for there is now no other to depend upon. Shall we be afraid of this – or shall we welcome it?'

'I confess the prospect inclines me to both emotions. I may be one-and-twenty, but I am not sure I feel it consistently. Sometimes I feel as staid and sober as forty; other times as foolish as fourteen.'

'I don't remember you foolish at fourteen,' he said gently. 'You were not permitted to be.'

Even so tentative a criticism of their father's rule left them guiltily silenced for a moment.

'Valentine,' Louisa said, squeezing his hand, 'if we were to have guests, I do not think we should inflict the fire-screen on them. The cherubs might give them nightmares. – That is, *if* we were to have guests.'

'Ah, I say again, who knows?' Valentine cried, with his keenest and most animated look. 'My dear Louisa, who knows what may happen?'

Mrs Lappage's suppositions about life at Pennacombe House were shrewd; but the picture her fancy painted was both gloomier and simpler than the reality.

For the children of the late Sir Clement Carnell, the period following his death was scarcely to be comprehended in any rational sense. They had existed in it as in a dream that held them baffled, paralysed and unable to wake. So accustomed were they to his daily direction that for some time they had drifted rudderless, unable without great trouble to make the most trifling decision. They even began to believe that he was right: that they were the feeble and disappointing creatures he had always made them out to be – and that they could not do without him.

And yet at the same time they were living on; and through that fog of bereft bewilderment, which Mrs Lappage had guessed at, came shafts of light in which Louisa and Valentine Carnell stood blinking and wondering. For they did not have to fear any more. The guilty starts, the hurried explanations and excuses, the dreary dread of a gathering temper-fit were gone: quite gone. They could sit at ease and think, and no harsh voice would break in on them demanding to know what the devil they were doing idling there. They could even, potentially, do what they wanted; though such was the impress of their father's domination that neither quite knew what that was, and could only contemplate it like a mysterious parcel not to be opened.

And all this had come about as the result of the death of their only parent! Such a terrible tangle of the feelings could not be quickly undone. The long silence and seclusion that had perturbed Mrs Lappage was inevitable; as inevitable, indeed, as its end. The disposal of the fire-screen, in itself a simple act, represented a momentous turning-point; though on this new path they had taken, Valentine stepped forth with more assurance than Louisa.

He had suffered, perhaps, more than she from Sir Clement's overbearing influence, and was correspondingly more impatient to escape it. But his own temper was in any case more volatile than hers. Though generous and warm-hearted, he had always been a prey to dark moods, and to finding refuge in gloomy introspection, where she found hers in a carefully guarded sense of the ridiculous. To laugh him out of his distresses had long been her cherished task. Now she found herself lagging a little behind him in the impetuosity of his spirits – though still with that perfect understanding of his feelings produced by their enduring and exceptional bond.

The months following their father's death had seen him of necessity taking on those duties that Sir Clement had jealously preserved to himself. Valentine was now master of the estate – the squire of Pennacombe, though there was very little that was conventionally squirish about his light, elegant, nervous figure or his sharp mobility of expression – and must learn the ways of the land-agent and the tenants' roll. This was all very well, but it was only being his father. Responsibility was solid, but it did not shine. His instincts were as liberal as his father's had been parsimonious, and so he was content to raise wages, order some gifts of timber and game, and leave the rest in the hands of the steward. Likewise the removal of the fire-screen was followed by some eager declarations about the tearing out of fusty old panelling, of the desirability of french windows and oilcloth; but it was plain to Louisa that the alteration he chiefly sought was to their sequestered and unvarying manner of living; that he craved stimulation, novelty, and company.

For her own part Louisa was very willing to encounter these: she had often sighed, though silently and inwardly, at the dullness of Pennacombe House – but she always had found a means of escape in the library, which had been well stocked by her grandfather, and had richly furnished her mind with amusement and wonder – and a capacity for dreaming besides, which would have shocked Sir Clement, if it had not been beyond his limited powers of imagination to guess at it. Valentine had no such resource. His eyes were turned devotedly outward: each day, following their agreement to begin living, revealed it in some new plan or project. She understood, she sympathised, for she longed also to encounter that greater world of which her reading had given her a tantalising and imperfect idea – but the voice of caution still spoke in her. It was, perhaps, inseparable from the remembered voice of her father, so particularly chill and cutting when either of them made the rare attempt to act independently of his wishes, and came to inevitable grief. The triumphant ring of that *I told you so* was not to be so easily disposed of as the fire-screen.

In one regard, however, Louisa was resolved to go further in defiance and boldness than her brother. There was one imposition of their father's that she was very ready to shake off – with no guilt, no lingering sensations of doubt or disloyalty, nothing but delighted vindication. It had a name, and the name was spoken when Valentine made his first solid plan for a change in their way of living.

'I have been thinking, Louisa, that the third Friday is coming up,' he said. 'And thinking that we ought to change it.'

The third Friday in every month was the appointed day on which their father had held a dinner – that is, he had invited the rector, Dr Sayles, to dine, and talked long with him on the necessity of stiff sentences for poachers, and the wiles of the poor, the rector being a man after his own heart in his detestation of greed and licence, and his appreciation of good port. Mourning had furnished an excuse for Valentine and Louisa to discontinue this custom, but the day was approaching when it must be renewed – or, as Valentine suggested, abandoned.

'For my part, I heartily dislike that self-satisfied old man,' he said, 'and I think he has had the run of his teeth at our table quite long enough. Instead, let us have people we like. I should be glad to see poor Mr and Mrs Lappage here: and I am sure the Tresilians will come. We may think of others – but this is surely a start. What do you say?'

'I would like to see them, certainly. But I wonder whether – well, whether Dr Sayles might not be offended at the omission.'

'Ah, Louisa, why do you fear to offend someone whose opinion you don't care for?' Valentine said gently. 'To be sure, I do know why. But that is something we must change. Else we cannot begin living at all. However, if your conscience is still tender on the matter, we could oblige Father's memory, and invite someone very much to his liking. I have had another letter from Pearce Lynley: he will soon be among us.'

Louisa turned away from his look of playful triumph. 'When is it to be?' was all she could say.

'Well, he informs me, in his characteristic style, that he is to depart from Nottinghamshire on the eleventh – which is today – and that he intends arriving at Hythe Place on the fourteenth; which allows just enough time to include him in the party, if our invitation is prompt.'

'I do not think,' she said carefully, 'that Mr Lynley would take up an invitation coming so short upon his arrival home. It would require him to be obliging and sociable, and to consider other claims than his own immediate comfort; a requirement that I cannot think will be met, unless during his absence in Nottinghamshire there has been a great transformation of his character.'

'Ah, that I doubt. His letter is much in the usual manner – regretting again that he has been unable to tender his commiserations to us in person since Father's death; but he promises that he will call on us as soon as he is able. Indeed he makes a point of it. You are not to escape him, Louisa.'

Not to escape him! These last words might have been expressly chosen to illustrate Louisa's feeling about Mr Pearce Lynley, and the relation in which they stood.

He was the man for whom Sir Clement had designed his daughter: whose claims her father had been urging since she was scarcely out of girlhood, and the only one, as he had made clear, that he would consent to her marrying while it lay in his power to control her choice. For many years, as it seemed to Louisa, Mr Lynley had been held out to her as the inevitable shape and image of her future, like a single door at the end of a passage. Her father had never seen any need for delicacy in representing his aims to Mr Lynley himself: had spoken much with that gentleman of his hopes for the future joining of their estates, and referred with his own peculiar species of facetiousness to the little defects of his daughter's temper and disposition, which it would in time be the pleasure of Mr Lynley as a husband to correct. Anything like an ordinary courtship would not, of course, have suited Sir Clement: he would at once have despised the indulgence of emotion, and mistrusted the liberty of being alone and unobserved that it granted to the participants. But he made sure that Mr Lynley was invited often to Pennacombe House, urged Louisa to help him to the best of the cutlets and to please him with music at the piano afterwards, and generally oversaw and encouraged the business, rather as if it were the progress of a law-suit that he did not doubt would be judged at last in his favour.

Louisa's own sentiments regarding this appropriation of her hand were so little regarded by her father that on the rare occasions when she was so bold as to hint at her misgivings he was almost bewildered; and it took him a few moments to recover, and to regain the safe ground of ferocity and intransigence. Once there, however, he was quite himself again, and able to inform her that the world was full of coxcombs and rogues whom she was unlikely in her ignorance to spot, and that in choosing Mr Lynley for her he was doing her a service, which he could only hope would not be quite beyond her stupidity to appreciate.

Mr Lynley was a notable man in the district. He had succeeded to the neighbouring estate of Hythe at a young age, and had at once proved himself more than equal to its responsibilities. Here was all the prompt forcefulness, and indisposition to have his will opposed for a moment, that her father must approve. Beyond that, Mr Lynley, though only five years Louisa's senior, possessed a degree of reserve, of cool self-possession and disinclination to think well of the world as befitted an older man; and all of these qualities recommended him to her father, who disliked youth on principle. That he was wealthy and of good family went without saying – her father esteemed no one who was not: but equally important, there was no fashionable extravagant nonsense about him.

The admiration was returned. Mr Lynley accorded her father a respect that, given his own fortune and standing, could have nothing to do with fear or calculation. He seemed to find Sir Clement's strictness perennially refreshing, and heard even his most extreme pronouncements with his dry thin smile of assent. As to his admiration of *her* – which was to be assumed, since Mr Lynley showed perfect willingness to go along with her father's plans – Louisa could only be grateful that he did not trouble himself to give it expression. She was scarcely equal to the prospect of being marked out for a man whom she disliked as much as she disliked Pearce Lynley; and could not have endured it if he had added to his vast assurance the urgency of the lover.

There was no sign of this, however. He seemed to have assessed her as a well-bred young woman who would be a thoroughly suitable match, whose fifteen thousand pounds would make a comfortable addition to a comfortable income, and who – being well trained by her upbringing – must be sensible of her good fortune in having her marital destiny so easily laid out before her. There had indeed been, shortly before her father's death, strong hints from Mr Lynley that he was ready to declare himself – or, rather, to enter into possession, like a man foreclosing on a mortgage. But circumstances had carried him quite out of the neighbourhood for the whole of the succeeding time. – He had been on a long visit to his maternal grandmother, who was in sole possession of a large property in Nottinghamshire, and was accustomed to rely on him for the direction of her affairs.

It had been for Louisa a blessed absence. Her detestation of Pearce Lynley was so complete that she could easily acquit herself of not liking him simply because her father wished otherwise. This was not rebellion: this was choice. There was nothing displeasing about Mr Lynley's person, for he was a handsome, imposing man; but the arrogance and superiority of his manner repelled her, and she found in his presence a chill, a want of humanity that jarred on her deepest sensibilities. He was, perhaps, all too reminiscent of her father; but where Louisa, being of a warm, quick, affectionate nature, could not help but love her father even when he was oppressing her with unhappiness, she was under no such obligation to Mr Lynley. The news of his imminent return to Devonshire roused at first the old feeling of dismay; but it was quickly followed by something much livelier and sharper: Pearce Lynley now lacked an advocate. Valentine did not much care for him, and liberty of choice was in any case to be the first principle of their new life together; and so when Mr Lynley next brought his vast assurance to Pennacombe House he would encounter only Louisa's true feelings, hitherto obscured by evasion and trammelled by duty.

So she joined in with Valentine's preparations for a revolutionary dinner; still she remained cautious enough to gasp a little at the number of wines he proposed, and when, on the Thursday, she passed Dr Sayles in the village on his high-bred hunter, she suffered a guilty pang. But when she thought of Pearce Lynley, the flag of defiance waved high. She even had a curious dream, in which the fire-screen was painted not with cherubs but with various representations of Mr Lynley's face; and instead of consigning it to a spare room, she was taking great pleasure in throwing it on to a merry bonfire.

Chapter III

'I am so very glad to welcome you to Pennacombe again,' Louisa told Mrs Lappage, 'and I am sorry that – well, I regret that we have not been able to do so for such a long time. The circumstances being – oh, Lord, how difficult it is!'

'My dear Louisa, don't say another word. I have never pretended to be a clever woman, but one thing I can claim to possess is discretion. Believe me, there is absolutely nothing that *you*, or dear Valentine, have the slightest need to apologise for. If offence lies anywhere, it lies in an *entirely* different quarter – but that I will not even allude to. And how well you are looking! Quite a brilliancy in your complexion! Valentine too – such elegance – such a taking figure. It has been a sad long winter for you, my dear, in more ways than one – but there, I won't allude to it. I hope I have more discretion than that.'

Mrs Lappage, a neat, small woman prettily faded, like good wallpaper in a sunny room, was all unaffected pleasure at finding herself in the drawing-room at Pennacombe House. Her smiles, her civility were universal – as was her observation; and her eyes brightened most keenly whenever their glance fell on some change or innovation.

'I cannot help remarking, my dear, how very much lighter and airier it is in here than my remembrance. The removal of those heavy brocades, I fancy. And was that not John Colley's youngest daughter I saw in the hall? A very pretty, pleasant girl, I am sure she will do well – and poor Mrs Deene has long needed more help, though it was never seen in certain quarters. But you need not fear I shall make any allusion to that, my dear. I should be a very blundering insensible creature if I did. Yes, Mr Lappage, did you want me?'

Mr Lappage, however, did not: this little appeal being a reflexive habit in Mrs Lappage, to make sure her husband had not gone to sleep.

The small party was completed by a family with whom Louisa and Valentine had long been on close terms. The Tresilians, as Valentine had said, would surely come. During Sir Clement's time they had been among the few visitors who were, if not exactly welcomed, at least tolerated at Pennacombe House. Old Mr Tresilian, dead some half a dozen years since, had begun as a merchant shipping china-clay out of Teignmouth, and had risen swiftly to riches and eminence. He had built himself a good house inland, a short ride from Pennacombe, and there lived in such a respectable manner that Sir Clement felt himself able to ignore his origins and speak well of him, his good opinion being further secured by old Mr Tresilian's temper, which tended to the dour and severe. His only son had inherited The Ridings, and the substantial shipping interests, and was a considerable man in the district – but he had revealed a terrible flaw in his character.

James Tresilian had married very young, and against his father's wishes. His bride was still younger: a delicate, entrancing creature, who was staying with relatives at Teignmouth, and was as pretty, giddy and fashionable as she was penniless. The couple had been united after the briefest of courtships, and to a general prophecy that young Mr Tresilian would rue. Seldom can a prediction have been so satisfyingly realised. The young lady rapidly repented of her choice, led her husband a merry dance of trouble, discontent and mild scandal, and made him as thoroughly unhappy as the most disinterested observer could wish, before succumbing within a twelvemonth of the wedding to a galloping consumption, and leaving Mr Tresilian a sorrowing widower, chastened by experience, at an age when most men were just contemplating matrimony.

Sir Clement, of course, had disapproved most heartily. James Tresilian, though some years Valentine's senior, had been his nearest friend since boyhood; and after this episode, one of Sir Clement's prohibitions might easily have been expected. Yet Mr Tresilian's fall so perfectly vindicated Sir Clement's beliefs about the consequences of wilful independence that he could not have borne to exclude him from his circle: to forgo the pleasure of saying, with a shake of his head, 'Ah! here's poor Tresilian – an example to us all, alas';

of moralising on Mr Tresilian's hollow cheek and muted manner; and above all of making his unfailing jests on the way in which the ill-fated attachment had begun.

Mr Tresilian, walking along the sea-front at Teignmouth, had rescued the young lady's hat, which had been carried away by the wind. This simple circumstance never lost its power to elicit Sir Clement's brittle mirth. 'Ah, Tresilian,' he would say, 'you have learned your lesson, I think, and will not go chasing hats again, hey?'; and if ever he heard in the neighbourhood of a rash or imprudent marriage – and to Sir Clement virtually all marriages were such – he would sweeten his outrage with the reflection: 'Someone has been chasing flying hats again – poor fool!' By the time of Sir Clement's death, the incident of Mr Tresilian's marriage was some seven or eight years in the past; Mr Tresilian had gone on with his solitary life, prospered, and ceased to be an object of general interest, but Sir Clement persisted in his acid pleasantries to the end.

Fortunately Mr Tresilian was a man of imperturbable temperament, who responded to the harshest of Sir Clement's sallies with his characteristic half-smile. Loyalty to Valentine, to whom he stood in something of the relation of an elder brother, perhaps accounted for it; but there might also have been a wish to see this relation made real. – He had a younger sister, Kate: a shy though not awkward girl, much accustomed to rely on his protection. A year or so ago, she and Valentine had danced much together at one of the rare assemblies the young Carnells were suffered to attend; and afterwards, the time being February, she had sent him a Valentine verse, partly inspired, it seemed, by the aptness of his name. This for Sir Clement was unthinkably bold, even if undertaken in playful fashion; yet it served as a useful warning. Well set up and respectable the Tresilians might be, but Sir Clement made it clear that when the time came for the heir of Pennacombe to marry, he must aim at a connection much superior to *that.*

What Valentine felt Louisa could not quite tell: that he was flattered was no less plain than that he was embarrassed; and Louisa suspected that he shared his father's views at least in this: that he did not look to find romantic attachment so close to home. His was an expansive and idealising temperament. 'When I marry,' he had once said to her, 'but then, you know, even to say those words indicates a dismal state of comfortable preparation. One *cannot* prepare – expect – anticipate. There is no planning an event that must begin like lightning striking from the sky, overturning and oversetting everything.'

Whether Kate Tresilian had intended a declaration, or whether Mr Tresilian still entertained any hopes in that direction, Louisa again could not tell. – Kate had returned to shyness, and he was always impossible to read. He was an odd, whimsical character; though gentleman-like, more at ease with sea-captains and ship's-chandlers than in society; and though Louisa liked him, was often amused by him and valued the unobtrusive friendship he had always shown to Valentine, she could not help but secretly deplore the spiritless way he submitted to her father's facetious contempt. He possessed fortune and independence, and owed Sir Clement nothing; and she for one did not consider those events of his past – of which, being then only a girl, she had a mere sketch of remembrance – to be an occasion of shame. Altogether she could not understand it: unless his unhappy adventure in matrimony had left him so defeated that his self-respect was quite extinguished.

There was something of that in Mr Tresilian's appearance: in his lean angular frame, his sadly scuffed boots, and the dusty-fair hair, which – to the impatience of Valentine, who was particular about his Grecian crop – he allowed to grow like a careless boy's. His habit of silence suggested it likewise; but he could speak with quickness and point when the subject interested him, as now, when on sitting down to dinner Mr Lappage mentioned the war news.

'It is an apt time for new departures,' Mr Tresilian said. 'The latest intelligence is that the Austrians are within a hundred miles of Paris, Wellington is far advanced into the south, and Bonaparte is at bay on all sides.'

'Surely he is finished at last,' said Mr Lappage.

'He may yet have a trick up his sleeve – but certainly he cannot produce new armies out of thin air.'

'That detestable monster,' cried Mrs Lappage, who felt warmly on every subject. 'I hope he will be brought sternly to answer for all the wrongs he has done.'

'Of course, the loser in any dispute is always in the wrong,' Mr Tresilian remarked.

'Come, Tresilian, never tell me you feel any sympathy for Bonaparte,' Valentine said. 'The war has been putting your ships in danger a hundred times.'

'Oh, I only wonder, as a matter of curiosity, whom we shall find to hate after he is gone: we have got so used to a good, comfortable state of loathing that I fear we may be bereft without it. For myself, I shall be glad to see him fall. All that tedious adventuring. Crossing the Alps and whatnot.'

'Well, there, for all his later tyrannies, one must admire the spirit of daring that animated him,' Louisa said.

'Really?' said Mr Tresilian. 'I don't see why. The Alps must have been put there for a very good reason. I have never wished to cross even a single Alp. He should have stayed at home and found an occupation: that was the trouble.'

'Well, we have had enough of war, that is certain,' said Valentine. He had already had his glass refilled several times, and it was with a dreamy inward look that he added: 'Aye, we have had enough of those times.'

'My dear Valentine, those are my sentiments exactly,' Mrs Lappage cried. Then, in a lower tone: 'Dear me – old habit – of course I should say Mr Carnell.'

'No, no, ma'am, none of that frosty ceremony,' said Valentine, eagerly. 'I would have only openness and ease at Pennacombe from now on. If the master of this house is to receive any respect, let it be earned by genuine esteem and affection. – Mr Lappage, I see your glass is not filled. Christmas, now – come next Christmas, I mean to observe it in the proper manner. I regret to say that lately even the village carollers have been frightened to approach the gate. Next time we shall see some true hospitality.'

'Watchmaking,' said Mr Tresilian. 'There's a proper profession. Plenty of interest and satisfaction. One never hears of a watchmaker crossing the Alps.'

'But, my dear James, he might want to,' gently suggested his sister.

'Then he would be a very silly watchmaker,' Mr Tresilian said gloomily. 'What do you think, Miss Rose?'

The lady thus addressed had been taken into the household at The Ridings a few years ago, being a second cousin of the Tresilians and having fallen upon hard times – meaning she had reached a certain age without anybody wanting to marry her. For Sir Clement this charity had been a slight further evidence of the softening of Mr Tresilian's brain consequent on the chasing of hats; but it might with justice have been a sorer cause of repentance for a man not possessed of Mr Tresilian's patience. Not that Miss Rose was any trouble: indeed, it was the very aim and desire of her life not to be so, as she was constantly asserting. An early attempt on the part of the Tresilians to acknowledge their relationship, and soften the sting of dependence by calling her Aunt, had been quite rejected by her aggressive humility; and though she had the dignity of the housekeeping keys, and the chaperonage of Kate, she could never sufficiently declare herself unworthy of them.

'I beg your pardon, Mr Tresilian,' she answered, 'and it is a great nuisance in me, I know, to be so particular where I can claim absolutely no right to consideration – but may I ask to what specifically your question refers?'

'Bonaparte,' said Mr Tresilian, drinking his wine, and raising his heavy eyes a little at its quality. 'What to do with him. Hang, burn, or drown. Or all three.'

'My dear sir,' Miss Rose said, with her little squeezed cough of self-deprecation, 'to consult *my* opinion on a matter of national moment is so very inapposite that I could almost bring myself to protest at it – if it were not for my consciousness that the enquiry is *meant* as a token of polite attention, but I hope I am very far from expecting any such tokens, or considering them my right in the least. If ever I did lapse into such unwarranted vanity, I hope I should drop myself in the river directly.'

'Dear Miss Rose, I wish you wouldn't speak of the river so,' said Kate.

'My dear Miss Tresilian, if *you* wish it, then of course I shall not do so. Anything other than a complete acquiescence would be shockingly unbecoming of my position. I hope indeed I should accept *any* prohibition of my speech without a murmur – even if it were an injunction to absolute silence,' said Miss Rose, in her most frozen and petrified manner, accompanying her speech with the penitential half-closing of her eyes, which suggested that even the power of sight she regarded as a presumption in a being such as herself.

'Well, ma'am, Bonaparte and the war and all of that is poor dull stuff, I'm sure you will agree,' Valentine said. 'Take a glass of wine, if you please, and think no more of it.'

'I beg your pardon, Mr Carnell, but your inviting me to take a glass of wine is an attention that I cannot with good conscience allow myself freely to accept, even at the risk of rewarding your condescension with ingratitude,' murmured Miss Rose, with a little drawing-in of her thin, tissuey form, as if to take up less room on her chair. 'I stand in a position of dependence, quite as much as a child to a parent, and I hope I shall never forget to refer any such question to my benefactor: indeed, the moment I do forget, I hope I may drop myself off a cliff.'

'Drink the wine or not, as you choose, ma'am,' said Mr Tresilian, with the bluff patience that never seemed to fail him. 'I'd advise it, for it's good and heady. You have made a proper start on the cellars, Valentine.'

'I hope I have,' said Valentine, colouring a little, 'for they have done little enough before now to justify their existence – which I take to be the fostering of conviviality and general enjoyment.'

But Miss Rose's determination to be ignored and slighted was not yet satisfied; and there must be a good deal more fuss about her taking a glass of wine, and her insisting that she did not expect such a privilege, before the matter was done, Miss Rose in this demonstrating the peculiar talent of those who proclaim their absence of self-esteem for getting a lot of attention by pretending they never get any.

The dinner passed pleasantly enough; but it was large and rich, neither Valentine nor Louisa being at all experienced in the planning of such things, and both of them inclined to liberality; and the wines in particular took their toll of Valentine. Louisa was just hesitating over that awkward responsibility of the hostess, of rising and inviting the ladies to retire, and wondering whether a parade-ground bark of 'Drawing-room – quick march!' might answer, when Valentine rose to his feet.

'I hope you will give me leave to say something,' he announced. 'It is this. I wish to apologise. Not for myself, but for – well, let us say only that most of you, indeed all of you, have at some time been subjected to unpleasantness, even insult, from a certain quarter, in this household. At the time I refer to, it did not lie in my power to express my regret for these proceedings; but now it does, and without for a moment wishing to speak ill of – of anyone, I must convey to you that sincerest regret, and to assure you that *those* times are quite gone.' Valentine's eye fell wanderingly over the company: their silence seemed rather to encourage than dismay him; and he was just embarked on a 'Furthermore . . .' when Mr Tresilian got up and clasped his arm in an access of warmth and gratitude, which almost looked like a determination to press him back into his seat before he could say any more.

Louisa took her cue to lead the ladies out, trusting that Mr Tresilian would be vigilant over the port; and though there were only Mrs Lappage, Miss Tresilian and Miss Rose to be entertained, all well known to her, she presided over the tea-things in some confusion, and not without some startling crashes, as if she were going at her task with hammer and chisel. In truth she was so unaccustomed to wine that the very little she had taken had dizzied her head; and beyond that, she was not as comfortable with the occasion as she had hoped to be. Acting the hostess felt strange; the very house felt strange with this unprecedented company in it; she wanted everyone to be easy and contented, but could not be so herself. Part of her regretted Valentine's outburst – yet she would have fiercely defended him against anyone who had questioned its propriety. Altogether she was in a thoroughly mixed state of feeling over their new enterprise of living.

It required only a little conversation with Mrs Lappage, however, to restore her to a consciousness of its one great advantage. That lady talked tactfully around the matter of Valentine's little speech – conveyed as delicately as she could that she did not take it amiss in the slightest, and that if it had been up to her, there would have been some much stronger expressions, and that when it came to *apology*, there had long been an apology due to Valentine and Louisa from a certain quarter; and then, brightening, appraised Louisa with a glance, and cried: 'But there, we look to happier times, as Valentine said, and I see *those* in your bright looks, my dear. Such a skin! And I like excessively the way you have trimmed your gown – that is the newest mode, I should think.'

'If it is, I have hit on it most luckily, for I know nothing of the newest modes,' Louisa answered frankly. 'Valentine spoke of my having a new gown from Exeter, but I – I had an idea for making something pretty of this one.' In truth she had scrupled to accept, because the voice of her father still spoke in her, sternly reproving the notion of fligging herself up in new clothes as soon as mourning was over.

'Ah, but you know how to dress, my dear, and that's something that no amount of new purchases can grant. All I can say is, I'm sure Mr Lynley will be as well satisfied with your looks as I am. You will know, of course – none better – that he is just returned to Hythe.'

'I know of it, ma'am,' Louisa said, after a moment.

'Well! I run ahead of myself, no doubt – I always do,' Mrs Lappage said, studying her closely. 'It's my failing. But when I observe that the relation between you and Mr Lynley is spoken of as a settled thing, I base my information not on gossip – heaven protect me from *that* – but simply from common report.'

'The relation between Mr Lynley and I—' Louisa faltered, performing more noisy tricks with the tea-things.

'It is not strictly accorded the title of an engagement – I think those cups have not been properly dried, my dear, and that's why they are so slippery. No, not exactly an engagement, and of course in the late solemn circumstances all such things must lie in abeyance, but there is a general expectation, shall we say? Now pray, my dear Louisa, don't suppose that I mention it from any desire to draw you out about the matter, because assuredly I do not.'

Mrs Lappage omitted to say why in that case she did mention it; and only went on smiling curiously into Louisa's face, so that she was forced to reply.

'There is certainly no engagement, ma'am, nor anything like it.'

'Ah!'

'I hardly know what to say. If the gossip— I beg your pardon, if the common report is that an understanding of any kind exists between me and Mr Lynley, then it is very wide of the mark; and I cannot think where such a report may have begun.'

'Can't you, my dear? I can. It is what I have suspected since the matter began to be talked of. To be sure, I should not even allude to this, here in this house, and with you and Valentine so circumstanced as you are – but, no, I will say it. I know very little of Mr Lynley beyond what everyone knows – that he is rich, and proud, and rather unaccommodating in his manner – but I do know that he was a favourite with your late father. And so I have always said to myself: It is of *his* arranging, whatever else may be the truth of it. Meaning no disrespect, of course. Now, I say nothing of your own inclinations on the question, my dear Louisa, because I know nothing of them: it may be that in *this* case at least, they coincide with those of your father. – Certainly Mr Lynley is a very handsome gentlemanlike man, and is spoken well of generally, though his being so much approved in *that* quarter does, I confess, a little prejudice me against him. But no more of that. Anything your natural candour might move you to tell me about it, I would, of course, be honoured to hear but otherwise I disclaim all interest in the subject.'

Louisa was at a loss how to answer: Mrs Lappage's inquisitiveness, though wholly good-natured, was inquisitiveness nonetheless; and her very decided feelings about Mr Lynley were such as she did not wish to share. They were so much her own, and no one else's: the one rock of certainty, amidst all the tides and cross-currents of feeling that had swept her about since her father's death. In many other regards, she knew, she was still Sir Clement Carnell's daughter – anxious to placate, doubtful of her own wisdom, and quick to suppose herself in the wrong. But in regard to Pearce Lynley, she was no other than Louisa – a thinking, feeling woman, who could not submit to have her whole future decided for her in a manner so contrary to her taste, understanding and heart.

That someone so well informed about the business of her neighbours as Mrs Lappage could speak of an engagement was a shock – but a bracing one. It renewed Louisa's determination.

'My father did, as you say, ma'am, hold Mr Lynley in high regard – and I cannot deny that he spoke of the match as a possible and desirable thing. But this is to leave out of account the feelings of both parties; and those, of course, no one else can direct.' As she spoke Louisa was conscious of a wish to make it plain that, even if her father had lived, she would not have supinely fallen in with his wishes – she was not such an abject being as *that*. The question thus raised, of how then she would have resisted her father, she could only answer by telling herself she would have found a way

– which was as much as to say, she would have hoped for it. A tendency to equivocate had long been a part of Louisa's nature: she could well remember one of her governesses trying to teach her the division of numbers, and her own eager reply on being told that three did not go into two, that it surely would with a little persuasion.

None of this could she convey to Mrs Lappage; she, however, was so happily absorbed in digesting the first delicious information that any more would have surfeited even her appetite.

The gentlemen were not long in rejoining them, and a glance assured Louisa that Valentine had drifted into a dreamy rather than a talkative state. The pianoforte was opened; and Louisa, being an ardent listener but an indifferent performer, was content to surrender it to Kate Tresilian, who played with skill and taste; and with a soft touch appropriate to her quiet character, and much appreciated by that large class of gentlemen, like Mr Lappage, whose enjoyment of music was enhanced by unconsciousness. Louisa invited Mr Tresilian to the seat beside her. She wished to say something in gratitude for his intervention at the dinner-table, but without suggesting that Valentine had done anything reprehensible; and when the moment came, in the applause following his sister's first piece, all she could manage was: 'Of course it was not ill-meant, you know. Not at all.'

Mr Tresilian only nodded.

'And I do not think anyone took it so,' she pursued. 'I'm sure everyone understands that it was one of those things that simply – comes out, and there is no help for it; and better it comes out than be suppressed. Come, you are Valentine's best friend,' she added, as he continued grave and silent, 'you, I'm sure, would be the last to disapprove him.'

'I do not,' he said. 'But it sounds rather as if you are trying to convince yourself.'

'Now you are being provoking, Mr Tresilian, but it won't work,' she said serenely, and then, with rather less serenity: 'After all, it was in part a defence of *you*.'

'Indeed! I am not aware of any need to be defended.'

'Well – considering that my father could be, at times, rather less than sensitive to your position.'

'At times? All the time,' he said, with a little twist of a smile.

'Very well, then. That is what anyone with a sympathetic interest in you must deplore, without any omission of respect to my late father's name.'

'Well, it's a curious thing. His raillery never troubled me in the slightest, because it was all based on a false supposition – that I must regret the past.'

'And you do not?' Louisa said, with an interest she could not conceal – for it was unlike Mr Tresilian to refer to the subject, still more to make a disclosure about it.

'Except in one particular,' he said, after a moment – then seemed to repent even of this candour; and his sister beginning to play again, he took the opportunity to retreat deep into silence.

This was tantalising – rather touching also. Louisa was so

accustomed to thinking of Mr Tresilian's marriage as disastrous, and his bride's early death as a sort of release, that she had never stopped to consider that perhaps *there* lay the real sadness: that even if the girl had made him unhappy, he might not have loved her a whit the less, and might have given anything to keep her by him. Still, he was a man so little given to the indulgence of emotion, except about the iniquities of ships'-chandlers and the fresh smell of a north-easter, that Louisa could not be sure. The one plain and unmistakable preoccupation of his present life was his attachment to Kate, and the cherishing protectiveness with which he regarded her. – Her dearest wish must be his. In this might lie the regret; for while Kate, with a faint blush, was now embarked upon Valentine's favourite song, and Valentine was gazing wistfully in her direction, Louisa suspected that his gaze was fixed on objects far more distant and beguiling than a girl he had known since childhood singing, 'Oh, had my love ne'er smiled on me'.

Chapter IV

Mr Lynley was home: there was no doubting that, for where an ordinary person would have relied on general report to disseminate this news among his neighbours, and indeed would not have supposed it as of more than mild interest to them, Mr Lynley's self-consequence required that he announce it. So thought Louisa, as Valentine laid before her the precisely written note in which Pearce Lynley presented to the Carnells his compliments, reassured their anxious minds that he was safe returned from the wild shores of Nottinghamshire, and promised to call on them at his earliest convenience.

'I doubt, however, that I will be his principal object in calling,' Valentine said. 'So never fear, Louisa – when he comes, I shall leave the two of you alone as soon as may be.'

'Valentine, this is not an occasion for jesting.'

'Isn't it?' Her brother smiled, but his look was penetrating. 'My dear Louisa, I suspect you are more averse to Mr Lynley than you have confided even to me. Which I quite understand: when our father was here, you were forced to be circumspect on the matter, simply to avoid trouble

– especially as that trouble was all too often deflected on me. Oh, yes,' he took her hand, 'I know you often suffered more so that I should suffer less. I remember well when I tore a hole in the knee of my breeches, and you responded by tearing your petticoat quite in half, so that you would come in for the scolding; and we were little children then.'

'And yet you still got the worst of it,' she said, squeezing his hand, and feeling sadly happy, or happily sad – the emotion would not stay still.

'Well, perhaps. But the important thing is, Louisa, those days are gone – and everything that went with them. We are entirely free, to choose and decide as we will.'

'Yes . . . though I do wonder, Valentine – can one ever be entirely free in that way?'

'Oh, you've been reading too much Byron.' He laughed, and she left unspoken the lofty and indisputable reply that one could never read too much Byron. 'But now *here* is a communication that promises much more satisfaction. It follows so exactly on my own dearest wishes – I was never more glad of a letter in my life. – It is from our cousins.'

'Our cousins!' repeated Louisa, not so much in surprise as to try the unfamiliar word on her lips: for that she and Valentine had such things was as certain as the fact that they had never been allowed to think of them as such; and she turned attentively to the letter that Valentine handed her.

'It has been my greatest regret – powerless though we were to alter it – that a friendly acquaintance with Mama's family was denied us,' Valentine said. 'It is not merely the deprivation to us, but the discourtesy, even the insult, offered to them – and beyond that, to Mama's memory. It has been in my mind how to repair the damage, and now comes this most opportune overture from the Speddings themselves.'

It was not the case that they had never seen these cousins: there had been a single occasion, when they were small, and before their father had quite retired to Pennacombe – a visit to London, and a call upon their relatives in Hill Street, of which Louisa could only remember that the two children of the house had tried to play with them, and had given up under the double discouragement of the little Carnells not being permitted to, and not knowing how to. – They were the offspring of Lady Carnell's sister, who had chosen a husband for his wealth and liberality, rather than his strength of character. Mr Spedding had died a few years since, leaving his widow and grown children very comfortably circumstanced; and from London Mrs Spedding had persisted in occasional civilities to the Carnells, writing her congratulations on Valentine's coming-of-age, or conveying new-year's greetings – all of which elicited the same response from Sir Clement: a stubborn silence, and a swift tearing of paper. He considered his late wife's kin a foolish, indulgent, fashionable set and, being the man he was, had doubtless told them so; and he could never sufficiently praise his own prudence in keeping Valentine and Louisa away from their contagion, nor cease to congratulate himself on having plucked his wife away from their pernicious influence.

The letter was jointly signed by Tom and Sophie Spedding,

but written by the latter. It was easy and good-natured, but lacking nothing in delicacy: the Carnells' loss, and the probable lessening of its worst pains, and the Speddings' difficulty in expressing their condolences, all were gently and lightly touched on, with a swift transition to a happier theme: the Speddings were staying at Lyme, no great distance away, Tom having taken a fancy that sea air at the very doubtful beginning of the spring would do him good; and it had done him good to the extent of his catching several colds, all of which, according to him, would have come out much worse otherwise: and now it wanted only one thing for the perfect restoration of his health. Sophie joined in his wish – to call upon their cousins at Pennacombe, and renew, or perhaps begin, an acquaintance they had long desired. They were travelling post, and if the Carnells could recommend a decent inn in the vicinity, they hoped to be with them in a few days – always excepting that if their cousins should wish instead to put this letter straight on the fire, they would not be offended in the least.

'Very friendly – very pleasant,' Louisa concluded. 'I should like to see them, certainly.'

'I sense a hesitation.'

'No, no – but I hope they will not be disappointed in *us*. They sound so very assured – so comfortable in the world, as is only natural for them, having lived in it.'

'Oh, as to that, I do not think we need to fear being found wanting,' Valentine said, with a faintly vexed laugh. 'We may not have lived in the world, but I hope for my part that I am not lacking in all assurance – in knowledge of how to acquit myself in society; really, I should consider myself a contemptible being else.'

Louisa, seeing his pride was touched, did not press the point, saying instead: 'Well, it will be, as you justly remark, a gratification to be able to know Mama's family at last. They ask about an inn. Do you suppose the Seven Stars . . . ?'

'It might do very well, if this were a distant connection, but as it is not so, and these are our nearest kin, who would in normal circumstances never have thought of an inn if they were in the district of Pennacombe – why, I see no reason why we should not invite them to stay here. Indeed, I feel it would be remiss if we did not. Certainly they do not angle for it – but in normal society, you know, the invitation would be such an accepted thing that it would hardly need extending.'

'Would it? No, Valentine, I am not in the least contradicting you. I simply don't know. We have so little means of comparison.'

'Exactly, and what I mean to demonstrate, Louisa, is that in our innovations we are only doing what others do. – Others who have lived in the world, I mean, and have not been so dreadfully confined to the same spot, the same circle, the same expectations. Oh, we have James and Kate Tresilian as an example, yes, with their eternal walking everywhere, and James deep in the talk of the wharf-side, and Kate with her music and books: this is very well. I do not disdain it, for a quiet life suits them: they have the art of limited contentment. But that won't do for me, and I have a strong suspicion it does not excite you either.'

'They do seem at ease with life, though – or, at least, not greatly desiring any change in it. Perhaps that is the definition of happiness.'

'Or of mere animal resignation,' said Valentine, with his most pricked, high-coloured look. 'But, no, don't mistake me, I think Tresilian the best of fellows, and I have the greatest of respect for Kate.'

Poor Kate! was Louisa's thought. If she still entertained hopes, this must end them. To excite in a man a state of violent loathing was, as any novel-reader knew, to stand in a fair light of winning him at last; but no woman could ever recover from the humiliation of being respected.

'I shall write our cousins at once,' Valentine went on briskly, 'inviting them to consider Pennacombe their home for as long as they choose. And we must have guest bedrooms prepared – no fire-screen, of course.'

Though Louisa was deeply curious about their cousins, and very ready to meet them, she could not yet enter wholly into his enthusiasm for the encounter. – There was first the matter of Mr Lynley, which divided her between relish and dread; for as the meeting approached, she found her triumphant resolution tending to trickle away at the corners, and to be displaced by a wish that she might somehow avoid the whole question altogether. He came to Pennacombe, however, the next morning.

The circumstances were, perhaps, unfortunate. Louisa had

a pet cat, which she had secured against her father's dislike of any domestic animals that did not come bounding up to you with a dripping corpse in their jaws by creating an entirely false impression of her as a great mouser. Sukey, having talents in another direction, had some weeks ago given birth to a litter of kittens, one of which was promised to Kate Tresilian. She and Mr Tresilian came that morning, armed with a basket, the chosen household addition having already approved its future mistress, to the extent that as soon as it saw her it chewed her finger and became riotous. The lawn immediately behind the house was the half-grown kitten's favourite arena, and there Kate and Louisa, attended with some masculine foot-dragging by Valentine and Mr Tresilian, went to find it.

With such an audience the kitten could not help but display all its tricks of stalking, running sideways, and climbing – this last with the result that it found itself in the lower branches of the crab-apple tree, and unable to get down. Mr Tresilian, sighing, made an attempt to climb up to it, but the spindly branches groaned ominously at his weight.

'No, James, you are too heavy – you'll fall,' cried Kate. 'Oh, what are we to do? Hark how she cries!'

'Cats can generally get down, you know, even when they look as if they can't,' said Valentine, laying a tentative hand on the lowest branch, seemingly equally doubtful of its bearing his weight, and the effect of climbing on his new superfine corbeau coat.

As the kitten was likeliest to let her approach it, and she was not heavy, Louisa decided the task was hers: she sprang up, and was reaching out to the animal almost before Valentine could call out to her to be careful. In a moment she had the squirming bundle safely tucked under her arm. Now came the descent, which, on looking down, she found to be further, and more difficult, than she had anticipated. A dizzy glance showed her the faces of Valentine, looking crossly anxious, Kate, looking amazed, and Mr Tresilian, wryly amused. Her pride overcame her alarm – it would be too ridiculous to have to be rescued in turn – and crying, 'No, no need,' to Valentine's declaration that he was going to fetch a ladder, she scrambled down, completing the descent with a jump that she flattered herself appeared easy and graceful, though it sent such a stinging shock through the soles of her feet that she had to bite her lip to stop herself yelping aloud.

She concealed her pain amid Valentine's reproaches and Kate's thanks, though Mr Tresilian's grey, observant eye seemed to suspect it; and then, on turning towards the house, had the disagreeable surprise of seeing Mr Pearce Lynley standing in the window of the breakfast-parlour, with an expression on his face suggestive of his having witnessed the entire spectacle.

'Ah, you have a visitor,' Mr Tresilian said. 'Come, Kate, stow that wild beast in the basket, and let's be off.'

'Oh, won't you stay?' Louisa urged.

'Why? Mr Lynley hasn't come here to see us,' Mr Tresilian said.

'But consider how it will look, if you go away without speaking to him – at least to give him good day.'

'It will not look like anything,' he said in his most phlegmatic way; and he and Kate departed by the shrubbery-path, leaving Louisa to her fate, and to the difficulty of getting into the house without limping.

In the breakfast-parlour Mr Lynley stood ready with his crisp bow and short words of greeting: tall, well-dressed, smoothly barbered – absolutely in possession of himself and of the room, though it was not the room in which callers were usually received, as he was prompt to point out.

'The girl showed me in here, for some reason. I did not recognise her. New, I think. It allowed me, at any rate, to view your activities in the garden. Miss Carnell, I hope you took no hurt.'

'None at all, thank you, sir,' Louisa said, reaching her seat with relief.

'One would have supposed the job more apt for a servant,' Mr Lynley went on, seating himself and glancing critically around the room. 'You have not suffered a general exodus from the kitchens, I hope. I have known it happen: when the strong hand of the master is removed, they miss it, and fancy themselves disaffected, and are often wilful enough to take themselves off to a worse place.'

'I don't know about a strong hand – but of course Pennacombe *has* a master, Mr Lynley,' Valentine said, quite temperately.

'To be sure: and I wish you well of it, Mr Carnell. Naturally anything more approaching to congratulation must be inappropriate in the circumstances. Even at the distance of many months, commiseration has the precedence. – I hope you are bearing up against your loss. It was no common one: men of Sir Clement's character are not often to be encountered. The news was a very great grief to me.' All this was pronounced with marble calm. 'My sorrow was the more intense in that I could not be here to pay my respects, and to offer you whatever service I might, at a time when you must have been sorely in need.'

'Thank you, Mr Lynley,' Louisa said, 'but we managed tolerably without you.'

'If it had only lain in my power to return to Devonshire,' Mr Lynley continued, taking no more notice of this than of a clock striking the hour, 'but Mrs Poulter was so ill, and her affairs so in need of direction, that I could not be spared.'

'Your grandmother is recovered now, I hope,' Valentine said.

'Her health is not secure, but the crisis is past. It is important that she suffer no agitation of the nerves.'

'And your brother?' Valentine asked. 'He is still abroad?'

'He is,' Mr Lynley said, with a further stiffening of his immobile features, 'but he is shortly expected home. I have received one of his rare communications. – He is wounded. Not severely: a ball in the foot during a skirmish before Orthez. The danger of the surgeon's saw is past, but he is lamed, and returns to England by the first ship.'

'Poor fellow! He will miss the final bout with Bonaparte,

then,' Valentine said. 'But he has served with honour, nonetheless.'

'He has remained three years with his regiment,' said Mr Lynley, in a tone of austere correction. 'It is more than was expected.'

The subject was plainly an uncomfortable one for Mr Lynley, and for that reason alone Louisa would gladly have seen it pursued; but Valentine, disappointingly, changed it.

'And how does Miss Lynley?'

'Georgiana is well enough; but I have been much disappointed in her governess, to whom her care was entrusted while I was in Nottinghamshire. There is not the improvement of manner and address that one looks to in a girl of her age, properly guided: indeed, I feel she has not progressed at all. I begin to wonder whether an effective governess is to be procured by gold – though I remember Sir Clement having like troubles. I must resolve the difficulty, I think, by applying to one of the agencies in London – and as soon as may be, for Georgiana cannot remain as she is, without an instructress.'

'Do you mean you have dismissed this governess?' Louisa cried, unable to prevent herself.

'Most certainly. Having presumed on her position so long, she could hardly expect the indulgence of notice.'

'But what is to become of her?'

'That, Miss Carnell, is scarcely my concern, once she is out of my employ.'

'But her situation . . . Has she family? Has she somewhere to go?'

'There is an aunt, I believe, in Bristol,' Mr Lynley pronounced, with a sort of comprehensive distaste. 'Mr Carnell, your late father was always a zealous upholder of the Game Laws. Have you been troubled with poaching here, as we have at Hythe Place?'

'Oh, very little, I think – Valentine, is that not so?' Louisa put in before her brother could answer. 'But if in future we should see the odd bird or hare go missing, I think we should not be hasty. It might after all only be a dismissed governess trying to procure herself a meal.'

'You have a lively fancy, Miss Carnell,' said Mr Lynley, in a way that implied he deplored rather than admired it; and turned the talk to politics.

Still his eyes dwelt on her: he continually presented her with an expression cool, ready and attentive, even when no reply was to be expected from her – which was not seldom, as his conversation was equally dry and categorical. – He spoke of dull things, and made them duller by his absolute assurance that he knew all about them. No curious question, no interesting sidelight was to be allowed: there was only the essence of a thing, and that once dealt with was to be put away neatly in a drawer of the mind. Valentine, who was playing his part well in spite of Mr Lynley's tendency to treat him as a boy dressed up in a man's clothes, responded courteously; but at last he caught Louisa's eye with a dark flash, and suggested that Mr Lynley might like to see the gardens – adding mischievously that he could positively engage for Louisa's not climbing any more trees.

The garden-walk, then, it must be: she must take Pearce Lynley's arm, and consent to that purposeful ambling, which, to any observer not acquainted with her mind, must look like the natural proceedings of courtship. Mr Lynley certainly seemed glad to have her arm, though his possessiveness was not so much lover-like as a sort of taking into intimate custody; and it was he who directed their steps, knowing the grounds of Pennacombe very well, and his the remarks on the growth of the timber, the trimming of the shrubs, and the condition of the lawns; so that to the same observer, it would have appeared that he was showing the lady around his own domain, and with a great complacency about how much she must like it.

His present contentment with talking at her, rather than with her, did allow Louisa to review his appearance, and examine her feelings. There was no gainsaying that he was handsome: his dark, strongly marked features lacked nothing but expression. His figure was good: he was a fine horseman, his usual mount being a superbly groomed and sinewy black thoroughbred, and somehow horse and rider had become interchangeable in her mind. If anything, his looks dismayed her, for she had strong doubts about the shape of her own chin and the tendency of her hair to do wild things within a minute of the curling-tongs. – She was conscious indeed that many a young woman would envy her position, and consider Pearce Lynley, who possessed in Hythe Place one of the finest establishments in the county, a great catch; but Louisa was not much interested in great catches, unless it were Selim the Turkish pirate in *The Bride of Abydos*, whose appearance in Devonshire society she must reluctantly accept to be an unlikelihood.

What chiefly occupied her, however, was what he had lately said about his sister's governess. In this she found all her aversion for Mr Lynley most potently distilled – the more so as, from what she knew of Georgiana Lynley, who was more than ten years her brother's junior. Louisa considered any governess who could tolerate the frosty little creature as thoroughly earning her salary and more. As for his dismissive references to his younger brother, she had to confess she knew very little of Francis Lynley; she had not set eyes on him since he was a mere youth, for after that he had spent much of his time at his grandmother's house in Nottinghamshire, where he was reputed a favourite – until he had done something, she knew not what, to incur the family disapproval; and subsequently, after trying various modes of life, and settling to none, he had taken a commission in the Regulars and gone to the Peninsula. He was always named as troublesome – her father, in his colloquies with Mr Lynley, would grimly shake his head at the very mention of his name; and there was, in short, everything to prejudice her in his favour, except his being a Lynley. Even if he shared in the family characteristics of coldness and pride she felt he deserved better on returning wounded from the war than the slighting remarks that were all his brother had seen fit to bestow on him.

But Mr Lynley did not recur to either of these subjects: having concluded his pronouncements on the state of the grounds, with some recommendations for a stricter supervision of the gardeners, he returned to the theme of her late father's virtues. 'You and Mr Carnell have contrived very well, I am sure: still, the absence must be hourly felt. As I said, I was conscious throughout my stay in Nottinghamshire of my inability to play such a part here as I could have wished.'

'It is good of you to think of us, Mr Lynley,' Louisa said, as evenly as she could. 'But I'm sure – as you have suggested – that you have many concerns more pressing and urgent than the neighbourly.'

'Neighbourly I hope I shall always be,' he said, after a bare moment, 'but I do not consider my position at Pennacombe to be so limited as that. I believe, Miss Carnell, that I possessed a good deal of your late father's esteem, trust and confidence. The legacy of the favourite gold-headed cane in his will, which Mr Carnell was good enough to send me, was a token of it. – Only one token,' he added, with a brief but for him significant look in Louisa's face.

But be assured that, though he might have wished to, he did not leave you *me* in his will. This was Louisa's bristling, unspoken thought; but she diverted herself from it with the memory of Valentine's wrapping up the cane in brown paper, and then remarking, as he contemplated the long thin parcel, 'I wonder if he will guess what it is?'

'This is why I was thankful of the opportunity to have some talk with you alone, Miss Carnell,' her companion pursued. 'To assure you that the degree of intimacy with which I have been received at Pennacombe is one I hope and expect will be maintained – even increased.'

'I am not sure I understand you, Mr Lynley. You were, as you said, one of my father's firmest friends – but my father is no longer with us.' An unworthy, half-hearted sort of response, but she found she was not so accomplished in rejection as she thought.

'My dear Miss Carnell, that is only one aspect of the case.' He gave his limited, satisfied smile; and she saw that he took her answer for nothing more than maidenly bashfulness. 'The intimacy I speak of is that which your father was good enough to encourage – even to speak of as his dearest wish: the intimacy that would in time see the estates of Hythe and Pennacombe united.'

The terms were perhaps more appropriate to a map-maker than a lover, but there was no doubting their import.

'Mr Lynley, I am aware – I have long been aware of my father's wishes in this matter. But I cannot too strongly emphasise that they were his wishes, and not my own.'

'To be sure, you have been so much accustomed to depending on his guidance that now you must be a little at a loss. I quite understand your hesitancy, Miss Carnell.' There was no diminution of his composure: no sign that he saw anything but a becoming modesty in her response. 'I am precipitate perhaps – a future occasion will be more suitable than this, our first meeting since the sad event, to speak at length of these things; but let me employ this one, if not to express my esteem and admiration, then at least to assure you, Miss Carnell, that you have it.'

There was nothing to reply to this: to thank him would be to convey that she was glad of his feeling for her, if feeling it could be called. Silence, on the other hand, might suggest that she was flattered, tremulous and overcome – surely *would* suggest it to someone so over-supplied with self-belief as Pearce Lynley. Instead Louisa found herself – to her own surprise as much as his – bursting out: 'Mr Lynley, your sister's governess – do you mean you dismissed her without a character?'

He looked as displeased at this as his habitual aloofness would allow. 'I was not aware that we were talking of the subject, nor of its pertinence. But, yes, I made it plain that I had found her services so unsatisfactory that I could not safely recommend them to another.'

'Then I think, sir, you have done an ungenerous thing. If circumstances compel her to be a governess, you may be sure she has no other resource. Is she young?'

He was reluctant. 'Quite young.'

'Only consider, then, that though she has not succeeded well with Miss Lynley, she may do better in another situation; she may improve, and will surely strive to do so, if she is granted another chance – which she will not get, I am afraid, without a character from her last employer.'

'To give such a character seems to me very like rewarding incompetence,' he said crisply, a little flushed. 'However, your womanly sympathy does you credit,' with a bow. 'And to please you, Miss Carnell, I will consider writing for her such a brief testimonial as is consistent with my regard for the truth.'

It was hard to be profuse in gratitude for this frozen gallantry; nor did she at all wish for it to be done to please *her* – but it was done at least, and she thanked him for it.

'You will allow me to remark, Miss Carnell, that you have much to learn in the ways of the world,' he said, with a return to smooth coolness. 'An open, trusting nature is indeed to be numbered among a woman's graces: one would not wish to see it changed; yet anyone with a particular interest in your future must fear to see it imposed upon. Hence my relief in being at hand once more. Naturally there is much at Hythe that requires my attention, after so long an absence – but I hope that will not prevent you, or your brother, from applying to me at any time when the advice and example of experience may be useful to you.'

'Again I am obliged to you, Mr Lynley; but as for lack of experience, is that not a thing everyone must remedy for themselves – by gaining it? And please do not allow thoughts of how we are faring to distract you from your many responsibilities. We shall shortly be much occupied ourselves. – We expect a visit from our connections in London – our cousins, the Speddings.'

'I know no connections of yours of that name,' he said,

with a look such as one might give to a child making up a particularly unlikely story.

'I dare say not,' said Louisa, her impulse to kick him restrained less by decorum than by the continuing pain in her foot. 'They are our cousins on our late mother's side. Presently they are at Lyme – but we welcome them soon to Pennacombe. We have not met since we were children, and you may imagine with what pleasure Valentine and I anticipate their coming.'

'Ah. These connections – I take it your father was not on terms with them.'

'He was not.'

Mr Lynley directed a frown of disapprobation at a squirrel scampering along a branch, as if it ought to be doing anything but that. 'What sort of people are they?'

She realised she hardly knew – but it would not do to say so. 'Tom and Sophie Spedding are of our own age – and young people of fortune; that is, our uncle Spedding was a rich man.'

'I see. – Of course, if you and Mr Carnell consider this attention due to your relations, I have nothing to say against it. I am sure you are never less than mindful of how your father would have *wished* you to conduct yourselves; and you will already have duly considered that if he severed the connection, he must have had his reasons for it.'

'Mr Lynley, you are, I think, five years or so older than me. I wonder, do you remember my mother? I have only dim recollections of her.'

Cautiously he answered: 'I was, let me see, at Eton when she died. But I recall Lady Carnell as an elegant, quiet-natured woman, generally well thought of.'

Well thought of – or pitied! thought Louisa. 'I have lost a father,' she said, 'but it remains the case that I lost a mother also, distant though the event is. And these are her sister's children.'

'Of course there is nothing to do with such sentiments but honour them,' he said, with another bow; but his jaw was grimly set, and he seemed reserving his real opinion for that future occasion to which he had alluded and on which, presumably, he would combine his declaration of love for her, with a thorough-going criticism of her character and judgement.

Now he noticed how heavily she leaned on his arm – the pain in her foot forcing the unwelcome proximity – and remarked that she must be tired, his tone for the first time approaching true warmth. Or it might have been approval, a disposition to feebleness being a commendable attribute in young ladies. – Louisa for her part was glad of the return to the house, and the escape it afforded her from his exclusive company. Escape, too, from the scene of her own failure. She might congratulate herself on having done something for the unfortunate governess, but for herself, she felt, she had done nothing; somehow she had fallen short of a plain assertion that she would not consider Pearce Lynley as a suitor, though the encounter had done nothing to lessen, and everything to strengthen, her aversion to him. The assertion was demanded not only by her own feelings, but also, she admitted, in justice to him. She doubted there was anything intense or profound in Mr Lynley's attachment to her, simply because it was Mr Lynley's – but such as it was, it must not in common kindness be allowed to rest on a delusive hope.

Chapter V

The unwelcome thought of Mr Lynley could be banished, at least temporarily, by one much more agreeable – the imminent arrival of their cousins; and at the last moment, this novelty of company received an addition: another bedroom must be hastily prepared. The Speddings were bringing someone with them.

It was a particular friend of Sophie's, whom she had chanced to encounter at Lyme, a lady currently unhappily circumstanced, out of health and spirits; and as she was finding some solace, however small, in her friend's society, Sophie had not the heart to leave her behind and alone; – and so, trusting to the generosity and good nature that she had already discerned in her cousins' invitation, she and Tom had included Lady Harriet Eversholt in their party, which hoped to arrive at Pennacombe on Wednesday.

'Pretty in them,' said Mr Tresilian, with a laugh, when Valentine read out the letter that purveyed this information. 'You must hope they don't fall in with a travelling fair between here and Lyme, Valentine, else you will be quartering a menagerie in your grounds.'

'Nothing of the sort, Tresilian. It is just the sort of generous spontaneity I should hope to find in our cousins, and we shall respond in kind.'

'Spontaneity is overpraised. When I sit down to dinner, I should not care to have the beef spontaneously replaced by roast octopus.'

'Tresilian, you are a perfect misanthrope.'

'No, I'm not, I'm still working at it,' said Mr Tresilian, taking a scrap of paper from his pocket, and making a sketch of ship's rigging, adding, at Louisa's curious glance: 'I have just had a thought about the cut of the *Minerva*'s spanker-boom.'

'How little I understand of that sentence,' she said, admiring his drawing. 'And is there truly something on a ship called a fo'c'sle? It seems to have an unwarranted excess of apostrophes. My suspicion is that when we landlubbers are not by, seamen do not use these words at all and talk quite normally.'

'An intriguing notion. I have often been entertained likewise by the speculation that when men are not by, women talk sense, for they assuredly do not otherwise.'

This was much in Mr Tresilian's usual style; as was his reply, on Valentine's urging him to come and dine once their guests were settled, that he would see how many other unbearable things he had to do that week. Louisa's own feeling about the unexpected addition was, however, not as uncomplicated as her brother's. Time and her father's obduracy had made strangers of their kinfolk, but kin they were:

this Lady Harriet Eversholt was all stranger. The aristocratic name was a further contributor to what she was dismayed to find was a paralysing shyness, as the hour of their visitors' arrival drew near; and she could only partly overcome it by the refreshing reminder that what she was doing was something Pearce Lynley would undoubtedly disapprove.

Valentine was in high, though nervous, fettle; he had altered the tying of his cravat half a dozen times, and was still toying with it when Louisa said uneasily: 'I suppose when we have begun to live – that is, when we have begun to live even more – something like this will be of very little moment.'

'Lord! yes. I have known people bring a party of twelve to a house with no notice, and stay a month, and no one has thought anything of it,' he said, though how and where he could have come across this singular instance of unstinting hospitality, he omitted to explain.

'Lady Harriet Eversholt – if she is styled so, she must be of noble birth in her own right, is that not so? I wonder what her unhappy circumstances are. Widowhood, perhaps. Or perhaps only her health. I hope the room is sufficiently aired—'

The sound of swift wheels and bustle put an end to suspense – and suddenly all was enjoyment. Even to stand at the threshold of Pennacombe House as hosts, and smile out at the smart post-chaise drawn up on the gravel, was a pleasure both simpler and keener than could have been guessed; Louisa was able to savour the liberation of the moment, with nothing of either guilt or bitterness towards the departed influence that had so long prevented it.

As for their cousins, she was very soon wondering that she had suffered even a moment's anxiety over their coming: Tom and Sophie Spedding alighted from the post-chaise, and hastened forward to shake their hands, and declare themselves delighted to see them, with such ease and frankness – so much eagerness, and so little ceremony – that the meeting seemed more a comfortable reunion of old friends than an introduction. Tom Spedding was a fair, fresh-faced, big-boned young man, mighty fashionable in his dress but all geniality in his manners; and Sophie, his equal in fairness but much more slight and quick, took on the responsibilities of greeting and explanation, of apologies for the quantity of their luggage and admiration of Pennacombe's drive and front, all with such volubility that there was no time for awkwardness.

'And now let me introduce my dear friend, Lady Harriet Eversholt,' Sophie concluded, 'who all the way down has been quite as severe with me as I dare say I deserve for imposing her presence on you.'

The lady thus presented murmured with a faint smile that she mustn't talk nonsense. She was certainly no widow, or not a recent one, judging by her dress, and might have been no more than twenty-five or -six; but she gave a curious impression, as she moved forward to touch Louisa's hand, of stepping out of a pool of shadow, despite the high brightness of the spring day.

'There can be no consciousness of imposition on our part, Lady Harriet, only honour,' said Valentine, with a bow; and though she thanked him cordially, in a voice both low and musical, she seemed glad to retire into the background again as they went into the house, and surrender the chief claim of attention to the Speddings.

'And here is Pennacombe at last,' said Sophie, 'and not at all as I had pictured it in my mind – which is a shocking piece of fudge because unknown places, and people too, never *are* as one pictures them, and it would be very surprising if they were. It would quite turn one into a gypsy fortune-teller. – Only I had imagined it handsome but not so light and airy – and you have the sweetest view across the park. Just before the turnpike we saw a most imposing place in the distance, but so very grey and frowning I rather hoped it was not Pennacombe. I fancied that staying *there* one would feel quite incarcerated.'

'That would be Hythe Place,' Valentine said, with a shrewd glance at Louisa. 'Certainly it is one of the finest seats in the county, but it is not to everyone's taste.'

'Splendid situation – but this, you know, is quite the thing,' said Tom Spedding, seating himself with all the care and deliberation that tight buckskins, narrow-waisted coat and starched cravat compelled. 'I was never happier to be in a place in my life. And as for meeting you at last, our very own cousins, I cannot conceive anything more agreeable. Almost feel as if I'm dreaming! For, you know, I did dream about it, just the other night at Lyme – didn't I, Sophie?'

'So you did, Tom; though that was the dream that ended unpleasantly – do you remember? – with the tiger chasing you.'

'So it was. Wretched beast. Sure it's going to catch me one day,' Tom said, his face only briefly falling, before assuming again its expression of sunny good temper. 'Fancy a great fellow of four-and-twenty dreaming about a tiger. Fierce one too. Teeth and claws and all. What do you think of *that*?' And, with a look of amiable surprise at himself, he began a slow-dawning laugh of deep enjoyment, in which it was impossible not to join.

'But now we are remiss,' Sophie said, having slapped her brother's knees, 'for though I know Mama wrote you when we read of your father's decease in the newspaper, we should not let this occasion pass without expressing our condolences.'

'Heavens, no,' said Tom. 'Dreadful thing. Never more shocked in my life.'

'And when I wrote Mama last week, she was most particular in her reply that we convey to you her kindest compliments and sincerest hopes that you are recovering from your loss. And now I shan't say any more: for I well remember after poor Papa died that in the end one hardly knew what to do with the commiserations. It all became rather mechanical – and then one felt guilty, because no matter how much one missed that person, still it was only human nature that one was not thinking of them *all* of the time.'

There was an understanding and a delicacy in this, which reinforced the conviction in Louisa's mind, that she was going to get along with their cousins very well. Valentine looked equally as pleased; and if there was any discomfort, it was in the presence of Lady Harriet Eversholt. Not that she did or said anything to create awkwardness: she joined in the conversation a little, civilly answering Valentine's enquiries about how she found Lyme, and whether it had been beneficial to her health, and expressing her pleasure at being in such a delightful spot. But her entire absence of relation to the family necessarily set her apart; and her looks, on which Louisa could not help dwelling with covert glances, sufficiently proclaimed the separation. At first sight she might have been judged no more than a moderately handsome woman, though exceptionally elegant; but the eye could not be satisfied with first sight, and must return with fascination to the strong profile, the full yet slightly indrawn lips, and the look of something both melancholy and forceful that suffused the whole.

It was probably a relief to her, Louisa thought, when the company broke up for the visitors to unpack, and for all to dress for dinner. She was not sorry herself to have a little space for solitary reflection: to feel the relief and gratification that their cousins were so congenial, to anticipate the further pleasures of their visit; and to wonder a little at her father's refusal to have anything to do with the family. Only a little, though, for while the Speddings revealed no affectation, they were undoubtedly town-bred, fashionable, independent, and thoroughly at ease with themselves and the world; and to that damning combination no superabundance of virtues could have been added that would in the least have redeemed them from Sir Clement's contempt.

Her solitude was not long, however. A tap at her bedroom door heralded Sophie Spedding, apologising for the intrusion, and asking for the loan of a pin.

'Of course you see I am full dressed, and don't want a pin at all,' she added, closing the door, 'but one feels the need of a pretext. – Louisa, I did so wish to speak with you alone. I should add, we are not going to be Miss Carnell and Miss Spedding, are we? Thank heaven. No, the fact is I have been a little anxious about our reception here – Tom too: though I cover it by rattling, and Tom is never uneasy even when he is uneasy, if you follow me.'

'I should be sorry to think we have given you any cause for anxiety. Is there anything not to your liking? For in truth we are not at all accustomed to entertaining, and I have been a little anxious myself on that score—'

'Gracious, nothing of that,' Sophie said, seating herself on a footstool as comfortably as if it had been an armchair. 'Why, Tom had a friend from Cambridge whose people accounted themselves *very* high, and we went to stay with them once; I had to wash my hands in a soup-tureen, and share my bedroom with an old wall-eyed pointer because it would sleep nowhere else. The creature conducted itself unspeakably all night, and I couldn't get the window open. No – it concerns my friend Harriet and my bringing her. I am sure it seems quite a presumption: and I fear there is already presumption enough in *our* thrusting ourselves on you.'

'But that was our wish, believe me, as soon as we heard you were at Lyme.'

'Well – shall I confess it was *our* wish too? If I refer to the past – to the estrangement between our families, and your late father's feeling about us – it is only to say I have no opinion about it, other than that it was a great pity; so Mama thinks too. But, yes, when we were at Lyme, and were debating whether to go on to Sidmouth, we did think: shall we not go a little further, and see our cousins the Carnells – because now, at last, we can?'

'So we happily thought alike,' said Louisa, smiling, for the charm of having her cousin sitting here in her room, talking so naturally and confidentially, was suddenly borne in on her. Kate Tresilian, for all her qualities, would never have done such a thing. 'And please don't give yourself any uneasiness over the past – over my father. He quarrelled with your family, as he quarrelled with many people: that was his way; I hope, with all respect to his memory, that it is not ours.' There must have been something invigorating about her cousins' presence, indeed, for she had never put the case, even to herself, so neatly; though she did not feel it quite as positively as she said it.

'You are excessively good,' Sophie said, gazing up at her with eyes that were, Louisa decided, larger and bluer than any others she had ever seen. 'Probably you will say I need not mind about Harriet either. Still, I feel I must explain myself, and the particular circumstances surrounding our friendship. We were first acquainted last winter in town. I met her at one of Mrs Manby's routs – which, by the by, do not at all live up to their reputation. I confess I was eager for the introduction, for there was a deal of fascination in what I had heard of Harriet's story. – Though, to be sure, this may be old news to you.'

'No – not exactly.'

'Well, she is the youngest daughter of the late Earl of Windham, who was quite a byword for high living. – If I say there was more than one acknowledged mistress, I mean only to inform and not to shock. It was the earl's eccentricity, which he made more a boast than a secret, that he could never remember his children's names. Oh, they lacked for nothing material, as Harriet has told me, but they were left quite to shift for themselves as far as guidance and affection went: he could not have been less interested in them, as long as they did nothing to incommode him, as he saw it. And this was poor Harriet's situation, when as a very young woman she met and fell in love with Colonel Eversholt. He was a good twenty years older than her – but dashing, spirited, and very devoted in his attachment; he was an equerry at the Court, and though temporarily embarrassed in the matter of fortune, still I should have supposed it a match to rejoice in. But the earl dismissed it, and so they eloped. And now will it be believed? The Earl, who had given no sign of caring in the least what his children did, went into a most dreadful rage against Harriet – abused her name shockingly in public – and swore she would not get a penny from him. Nor did she: for when a twelvemonth later he died – literally of cherry brandy, they say – Harriet was cut altogether out of his will; and her brother who succeeded him would do nothing for her. Is it not monstrous?'

Louisa was very ready to agree that it was. There was for her a keen interest in this tale of a father, very different from her own in his habit of neglect rather than control but no less capricious and arbitrary in his dispensation of his children's lives. She was thankful at least that their treatment had thrust her and Valentine closer together; the young earl's unbrotherly conduct seeming an inevitable result – shocking, but not surprising – in a family where natural feeling was so little promoted or valued.

'For my part I cannot conceive of anything so inhuman,' Sophie went on, 'but then Papa was always so fond and indulgent with us – too much so, I dare say. I surmise – can we be confidential? – that your own experience was different. Mama always said that Sir Clement tended to strictness – oh, but she said so only in terms of respect—'

'My father was strict and severe in everything,' Louisa said simply.

'Yet you are so good-tempered! But there, I'll say no more of that. – I was telling you of Harriet. Well, her marriage stirred a good deal of talk in society: ordinarily it would soon have died down. But they remained very conspicuous: Colonel Eversholt, I fear, was quite as addicted to high living as the old earl had been; and she, as she has readily confessed to me, was dazzled at being his bride. Being, as you see, a considerable beauty – though her late trials have sadly darkened her looks – she was glad to dress, and go about, and shine, and feel herself the object of regard and attention. Alas, the spirited temperament that had so captivated her in Colonel Eversholt began to reveal itself in less pleasing ways. – He had threatened to horsewhip the young earl when he slighted Harriet – gallant enough, if hot-headed; but such violent outbursts became more frequent, especially as his income began to prove unequal to his style of living. He soon acquired a name for being unapproachable, particularly when he had lost heavily at the tables; and I regret to say that the wife he had won with such ardour at last became the frequent victim of the worst excesses of his ill-temper.'

'This is terrible,' breathed Louisa, though it was not so terrible that she was not eager to hear more.

'Mind, Harriet has never been forthcoming on that last part; but I know how to read a painful silence as well as the next woman, I hope. It was at this time that I became acquainted with her, having often seen her in town, from a distance; and observed the swift change from a brilliant bride to a woman reserved – sorrowful – and, as I found, sorely in need of a friend, who could listen without leaping to judgement. For there was no lack of voices to say that she had reaped what she had sown, and had no one to blame but herself.'

'Yes. I can just hear them,' Louisa said, with warmth. She could hear *one*, certainly. 'But no woman can be held to deserve that, surely – not for any reason; and certainly not for acting on the heart's impulse.'

'I knew you would be of my mind. Yet it was from other

women that I heard the harshest reflections on Harriet's character – which I confess endeared her to me all the more. If I wished to be part of a herd,' Sophie said, drawing herself up with elfin solemnity, 'I should have been born a cow. I have often told people that, and they never know how to answer it. Harriet is a delightful creature – tender-hearted – and no one more amusing when she is in spirits. Those, however, are now quite sunk, as you may have divined. My dear cousin, here is where I must test your liberality of spirit. – Harriet is living apart from her husband.'

'So I should hope,' cried Louisa, who was growing bolder by the moment. 'That is, if his conduct has been as you describe.'

'All of that and worse,' said Sophie, opening her eyes even wider, if that were possible. 'Still, some might say it was her duty to endure it. But she could not sacrifice self-respect on the altar of convention. That's rather a good phrase, isn't it? I must have read it somewhere. – Yes, she left his house when she could bear no more, making no complaint of his cruel treatment – common report had sufficiently established that – but only to secure herself from further outrages. Her brother persisted in his opinion that she had made her bed; and Colonel Eversholt has been as furious against her as may be expected, abusing her as an undutiful wife and, what is worse, denying her any decent maintenance.'

'But he is not obliged to do so?'

'If the separation were to be placed on a legal footing, then he might be brought to it. But Harriet is reluctant to subject herself to the further publicity and scandal of the courts; and besides, though she is the last woman to prate of her feelings, I suspect that though she cannot bear to be any longer under Colonel Eversholt's roof, her heart is not entirely closed against him; and that love can sustain the greatest injury, and still not die. I suspect she nurtures a secret hope that he may change, that her situation may resolve itself as happily as it seemed to begin. But in the meantime she must support herself as best she can; and, as she candidly admits, her education fitted her for nothing. So, Louisa, she is obliged to keep a faro-bank.'

'Really?' said Louisa. Not knowing what a faro-bank was, but hating to admit it, she tried to include in her tone everything from outright shock to easy acceptance, with a result almost operatic in effect.

'Yes: she took a lease on a house in Jermyn Street, and there presided – at a cost to her reputation, you may be sure; though she has friends, among whom I hope I am numbered, who are compassionate rather than condemn her. And, in any case, no one can despise her more than she does herself; and it was a crisis of the nerves, brought on by her wretched consciousness of her situation, that resulted in her physician ordering her to the sea for her health. – And so I came upon her again at Lyme. I was shocked to see her so low – so changed; but in truth it was a happy circumstance, for at Lyme solitude was beginning to undo what sea air had repaired. Our intimacy rapidly increased: much that I have told you I learned fully only while we were so much together at Lyme. I dare say any sympathetic presence would have had the same effect on her, poor thing – it happened to be me. But such was the attachment that I could not bear to think of her left alone again. Though neither could I bear to abandon the opportunity of meeting my cousins at last: hence the result: hence my presumption, my dear Louisa, in bringing her here.'

'It is an unhappy story indeed. I hope we should have welcomed any friend of yours, even without it; so you may believe I am very far from seeing anything like presumption – and I can answer for Valentine's being of the same mind, for we always feel alike. But I do have one anxiety. – From what you have told me of Lady Harriet, I am afraid she will find life at Pennacombe very dull.'

'My dear, have no fear on that score. It was with difficulty that I overcame Harriet's own scruples about coming here unintroduced – but it was the very thought of a healthful, kindly, retired spot, and the balm it might offer to her nerves, that seemed at last to overcome them.'

There was so much in the story of Lady Harriet to appeal to Louisa's strong sense of fancy – not unmixed, perhaps, with a guilty thrill in imagining her father's reaction at having her under his roof – that it might almost have displaced her fascination in meeting her cousins. On their going down to dinner, however, the Lady Harriet of Sophie's narrative gave way again to the quiet, undemonstrative woman, elegantly but soberly dressed, who seemed to wish only to be noticed as little as possible; and attention fastened again on the

Speddings, who revealed themselves to be excellent company, and who made the dining-room so talkative, animated and cheerful, that it was hard to remember that it had once been the most oppressive place in the house, the scene of freezing silences, needling interrogations, and servants in such stiff terror of clattering the crockery as made clumsiness inevitable.

'Capital – couldn't be better,' was Tom Spedding's reply, on Louisa's asking if he found his room comfortable. 'Only I hope you haven't gone to the trouble of giving Sophie a bed: for she doesn't sleep, you know: not she – never a wink!'

'Oh, Tom, you shocking fibster – pay no heed to him, I beg you. I certainly do sleep, though it's true I have never much cared for it, and see it as a thing to be got over. Besides, Tom, *you* go to the opposite extreme: *you* once fell asleep sitting on a stile, which in anyone else but you would be a physical impossibility – now don't deny it.'

Tom, laughing, did not. – His good humour seemed unassailable. Everything met with his hearty approbation: not only was his room capital, but the house, the dining-table, the fire in the grate, the entrance of the roast mutton, all received from him the tribute of being splendid, famous, or just the thing. The minute attention he had given to his hair and clothes before coming into dinner, and his surreptitious and doomed attempts to see the back of his head in the pier-glass, suggested perhaps that his mind was not as developed as his figure; and he had an occasional tendency, when narrating an anecdote, to presuppose that everything familiar to him was familiar to his hearer; as, when describing a favourite dog, he added to Louisa: 'Got him as a pup from old Southwood. Not his brother, the other one. Queer old cove. Had half a finger missing. Gave me a whipping once for stealing greengages. No?' But on discovering that Louisa did not share these entirely personal memories, he laughed at himself with the same good humour.

It was only after dinner that Lady Harriet came a little out of her shell, seating herself beside Louisa, and saying, in her cool shaded voice: 'Miss Carnell, I will not embarrass you with thanks for the welcome you and Mr Carnell have given me. It is more than I could wish. But if any misconceptions concern my presence here, I must correct them. Sophie, I am sure, has told you all about me.'

Louisa, in some discomfort, hesitated over her answer; but Lady Harriet surprised her by quickly squeezing her hand.

'I see from your look that she has. Good, because I wished it so: nothing less than a full account of my situation is owing to you. But what I wish to make plain is that it was my importunity that brought me here. Knowing Sophie, she will have taken the blame to herself, and said she could not part with me. But I fear I have lately been so very dependent on her – clinging, call it – that she was left with little choice.' Lady Harriet gave a brief, bare smile, in which the beauty for which she had been celebrated was startlingly renewed. 'There, that is all I have to say. You need not fear that I will be always remarking on these circumstances.'

Nor did she, at least for the rest of the evening. Evidently Lady Harriet was so dead to pleasures that even the one most universally enjoyed – talking at great length about oneself – was denied to her.

After their guests had gone to bed, Louisa and Valentine stayed some time in the drawing-room that had seen the removal of the fire-screen, reflecting on the swift changes that had followed it, and expressing their equal pleasure in the society of their cousins: Valentine finding Tom extremely well-bred, agreeable, and refreshing in the ease and openness of his manners. Louisa had had a hint from Sophie after dinner that it would be only proper if Valentine also knew the history of her friend; and so she told it, as nearly as possible in Sophie's words – not feeling equipped by experience or understanding to put any of her own gloss on them and, besides, rather liking her cousin's light, rapid way of speaking, and wishing it were her own.

Valentine heard Lady Harriet's story as attentively as he had looked all evening at the lady herself. 'No,' he concluded, with a sigh, shaking his head, 'none of this surprises me. Her sorrows are there to be read in her face.'

'Even her being obliged to keep a faro-bank?'

'Oh, I do not think that the worst of it: do you?'

'Well, it depends on what *sort* of faro-bank it is, to be sure. If it is a – oh, Valentine, I am trying to convey to you that I don't know what a faro-bank is, and you are supposed to help me to an understanding without my having to ask you.'

'Ah, forgive me. That was too subtle for me. A faro-bank – well, faro is a game at cards—'

'I *thought* it was. But the keeping of a bank confused me.'

'Faro is a banker's game: that is, when you bet on the turn of the cards you bet against the banker, or dealer. If you lose, the banker keeps the stake. So it can be profitable, if someone sets up a house at which faro-games are regularly conducted, and they can attract a good number of players to it.'

'So you mean Lady Harriet keeps a gaming-house? Is that not against the law?'

'Oh, it depends on the zeal of the magistrates, I think. It can plausibly be presented as the holding of a private party, after all, at which the guests happen to be gaming at cards. I have often heard of ladies of quality doing this, when they – well, when they are in an unfortunate position, as Lady Harriet is. I for one would certainly not condemn her for it.'

'Oh, neither would I,' said Louisa, quickly.

'You know, I grow more and more disgusted at the illiberal thinking of the world,' Valentine said, frowning and raking the fire. 'The haste to leap on the moral high horse – the disregard for the honest impulses of the human heart. Well, we shall set a different example at Pennacombe, I hope. – Louisa, we must have a dinner. I should not want Lady Harriet to feel in the least that we are constrained by her presence: no, she shall be treated as an honoured guest. We shall invite our friends – aye, and let that old humbug Dr Sayles come too. And then Pearce Lynley – an invitation is surely owing there.'

'I do not consider anything as particularly *owing* in that quarter.'

'Perhaps not. – Still, he is a notable man after all, and we surely don't want our cousins thinking we know no one of consequence.' He shrugged away from her look of mild surprise at this, coughed, and recovered himself by adding, with a teasing smile: 'And besides, Louisa, you must know you cannot avoid him for ever.'

Chapter VI

The Carnells and the Speddings were very soon on terms not merely of cordiality but of intimacy. At least in the case of Valentine and Tom, they were much together; shooting was over, but they rode every morning; before and after dinner they often talked together for minutes at a time; and each referred to the other as an excellent fellow. Even Louisa's limited experience recognised in this the ultimate expression of masculine sentiment; and when Tom began to teach Valentine the newest and most fashionable methods of tying the cravat, their friendship was plainly placed on unshakeable foundations.

As for Sophie, she was so forthcoming, so free of reserve, and so gratifyingly inclined to like her, that it was impossible for Louisa to imagine being anything less than confidential with her. Whether Tom's assertion that she did not sleep were true or not, she certainly possessed great vivacity: but it was not of the relentless sort that leaves one longing for a little lifeless silence. She was as eager to listen as to tell – a fact that occasioned in Louisa, at first, some constraint; for Sophie had been accustomed to going about with her brother since he was at Oxford, and clearly knew so much of London, of Bath and all the watering-places, of country-house parties and town crushes, that Louisa feared she had little of interest to offer in return. – But Sophie, in her affectionate way, would have none of this. She was hungry for everything Louisa had to say, and found equal fascination in all of it. It was a stimulating thought, that even having a great deal of experience did not diminish the appetite for more.

Instructive, too, was the manifest ease between Tom and Sophie, which must be a reflection of their very different upbringing. They could abuse each other with the greatest good humour, rising to such epithets as *great starched booby* and *prattling featherhead*; and their true affection was unimpaired. Between Louisa and Valentine, the very tightness of the bond precluded such freedom. They had both received too many insults in earnest. If Louisa could speak with anyone in that way it was, curiously, Mr Tresilian; but with her brother, it would have been like playing with knives.

The presence of Lady Harriet might have acted as a check on the rapid familiarity of the cousins, but she conducted herself much as she had hinted on that first evening – seeming only to seek quiet and retirement. She did not monopolise Sophie's attention: spent a lot of time writing letters, but did not receive any; and would sometimes smile distantly but tenderly at the high spirits of the others, as if a great number of years separated her from them. – Her situation brought out all the warm chivalry of Valentine's nature. His brow would cloud if ever Sophie, in whom volubility occasionally overleaped tact, happened to mention the name of Colonel Eversholt; and he exerted himself constantly in attention to Lady Harriet's comfort – though always with a delicacy that would not render her conspicuous.

Her presence must excite remark, of course, at the dinner Valentine insisted on, but this would be lost in the general novelty of their being company at Pennacombe House. Curiosity brought a ready attendance from their guests, except the rector, Dr Sayles, who came only to be offended and disapproving, and remained throughout as much on his dignity as was possible to a man with horse's teeth and large bunches of hair growing out of his ears. The occasion went well; Louisa felt that with the Speddings there, it could hardly go otherwise. Before the first course was over, Tom was confiding to her that he had never met such a thoroughly agreeable set of people in his life. This was in spite of his having on his other side the doleful shawled figure of Miss Rose, emanating murmurs about preventively throwing herself off ledges and into lakes before she would be a nuisance to anyone. But in her determination to be disregarded she had met a stiff enemy in Tom, who persisted in helping her to the choicest slices of meat, and in finding everything she said interesting, to her almost complete bafflement. There seemed in the end no recourse for her except to be civil, pleasant and cheerful in return. Miss Rose managed to avoid *that*, naturally, but it was a close-run thing.

'Well, my dear, I was never more delighted,' Mrs Lappage

cried, seizing on Louisa when the ladies withdrew. 'Such very charming young people! Such elegance, without the least affectation! I heartily congratulate you for improving the acquaintance; and indeed there is such a degree of amiability and good manners that one can only wonder why the acquaintance was rejected before, in a certain quarter. But then one does *not* wonder, on recollection – amiability and good manners being not at all esteemed in that certain quarter: but I will not allude to that. And as for their companion –' lowering her voice '– I feel sure I have seen her portrait engraved in a London paper, illustrating notable beauties. There is certainly a good deal more reserve in her manner; and if I thought that was in any way to do with her finding some of her company beneath her, I should be a little dismayed – but your look tells me it is nothing of the sort, my dear, so I say no more of it.'

Certainly Lady Harriet had said little at dinner but, then, she had not had the most engaging of companions. – Mr Lynley, at Louisa's instigation, had been at her side. She was sure that his pride, at least, would be gratified in taking in to dinner the lady of the highest rank there: rank was always a first consideration with him; but Louisa had not acted to oblige him, only to deliver herself from his society. It was true, as Valentine had hinted, that she could not for ever evade him or, rather, that formal avowal of his intentions which he had given her notice to expect; but he was unlikely to make it in the course of a dinner-party, and she could at least secure the temporary comfort of not having to talk to him. He had appeared, however, not at all put out, as far as his immovable expression could be judged; and seemed chiefly occupied with a minute observation of the newcomers, and the storing up of his gathered intelligence against a conclusion.

'And I fancy I am not the only one favourably impressed,' Mrs Lappage went on. 'Mr Tresilian, I could not help but observe at dinner, was most forcibly struck by Miss Spedding.'

'Was he?' cried Louisa, in surprise. 'I did not remark it.'

'Oh, nothing *demonstrative* – that is not his way; but I saw him several times absolutely gazing at her – I would almost say, as if he were lost in admiration.'

'Mr Tresilian? Well, perhaps you are right, ma'am.' It was quite a new idea – but, Louisa thought after a moment's reflection, a mistaken one. When Mr Tresilian gazed in that abstracted way, it usually meant he was thinking about the new excise duty.

No, she strongly doubted that Mrs Lappage had read Mr Tresilian aright; still, with a sharpness of curiosity she could hardly account for, she resolved to be watchful when the gentlemen rejoined them. – Alas, when they walked into the drawing-room her attention was promptly claimed, or appropriated, by Mr Lynley, who took his seat by her as if by right; and receiving from her hands his tea, which by unhappy lack of foresight she had neglected to fortify with poison, declared: 'Well, your cousins seem tolerably well-bred people on the whole. They are rather inclined to fashion, I think; but I have had some conversation with Mr Spedding, and it appears their fortune is at least equal to it.'

'I dare say: I have not thought of it. I have been chiefly occupied with the simple pleasure of getting to know them, as they are our nearest family.'

'Very proper. That is not, of course, a consideration that can be extended to their companion. I am curious to know how Lady Harriet comes to be travelling with them. I have been thinking on her name. Eversholt is not, as I recall, a family name occurring in the peerage, which suggests she must be married, or widowed.'

'I congratulate you on your detective skills, Mr Lynley: I'm sure you may become a Bow Street Runner whenever you choose to apply.'

'Naturally,' he said, ignoring this, 'neither you nor Mr Carnell would have welcomed her to Pennacombe without some previous assurance as to her character and situation in life.'

'She is a guest, Mr Lynley, not a governess.'

He made no answer to this, but sat regarding her with a look more quizzical than his usual coolness admitted. Perhaps it was the dressing of her hair, which she had done rather after Sophie's fashion; whatever the reason, it made her sufficiently uncomfortable.

'So, have you any more news of your brother, Mr Lynley?'

'I hear, through an Admiralty connection, that he has taken ship: he will be in England as soon as the winds permit.'

'No doubt it will be a great comfort to you to have him restored.'

'I am happy that he is safe, certainly. Comfort is not a

term I would apply in this instance, nor in anything connected with Francis,' he said, with his severest composure.

'I'm sure I should be greatly agitated if my brother were to be returning wounded from overseas.'

'Your familial feeling does you credit. – Allow me to remark, however, that the situation is quite different.'

That *allow me to remark* was a characteristic phrase of Mr Lynley's that in Louisa's view contained, in little, all that was detestable about him. There was, after all, not the slightest possibility of his *not* being allowed to remark, ever – as he well knew; but the phrase established his superiority, put you in your place, and cast over the conversation the deep chill that he appeared to consider the median temperature for human relations. – Fortunately she had not long to remain at this pitch of vexation with him. Mr Tresilian came to entreat her to play, and conduct her to the pianoforte.

'The fact is,' he confided, 'they're talking of Kate playing; but the newcomers have made her shy so I thought if we had you, it would cover it over for now.'

'There is no resisting such a gracious invitation. What do you like best about my playing, Mr Tresilian? The wrong notes, or the splendid force with which I hit them?'

He thought. 'No: the way you look at the music, as if it were a threatening letter written in blood.'

She was not so diverted by this as to forget to watch him when he returned to his seat by Sophie; and having got creditably to the end of her first piece without taking too many musical wrong turnings, she observed them further.

There was certainly a marked attention in his manner; but the gaze he fixed on Sophie struck Louisa chiefly by its wistfulness. – It seemed the look of a man remembering, rather than admiring. As a girl she had only glimpsed the late Mrs Tresilian once or twice, Sir Clement not in the least inclining to bridal visits; but putting that together with all she had heard of her, she wondered if Sophie, with her dainty vitality, was reminding Mr Tresilian of his unfortunate choice, and with what emotions he contemplated the likeness.

Presently Kate was prevailed upon to play – it was Lady Harriet, with a few discreet and skilful words, who achieved it; and as Mr Tresilian's attention was now claimed by Miss Rose, who was looking unhappy so that she could deny looking unhappy, Louisa took the opportunity of asking Sophie how she liked her dinner companion.

'Oh, excessively! I thought at first I should get nothing from him – but he is quite a delightfully whimsical creature; and when I asked him about his name, and whether it is Cornish, he said yes, but I must be quiet about it, because the men of Devonshire and the men of Cornwall have disliked each other since time immemorial, and he was liable to be put in a sack by night and dropped in the Tamar. His face was so dreadfully solemn that for a moment I thought he was serious.'

'Mr Tresilian does not often say serious things.'

'No – and yet there is the most interesting melancholy about his face; and then something boyish too, when he smiles – though at first I supposed him past thirty.'

'He is, I think, eight-and-twenty.' Louisa doubted that it was appropriate for her to give Sophie his history; and indeed found herself feeling a little proprietorial about it, and faintly resentful of such speculations from a newcomer, when she knew him so well. But she was doubtful also whether it was something her cousin actively sought. If anyone else had spoken so, she might have suspected a partiality; but in Sophie's words and expression, she discerned nothing more than the Spedding tendency to find everybody likeable.

The party broke up early – much earlier than suited Valentine, who wished parties to go on for ever – at the instigation of Mr Lynley, who asked for his carriage to be brought round. The Tresilians, who only used theirs when there was Miss Rose to be conveyed, thought they had better go too, to save troubling the servants twice over; and so started a general leave-taking. Mr Lynley, who still wore an air of privately drawing conclusions, chose a moment in the hall to speak to Louisa alone.

'I hope, Miss Carnell, that the demands of your company will not prevent me from calling at Pennacombe in my accustomed manner, and having some talk with you alone,' he said, in a tone very little like that of a man asking a favour, and much like one asserting a right.

'Certainly: though as you remark, Mr Lynley, the entertainment of our guests must have the first claim.'

She thought she had done rather well in answering him with his own cold propriety of expression; but she could not be comfortable under his steadfast regard; and she hardly knew how to answer when he went on: 'As to *claims*, there are those which are incidental and temporary – and those which are of long standing, and reinforced by the strongest authority. The balance between them, my dear Miss Carnell, I leave to your good sense to judge; but as this touches on the matter I wish to discuss, I shall not anticipate.'

For some time afterwards she felt as drearily crushed and helpless as she had after her father's worst rebukes – a sensation very unwelcome in its return; and it took all the liveliness of her cousins to restore her spirits, before the hour of retiring. Here, indeed, lay her best remedy: for she was reminded that this was an acquaintance begun and maintained by happy choice, not by compulsion. The question of choice was still in her mind when at last, being alone, she told Valentine of Mrs Lappage's conjectures about Mr Tresilian.

'I don't know – but I fancy Sophie may have set him thinking, perhaps, of his late wife, and that is all the reason he was struck with her,' Louisa said. 'And yet it occurs to me – Mr Tresilian *might* marry again: there is nothing to prevent it; he has an easy fortune, and though he has a peculiar provoking sort of temper, that might be no obstacle to a woman who could see past it.'

'Tresilian and Sophie? It is an intriguing notion. – But no, I know Tresilian as well as anyone, and I am almost sure that romance is quite dead for him. And even if it were not, I cannot imagine Sophie consenting to the steady, plain sort of life that Tresilian could offer. – There is Kate besides. He cherishes her to such a degree that he would surely not bring a wife to The Ridings, and see Kate relegated to that second place in his duty and affection, which must necessarily be her lot. No, he would not do it.'

'I confess I cannot picture him in the character of a lover: he would be too inclined to laugh at himself; and I suspect a woman generally requires a man who is in love with her to be made satisfyingly miserable by it. But, then, Kate might not be an impediment – Kate might marry also.'

Valentine did not answer this directly, only shaking his head and remarking: 'I fear Tresilian shelters her too much: you can plainly see the difference between her and Sophie, in ease and manner. Lady Harriet, of course, I do not mention: it could hardly be expected that she should match *that* degree of elegance and self-command. It can only be admired, as an example, from a distance.'

There was no doubting, from Valentine's look, and the urgent tone in which he pronounced these words, that the admiration he referred to was his own. It suggested more strongly than ever that any lingering attachment to Kate must take its lean chance in the new world opened to his mind by their cousins: even suggested, perhaps, that when he came to fix his heart, it would be on a woman possessing Lady Harriet's qualities. That he should fix his heart on Lady Harriet herself was, of course, out of the question: their enterprise of living, bold though it was, surely did not run to impossibilities.

Chapter VII

From their first arrival, Sophie had remarked on the inviting views that opened up beyond the park. Certainly Pennacombe House was situated at the foot of some beautiful rolling country – though Sir Clement had always lamented his ancestors' not building on high ground, presumably because from a hill one could always look *down*; but, as Louisa knew, the green richness of Devonshire was equally rich in mud for a good part of the year. The strengthening spring continuing dry, however, it was possible now to make an exploring-party without the addition of stilts.

A family picnic on the downs must be, Louisa supposed, a very mild amusement for someone of Lady Harriet's experience: yet it was this that occasioned a notable lifting of her spirits. Valentine had just chosen a spot for the laying-out of their collation, and Tom had agreed that it was famous, the very thing, and could not be bettered, when Lady Harriet burst out: 'No, no – not here.' With a rueful smile she went on: 'Forgive me, I know I have no right to dictate – but do look around: we are so beautifully free of the world – except *there*.' She pointed to a fold of pasture, above which could just be seen a cottage roof. 'Is it not a pity? If we were to descend a little further towards that covert, then I think it will be quite out of view – and we shall be free.'

'I'm sure I have no objection,' Sophie said. 'But, my dear Harriet, we have walked a fair distance: will you not be tired?'

'Tired? Not in the least. This is so magnificently refreshing – I feel new-made.' There was indeed a brilliancy in Lady Harriet's look, a glow in her complexion, that Louisa had not seen before: it was engaging; though she felt it was a little hard on the blameless cottage, which belonged to Mr Tomms the bee-keeper, supplier of excellent honey. 'But you are too gentle, Sophie, to reproach me as I deserve. At Lyme, Miss Carnell, I was always the first to declare myself fagged: I wanted to walk, and then complained I was unable to walk. I was a great trial to your cousin's patience. But you need not fear a revival of *that* vexing creature: she is gone. Mr Carnell, will you indulge me in going a little further?'

'If indulgence were called for, Lady Harriet, I hope you might always depend upon it from me,' Valentine said, smiling, 'but as it happens, I think you have chosen best.'

He gave her his arm as they made the descent; and as the roof was blotted from sight, she cried: 'There – it is complete. Now there is nothing but us, and the living earth – just as it should be.'

Her enthusiasm was infectious; though Louisa had to suppress a smile at a notion of wild nature that could be fulfilled in a Devonshire meadow, with the busy Dawlish road just beyond the ridge, and behind them the manservant bringing the laden picnic-basket.

'"Under the greenwood tree, who something something me", tum-te-tum the weather,' Tom remarked. 'Shocking memory for poetry.'

'Now, let us sit down on the grass, with nothing to remind us of the world; and forget everything,' Lady Harriet said, looking round at them all with rapturous urgency. 'See if you can do it.'

'Everything?' cried Sophie. 'I am afraid there will be nothing left of me.'

'Oh, but there will – there will be the essence, and that is what we so sadly lose.'

Tom, once his coat-tails were properly arranged, looked as if sitting and thinking of nothing were comfortably within his range of accomplishments.

'Are we not permitted to remember the good things of the world, Lady Harriet?' Valentine asked, with a look at once smiling and serious. 'The pleasant, the hopeful – the beautiful?'

'Ah, no,' said she, shaking her head, 'they are the most delusive of all.'

Louisa, in trying to think of nothing, found she had never thought of so many things at once in her life; and was glad when Tom brought the experiment to an end by declaring that he was famished for pigeon-pie.

Among the countless thoughts that had crowded into her mind, that of Pearce Lynley was not the least prominent.

Cold meat and hock effected its temporary banishment; but the unwelcome theme was taken up by Sophie who, drawing closer to her, began: 'Louisa, do you mind if I ask? Indeed, I don't know why I say that, because I always *do* ask. That very impressive gentleman Mr Lynley – is there something in the nature of an attachment? I could not help but observe, when he dined the other day, that he had eyes only for you during the whole evening.'

'I dare say he did,' Louisa said. 'The eyes of a strict overseer for an apprentice, perhaps, or a cat for a mouse-hole.'

'Dear me – revealingly expressed,' laughed Sophie. 'I was right then to call it something in the *nature* of an attachment. I confess I did not find him as agreeable as Mr Tresilian – though he is undoubtedly well-bred, and has a great deal of air and address, and is uncommonly handsome; and I take him as having a large fortune.'

'Just so: you have now enumerated all Mr Lynley's attractions; he could hardly have done it better himself, though I am sure he would be willing to try. I may as well say that Mr Lynley *considers* there is an attachment: it was a match much promoted by my father, whose feelings about the matter are the only ones Mr Lynley regards as important; and I am tolerably certain that he intends making me his wife, whenever his judgement deems it appropriate.'

'Ah, so that's how it is! And you intend refusing him, I collect.'

'I would hope I have already given him sufficient hints of my feeling to make a proposal unlikely. But Mr Lynley is not a man to pick up hints: probably it is too much like stooping.' With a little bubble of irritation, directed less at Sophie than herself, she added: 'You are about to tell me, perhaps, that I ought to be flattered by the admiration of such a man, even if I cannot return his sentiments.'

'I should hope not,' Sophie said earnestly. 'Undoubtedly I would be flattered, because that's the kind of goose I am; but as you have told me, you have lived retired, and known little society – so I would be more concerned if you *were* quite overwhelmed by the first eligible man to approach you. There are many more Mr Lynleys in the world, believe me.'

'That is what above all I should not wish to believe. – But come – you don't mean that you have any inclination towards him?'

'No, no: only that when a man favours me with his attentions, I cannot help liking it, even if I cannot like him. Utterly nonsensical of me, I know. And as for proposals, they are so very exciting – at least, the four I have had were so—'

'Four?' put in Tom, overhearing. 'I thought it was three.'

'There was one I didn't tell you about, and now kindly return to your pie, sir. – No, there is something very beguiling about a proposal: just the proposal in itself, without its leading to anything. For to accept one, of course, is to exclude the possibility of any more.'

At this Lady Harriet slightly turned her head, and Louisa saw a look both wry and sorrowful cross her face, before she returned her attention to Valentine. He was talking of London – with a very creditable appearance of knowledge for someone who had scarcely been there in his life. Louisa did not take what Sophie had said with entire seriousness: her cousin was habitually light-hearted, which Louisa felt was a different thing from being light-minded; and though Sophie had spoken warmly again of Mr Tresilian, she remained convinced that nothing was to be apprehended in that quarter. – The real imperviousness of Mr Tresilian's temperament, and the apparent disposition of Sophie to like liberally without feeling deeply, preserved her from any anxiety. But in one regard Louisa found herself unyieldingly serious. She might imitate Sophie's method of dressing her hair, and even emulate her happy nonchalance towards those great questions of life that Sir Clement had always believed difficult beyond his children's capacity; but no matter how hard she tried, the prospect of a proposal from Mr Lynley was not something Louisa could conjure as exciting or beguiling.

Still, her mind remained supple enough to wriggle away from the question until she was unavoidably confronted with it: which happened the very next day. She had stayed at home while Valentine and their guests took their morning walk, recognising that a consultation with the housekeeper was long overdue; and having looked over the accounts, ordered the meat and flour and candles, and shrugged off the spectre grumbling over her shoulder about their increased spending, she had seated herself with a book when Mr Lynley was announced.

'I am glad of the opportunity to speak to you alone,' he said, after his usual austere civilities; but what came next, though equally unwelcome, was widely different from what she had anticipated. 'I am in possession of some intelligence about one of your guests, which, while unpleasant and even abhorrent, I feel I have a duty to communicate to you. The special position towards you and your family in which I have the honour to be placed, by the confidence of your late father, renders it absolutely necessary; not to speak of my own feelings, which are engaged in such a manner that I cannot stand silently by, where I may warn, advise and protect.'

He left a pause, which she presumed was to be filled with her acknowledgement and gratitude, but Louisa, as much surprised as displeased, gave him only the very limited satisfaction of saying: 'Go on.'

'I have nothing to say of your cousins: your choosing to acknowledge the relationship is, as I have previously remarked, a matter for you and Mr Carnell to balance between your own inclinations and the wishes of your father. But there is no tie of blood to plead the case of Lady Harriet; and there, I am afraid, you have erred greatly, though I think inadvertently, in receiving her as a guest at Pennacombe, where a scrupulous regard for propriety has always been the admirable rule. – I thought, on first hearing the name of Lady Harriet Eversholt, that I had heard it mentioned in some undesirable connection, but I could not be sure: so I took the trouble of writing a confidential friend in London, who has a broad knowledge of the affairs of the town, to see if he knew anything of her history. I am sorry to be the bearer of this news, Miss Carnell,' Mr Lynley said, walking to the fireplace, and looking more triumphant than sorry, 'but Lady Harriet is a woman whose situation is such that even her rank cannot rescue it from disrepute. I should be willing to spare you the details, if you would be content to believe that I have this on the strongest authority, and to accept my word that the acquaintance should not have been begun, and must now be discouraged as far as it lies in your and Mr Carnell's power.'

'I am sorry, Mr Lynley, but I cannot accept your word, or anyone's, on such a matter. I would be most perturbed if someone were to decline *my* acquaintance, simply because someone else had told them they must do so. I must know the grounds on which you seek to make this prohibition; but I should add that Valentine and I know Lady Harriet's circumstances pretty well.'

'That I crave leave to doubt,' he said, frowning down at her. 'But since you compel me, I must ask whether you know why Lady Harriet travels alone, though her husband is living.'

'Certainly: Lady Harriet is separated, though not formally, from her husband – Colonel Eversholt, an equerry in the royal household.'

Mr Lynley's eyebrows rose. 'He has been an equerry, though my understanding is his services are no longer required, such is his reputation. – But surely you have said enough, Miss Carnell, to corroborate me; and if you have not reflected seriously on this, as I can only conclude you have not, then I urge you to do so now. The separation is not, as you remark, made formal, which consigns Lady Harriet to a very dubious status – a married woman, yet one who goes about independently. But even a woman legally separated from her husband – even one nobly born – cannot be an entirely unobjectionable figure in society. There is a loss of that complete respectability, which a young person in your position cannot too strictly enjoin as a condition of your acquaintance.'

'Mr Lynley, I hope I shall never begin setting conditions on my acquaintance – unless that they be pleasant and amusing. And if this is all you have to urge against Lady Harriet, then assuredly you have wasted your time. I am sorry for that, and I would be more sorry if you had undertaken these researches at my request, instead of by your own choice.'

'You astonish me. I can only suppose your want of experience, and Mr Carnell's likewise, has inclined you to this liberality of judgement; that it proceeds from an innocence of what is fitting, rather than a disregard of it. If such is the case, I must be sensible that further enlightenment may give you pain; but I cannot do justice to my conscience without telling you all. Miss Carnell, the circles in which Lady Harriet has been accustomed to move are those to which tolerance would accord the title fashionable, though I should rather call them rakish. Believe me, I have no pleasure in speaking of this; but how do you suppose Lady Harriet supports herself?'

'Oh, she is obliged to keep a faro-bank,' Louisa said, with the easiest unconcern.

Mr Lynley stared; but he quickly recovered at least the appearance of composure and, shaking his head, said in a tone of superior forbearance: 'Well, well, I perceive you have heard those words, but plainly have not attached any proper meaning to them. If you knew—'

'I know very well what a faro-bank is, Mr Lynley,' cried Louisa, all the more indignant because he had inadvertently touched on the truth. 'And I dare say it is not what some people would consider respectable; but then we are country-bred, and may perhaps be narrow in our views about such things. My chief feeling is that it is a great pity Lady Harriet has to live in that way: it does not alter my opinion of her in any other direction. If *you* do not wish to continue in her acquaintance, then that is up to you: I do not consider myself in the least entitled to direct your choice – any more than you are entitled to direct mine.'

Her anger on Lady Harriet's behalf, though real enough, was now diverted into a much stronger channel: against Pearce Lynley, against all the presuming arrogance with which he oppressed her, against all the harsh, cold certainty he represented – and even, perhaps, against that one overbearing influence, which until now she had only permitted herself to regret. – Finding herself on the verge of actual bitterness against her father shocked her: she was silent, where she had meant to go on. – Mr Lynley's look of high mortification sufficiently revealed how unexpected, and ungratifying, had been her rebuff of what he doubtless considered his good offices: whether he read a more flattering remorse in her silence she could not tell – for at that moment Valentine entered the room.

'Oh! hullo, Lynley, I didn't know you were here,' he said cheerfully. 'Have you heard the news? I had it from old Jarrett, who had just come from Teignmouth, where there was a cutter just put in from London – in short, it is as certain as anything: Bonaparte has signed the instrument of abdication. It is all over – we have peace at last. A wonder, is it not? I must send to Dr Sayles about having the church bells rung – and there must be a bumper of ale for everyone in the village. I wonder if there are any fireworks to be had hereabouts – Tresilian might know. Now, you must positively engage to dine with us tomorrow: we must mark the occasion in the proper manner.'

Mr Lynley signalled his acceptance with short thanks, and a shorter bow: whether from the prospective moral pollution of dining at the same table with Lady Harriet, or from the continued discomposure of his conversation with Louisa, he could not be easy; and after a very few remarks, which in their suppressive tone could hardly have been further from Valentine's generous elation, he took his leave.

'He is a stiff-necked fellow,' Valentine said, 'but I mean to have a large party, so he will be well diluted. Well, what grand wisdom has he been handing down to us today, Louisa?

Or was he paying you those compliments I know you take so much delight in?'

Louisa laughed, or tried to; and turned the conversation back to the news of the peace. She decided, almost instantly, not to repeat to her brother what Mr Lynley had said. His indignation on Lady Harriet's behalf would surely be greater than her own; and something – perhaps the tedious voice of caution, which she still could not stifle – told her that it could do no good to engender in Valentine's heart any warmer feeling towards Lady Harriet than he already possessed.

Chapter VIII

A mere dinner, to celebrate the great news of victory and peace, could not satisfy Valentine. For much of that day and the next he was engaged in riding about the neighbourhood and into Teignmouth, personally to deliver invitations, and to secure the services of a small band of musicians. – There was to be dancing at Pennacombe after dinner. The ceremony and parade of a formal ball must await another time: it had indeed been one of his many projections; but he was far from considering this mode of arranging an entertainment inferior. There was a spontaneity and flexibility in it that was much to his taste; and it raised a willing response, especially among the young people of the district, for whom short notice only added to the prospective excitement of such an evening, little to be encountered outside the accustomed winter balls of Newton Abbot.

He had cast his net wide; and the sons and daughters of lawyers, land-agents and merchant-captains were bidden welcome to the hospitality of Pennacombe House, with a freedom that would have appalled its late master. Valentine even suffered a moment of anxiety himself, in which his natural liberality contended with his wish of appearing well in the eyes of their visitors; but it was quickly got over. The Speddings were much more sociable than exclusive, and inclined to like large parties; and Lady Harriet, continuing in revived spirits, commended his plan fully, and with such lively looks as might have led him to increase the number of guests, if there had been anybody left to invite.

Of the dinner guests, James and Kate Tresilian were the first to arrive – but without Miss Rose, who had insisted on staying at home. She had protested that she would be quite superfluous in such a large gathering: – had probably foreseen, indeed, that there her settled purpose of being overlooked might be too fully realised, and had calculated that in deliberately absenting herself from a special occasion lay her best means of ensuring she would be missed, thought about and worried over, to the general detriment of the Tresilians' pleasure. With Kate, certainly, she appeared to have succeeded.

'I do think it a pity that she is sitting there alone.' She sighed. 'I ought to have stayed at home with her: it was rather selfish of me to have come.'

'Nonsense,' said Mr Tresilian. 'Miss Rose will be having a thoroughly pleasant evening. She can put out candles and make do with one, and decline to have a fire lit or the cloth laid just for her, and indulge in every discomfort.'

'These are surely circumstances in which age must accommodate youth,' Valentine said. 'Respect for our elders is a very good thing – but it might be more willingly given if our own feelings were respected in turn. I should have hated the thought of you missing the music and dancing, Miss Tresilian – you who are so fond of it; and I hope you will promise me the favour of the first two dances, as earnest of your intention to enjoy yourself, and not be put out by any such reflections.'

Kate assented with a readiness that, in a young woman less inclined to quietness of temper and more inclined to display, would have rendered unmistakable the strength of feeling behind it. Louisa certainly did not mistake it, and nor, she was sure, did Mr Tresilian; but how much Valentine saw, how much or how little he meant to distinguish Kate by this attention, could not be determined. – He was off again in a moment, to welcome another guest, and to exert himself in nervous, happy sociability.

'Well, there will be a regular crush after dinner,' Mr Tresilian said to Louisa, watching him go. 'Does this mean, by the by, that I now have to ask you for the first two dances?'

'Why should you think that?'

'I don't know. Symmetry, I suppose.'

'Do not allow that to trouble you, Mr Tresilian. I am content for us to be a little lopsided, rather than put you through such agony.'

'Mind, Pearce Lynley has the first claim anyhow.' At her look he went on: 'Well, does he not? It is common knowledge that Sir Clement favoured him; and now he is back in the county, and being generally attentive to you, one draws the obvious conclusions.'

Somehow there was more to dislike in hearing this from Mr Tresilian's lips than any other: perhaps because she was used to plain truth from him. – But with this in mind, indeed, she gathered courage to ask: 'Tell me, Mr Tresilian, what do *you* think of Mr Lynley?'

'Think of him? I should have to ask you precisely why you sought my opinion before I could answer that.'

'Now I must ask you why that is the case, and we shall just go round in pointless circles.'

'Rather like dancing, in fact. Oh, I think well enough of Mr Lynley: he has committed no murders that I am aware of, and he gives me good-day quite as if I were human. I cannot conceive what else you want from me. You surely do not seek to be influenced in any direction, now that the liberty of choice is yours. If I disliked him, I hope that would have no more bearing on your own feeling than the fact that your father liked him.'

'To be sure it would not,' she said, a little disconcerted. 'Only – only our feelings always are influenced, surely: it is no simple matter to disentangle them.'

'You want me to tell you that you are right, and I am not going to. My own rule with feelings is always to mistrust them. Now we had better stop talking about Mr Lynley, for he is here.'

He was – and there was an end of Louisa's peace. She was curious, in a savage sort of way, to observe how he would greet Lady Harriet. There was certainly a further degree of aloofness – which seemed to extend also to Tom and Sophie. But after a few moments she discerned what was chiefly troubling him and making him prowl so unconscionably about the room, and bestow his pale stare even on innocent Mrs Lappage, who attempted a civil enquiry about his sister. – They were receiving in the summer parlour, the large drawing-room having been swept clear of furniture for the dancing: it could be glimpsed across the passage, whenever a guest arrived, in all its inviting vacancy; and there Mr Lynley's gaze kept returning, with a hardening expression of disapproval on each occasion.

This brought Louisa's vexation with him to a sharper point; and when he made his bow, she could barely return his civilities. These were brief indeed, however, and he at once went on: 'I appear to be under some species of misapprehension. Mr Carnell was good enough to ask me to dine. Yet I see preparations suggestive of a ball.'

'Not a ball. But dancing, yes, after dinner. We mean to have a good deal of company, you know, in tribute to the exceptional news.'

'I see,' was all his answer; but he resumed his pacing, and his hauteur increased to the extent that even Tom came away from speaking to him with a slightly crushed look, and remarked to Louisa: 'Splendid fellow. A little on the high ropes, perhaps, but still. Sterling fellow at bottom, I feel sure,' and he was obliged to look at himself several times in the pier-glass, and reassure himself as to the sweep of his hair and the set of his cravat, frontally and in profile, before he could be quite composed again.

It should have been – in many respects was – a convivial dinner: Valentine as host was on his best mettle, the Speddings lively company as ever, and everyone inclined to the cheerful and celebratory spirits that the occasion naturally called for; but there was an exception, and it was an exception that Louisa could not long contemplate without feelings so powerful, so heated, as to threaten their breaking out if she did not quickly wrest her attention elsewhere. – To behold Pearce Lynley distributing his cold looks, quelling the exuberance of his neighbours, and creating a peculiar patch of shade at his end of the brightly lit table was almost more than she could endure. It brought on a sensation, as unpleasant as it was tortuously complex, of her father's still being with them. She heard again the grating voice of reproof, felt again the tight tension of being studied and weighed, tasted again the dry, coppery mouth that always impeded her before one of his long sardonic questionings, with a vividness unequalled since the first distracted weeks after his death. That Mr Lynley should have introduced such a feeling, where there should only have been comfort and pleasantness, seemed the heaviest charge against him yet; and she found her ingrained inclination to make the best of matters, and to round sharp edges with caution and tact, giving way before an anger that was no less potent for being diffuse in its object, and uncertainly divided between past and present.

The interval after dinner was not long: plainly Valentine had discouraged the gentlemen from sitting over their wine, when there was dancing to be had; and soon the hall was busy with new company, Valentine no less busy in greeting them, and there began a general removal to the transformed drawing-room, where the musicians were trying over patriotic airs apt to the occasion. Such a concentration of eager, chattering youth Pennacombe had never seen: all was animation and delightful nervousness, all was flickering glances, choked laughter, adjusting of head-dresses, flexing of toes in dancing-pumps; and every eye was on Valentine moving among them as host – here and there, among those unaccustomed to such splendour, with momentary apprehension: but it was momentary indeed, and gave way to gratified and admiring looks. To Valentine's natural charm was added a new ease learned from the Speddings, and Louisa had at least the true satisfaction, in the intervals of her mounting vexation, of hearing her brother commended on all sides, and even seeing him promptly fallen in love with, in several quarters where the name of Carnell would formerly have excited only a fearful curiosity.

The whole scene, meanwhile, was observed with the most patent distaste by Mr Lynley. His determination to hold himself aloof from the proceedings was observed by Mr Tresilian, going in with Louisa, who remarked to him with amiable gloom: 'You do not intend dancing, Mr Lynley? Very wise. No more do I. A man of my years must allow the roast mutton and his stomach to get on tolerable terms before he thinks of moving about.'

Mr Lynley lowered his brows at the mere mention of the word *stomach*; and Louisa entertained herself for a moment in wondering what alternative might be deemed acceptable, or whether in Mr Lynley's world the very existence of such a thing was altogether denied. But this could not long divert her from her real disgust with his conduct, which was only heightened by his concluding another raking glance about the room with a short bow to her, and the words: 'I do not intend dancing, certainly. My invitation here comprehended no such thing. However, I will dance with you, Miss Carnell, if you wish it.'

'Thank you, Mr Lynley – but if you were to do such violence to your principles, merely to oblige me, I should be so little able to forgive myself that my pleasure in the evening would be quite destroyed.'

He caught something new in her tone and expression: his own was perturbed, though he tried to recover himself. 'Believe me – Miss Carnell, it is very far from a matter of obligation—'

'Surely the lady must always be the judge of whether an attention is flattering or otherwise,' she said, cutting him off. The music struck up, the set was beginning to form, and she was almost too put out to dance herself: – but that would be yielding Mr Lynley an advantage; and so she stood up with a very young and anxious midshipman who had been hesitating about asking her, and who found the question abruptly decided by her seizing his hand and fairly hauling him into the set.

Insufferable man! And insufferable the unfeeling tyranny that had matched her with him! With such dark and explosive feelings upon her, she was afraid her poor midshipman must soon be regretting his choice: but she could not lighten her demeanour. Even Mr Tresilian came in for a little of her irritation: she wished he would not pretend to be older than he was, and sit out in that stupid way, when he was more than the equal of the various young puppies and striplings taking the floor. If pleasure was to be found, it was in the sight of the evident delight with which Kate Tresilian danced the first pair with Valentine: yet even that must be witnessed with a divided hope – either that her delight was not too great, or that Valentine meant more by it than was apparent.

Kate's spirits continued so high after the first dances, however, that she was soon to be seen urging her brother out of his seat, and in the direction of Sophie Spedding, who had no dearth of applicants for her hand, but who assented at once on beholding Mr Tresilian's bow, with a smile whose brilliance could be felt across the room. Mr Tresilian could not be said to dance easily; but he looked so surprised at his doing it at all that the effect was not uncongenial.

On the set's ending, she went to him, meaning to tell him how pleased she was, but her temper must still have been unsettled, for she could only remark: 'Bonaparte defeated, and Mr Tresilian dancing – this is a memorable week indeed.'

'Ah, you are not the only ones to undertake the enterprise of living, you see,' he said, seating himself and consulting his watch. 'And now that it is over, I can say the experience was not so very bad, all in all. Though I confess I did begin to feel a little jaded about the third or fourth minute.'

This was excessive even for him. Louisa could not believe in the indifference of so much indifference: she noted his flushed looks, and the heightened blue of his eyes, and would willingly have given the tantalising question more attention. But no: – like a stone in the shoe, or a cold draught blowing, the presence of Pearce Lynley could not be ignored. He was now walking, or rather patrolling about, in clear sight of Lady Harriet seated alone: making it equally clear that he would not dance, and would not speak to her. – This was beyond bearing. Louisa politely refused several requests for the dance just beginning, and took the seat by Lady Harriet's side.

'My dear Miss Carnell, don't tell me you are tired already.'

'No: only tired of ill-mannered presumption,' Louisa said, in a carrying voice. 'And even where there is dancing, I hope I shall never forget civility, and the value of cordial conversation.'

Lady Harriet's dark eyes seemed to see much; but she said only, with a gentle smile: 'I'm sure you never do. Still, I regret to see you sit out; though to be sure there will be many more dances for you.'

'Believe me, I shall not mind if there are not,' Louisa said, seeing from the corner of her eye Mr Lynley drawing stiffly away.

'I do not mean only here. You have youth, fortune, beauty and spirit; and I do believe you are not vain of them. In society, trust me, they would secure you such attention as would leave you very little time to sit by with the old married ladies.'

It was said with all Lady Harriet's quick, quiet grace; but Louisa was so little accustomed to compliments as to be thrown into some confusion. The picture of herself thus presented was too strange for vanity to find a likeness there; but the very words, even if there were scant truth in them, fortified her further against the overweening proprietorship of the man stalking about at her back. – She had not long, however, to hesitate over a reply. Suddenly Valentine was before them, and inviting Lady Harriet, with a deep bow, to dance; and Lady Harriet, after what seemed a momentary shake of the head, was accepting him.

Louisa watched them take the floor. They were well matched in their lustrous darkness of looks, in their height, and in their grace: such must be the reaction of any who beheld them, even knowing the unfortunate circumstances of the lady; and Valentine's gallantry in refusing to see her neglected was surely to be admired. If there was anything to cause disquiet in the sight, it was very soon thrust aside by a feeling much more distinct and bracing, as Mr Lynley took the seat by her, uninvited, and pronounced: 'And now she is actually dancing! I should not have believed it, even of *her*. It is a private rather than a public occasion, to be sure: but to expose herself in this way – a woman in all the dubiety of her situation – shows her to be more shockingly dead to propriety than I had supposed.'

'I do not observe anyone else being shocked, Mr Lynley – everyone seems too preoccupied with enjoying themselves. And Valentine and I would never, I hope, have a guest in our house, and then set limits on what that guest could do.'

'Allow me to remark, Miss Carnell, that you should not need to. A sense of what is right and fitting should operate on both sides, to the prevention of such unseemliness. – Indeed, I cannot restrain myself on this matter – on other matters also: I must beg, Miss Carnell, that you will favour me with a word in private. Let us step back into the parlour.'

There was real urgency in his tone; and though a part of her wanted to retort that it would surely be unseemly and improper for them to take themselves off, she restrained it as childish. – If he wished to speak to her seriously, she was no less willing to address him in the same terms. She rose, and with a stiffness of back that even he could hardly have emulated, went before him into the parlour, where the noise and gaiety of the dance, appropriately, was distanced and subdued.

'I must take what may seem to you an inopportune moment to speak to you,' he said, closing the door almost to, 'because of the course of my own affairs. I may not be much longer at Hythe. I anticipate an early removal to town; and that being the case, I must have things made plain between us.'

'To town? Not bad news, I hope,' she said, with very effortful civility.

He gave a bare shrug. 'As I have said, I must engage a

reputable governess for Georgiana; and then there is my brother. His ship is in, and he intends lodging in London; but he is doubtless distressed for funds. It will be best if I take a house in my usual neighbourhood – I have acquaintance who will secure it – so that Francis can be decently accommodated with us there, while we consider his future.' His expression, as he sat down, was that of a man contemplating an ill-cooked meal. 'I have friends who possess influence in the Excise, for example, that might be exerted on his behalf. Or something else might be found to settle him. Above all, he must be forestalled from applying to my grandmother. Her health is not equal to *that* trouble again.'

'Certainly it sounds as if you have a good deal to arrange, Mr Lynley; and so I'm sure there should be nothing to delay your departure.'

'Only yourself, Miss Carnell,' he said, with a penetrating look. 'Some of the things I have to say to you on that score you will not like. But believe me, I urge you to these considerations not in any spirit of criticism but out of a wish – a cherishing wish – to protect you: to protect you from error and danger – to protect you, perhaps, from yourself.'

'You say I shall not like some of the things you say: I have rather a presentiment I will not like any of them. Your disapproval of Lady Harriet's presence you have already expressed – and have now demonstrated, I should add, with a disregard for her own feelings that I find difficult to reconcile with the actions of a gentleman. I assume you have further reproofs ready; but before I hear them, I must ask what right you suppose yourself to have, Mr Lynley, to make them?'

She had stung him: it was with a flush, and unwonted quickness that he answered: 'My right is surely plain – though I should consider it more an honour. The implicit trust placed in me by your late esteemed father, whose watchful care of you I have the happiness to consider now a portion of my own duties—'

'It is not at all. Dismiss that from your mind, Mr Lynley, I beg of you. I do not stand in need of a guide or guardian.'

'Allow me, with the greatest respect, to dispute that. You have lost a great prop and stay, after all—'

'Mr Lynley, you force me to be truthful. I know you admired my father: you considered him, I think, a great and singular character; but I must assert that in that character was comprehended much harshness, injustice, and even cruelty. Perhaps you think I should not say this: indeed, I don't want to; it gives me every pain that disloyalty can inflict. But you must at least consider that not every proscription placed on us was well meant: that in his forcefulness there was a love of power, and of directing for directing's sake, which was no less apparent in the arrangements he saw fit to make for our future. Yes, there has been a loss; but if you and I are to understand each other at all, you must recognise that there has been a gain also.'

Even through the mist, half anger, half wretchedness, that swam in her vision, Louisa saw that Mr Lynley's mind was struck – that he was actually listening; and it was with some caution in his tone that he at last said: 'I do not dispute your right to say this, Miss Carnell, not at all. My knowledge of Sir Clement was that of a family friend; but yours, of course, was different in kind and degree, and must be honoured. I do not doubt there were oddities and excesses in his temperament: there are few, very few, of whom that cannot be said.' He paused as if mentally reckoning the number, and limiting it, on reflection, to himself. 'And you have, indeed, helped me to a better understanding. If your father's treatment of you was all you say – and I do not doubt you –' with a hasty bow '– then I fear he did, most regrettably, and with the best intentions, sow some unhappy seeds. A little more moderation might have prevented all this.' Rising to his feet, and pacing, he gave an inclusive wave of his hand. 'It was, perhaps, inevitable. This reaction – this rebellion you are suffering—'

'I am not suffering, I am enjoying it. Though, really, if an impromptu dance for twenty couple is to be accounted evidence of rebellion—'

'I refer to all of it. All of those misjudgements – those lapses of decorum I have been constrained to observe at Pennacombe since my return to the county. Consider, Miss Carnell: on my very first call here, I encountered you in such a situation as can only be described as—'

'Up a tree,' Louisa said; and, at his mortified look, 'Do go on, Mr Lynley.'

'I refer to a trifling instance; but I might with much greater pertinence point, though I have refrained from doing so, to your putting off blacks after six months. To be sure mourning is a convention that can be too scrupulously observed; and I hope I can forgive the natural desire of a young woman to look well, which cannot long tolerate a restriction on dress, even at the expense of conscience.' He seemed to take encouragement from Louisa's silence at this; though it was rather as if a man should conclude that there was not going to be a storm, because the air was so very still. 'But when it is added to these other deviations – of which, yes, I count the acquaintance with Lady Harriet Eversholt not the least disturbing – then I cannot help reprehending the course you are set upon, even though I understand it in part.'

'Very well; you have set out my failings, and I am ready to own them, Mr Lynley, if you will now undertake not to suffer another moment's anxiety over them. You have done your duty by my father, and we have spoken enough of that. Now let me bear the consequences myself.'

'That is exactly what I do not wish. You asked by what right I spoke; and I should have said, by the right of my attachment to you. If I did not esteem you so highly, I should not be so careful of you. You have a lively and developed mind – indeed, your father used to lament to me that you spent too much time with books –' he quenched at once the reminiscent smile this occasioned '– and though you are inclined to a certain playfulness of fancy, I know you to have abundant sense, discernment and discretion; indeed, with no disrespect to Mr Carnell, I have always considered yours the greater portion. These are qualities I know how to value;

and I should not wish to see them neglected, in a mere giddy rush after novelty and pleasure.'

'I thank you for the compliments, Mr Lynley – all the more so, as they are plainly wrung from you quite against your inclination. But an attachment that seems chiefly to consist in knowing what is best for me is not one I can bring myself to prize; and its proceeding so little from the heart, and so much from the will, reassures me that it will cost you scarcely any pain to give it up, as I earnestly hope you will do.'

There was no pacing now: he was all rigid, sharp-jawed attention. 'Miss Carnell, I hope I know my own worth. I do not consider my attention and regard as something either to be lightly bestowed, or lightly abandoned: that is not my nature. Nor is it in my nature to see my true esteem and affection slighted with any of that indifference you attribute to me. A man must value himself very poorly, who could receive it so.'

'Then I am sorry,' she said, feeling as if she had stepped out on to a path that looked merely a little wet, only to find it treacherously iced. 'I have no wish to injure your feelings, Mr Lynley; and if, as you insist, they are more developed than I have had any evidence to suppose, then my regret is all the greater. But I hope I value myself also – though the sense of self-worth has never been encouraged in my upbringing; and therefore I cannot simply accept the attentions of a gentleman, either because my father told me to, or because the gentleman tells me I ought to.'

'This is still to place my attentions in a very disparaging light,' he said, frowning. 'I do not think when your father was alive you would have expressed yourself so, Miss Carnell. And I cannot help but conclude that this alteration is the result of an influence – recent, ill-advised and pernicious – that I was right to mistrust from the very beginning.'

'I could not express myself when my father was alive, sir, because I was afraid of him – afraid for my brother's sake and mine; and just now I heartily wonder that that fear never turned to hate. But here is another charge to lay at my father's door, perhaps; for if, Mr Lynley, you gained any impression that your sentiments were returned, it must have come from him. I apologise if I did not make it plain *then* that I do not care for you; but apology is superfluous *now*, for I am telling you very plainly that I do not; and if this is to inflict a wound, I am convinced that your vanity will very soon repair it, to the perfect restoration of that splendid self-regard, which you have been good enough to recommend to me as one of your attractions.'

As unfortunate punctuation, a loud, shrill laugh carried from the drawing-room at that moment. The incensed glare that Mr Lynley threw in its direction was, Louisa saw, at least partly intended for her; and its force was little diminished when he turned back to her, and said with an almost crackling composure: 'You refer to my vanity: I would prefer to call it pride; however we name it, you may be assured that it will prevent the renewal of these addresses, which are apparently so unwelcome to you. The vigilant care for your interests, which I consider was enjoined upon me by your father, I relinquish likewise; though, believe me, Miss Carnell, with no very sanguine hopes of how you will fare without it.'

He was gone: gone altogether from the house, as she discovered when, after sitting frozen and breathless for some unguessable time, she returned to the drawing-room. The dance was still in lively progress, but she could only creep to the furthest chair, and hope to escape notice while she tried to collect herself.

It was done: relief, overwhelming relief, there must surely be, at the simple ending of suspense. Yet for now a stifling multiplicity of feelings pressed on her – just as a number of gentlemen began urging her to dance, when she wanted only to be still. There was nothing of positive regret – nevertheless, she had given pain, and she could take no satisfaction in that. Anger remained: – anger at Pearce Lynley's presumption, and anger with her father that he had ever placed her in this position. An alarming emotion this last; and crowding close behind it, and refusing to be denied, was guilt – guilt muttering to her that she was an unnatural, ungrateful daughter, who deserved never to know peace again. But one sensation she did not recognise: it wore something of the aspect of freedom – something even of power; and though it hovered in the background, there was that in its look which suggested their acquaintance would soon ripen.

Chapter IX

The dancing continued until the early hours, but Louisa sought her bedroom by midnight; and there Valentine soon came tapping.

'Are you quite well?'

'Oh, yes: only fatigued. Go back to our guests, Valentine, you'll be missed.'

'They're footing it happily without me. Your midshipman declares he will not leave off until he sees the sun.' He came in and sat on the foot of the bed. 'Lady Harriet was concerned about you. She feared there had been some dissension – some unpleasantness – and that she was the cause.'

'Not at all – not in the sense of being to blame. She was *referred* to this evening in terms I found objectionable. But that was only one of my manifold errors, which I have had the pleasure of hearing recited.'

'Pearce Lynley, I collect,' Valentine said; and then, with a darkening expression: 'I hope the man was not insulting to her. If so, I shall—'

'No, no,' Louisa said hastily, 'nothing of that. He was – he was simply being Mr Lynley, with all the officious propriety one expects. But we had a very uncomfortable interview, in which he declared himself to me, as far as such a man can, and I rejected his addresses. – Dear me, his language is catching. Well, all is made plain between us, at any rate.'

'Good,' said Valentine, firmly. 'Good, first and above all, because you have exercised your free choice – which is a wonderful thing, is it not?'

'Yes,' she said – but the wonder of it was still clouded. 'I am afraid, though, you are not to be rid of me yet; and you must be a little troubled, lest I contract a habit of rejecting eligible gentlemen.'

'Rid of you? Such talk.' He saw she was perturbed, and squeezed her hand. 'Look here: now, I can say it. I can say that I should have hated to deliver you into the matrimonial custody of Pearce Lynley. But I have been careful not to influence you in either direction. No, I want us to enjoy life together a good while yet – to taste the world fully, as we resolved to do. And not just here. Louisa, I have been talking to Tom. He tells me, with regret, that he and Sophie must return to London – Lady Harriet also. But this need not be an end: rather, a beginning. Our cousins very much wish that we would go with them.'

Valentine was all shining animation; and though Louisa, from the agitations of the evening, was unable to match it, she experienced a moment of leaping thankfulness. – Yes: let them get away, far away from the scene of this horribly unsettling business with Mr Lynley. Another moment's reflection reminded her that he also was planning a removal to

London; but, then, that was different: there he would be one among a multitude, here a continued neighbour, presence, and irritant.

'Well, what do you think?'

'I hardly know. Yes – yes, I should like to go of all things. But how long? Where would we stay?'

'With the Speddings, of course. Tom is most insistent that he return our hospitality – will not be easy until we accept. And for as long as we like. You know they are not the sort of people to set quibbling limits. To be sure, we shall only come in for the end of the season – but, then, they say town will be very different *this* summer: none of the usual deadness, with the peace celebrations coming on; so it could hardly be better.' He kissed her and sprang up. 'Well, we shall speak more of it tomorrow. Lady Harriet has promised me one more dance.'

Louisa lay long in the dark, listening to the sounds of a party coming to a close – hilarity turning a little quarrelsome, and fiddles going out of tune. The transformation of the house struck her afresh – her own transformation no less: she saw, as if beholding another person from outside, the abandonment of caution and submissiveness, the adoption of boldness and independence; to these were added visions of London, as vague as they were grand, which presently melted into dreams. Such a tumultuous activity of dreams did she have that night, in fact, that she woke late more exhausted than refreshed.

The subject of a removal to London was already under

discussion when she joined the others at breakfast. Every voice was for it: and Louisa had nothing to urge against the project. The first impulse of last night – to quit a place where something troubling had happened – was present in maturer form: the change must be of benefit in raising her spirits and diverting her thoughts, so that she would not be forever dwelling on it, and making her company tedious for others. In its train came a very real excitement at an idea that promised so much of novelty and interest: to see places that her reading had painted before her mind's eye in almost fabulous colours: to go into society, not through the imaginative accompaniment of a novel-heroine, but in her real self; and the cheerful encouragement of her cousins, their ready engagement for the unstinting welcome that would be extended by her aunt Spedding, and the relish with which they set forth plans for the Carnells' entertainment while in town, were not to be resisted. She was soon joining in, not only in acquiescence but in actively considering dates and times and travelling arrangements; and, in this pleasant flurry, she was able to give only passing attention to a little inner voice, which told her that what she was really doing was escaping from her father.

Lady Harriet, though good-humoured enough, could not participate entirely in their elation. She smiled, but sighed also; and on their quitting the breakfast-room, spoke aside to Louisa.

'I am afraid I have been a check on your spirits, Miss Carnell. Pay no heed to it. The fact is, I like it so well at

Pennacombe that I cannot contemplate a removal without sorrow. Here there has been peace and cordiality – that is, *I* have been fortunate enough to feel it –' with a gentle touch on her arm '– though I fear my presence has not always occasioned it. As for returning to London, it is a thing I must do, rather than a thing I wish to do. But it will be some recompense if I can count on my new friends there – though even in that there will be alteration. In town I must lose the person I have been here, and find the old one I despised.'

She said no more in this strain, however; and once preparations were thoroughly under way, became lively. – The sheer stimulation of change, perhaps; or perhaps the compensations she spoke of impressed themselves more vividly on her mind, for she spent much time in conversation with Valentine, discussing the best means of travelling, and describing what was to be expected in town at this part of the season, to his evident fascination.

At last the day was fixed for their departure: Valentine, with some impatience, occupied himself with instructions for the steward and housekeeper during their absence; and its soon being given out that the Carnells were to leave Pennacombe, callers came to give friendly wishes. Mrs Lappage was among the first, and the most sincere.

'It is quite what I have always wished, my dear, that you and Valentine, Mr Carnell I should say, should see something of society; and indeed if I were truthful, I would say it was a great pity that two handsome young people of fortune should have been forced to wait till *now*, because of the unfeeling obstinacy prevailing in a certain quarter. But I shall not allude to that. However, I shall miss you, my dear: indeed, we shall be quite depleted in the district, for as you may know – as indeed no one is better placed to know – Mr Lynley leaves shortly for London also. Whether you may see anything of him in town I can hardly conjecture – as I'm sure that depends on a great many things, you know, which are really none of my affair.'

'It is possible we may do – only by chance,' was Louisa's answer: which gave Mrs Lappage such delightful room for speculation that she could hardly wait to prod Mr Lappage awake so she could go home and take possession of it.

There was no call from Mr Lynley himself: only a short note presenting his compliments, wishing Mr and Miss Carnell a safe journey, and announcing his own departure next week, for a residence in Brook Street, Grosvenor Square. He expressed no hopes or wishes of waiting upon them in town; an omission which was so far from a disappointment to Louisa that she considered this note the most satisfying communication from Mr Lynley she had ever received.

The day before their own removal, the Carnells and their guests fulfilled a promise, and called at The Ridings, the Tresilians' house near Teignmouth. In this there was, for Louisa, always pleasure: there was nowhere quite like it. Old Mr Tresilian, on coming to wealth and gentility, had built his house out of sight of the sea, as if to assert that he belonged now to the country and not the port; but his son had added, just behind the house, a round tower with steps leading to a platform, whence the sea was visible, and where he spent many contented hours with a telescope. It had been one of Sir Clement's favourite jests that this building might have been called Tresilian's Folly, if the term had not already been appropriated by the fellow's marriage; but even he must have perceived this as harsh, for he only repeated the sally to Mr Tresilian himself once or twice a month, and always added that he meant no harm by it.

The old merchant had built likewise in a formal style, the severity of which extended to the grounds; but since coming into the inheritance, Mr Tresilian had softened this appearance with profuse planting and trellises, seats and arbours, so that what had been chill and stony was generous and woody; and within, he had indulged his taste for the curious, filling the lofty rooms with collections from all across the seas, from maps and engravings to shells and corals. He had fitted out also a handsome music-room for Kate, complete with a portrait of Handel, signalling transcendent genius in the usual way, by his wearing a very loose coat while holding a pen.

Here the Carnells and their guests were made comfortably welcome. Mr Tresilian was an attentive host, and Sophie a most satisfying guest to be shown the curious collections – vastly interested in everything, not shrinking from the Turkish sword but wanting to take it down from the wall and flourish it about, and very ready to climb the steps of the tower and train his telescope on the sea, while he pointed out the beauties of Teignmouth harbour, including the masts of one of his own ships. Yet for much of the time he seemed deep in thought, or rather deeper than usual: and even a little dejected. When they all came to take a walk about the gardens, Louisa manoeuvred herself so that it was her arm he took. It was not that she wished to separate him from Sophie: rather, she wished to satisfy herself as to how much, or if at all, his affections were engaged. Simple curiosity accounted partly for this – but there was concern also; for delighted though Sophie clearly was with Mr Tresilian's company and with his house, all her thoughts, all her conversation these last days had been fixed upon London, with an anticipation of unalloyed pleasure, and with only such regrets at leaving Devonshire as were natural on quitting a place where pleasant times had been passed, and pleasant new acquaintance made.

'So the enterprise of living quickens,' he remarked, with his eyes on the grass.

'Yes: but it is nothing wild, after all. We are only going to stay in London with our cousins. We have come to know them so well that it seems rather natural than otherwise.'

'They are agreeable people,' he said reluctantly, glancing back at Tom, who was inflicting on Miss Rose all the agony of his unfeigned politeness and attention. 'Not at all like you and Valentine, though.'

'Do you mean in agreeableness, or in some other quality?'

'I mean that they seem to have no fear of life.'

'Neither do I – or at least I should hope not.'

Mr Tresilian gave her a short, sceptical look. 'I think it is salutary to have a little,' he said, and fell silent.

'It is surely allowable to follow the impulse of the heart *sometimes*,' she resumed.

'If you are looking to me to disapprove of your project, so that you can be grand and defiant about it, I must disappoint you. A scheme to London sounds very well: it will be worth seeing this summer, I hear. Visiting dignitaries, reviews and parades. Junketings. Ah, I'm glad of the opportunity to say that word. Let me do it again. Junketings . . . No.' His face fell. 'Not so good this time. One should never take a second sip from the cup of pleasure. Valentine: I am a little uneasy about Valentine.'

Louisa looked at her brother, who was walking some distance ahead with Lady Harriet on his arm. 'Are you? I cannot comprehend why,' she said, with such a sensation that, if it were not uneasiness, was something wonderfully like it.

'He is headstrong. Let him fix on an idea and he will not be moved from it. Whereas you may talk high-flown nonsense like one of Byron's creatures, but you remain a rational being at heart.'

'I *think* there is a compliment there somewhere, but it is very well disguised. Well, you may be assured, Mr Tresilian, that whilst we are in town I shall try not to let the nonsensical overwhelm the rational. But if you are troubled at not having Valentine under your eye, who do you not essay a visit to London yourself? Then you and Kate might enjoy the junketings also.'

'London? No, no. I have far too much business on hand here to consider anything like that. No, indeed.' Again she found something telling in the very promptness of the refusal, and the frowning silence that followed. 'Besides,' he resumed, 'Pearce Lynley is going also, I hear – so you will not lack for the comfort of the familiar.'

'Even if I wanted it, I should not seek it *there*.'

'Ah!' he said on a long bass note; and then in his most cryptic manner: 'You are doing it all, then . . . Well, all I can say is, it will be damnably odd without you.'

'It is damnably odd to be going,' Louisa said, experiencing a shiver that was only partly excitement. 'I hope London will not open its mouth and eat me up.'

'The other way around, I should think,' said Mr Tresilian. A short distance ahead Valentine and Lady Harriet were crouching by the fish-pond, pointing and laughing together. Mr Tresilian sighed. 'A pretty picture. I do not like to disturb it; but I had better be true to my character, and take him aside for some dull, heavy words about being prudent, and mindful of the temptations of London and whatnot.'

In the subsequent rearrangement of the party, Louisa found herself walking with Kate Tresilian; and in her paleness of cheek and muted utterance were to be read all the disappointment that in another young woman might have proclaimed itself to the skies. If the strength of Mr Tresilian's feeling for Sophie was still inscrutable, no such doubt attached to Kate's, on the prospect of Valentine's going away.

Kate, however, tried to speak composedly on the event

that was giving her pain. 'You will be gone a good while, I dare say.'

'Our cousins are kind enough to invite us for as long as we wish to stay. But, of course, we shall not remain in town for ever.'

Kate smiled faintly; and looked as if it would seem so, for her.

'I was asking your brother whether he might not contemplate an excursion to London at some time,' Louisa said tentatively. 'He was not much inclined to it – though I fancy *your* inclination would weigh much more heavily with him.'

'I should like to see London,' Kate said, with a little shake of her head, 'but – I know this is absurd – I misdoubt whether I would be homesick, if I stayed long; and of course one cannot see it all in a few days.' Her eyes on Valentine and Lady Harriet, she added: 'And we know no one there. Your cousins, I dare say, have a good deal of acquaintance in society.'

'I dare say. But for my part I do not mean to be impressed by society, unless it truly is impressive. And I doubt we shall reach so very high, after all: no royal levees, or anything like that.'

'But you never know,' Kate said, brightening in spite of herself, 'you might even see the Prince Regent.'

'Well, we might see a part of him: of course one could not see him all in a few days.'

This occasioned in Kate one of her quiet, helpless fits of laughter; and when she had squeezed and cajoled herself back to sobriety, she said curiously: 'I wonder how much, exactly, you have to eat to become so prodigiously fat? And if you indulge an appetite so much, does it not sicken? It is a strange pleasure, indeed, that must be pursued until it becomes a positive pain to you.'

Strange, certainly: but as they took their leave, and Kate gave Valentine her hand with brief, white, sad confusion, and watched him turn eagerly to hand Lady Harriet into the carriage, Louisa thought it was not so very strange: or so very uncommon.

She sat up late that evening, talking with Valentine, whose spirits were unquenchable; and of his interview with Mr Tresilian, he said only with a pitying smile: 'I did not tell him so, of course, but really Tresilian is turning quite the old woman. I almost felt I should promise him to wear a flannel waistcoat, and sew my purse into my pocket.' After he had gone to bed Louisa extinguished the candles, then sat on for a while, reflecting that this was the very room where she and Valentine had made their decision about the fire-screen, and about the enterprise of living. Of the many changes since that day, passing swiftly through her mind, it was the internal that struck her with most force. 'And all changes for the better,' she said aloud; but the sound of her own voice, in the silent blackness, afflicted her peculiarly, and she hurried to bed.

Chapter X

Travelling post to London was, as Valentine pronounced, the only way. It was many years since either the Pennacombe coach or coachman had ventured further than Exeter; and going by post-chaise was, besides, swift, dashing and comfortable – everything indeed to arouse Sir Clement's mistrust.

The degree of comfort was, Louisa found, somewhat overstated. The heroines of novels were always whirling along in post-chaises, but the whirling never seemed to include such bumping, joggling, lurching and bone-aching; nor was there complete relief to be found in the two nights they spent at inns – establishments that, though reputable, seemed to have become thoroughly infused with old gravy, from the rafters to the bed-sheets. The enforced confinement with companions that such long travel required was also, she found, a great test of tolerance; though after three days on the road, she hoped she was no worse affected to them than in finding a good deal of the town tattle exchanged by Sophie and Lady Harriet rather vacuous, and in considering that Tom's habit of genial smiling might easily have been restricted to four or five hours a day, without any risk to his general amiability.

Under such circumstances, the wonder of her arrival in London was tempered with relief at their having got there at all: the great straggle of suburbs, where everything was either falling down or being new-built, the river with its teeming of craft, the dome and spires of the City heaving up through the smoke, all received from her a weary hastiness of admiration that must wait its time for proper expression. After a fierce battle with an army of hackneys, they drew up at last before the Spedding house in Hill Street, in all its substantial gentility.

'Going away is delightful – but still there is nothing like coming home,' cried Sophie. 'Now, Harriet, I will not hear any more of it. You simply must dine with us, and rest yourself a little, before you even think of returning to Jermyn Street. Now I insist: and if you refuse, I shall become fierce. I am terrible when I am fierce, you know.'

'No. It is only postponing it,' Lady Harriet said, with a grey smile.

'Let me add my own entreaties,' put in Valentine. 'After such a long, fagging journey, Lady Harriet, going home alone to an empty house is the very worst thing for your health and spirits.'

'You must not suppose me so fragile, Mr Carnell,' she said, shaking her head, 'indeed you must not. Besides, you are a family party: you and Miss Carnell have your aunt to meet. I have played the cuckoo in the nest long enough.'

She would not be moved; and with a brief nod at Sophie's assertion that they would see each other again soon, she drove away in the first of the chaises, while the small luggage was being brought down from the other. This, indeed, was all Louisa would have thought to bring; but Valentine had insisted that people who did things in style always had a great deal of luggage, and so there were several trunks being sent on by the public coach – which, containing as they did some of his best shirts and waistcoats, he had then been anxious about all the way, and continually imagining being tipped into ditches, or despatched to Lisbon by short-sighted postmasters.

The Spedding house was richly fitted out: nothing was wanting either in comfort or elegance; and their aunt, Mrs Spedding, who received them in a drawing-room full of lustrous reflections, was as welcoming and hospitable as Tom and Sophie had promised.

'It is a very great pleasure to see you at last, my dears,' she said, taking their hands, and searching their faces with a wondering smile. 'Dear me, yes, there's my poor sister, to the life! It's such a pity we have been so long unacquainted – but there's an end of that. You must consider this absolutely your home, you know, as long as you are in town. I am very fond of company, and there is after all no company like family. Bless me, we shall have a thoroughly pleasant time of it.'

To the novelty of cousins was now added that of an aunt: though it was soon clear that the august quality that that word bestowed was not much sought by Mrs Spedding, who wished rather to look young. She was a pink, rounded, daintily smiling woman, with eyes very open, perhaps so that they should not wrinkle, and a little light hair artfully made much of: fashionably dressed in a high-necked gown, with many tinkling bracelets: serenely easy in her manner, full of civil enquiries, happy responses and ready agreement. Sophie and Tom treated her with great fondness and indulgence, reassuring themselves that she had not suffered a moment's loneliness without them, commiserating her small ailments, loading her with presents they had bought at Lyme, and generally according her every sort of attention, compatible with not really taking any notice of her.

'Well, you tell me you had a safe journey, my dears, and so I believe you; but I am always a little anxious about these things, ever since the time you got lost in Scotland.'

'Dear Mama,' laughed Tom, 'that was Wales: and we did not get lost – one of the carriage-horses lost a shoe; quite different, you know.'

'Is that how it was? How very surprising: I had Scotland quite fixed in my mind. But of course you must be right, my dear – and it is still very disagreeable when a horse loses a shoe. One must wait about for an age. I know I had to wait a good half-hour at Vauxhall once; and I always suspect damp at Vauxhall. How do you like Vauxhall, Louisa?'

'I'm afraid I have never been there, ma'am: I have never been in London since we came here as little children.'

'To be sure – exactly what Sophie wrote me. Well, here

is your opportunity, my dear, to try all the diversions of the town. For my part I live pretty quietly, but these children of mine are the most sociable of creatures. I dare say they will be taking you everywhere.'

'Exactly our plan, Mama,' said Sophie. 'It is our determination that not a single day or night shall pass without its engagements, as long as our cousins are with us.'

Fatigued as Louisa was, there was more just then to oppress than to excite in Sophie's promise of their entertainment; but after being shown to her room, and enjoying the comforts of hot water, a change of clothes, and a luxurious stretch of her limbs on the ample bed, her spirits were almost restored; and an excellent dinner completed the revival. Even the sounds of London, the continual undertone of carriage-wheels and rapping doors and street-criers, began to act not on her nerves but her imagination, and to speak a promise.

A comfortable couple of days of settling in succeeded: – enough to reveal to Louisa whence came the assurance of address, the confidence of belonging in the world, that characterised her cousins. The ease and liberty prevailing in the Spedding house could hardly have presented a bolder contrast with her own experience of home. Mrs Spedding was the mildest of châtelaines; and her untroubled references to her late husband, and the portrait of him in the hall, which appeared to show a smiling man melting apologetically into his cravat, suggested that his own temper had been no more exacting.

Not that Mrs Spedding was spoiled or selfish; but generally she presented the appearance of a woman who had never suffered any greater inconvenience than was occasioned by the bringing of two children into the world. There was that, indeed, about Mrs Spedding's pretty smile, which suggested that her cheerfulness was private and interior, and not much altered by seeing you, or hearing what you had to say: – but this was to quibble. She made Louisa and Valentine very welcome: listened devouringly to anything they had to tell, and promptly got it entirely wrong in retailing it to someone else; and gave every indication that if either of them were to fall under the wheels of a carriage tomorrow, she would find it thoroughly regrettable.

'You know, I feel as if I have lived here all my life,' Valentine remarked to Louisa, a few mornings after their arrival, as he stood at the breakfast-room window looking down at Hill Street. 'Pennacombe seems very far away!'

In fact Louisa had just been wondering whether the housekeeper was being kind to her cat, and whether Jane Colley had heeded her instruction to call in the surgeon to look at her gammy knee, and not go to that old woman in the village who brewed noxious nostrums out of snails. – Valentine, however, was plainly not so encumbered by recollection. He was all eager receptiveness: was already speaking familiarly of the Strand and the Monument, of hackney-stands and link-boys, even with a note of true London world-weariness; and last night had been talking with Tom of the advantages of a town residence every winter, with a ready agreement that a neighbourhood east of Soho Square was not to be considered. He had only one dissatisfaction – they had seen nothing of Lady Harriet since their arrival; though Sophie assured him that her friend had not deserted them, and that she must have a thousand things to attend to in Jermyn Street.

Not the least of these, Louisa surmised, was the reopening of the faro-bank by which she supported herself: though there might also be, for all she knew, negotiations with her estranged husband to be dealt with. Certainly there must perforce be an end to the holiday-time, the retreat from the world, which Lady Harriet had enjoyed in Devonshire; and Louisa found herself several times on the brink of hinting at this to Valentine. But on second thoughts she trusted the general fascination to displace the particular. Lady Harriet had appeared at Pennacombe as a brilliant fragment of the greater world: that world now lay all about him, in its vastness and variety. Her significance must surely be crowded out by a host of other impressions. There was more safety, Louisa felt, in being universally dazzled than in following a single light down a doubtful and unpropitious path.

For her own part, Louisa was very soon thrust into the bustle of a town season. Sophie, of course, was voraciously social; and Mrs Spedding, in spite of her avowal of living quietly, scarcely less so. Her especial addiction was shopping, for which she made a daily expedition; and once Louisa politely accepted an invitation to accompany her. – Once was enough. Louisa could find only so much interest in looking over hats, ribbons, fans, scent-bottles and gewgaws, and was heartily glad when Mrs Spedding had done. Her aunt's appetite for buying never diminished, however; and on every subsequent occasion, she returned to Hill Street with something new and prodigiously pretty that she could not live without; and which would make an appearance once, in her costume or on her work-table, before being entirely forgotten.

Paying morning calls was another rite that Louisa found less than stimulating, though its complexities greatly exercised Sophie, who was deep in the matter of who had called on them and when, who had left cards, who had departed from town, who had arrived, who was expected. – The culmination of all this activity was often nothing more than half an hour spent sitting in a cold drawing-room on a hard chair, exchanging commonplace enquiries with people who seemed to Louisa quite as bored as she felt, before rising, expressing delight in the visit, and going on to the next, where the only expectation of novelty was that the hard chairs might be differently distributed.

Much more to Louisa's taste, indeed, were the galleries, concert-rooms and theatres, and here her cousins were invaluable guides and arbiters. May, and the end of the season, it might be; but as Mr Tresilian had said, there was to be no tailing-off into summer this year. – Preparations were afoot for a great round of celebrations: foreign dignitaries and even crowned heads were to descend on London to mark Europe's final crushing of Bonaparte; and even Sophie admitted she had never known town so lively. It was the theatre, above all, that convinced Louisa she had never properly lived until now. Even to step into the lobby at Drury Lane was an excitement; though Sophie delicately cautioned her, indicating the concourse of gauzy females, that this was not a place to linger.

'Because they do rather tend to use this as a place of resort,' she said; and then, at Louisa's enquiring look: 'Demi-reps, my dear. Cyprians. Votaries of Venus. The muslin sisterhood.'

'Oh,' said Louisa, in an impressed tone. 'I thought they were just prostitutes.'

As for the performance, she could have dispensed with the patriotic prologues, but *The Merchant of Venice*, with Mr Kean as Shylock, was another matter. She was so incensed by the gentlemen who came in yawning at the last act, and talking loudly to their friends, that she could have turned Shylock herself, and divested them of a pound of flesh each without compunction.

For some time afterwards she remained wrapped in the high-coloured world that had been presented on the stage; and, on returning to reality, found everything about herself drearily everyday. Even a dose of tragedy, she thought, would be a fair price to pay in order to feel life that intensely. No such exaltation of emotion intruded at Hill Street, of course: still, there came some ripples to its untroubled surface. Among the many calling-cards that adorned the hall table, that of Mr Pearce Lynley one day appeared.

'Ah, yes, one of our Devonshire acquaintance,' Tom informed his mother. 'Has the neighbouring estate to Pennacombe. Capital fellow. Never known a better, taken all in all. His place is called whatsname, no, Valentine, don't tell me. Begins with a – what's the letter? – jolly old B.'

'Hythe Place,' supplied Valentine, smiling. 'Mr Lynley is indeed our neighbour at Pennacombe, Mrs Spedding, and was a friend of my father's. He came up to town, I believe, shortly before we did.'

'Well, it is a thoroughly pleasant attention in Mr Lynley,' Mrs Spedding said, 'and I shall be very glad to have his acquaintance. It would bring me a little closer to Pennacombe, indeed, and to my poor sister.'

Louisa was silent, though she felt the eyes of both Valentine and Sophie turned to her. The card was only a card – the name only a name: still, they released a flood of unhappy feeling, which she was at some pains to disguise; but at last she forced herself to recollect that Pearce Lynley was nothing if not punctilious, and that the leaving of a card at an address of his acquaintance in London he would consider an imperative form, even if he had to dodge through a second Great Fire to do it. – This duty once performed, there was nothing more, she thought, to be apprehended. He seemed to have viewed the Speddings as, at least, tainted by their association with Lady Harriet Eversholt, and would surely not expose himself to the potential corruption of a house where she was welcome.

But of that welcome Lady Harriet herself did not seem sure: she called at Hill Street, at last, and was comfortably received by Mrs Spedding, and overwhelmed with attention from Sophie – but she could not be easy.

'Your mother is the kindest of women,' she said to Sophie, while Mrs Spedding was occupied with fetching her maid to come and disentangle her bracelets, which had tortured themselves into a sort of chain-mail halfway up her arm. 'And for that reason I would not see her reputation in the least endangered by my presence. I know, she does not mind: still, it is much better if I do not come. My time in Devonshire has taught me how to value good, kind, decent society and not to be so thoughtless as to see it threatened. You will understand, my dear – and I flatter myself that Miss Carnell will likewise. Of Mr Carnell I do not speak,' she added, her voice falling. 'I am afraid he is too chivalrous. I must rely on you to bring him to an understanding that our country acquaintance was one thing – our town acquaintance quite another.'

'She is very hard on herself, poor creature!' Sophie said, when Lady Harriet had gone. 'But I know we shall not see so much of her in any case: her time is much taken up. Yes – the faro-bank is begun again. She has the greatest distaste for it, but what is she to do? Colonel Eversholt remains obdurate – allows her nothing. I know he has returned to town – he has been at Bath – and that there has been a meeting: productive only, I collect, of more unhappiness. His temper is worse: at Bath, they say, he fought one duel, wounding his man horribly, and threatened another; only the gentleman would not fight – declined, on grounds that a challenge from a madman was no challenge. Why he went to Bath I cannot devise; if it was for the waters, I fear it was only so that he might mix them with his brandy.'

The picture thus presented of Colonel Eversholt was an alarming one: it could only reinforce Louisa's conviction that Valentine was better out of Lady Harriet's society, gallant and disinterested though she believed his feeling for her to be. She might have said something of this to him, but that would be to act in the heavy, carping manner of their father, which they were done with; and there was, besides, a diminishing of their intimacy as their time in London wore on. – It was the one alloy to her very real pleasure in the new scene. He was no less fond as a brother, but he was more distant. He went about much with Tom who, besides coaching him in the latest modes of tying the cravat and dressing the hair, was securing his admission to White's club, and introduced him to Limmer's, and Tattersall's, and other haunts of fashionable males – all of which, Valentine laughingly assured her, were a good deal more steady and commonplace than their reputation, though that did not stop him resorting to them frequently, and returning late, and often a little foxed.

But any disquiet she might have felt at this could be easily banished by summoning an image of Pearce Lynley glaring in disapproval; and besides, she herself was beginning to resemble Sophie in finding sleep a rather dull interruption of living, and often found herself at the earliest of hours impatiently throwing back the bedclothes and springing up, as if someone were calling her.

Chapter XI

Mrs Spedding had a great many friends, all of whom seemed to be her very oldest and dearest; but the lady on whom these epithets were most liberally bestowed, and who was the most frequent caller at Hill Street, was a Mrs Murrow. She was a lean, dry, sallow woman: much given to feathery, flowery caps fastening under the chin, and with her head always staringly on one side, so that it looked as if someone had tried to strangle her with her head-dress. Like her friend, she was a widow: very soon into Louisa's acquaintance with her, she gave it out, with emphasis, that she had buried two husbands; and even that degree of acquaintance was enough to create the ungenerous suspicion that they might well have submitted to the interment without the formality of dying first.

She was not an easy conversationalist. 'Carnell?' was her cry on first introduction to Louisa and Valentine. '*Carnell*, did you say?' – with a look as if a poor joke were being played on her, and they had pretended to some absurd surname like Butterfingers. The mention of Devonshire brought the same uncomprehending, deprecating look; and on her being brought at last to accept the existence of such a place, she could only say: 'I should think it is dreadfully cold down there.'

'Oh, we have had our share of snowy winters,' Valentine said, at his most agreeable, 'but generally, ma'am, being near the sea, we are lucky enough to enjoy a mild climate.'

'I should think that is worse. It is just the sort of climate to breed fevers and agues, and I don't know what else: upon my word, I can hardly bear to think of it,' said Mrs Murrow, with a pained look at Valentine for making her do so. 'And so, when do you go back, Miss – Miss—' Mrs Murrow, with a shudder, gave up on the unpronounceable name.

'The midsummer perhaps,' Louisa said. 'Aunt Spedding is kind enough to set no limit on our stay.'

Mrs Murrow shook her head. 'I should not like that sort of uncertainty. I think there is nothing worse. Then, to be sure, when you do go back, I should think you will find it horribly dull.'

'Well, and how does your sweet niece?' asked Mrs Spedding, whose patience with her friend's habit of poisoning the wells of conversation appeared limitless. 'People still talk of her triumph at Almack's, you know. They say there never was such a coming-out.'

'Dear, dear, no wonder at that – with her beauty and elegance,' sighed Mrs Murrow, as if referring to a sad deformity. 'And such a round of engagements as she still has – there is never an end to it. I fear it may tax her strength at last; and if she *were* to be ill, I don't know what I should do.'

'Bless me, but there is nothing to be feared in Miss Astbury's constitution, I hope?' Mrs Spedding said.

'Oh, no: thank heaven, her constitution is very good – but if it were *not*, you have no idea how dreadfully alarmed I would be: dear, dear, you really cannot conceive it!'

Mrs Spedding hastened to commiserate with her friend on the alarm she did not feel; and went on: 'She is young, you know: at her age, I was ready to dance all night, and do it again the next. But she is well guided by her aunts, I am sure; and as she is quite the belle of the season, let her enjoy it. There will be a very good match made in time, I do not doubt. I have asked Tom if he did not find Miss Astbury a delightful creature,' she added, laughing, 'but he only shrugs and chuckles, and says he is content to be a bachelor. I think all young men should be eager to marry. Valentine, you are not so stuck in your ways, I hope.'

'Well, I am in no hurry, ma'am,' Valentine said, laughing a little consciously. 'I should hope to emulate the position of Miss Astbury, and to enjoy my liberty for now.'

'The young will have these ideas,' Mrs Murrow said, clucking her tongue. 'I am sure when I was young, I never had any,' which Louisa was very ready to believe.

This Miss Astbury was, as Louisa soon learned, quite the prodigy of the season. She stood heiress to her grandfather, who lived reclusively in the far north of England: not only a large fortune, but vast coal-bearing estates would descend to her, and so to any gentleman who could win her hand; and thus it was not only in tribute to her renowned fairness that she was known in society as the Golden Miss Astbury. Fortune-hunters there would certainly be: but old Mr Astbury had sensibly decided to declare a sort of open season, rather than sequester his heiress. She had been despatched to the care of her maternal aunts, Lady Carr and Mrs Murrow, who, being both widowed and well-off, kept together a good house in Portman Square. From there Miss Astbury had made her entrance into society in high style. The Portman Square receptions maintained their fame even at such an exceptional time – for the town, far from emptying, was now crowding with company for the arrival of the Allied Sovereigns to celebrate the peace – and Louisa was as curious as any, when the invitation came, to behold the golden heiress in state.

It was a close, noisy occasion. 'Just the sort of crush I like,' Sophie declared on their going in; but the unseasonably warm weather made Louisa wish for a little less crush, and a little more air; wearing a train, and being unaccustomed to managing it, she experienced several times the startling immobility of having it trodden on. Lady Carr was a little nervous woman, as much occupied with promoting her guests' comfort as Mrs Murrow was in detracting from it; but the chief attention of both was devoted to their niece. Miss Astbury was indeed the queen of the evening. Louisa was in due form introduced; and several minutes of talk ensued, being nothing much beyond civil enquiries, commendation of Mrs Spedding's qualities, and agreement on the happy prospects of the peace. We are always apt to find fault with the manners of those handsomer and wealthier than ourselves: – still Louisa could not warm to her. She was very tall, slender and glacially fair: her bare, thin-muslined Grecian costume, complete with sandals, showed her to great advantage, and even rendered her Christian name – Parthenope – rather appropriate than awkward; but there was about her a deadly sort of haughtiness that could not please. It was understood that Miss Astbury, in preparation for her entrance into society, had been polished at the best schools; and Louisa could not help feeling that the polish had been too liberally applied, with results that glared rather than shone.

Valentine seemed scarcely more impressed. 'Quite the beauty – and thoroughly conscious of it too,' he remarked. 'Well, I have had my audience, and I gladly give place to the rest of the eager courtiers, lining up to kiss the ring. Great heaven, a man must be dead to all self-respect, who can go crawling after her and her guineas like that. I say, Tom, isn't that The Top over there? Now *he* has more sense, at any rate.'

Louisa had heard this singular name mentioned before as a close friend of Tom's, but had thought she must be mistaken, and that it actually referred to one of their fashionable places of resort, like The Corner and The Finish. But soon she was being introduced to the gentleman who rejoiced in this sobriquet. 'Bellingham is the name,' Tom explained, 'but to everyone of the *ton* he is simply The Top, you know: no one would think of calling him anything else.'

'I should think not!' said The Top; who was a very crisp-starched, high-booted gentleman, not young, and rather fleshy, wearing such a tightly tailored coat that Louisa doubted it could be taken off in the usual way at all, but must be escaped from with applications of bear's-grease, and perhaps a rope. 'Now come to the mark, Spedding, what in the name of blazes do you call *that*?'

With an appalled glance he indicated Tom's cravat, which to Louisa's eye only looked slightly more complicated than usual.

'Why, it's the Imperial,' Tom said, a little doubtfully.

'Is it indeed! Lord, Spedding, that's doing it too brown! Unless I miss my tip, you've been studying for it in the fashion-papers! Look at your friend Carnell there – that's the way to wear it. Imperial indeed! Never heard such a Banbury tale!' The Top concluded with a short metallic laugh; and turning to Louisa, continued: 'Well, Miss Carnell, what do you say to this precious squeeze? A dead bore, is it not? But I felt I had to see the famous Miss Astbury for myself. Wouldn't have been half surprised if she'd turned out to be a shocking quiz! The fact is, for all her blunt she's not of the first stare. So I told young Rivers, who's dangling after her: not up to the scratch for the son of a marquis, even if he is lodging in Queer Street just now. Too much splashing at Lady Harriet Eversholt's faro-table! He should learn to bet like a gentleman: always stand up after the first five hundred. What do *you* say, Miss Carnell?'

'I am afraid I cannot be easy at the thought of anyone betting five hundred pounds on the turn of a card,' she said frankly.

'You think me pitching it rum!' he said, in his hard-smiling way. 'Not a bit – happens every day! Oh, my dear Miss Carnell, I could tell you a tale or two!'

She was sure he could; and it only took a little longer in his company to convince her that none of them would be interesting. He was, she supposed, very much the man of fashion, and could understand that someone of Tom's tastes would admire him; but it surprised her to see Valentine deferring to a man in whose character there appeared so little of substance. His talk soon moved on to horseflesh, pugilism, single-stick and ratting-matches, in all of which he was as expert as in the finer points of shirt-linen and boot-blacking: but of thought and feeling there seemed nothing; and though she gathered he was accounted a great wit, she could not devise wherein the reputation rested, unless in his habit of saying things in abrupt slang, and peppering everything with audible exclamation-marks.

He did not remain long at the reception, declaring that it was such a bore it put him flat in the dismals; and afterwards, on Tom's asking how she liked him, she could only say: 'He is certainly very well dressed.'

'That he is,' said Tom, reverently. 'The absolute nonpareil. I feel a proper tomnoddy about the Imperial. I *thought* it didn't look right.'

'Tell me, when you get to know The Top very well, can you address him more familiarly? Can you simply call him The?'

Tom seemed about to give the question serious consideration; but Valentine smiled and said: 'He is a little extravagant, to be sure. But he is a man who knows a great deal of the world, and a capital companion, all in all. He has the *entrée* everywhere.'

Louisa made no demur at this: loyalty to Valentine remained her first consideration, and if his tastes and pleasures were not her own, she was not about to reproach him for it. But from the conversation of The Top she drew one anxiety. Lady Harriet's faro-bank, and the large stakes laid there, appeared to her mind for the first time as a reality, and not as a yardstick of worldly toleration. She hoped that Valentine and Tom did not take it in during their nocturnal jaunts; and she was almost ready to ask Tom about it: – but she made the mistake, on Tom's enquiring again what she thought of his friend, of referring to him as a dandy; and this set him off on such a painstaking explanation of the subtle differences between a dandy, a swell, a beau, a buck, a blood and a Corinthian that she gave it over.

There was a further distraction. – Sophie took her aside, and astonished her with the information that several gentlemen to whom she had not been introduced were longing to meet her, and several more to whom she *had* been introduced had been warm in their praises.

'No – you are funning,' was all Louisa could say; for as far as she was conscious of herself at all, she suspected she was hot and cross-looking, and inclined to say very stupid things.

'Not in the least: I never joke about the important matters of life, my dear – and you may ask Valentine, if you like, for he heard them too. No, the Golden Miss Astbury is not to have the field all to herself, believe me.'

This Louisa could not believe: and it was on the tip of her tongue to say that where Miss Astbury was Golden, Miss Carnell could claim only the title of Bronze, or perhaps Tin; but on second thoughts, she reflected that she had known sufficient disparagement over the years, without turning it on herself. She would not allow praises to go to her head: – but they might be allowed to reach as far as her eyes, which, when she saw herself reflected in the hall mirror as they left, certainly seemed uncommonly bright.

Chapter XII

Mrs Spedding's avowal that she would be glad to meet Mr Pearce Lynley of Hythe Place was something that lay in abeyance, very happily to Louisa's mind: there were so many other things to gladden her aunt, she felt, that there was no need for a reminder. – Fortune, however, decreed otherwise. On Sunday afternoons it was Mrs Spedding's fashionable habit to drive in Hyde Park, where she was always certain of seeing a great number of acquaintance, and of styles of bonnet and mantle to be admired and sought on the next shopping-expedition. Louisa and Sophie accompanied her in the barouche, while Tom and Valentine rode alongside: Tom having secured from a friend the loan of a mount for his cousin that he described, with more enthusiasm than intelligibility, as 'the primest goer, excepting the little feather on her legs'. Valentine looked extremely well as a horseman, and quite the equal of any of the smart young bloods riding the ring; and this particular Sunday Louisa was just reflecting on how far they had come from the staid retirement of Pennacombe when the emblem of that past appeared before her.

It was Pearce Lynley: – with him, a young man in regimentals, and his sister Georgiana. All three were mounted, Georgiana on a pony that looked as prettily ill-tempered as herself: the fourth of the party, a young woman, walked beside her. There was no escaping the introduction. Tom was already hailing Mr Lynley, before Louisa's eyes met his. He coloured slightly, and snapped at his horse's reins, though the animal was quiet: how much was revealed in her own expression she could not tell, but the force of the tingling, unhappy memory that the sight of him revived surprised her; and she realised how effectively the London adventure had worked in suppressing it, and how signally it had failed to replace agitation with indifference.

For now all was outward civility. Valentine introduced Mrs Spedding, and Louisa had the small satisfaction of observing that Mr Lynley, taking in her dress, carriage and manner, could not fault her in point of respectability. Meanwhile her own attention turned, with sharp interest, to the young officer, whom Mr Lynley introduced as his brother Francis. In him there was nothing to be seen of Pearce Lynley's remote, finished handsomeness: there was a want of symmetry in his dark, thin face with its prominent jaw; but something both keen and sardonic in his looks drew the eye. And when he heard her name, a glance of intense curiosity lighted first on her, and then on the marmoreal face of his brother.

'Miss Lynley,' concluded Mr Lynley's introductions: apparently the young woman accompanying her no more merited a name than a mount. Louisa could only suppose her the new governess that had been sought, and pitied her: though her pale, composed look suggested she had already cultivated stoicism.

Like her children, Mrs Spedding was very ready to find everyone agreeable; and Mr Lynley being impressive besides, and having known her late sister in Devonshire, nothing was wanting for her to take to him thoroughly. Soon she was speaking of the musical party she was to hold at Hill Street the next evening, for which a famous harpist had been engaged, and extending an invitation to the Lynleys to join them. While Mr Lynley was still bowing his stiff acknowledgements, his brother spoke for the first time.

'Georgiana would greatly like that, I think: she is very fond of music.'

'Oh, is Miss Lynley out?' cried Mrs Spedding. 'In that case, I should be even more delighted.'

'Miss Lynley is not out, in the sense that she is able to accept evening engagements in town,' Mr Lynley said, in his most repressive tone. 'However, the case of a musical party is, I allow, somewhat different: if she may be properly accompanied by her governess, ma'am, I do not see the harm in it: thank you.'

'I am glad to know you are a lover of music too, my dear,' Mrs Spedding said to Georgiana, who was looking half pleased and half sulky, 'for I am devoted to it; and you may be sure of hearing the very best, for this harpist has played before the Prince, I hear, and was taught by Mr Handel himself.'

'She must be prodigiously old, in that case, Mama,' said Sophie, 'for Mr Handel died some sixty years ago. Perhaps it was Mr Haydn.'

'Really? I was absolutely convinced it was Mr Handel – but I am sure you are right, my dear. And so you knew my poor dear sister, Mr Lynley? It is a lasting regret with me, that I was never able to see her at Pennacombe.'

'I recall Lady Carnell as an estimable lady, ma'am,' was the short reply.

'I can never look at my niece without bringing her to mind, and seldom without a sad tear,' Mrs Spedding said, turning to Louisa with a countenance altogether cheerful. 'It is the sweet shape of the face – and those very expressive dark eyes; do you not agree, Mr Lynley?'

'Anyone who has seen either lady must acknowledge these and other merits,' Mr Lynley said – as near to handsomely as was possible to him. 'Miss Carnell, I hope you find the London air as agreeable to you as your looks suggest.'

To find him courteous, even in his steely way, cast her into such confusion that she flew to the opposite extreme, and said without warmth: 'Yes, thank you, Mr Lynley. But you have made an omission – there is one of your party you have not introduced.'

This he plainly did not like at all; and she saw Francis Lynley looking satirically up at him from under his arched brows. But he recovered himself, and said: 'My apologies. Miss Bowen – lately joining our household as Georgiana's governess.'

If he was discomfited, however, Miss Bowen did not appear at all gratified by Louisa's intervention on her behalf: she merely inclined her head, and resumed her appearance of fixing her mind at a great distance. Perhaps, indeed, she was as chilly in her way as her employer, and so was well matched with – Louisa would not say the family; for she suspected, even on so slight an acquaintance, that Lieutenant Lynley differed a good deal from both his brother and sister.

With compliments on both sides, the two parties moved on; and Louisa was left to ponder on why Mr Lynley had accepted Mrs Spedding's invitation, when it must be thrusting him back into the society of the woman who had rejected him, and whom he had apparently forsworn with all the unbending resentment of a proud nature. Politeness: the prompting of his brother on Georgiana's behalf, which had rather pushed him into a corner: a self-respecting determination to show that he was perfectly equal to being in her company: – all these answers she considered, without finding satisfaction. It was Sophie who as they drove on confided in her ear a different possibility.

'Oh, my dear girl, how Mr Lynley still looks at you! I am afraid you have made a conquest there, more lasting than any of Bonaparte's.'

Louisa started in surprise, and was very ready to call this nonsense – yet not with such a reflex of discomfort as would formerly have been the case. – She felt more sure of herself. Let him come to Hill Street: she was better able to meet him on this neutral ground than at Pennacombe, where long habit made him proprietorial: he might see for himself that she was faring very well, where he had darkly hinted that she would do very ill. As for his feeling towards her, she could not believe it was as Sophie represented it; but if it were even partly true, a voice spoke in her to say that a little deprivation and suffering would do no harm at all to someone so entirely unaccustomed to them as Pearce Lynley.

The next day, before the musical party that was to put these conclusions to the proof, there came unexpected news. Valentine, opening his letters as they sat after breakfast, came upon one from Mr Tresilian.

'Here's a wonder! Hark to this, Louisa. "My dear Valentine, I hope this finds you et cetera." His words, I am not summarising. "Believe me, I am as grateful for your letters as if you had written any." He doesn't mean it, of course,' Valentine said laughing, very heartily, and looking around, 'and you know, Louisa, since we came to town there really has hardly been a moment. – Well, he goes on. "Tell your sister that when she talked of our going to London, she planted a seed that has grown into a mighty oak. Or a middling sort of oak at any rate. – Kate, Miss Rose and I are hey-ho for London. Though I detest the notion of being hey-ho for anything, and I hope that the moment I declare myself hey-ho you will, as Miss Rose would say, drop me off a cliff directly. Still, we are coming. The times are exceptional. I want to see my banker, for Boney's fall has set off fireworks in the funds, and I'm afraid of them, and want to be sure. And then you have all the Crowned Heads of Europe, and generals and whatnot arriving, and we shall not see such a thing again, and Kate must not miss it. It's the Tsar of Russia coming that has decided it for me, and Kate too. It is one thing to see a king, another to see a tsar – or, as Miss Rose insists on calling him, a Star. Her English tongue is affronted by the reversal of those letters. We come by the stage. Expect us in four days. If you know of a decent lodging, I will be obliged. Yours, James Tresilian."' Valentine, impatiently smiling, tossed the letter down in front of Louisa. 'A decent lodging! That will be hard to find, with town so full of company. I'll ask Tom. The Top, too. Coming by the public stage – dear God, they will be an age upon the road. – I do wish Tresilian would go at life with a little more style.'

'Still, it will be a great pleasure to see him again,' Louisa murmured, picking up the letter for herself, and smiling over the postscript: *Acorn, I meant, not seed. Dunderhead*, 'Kate too.'

'To be sure – though let that be an end of our Devonshire acquaintance descending on us, else we shall have Mrs Lappage knocking at the door next, and we shall feel we never escaped at all.'

Sophie protested at this; for her part, she would have them all come to town – nothing could be nicer: and she went on to describe Mr Tresilian in vivid and comprehensive terms to her mother, recalling with especial delight the view of one of his ships from his tower look-out. Mrs Spedding listened avidly, and said she could not wait to meet him: – and, doubtless, stored away the impression that Mr Tresilian was a small, talkative clergyman, who lived in a forest.

Louisa noticed Tom giving his sister what was, for him, a penetrating look. She wondered too whether Sophie anticipated Mr Tresilian's arrival with something more than her usual eagerness for company; and whether it was the promised sight of someone altogether prettier and more graceful than General Blücher that was bringing him to town. If it were so, she was not sure how she felt. Something of foreboding: for Sophie, as she had seen, was a prodigious flirt, and without any ill-meaning could find three men in an evening equally fascinating. Part of her, though, registered a curious irritation at the notion of James Tresilian coaching a hundred and fifty miles in pursuit of an amorous vision. Somehow it lowered her opinion of him. – But she caught herself up: surely this was to think like her father – she would be talking of chasing hats next.

If it were Kate, however, who was behind the enterprise, she could only shake her head sadly. Watching Valentine preparing for his morning ride, pulling on skin-tight gloves and dusting specks from his mirror-like Hessians, she doubted whether his mind entertained a thought of any such person as Kate Tresilian existing in the world.

Mrs Spedding's musical party was well attended: her large reception-rooms were filled to bursting. Accomplished amateurs of pianoforte and voice were to precede the harpist – a much-dressed lady, who seemed to have solved the question of choosing a costume for the evening by putting on everything at once. Among the guests were Mrs Murrow and her niece, the Golden Miss Astbury; who revealed herself to be a superb executant, but would play only a single piece, and calmly refused to return to the pianoforte afterwards. Mrs Spedding, who genuinely did like music, to the extent of tapping her fan in time and only talking quietly while it was playing, was in raptures; but Mrs Murrow at her side shook her wrapped-up head.

'Well, well, I dare say she ought to receive some credit, indeed – for she practises dreadfully hard.'

'Oh, but that is because she loves it – do you not, Miss Astbury?' cried Mrs Spedding. 'That is what you call a labour of love.'

'Then I am afraid she loves it a good deal too much. I know it would give me a shocking headache to be always peering away at those little black notes: dear me, I can hardly bear to think of it.'

But Mrs Murrow reserved her dullest incomprehension for the harpist, about whose spirited performance she could only say: 'I should think it must hurt her fingers dreadfully.'

'The fingertips harden with use, Aunt,' said Miss Astbury, who seemed to accord Mrs Murrow a firmly patient attention, as if she were a not very bright child.

'Then I am sure her needlework must suffer for it – and then how will she contrive when she is old?'

As there seemed no appropriate reply to this, short of placing a bag over her head, Mrs Murrow's question went unanswered; and Miss Astbury turning to Louisa asked: 'Are you musical, Miss Carnell?'

'Oh, not very – that is, I play indifferently and I listen with pleasure, but not much comprehension.' This sounded to Louisa's own ears faintly imbecilic: she added quickly: 'I am fonder of reading.'

'Indeed? Novels, I suppose.'

'Some: but I much enjoy poetry – Cowper and Crabbe, and Scott too, but above all Lord Byron.'

'Ah! I have met Lord Byron.'

'Indeed? You astonish me. Not the circumstance, I mean, but – is he as fascinating as they say?'

Louisa was all agog: – but Miss Astbury's smile was cool and quelling. 'He is made a great fuss over, as man and poet; but the simple fact is, the irregularities of his private life cannot redeem him in either regard; and though there was a certain piquancy in the introduction, he was not a person with whom I could continue an acquaintance.'

And there was Byron dealt with! Louisa need no longer envy Miss Astbury's having met him – it would be like envying a blind man the view from his window; and she did not trouble to defend her hero against so pitiable an attack. The supper interval was beginning: and Pearce Lynley, who so far had paid Louisa no further attention than a bow and greeting, was to be seen approaching. Whether he intended taking her in to supper there was no telling – for Mrs Spedding was quick to speak to him, and to introduce him to Miss Astbury. Here, Louisa thought, was an apt conjunction: in lofty self-regard and withering propriety they were evenly matched; and it was fitting that

Mr Lynley presently gave Miss Astbury his arm to go in to supper, where they could ice the soup and chill the cutlets in concert.

As promised, Georgiana and her governess Miss Bowen were there also; but Louisa had failed to observe Lieutenant Lynley in the throng – and was sensible of a certain disappointment, which turned abruptly to surprise. – Francis Lynley was by her side. She had been expecting to see his red coat, as her look must have shown. He glanced down at his plain black, and said, with a faint smile: 'Yes, I have put off regimentals. My sick-furlough will become discharge soon enough – but in truth I abandoned the red coat because I am tired of people coming up and congratulating me.'

'I suppose it is very natural, when we are celebrating victory.'

'I am not sure I did anything to contribute to it. My foot arrested the progress of a musket-ball, which might otherwise have lodged in an innocent tree or fence-post: there is that. Well, shall we get over the civilities about a delightful evening, and so on? They do get in the way of what one really wants to say.'

'I can happily dispense with them. What *do* you want to say, Lieutenant Lynley?'

'Oh, ever since we met in the park, I have wanted to convey to you the full strength of my amazement. I have at last encountered the fabled Miss Carnell – a creature as rare and incredible as a real military hero.'

Louisa faltered. – His face, with its wryly twisted lips, was alive with expression, in complete contrast to his brother's:

yet still she was uncertain how to read it. 'I had no idea I was such a monster,' she said dubiously.

'Think of mermaids and enchantresses rather. May I take you in to supper? You look perturbed. It is only my rather nonsensical way of saying I have heard a good deal about you.'

Between doubt and fascination, she gave him her arm. His limp, as they went in, was very noticeable; but she did not think his lean figure any the worse for it.

'You probably know my brother and I are not generally on the warmest of terms,' he pursued when they were seated. 'But we do correspond, you know: indeed, for two people who do not understand each other in the slightest, we rub along pretty well. And the great theme of his letters – besides my own shortcomings, on which there can never be enough to say – has long been Miss Carnell of Pennacombe. I had only the vaguest memory of you from my residence at Hythe: your family were very little seen about; and this only increased my curiosity to behold the object of such singular praises. Do I speak out of turn?'

'No: that is, I hardly know what to say. I am not sure whether you are in earnest.'

'Dear God, I hope I am never that; but I am not making a game of you, I assure you. Nor of my brother's attachment – though it is so little in Pearce's way to be liberal with the expression of his feelings that I had to do a little reading between the lines to be certain of it.'

'Lieutenant Lynley, this is all very difficult.' Not the least difficulty was accommodating the idea of Pearce Lynley praising her: if there were praise to be bestowed, she had always supposed he reserved it to himself, for his condescension in noticing her. 'While my father was alive, there was some promotion of a match between Mr Lynley and myself, because it was his wish – but that is really all I can say. Certainly – though I do not doubt you – I have never had reason to believe that your brother's attachment was such, in kind or degree, as to be at all troubling to him.'

'I do understand you. He always spoke of it as such a settled thing that I wondered whether it was so settled after all. And as we are being so thoroughly and improperly frank, Miss Carnell, I may as well add that there has lately been an alteration in Pearce, from which I collect there has been an alteration in his expectations. In short, I suspect he has been refused. This, of course, is the moment at which you may well decline to speak of the matter, deplore my impudent curiosity, and sever the acquaintance: by all means do; but let me at least help you to some of this excellent pie before I withdraw discomfited.'

She shook her head, laughing a little sorely. 'I will not have any pie – but I shall not send you away either. – A glass of that Madeira, though, if you will be so good. You have spoken the truth of it, Lieutenant Lynley: the attachment was – was not mutual; and I am only a little concerned, from what you have said, that your brother was made more unhappy by the matter than I had supposed.'

'Oh, as to that, it is difficult to tell with Pearce. I know he thought very highly of you: but if I can say this with respect, I wonder whether he can continue to think highly of anyone who has refused to give his merits the proper adoration. Certainly you have knocked him back, and his pride is hit. But I would not be uneasy. A woman is entitled to some conquests, surely.'

'I don't know – I fear I shall sound priggish, but I am not happy with this notion of conquests,' she said, recalling Sophie's hints in the park. 'It is altogether too warlike – though perhaps I should not say that to a soldier.'

'Now this is what has given me such pause,' he said, sitting back and contemplating her. 'Because you are not at all how I had fancied you. – And please, don't embarrass me with the title of soldier. It was something I did because I couldn't think of anything else, and it was nine-tenths humbug and one-tenth fear.'

'If you say so – though I am sure you ought to be more proud than ashamed.' With irresistible curiosity she added: 'Then how *did* you fancy me?'

'Oh, rather along Pearce's lines, translated. Somewhat grand and unapproachable.' He lowered his voice. 'In truth, rather like that imposing creature he is sitting with. That *is* the famous Miss Astbury, is it not?'

'It is.' Louisa glanced over to see that Mr Lynley and Miss Astbury were conversing with ease, if not animation: though that was hardly to be expected. 'But I cannot help wondering, Lieutenant Lynley, if I am not grand and unapproachable, what that makes me instead. Insignificant and humble, perhaps.'

'You must determine that for yourself,' he said, with his narrow, cat-like look. 'I shall only say that I did not expect to like you very much. Well! Miss Astbury is actually smiling. Pearce must be exerting himself. He can *be* pleasant, you know: it is only that somehow he does not see the need for it. It would not be such a great surprise if he chose to pursue a golden dolly like that.'

'No – you do not think so? Your brother has an ample fortune.'

'Just so – but I am sure, like all of us, he would be happy to have more. He has often spoken of going into Parliament, which is an expensive business. And Miss Astbury would not be above his touch, you know. For all her airs, I understand the gentility of her family does not go back very far; whereas the Lynley name is ancient and irreproachable. Lord, the Lynley name: how much I have heard of it. And then a man who has been refused will often seek to demonstrate that other women find him thoroughly acceptable. This is only human nature – of which my brother, despite plentiful evidences to the contrary, is certainly a sharer.'

Louisa looked again at Mr Lynley and Miss Astbury in colloquy, with a peculiarly mixed emotion that she could not identify. Though she quickly dispensed with any suggestion that by these attentions he might succeed in inclining her either to jealousy or regret, she could not be flattered that his affections for her, which his brother had represented as more powerful than she had guessed, might be so quickly superseded.

'Well, you know him a good deal better than I,' she said, with rather strained carelessness. 'And I may as well say, Lieutenant Lynley, that you are not at all what I expected either.'

'Ah, no horns or cloven hoof, eh? No, you need not try to explain, Miss Carnell. If my brother has mentioned me at all, I'm sure it is in terms of disapproval; and by Pearce's standards, they are I dare say entirely warranted. If there is a black sheep of the Lynley family, I must accept the title. I was never able to measure up to my father, or to Pearce, and perhaps I did not try enough. But I would contend for being a *grey* sheep. I have never settled to anything very well: that I cannot deny. I would say it was in my nature, if I did not loathe people who talk about things being in their nature, and get so tremendously interested in themselves. I have never been able to keep hold of money, but then I have never laid out vast sums of it either. Gaming I find dull, and in the regiment I was accounted a poor fellow because I could not drink my bottle without turning green. That inability to apply myself extends, I fear, to vice. I should very much like to be a complete rogue: at least it would mean I had finished something.'

The picture of his being unable to equal the expectations of his family was one that struck forcibly on Louisa's mind, knowing his brother, and remembering her own father. 'But you applied yourself to the army, surely – even if it was not something you would have freely chosen.'

'Well, I did not desert. If you will allow me to take a little pride in that, then thank you: believe me, I will take any pride that is going. I confess I often wished to – but it requires a particular kind of courage to desert, so I chose instead to cultivate the art of dodging and ducking.' He put away his plate scarcely touched: he seemed to find food uninteresting. 'But you are too good-natured, Miss Carnell – or else more impervious to gossip than any normal person can be. It must have been well known in Devonshire that I was much with my grandmother – and then, suddenly, not.'

'I confess I am too curious to deny it. But that was all that was positively known.'

'And a great deal more speculated, no doubt,' he said, with a harsh, clouded look. 'Forgive me – the whole business is something I cannot recall with equanimity, perhaps because no one comes out of it well, least of all me. I was very young: my grandmother, Mrs Poulter, spoilt me excessively: there is an end of the excuses. She has always been generous; and at that time she extended her kindness to a young woman of the district, whose late father had been a poor curate, and was distressed for means. Mrs Poulter had her there several times a week to read to her, and do a little sewing – anything, in fact, for which she could pay her, without the degradation of charity. You may possibly guess the rest. The young woman and I formed an attachment – or fell in love – or took a liking to one another, which the romanticising of youth and inexperience were quick to elevate into something beyond its true level: choose as you will. Nothing would satisfy us but an elopement: fortunately our preparations, which were hopeless enough, were discovered, and we were prevented.'

'You say fortunately. – Do you regret this scheme, then?'

'Regret? Absolutely. It was folly and nonsense. We would not have done well together at all; and as for what we were to live on, I had no firmer notion than a hope that my grandmother would do something for us. Yes, it is rather sad and grubby, is it not? But I suspect I had some confused idea that at last I was striking out on my own, and deciding for myself, and so on. Well, as soon as it was known, Pearce hastened up to Nottinghamshire, and took charge. He had not long succeeded my father to the estate, and was determined to show himself master of every situation. As indeed he was, and always has been: I do not quarrel with that: if I say I wish there were a *little* fallibility in his nature, it is probably because I recognise too much in my own.'

It was a relation intensely interesting to Louisa: she could well imagine Pearce Lynley *taking charge*, and the picture was not one that softened her feelings towards him. 'But what happened? Were you forcibly separated?'

'Ah, now you are looking for a tale of unfeeling tyranny, in which my wrongs are painted in the liveliest colours. No: I was read a great lecture on responsibility, which was probably sensible, if lacking a little in sympathy: my grandmother, whose distress at the whole episode is what I most blush to recall, took the girl aside, and represented to her the recklessness of the project. We were both made to feel the abuse of trust that we had demonstrated; and I was despatched to London, to read in the chambers of the most appallingly dull lawyer that ever sharpened a pen. I mean that he was dull when he was drunk, which was most of the time: when he was sober, he was only ferocious.'

'What became of the girl?'

'Oh, for a time we were rebellious enough to correspond, in spite of its being forbidden – or, rather, because of it; but it is wearying being on the high horse all the time, and we could not keep it up. I understand, from my grandmother, that she married an attorney's clerk in the end. There: now I have talked about myself sufficiently for three bores, and you have borne it very well, so let us turn to the weather, or the Duke of Wellington.'

'You talked because I asked; and I do not find it a grubby story in the least.'

'Well, don't go looking for heroes and villains in it, because there aren't any. What I don't like about it, if I may sound one note of self-pitying complaint, is that I have never been allowed to be anything other than that idiot stripling of nineteen, though now I am nearly five-and-twenty, and have seen men get their heads shot off, and may have killed some myself, though all I ever did was fire blindly in the smoke and pray for it to end. I am quite fenced off from my grandmother, as if I will take some disastrous advantage of her, when she is a perfectly sensible woman, who knows well what she is about. As for Georgiana, I think she would almost like me if she dared, but she turns into a ramrod in my presence.'

'And now you are to be taken charge of again, I collect.'

'Pearce has said so, has he? No, Miss Carnell, don't fear

you have committed an indiscretion.' Lieutenant Lynley laughed gently. 'His responsibilities are, I know, always the great theme of his conversation, and he chooses to see me as the weightiest of them all. Well, let it be so, if it pleases him. For now I want only to enjoy my freedom from that detestable army: hear some talk that is not all boasting and oaths, and see sights more elegant than a private's back cut in pieces by a flogging.'

'You would not contemplate a return to Hythe?'

Lieutenant Lynley shrugged. 'I think I should rather like it. I have been a wanderer enough to value the idea of a home, though black sheep are not supposed to think that. But as for Pearce and I residing together . . .' He shook his head, his face darting with wry bemusement. 'And then, you know, if he does marry – as I don't doubt he will, for he may surely take his pick – I should be even more *de trop*. No, I think a better course for me would be – well, the same course. I shall try to marry, and marry well. Does that not sound sensible?'

'I am not sure. If you mean to marry for money, then I suppose it is sensible – but altogether cold and mercenary; and I cannot quite believe you serious.'

'Why, it is only doing what everyone does, more or less. Oh, if there is love also, then so much the better – I presume, anyhow: for all my reputation, I have never known what the poets call the pleasing passion, unless you count that piece of youthful folly I have tired you with. But love in a cottage is, I am reliably informed, not a prescription for happiness.'

Louisa was at a loss how to judge this. Everything in her, of both reason and sentiment, had taken his part entirely, in hearing his narration: everything in it accorded so well with what she knew of Pearce Lynley that she could only wonder she had not guessed at such a truth before, behind Mr Lynley's veiled disdain and dark hints about his brother's character. She could only conclude that this last declaration of his, and the half-playful, half-scornful look with which he had said it, was the result of more disappointed hopes, and a more embittering experience than he would allow.

Supper being over, she was detached from Lieutenant Lynley – though she would gladly have had more of his company – by Sophie, who besought her aid with Tom. He had lately affected an eyeglass; but had the greatest difficulty in fixing it, and keeping it in; and had been tussling with it throughout the evening, to such painful effect on his face that it looked as if someone had attacked him with it. Louisa was to join her entreaties to Sophie's, that he abandon the innovation, even though he had heard it was quite the latest and smartest thing. They were successful at last, though not without some difficulty; and Louisa would have enlisted Valentine's aid, if he had been anywhere to be seen.

'Why, I think he took himself off,' Tom said, regretfully consigning the eyeglass to his pocket. 'Meeting The Top at the club, perhaps. They are a good deal together, those two: which is no surprise – sterling fellows, both. Hardly know which I love best.'

The discourtesy of his leaving their aunt's party, and the

thought of Valentine choosing to spend his time instead with so vacuous a companion as The Top, were equally disturbing to Louisa: – but she would not allow herself a conscious reproof. Lieutenant Lynley's story had sharpened her distaste for sitting in moral judgement. She was reminded of an earlier promise to herself – to take notice of Georgiana's governess, Miss Bowen, who had been confined to her pupil's side the whole time. Seating herself by them, she took care to address her remarks to Miss Bowen as she would to any other guest – not with total success: Miss Bowen, pale, plainly dressed, reserved, seemed bent on maintaining her subservient place. But she had surprisingly large grey-green eyes, which when she lifted them revealed a strong spark of intelligence, and even force; and Georgiana manifested a notably decreased tendency to pout, sneer and toss her head, which suggested that Mr Lynley had perhaps chosen well. A chance remark about reading revived something that had been niggling at Louisa ever since she had spoken with Miss Astbury; and she found herself abruptly asking: 'Miss Bowen, what do *you* think of Lord Byron? Do you think the genius of his works in any way vitiated by – well, what is rumoured of his private character?'

'No: I think that is a great nonsense,' Miss Bowen said promptly.

'I am glad to hear you say so. There is such humbug talked – and surely no true critic would sit down to assess the worth of a poem or a book on such grounds.'

'I agree. The true critic, indeed, would do better to put

aside the adulation that the undoubted novelty and energy of Lord Byron's poetry excites, and address instead its very real weaknesses.'

'Weaknesses? I do not understand you.'

Miss Bowen smiled a little. 'I do not deny that he has genius, and it may in time achieve a fuller expression. But there is a want of unity and design in his works, which one would hope to see corrected; and sometimes taste is sacrificed to a desire for cheap effect. In this last he might profitably learn from the graver, purer style of Mr Wordsworth, the poet of the Lakes.'

'I have read a little of his work,' said Louisa, by which she meant she had not read any. 'Is he not accounted rather dull?'

'He can be: that is his weakness. I am not setting one up against the other. That would be as superficial as judging an author by his private life.'

'Yes: certainly it would,' said Louisa, who was beginning to find Miss Bowen rather formidable, and certainly not in need of any such reinforcement of self-esteem as she had hoped to communicate.

'You need not agree, you know. These are simply the opinions of Mary Bowen: they are there to be challenged.'

Louisa was about to agree to this – but saw that that would not do; and very soon made an escape, on the pretext that she was wanted by her aunt. It was an unlucky choice: – Mr Lynley was with her; and Mrs Spedding surrendered his company at once, cheerfully remarking that, as such old acquaintance, they must have a great deal to say to one another.

This appeared, at first, so very far from the case that they sat in silence for a time that would have been for Louisa unendurable, if the prospect of speaking to him had not been equally vexatious. Her opinion of him tonight had been set upon a see-saw: the idea that he might really have loved her, and that he might seek to assuage his wound by a hasty declaration in another direction, could not fail to move her in some degree; but her conversation with his brother had reminded her of the character of this man over whom she had such apparent power, in all its cold officiousness. It was this aspect of Mr Lynley that came to the fore when at last he spoke.

'I could not help but observe, Miss Carnell, that you sought to engage Mary Bowen in conversation. I have no doubt that this was kindly meant; but you need not give yourself the trouble. It is very well understood that she appears here as nothing more than companion and preceptor to Georgiana's youth: it would be a very unhappy derangement of propriety if she were to be addressed in any other way – unhappy on all sides; for no one knows better than Miss Bowen herself what is appropriate to her position, and it cannot be to her comfort to have these matters set at variance.'

'As to that, Mr Lynley, I can make no more courteous reply than that I talk to whom I choose. If I made Miss Bowen uncomfortable, I am not aware of it.'

'It would not be her place to betray it. It was her strong sense of these distinctions, alongside her other qualifications, that led me to engage her as governess. Her father was secretary and librarian to the scion of one of our noble houses; and thus, though of modest birth herself, her upbringing has naturally produced in her a consciousness and comprehension of due degree that cannot be too highly commended.'

'Then I myself lack this comprehension: very well, Mr Lynley – leave me to the consequences of it. I am sure you cannot fail to recollect the substance of our last conversation at Pennacombe, in which you forswore these attempts to oversee my conduct.'

'I recall it,' he said, his eyes very pale, 'and it has been, and remains, my settled resolution never to allude to that conversation again. I would be grateful for the acknowledgement, Miss Carnell, that the reference came from you.'

'Certainly, whatever you wish: only if we are to meet at all on tolerably civil terms, you must stop observing me in this way. I have seen too much of the urge to direct and control for me to like it, even when it is represented as responsibility.'

His chin went up. 'You have, of course, been having a long conversation with my brother.'

'Yes: I do not suppose *that* escaped your observation either. But you need not fear, he has not told me any tale of woes or wrongs, or spoken of you with anything but respect. I now understand the shadow attaching to Lieutenant Lynley's name; the circumstances surrounding his departure from Mrs Poulter's house: nothing pleasant: but nothing so very dreadful either.'

'Not in consequences – for luckily the scheme was discovered. But there is much to reprehend in the betrayal of my grandmother's trust, the heedless unconcern for her repose of mind—'

'Which he is very sensible of, Mr Lynley.'

'I see. You are a swift convert to his cause: so I shall not even ask the question, whether you found much that was improving in my brother's conversation.'

'He has contracted, I think, an unhappily cynical turn of mind – but that I conceive a result of the influences operating on him. If a man is to be always mistrusted, it is not wonderful that he falls out of the habit of believing in anything himself.'

'I think trust must be earned.'

'And I greatly wonder what your brother would have to do finally to earn it,' Louisa cried. 'Really, Mr Lynley, I could like you a good deal better if *you* had ever committed an impetuous folly.'

'I consider that I have,' he said, with a full look that seemed to blister her; and, with only the shortest of bows, walked away from her.

Louisa was not sorry, after all, for the musical party to end; and even envied Valentine his masculine privilege of going on somewhere, when she was afraid that sleep would not be soon summoned. She occupied herself by taking up her volume of Byron, and reading it again with an eye for unity and design; but she was not convinced – and was preparing some smart replies for Mary Bowen, when at last she heard Valentine come in. She saw with a start that it was past three in the morning: he had never been so late before. His footsteps sounded in the passage, and then paused outside her door, as if he had seen the candlelight, and was about to tap and come in. But this was less and less his habit; and after a further pause, in which she could not be sure whether she detected a sigh, he moved on to his own room, shutting the door softly.

Chapter XIII

'It was very obliging of them,' said Mr Tresilian, referring to the arches, banners and garlands with which the principal streets of London were now decorated, 'but they need not have made such a fuss about our coming. Just a trumpet or two would have sufficed.'

'Oh, my dear sir, you are very welcome indeed,' said Mrs Spedding, 'but I think those preparations are in honour of the visit of the Allied Sovereigns, who began landing at Dover yesterday – oh, but you are funning. You looked so grave I mistook you! Well, you have certainly come at the most remarkable time. There will be the Tsar of Russia and the King of Prussia – Tom, have I got those the right way round? – and Prince Metternich and any amount of generals. It will be a gala – quite a gala. And to think at this time of year there is usually not a soul to be seen in town!'

Mr Tresilian, Kate and Miss Rose had called at Hill Street as soon as they were settled at the Golden Cross Hotel – a venue that Valentine allowed as acceptable, though not as elegant as Stephen's; but both he and Tom were amazed as to how they had secured rooms there. 'For everywhere was full

– shockingly full. Only by a word in the right ear, only by a useful connection could one get a decent berth anywhere.' Mr Tresilian deferred to their superior knowledge, but resolved the mystery quite simply by saying that he had asked the landlord if there were rooms, and given him a half-sovereign as he did so, and that had seemed to settle the business.

'But, my dear Tresilian, how long do you intend to stay?' Valentine pursued. 'The comforts of an inn-lodging, even the best, are limited; and I have been asking around for a decent house, and there is nothing – simply nothing.'

'We shall stay as long as there are interesting things to see,' Mr Tresilian said. 'As for lodgings, my banker writes me that he can secure us some pleasant rooms for Monday, hard by Lombard Street.'

Valentine winced a little at the naming of an address so very City, and so little fashionable; but on the whole he was unreservedly delighted to see his friend, and was thoroughly cordial to Kate and Miss Rose: and while the visitors were occupied with Mrs Spedding, he murmured to Louisa: 'I am glad he has a new coat. He would have appeared excessively countrified in that old blue thing without a waist; and you see how well he looks when he takes a few pains.'

Louisa said nothing: she had never thought Mr Tresilian looked ill in his old coat; and she could only suppress a sigh that Kate's new gown and spencer, fresh complexion, and bright shy glances, went quite unremarked.

As for Sophie, she was extremely attentive to Mr Tresilian,

asking with great minuteness after his neighbourhood, his household and his ships. In his replies he was agreeable – but composed; as if, Louisa thought, he were setting out to measure and test his own fascination. He cordially accepted Mrs Spedding's invitation to dine with them later; but once there, it was the Carnells to whom he devoted his chief attention. Naturally enough, perhaps: they were the oldest of friends, and he had many things to tell of their Devonshire neighbourhood: items of news, and the kind regards and compliments of their neighbours. To all of this Valentine listened with a very limited patience; and when Mr Tresilian added that he had ridden over to Pennacombe House most days, to see that all was in order there, Valentine snapped with a little laugh of irritation that there was not the slightest need for him to be fussing with that, as the steward knew his business very well. – After this Mr Tresilian was less inclined to talk to his friend, and more to observe him quietly. Louisa, who could not bear to have Valentine thought ill of, and least of all by Mr Tresilian, at last intervened on his behalf, saying at dinner, with attempted lightness: 'You must think, Mr Tresilian, we have become thoroughly townish. But the fact is, there is always such a great din of talk here that one becomes somehow deaf to country news, much as one likes to hear it. You will soon find it so yourself.'

'I do not think I shall find anything of the kind,' he said, 'but I congratulate you. That piece of tact was ingeniously worked out.'

'I'm sure Valentine did not mean to offend—'

'He did not: and even if he did, he can always rely on you to avert it. So, have you seen Pearce Lynley in town?'

'Yes, we have met the whole family. Well – I find London is a smaller world than I had imagined, and there is really no escaping the acquaintance,' Louisa said: conscious that, for various reasons too ill-defined to be examined, she did not wholly wish to.

Mr Tresilian nodded. 'Yes: we had better leave a card,' he said, with an expression of fathomless gloom. 'What I would really like to do some day is leave a blank card – perfectly blank – on every hall table.'

'What would be the purpose of that?'

'Benevolence. It would furnish everyone with the opportunity for intriguing speculation: it would promote sociability, as they would be asking their friends if they had got one too: and children could draw on them. I always longed to draw on calling-cards when I was a boy, but it was never allowed. How does Lady Harriet?' he added, with a sharp look.

'Tolerably well, I think: we have seen little of her,' Louisa said carefully.

'I wondered if she were reconciled with her husband. Oh, yes, I know her history: Valentine told me when we were at Pennacombe. He was always harping on that string.'

'I do not think a reconciliation likely. Colonel Eversholt continues very violent, they say. But Sophie, you know, is her great friend, and she could tell you more of that, Mr Tresilian.'

'Oh! it doesn't signify,' he said quickly, as if a little breeze had blown through him. 'Lady Harriet is doubtless much occupied with her faro-bank; and that is not one of the sights we are bent on taking in. Oh, yes, we mean to be thorough country visitors, you know, and to go steadily about, gaping at everything from the lions in the Tower to the dear fat Prince himself, and grumbling about the prices. I told Valentine so: naturally his delight is not to be expressed.' Mr Tresilian's face was impassive: probably only someone who knew him as well as Louisa did would have seen the devilish spark in his eye. 'Well, Kate is all excitement – and I hope that the change and novelty, at least, will do her good. She has been a little low. And though we had the greatest difficulty in persuading Miss Rose to accompany us, rather than stay at home and live on boiled nettles, I want her to drink the full measure of the experience, now we are here.'

'I doubt she will thank you for it,' Louisa said, glancing across at Miss Rose, who had been placed next to her old nemesis, Tom, and who was resisting his gallant delight in her company with every self-hating weapon in her armoury. 'Or, rather, she will thank you in such terms as will make you feel more uncomfortable than if you had done her an injury.'

'Oh, yes, that is certain,' said Mr Tresilian, easily. 'But I cling to the hope that somewhere, underneath it all, she may at last enjoy herself. I could cheerfully knock her on the head, sometimes: but still, allowances and all that. I remember my father telling me she was a great beauty in her day. You needn't stare: you people who have beauty can never quite conceive it in others. *I* was a beauty in my day, and a baronet once called me an enchanting faun – but there were objections to the match, and my bloom quickly faded.'

Diverted as she was, she had a moment to register the strangeness of Mr Tresilian's referring to *her* as a beauty; but his talk was so steeped in the ironical that it surely meant nothing.

Louisa and her cousins were much with the Tresilians over the following days, for all were eager to witness the spectacle of the foreign princes, and they made up a regular party to view the processions and parades. Valentine accompanied them sometimes; but he yawned even at the sight of the Tsar driving in the Prince Regent's chariot to the Carlton House banquet, agreeing with ready cheerfulness, when Mr Tresilian accused him of having no sense of history.

'I must ask Valentine to take me on one of his town jaunts,' Mr Tresilian remarked to Louisa, thoughtfully. 'There must be a powerful attraction in them: they cannot all be dressing up, jawing, and lounging. Mr Spedding, perhaps you will secure my admittance.'

'Certainly, my dear sir, nothing easier: would like nothing better. But I must caution you, Valentine goes the pace – Lord, he goes it! Frankly, I flag, and want my slippers by midnight. But he will always go on somewhere.'

'I wonder where,' Mr Tresilian said mildly; and Louisa found herself avoiding his eye. His words – *a powerful attraction* – had stirred in her an uneasiness she did not wish to acknowledge.

There came the morning when the Tresilians were engaged, in moving to their new lodgings, and Tom with an unbreakable appointment at his tailor's; so it was Valentine who accompanied Louisa and Sophie to see the Allied Sovereigns riding in Kensington Gardens. The crowd along the avenue to the Serpentine was greater than any they had yet seen – greater, noisier and, under the hot midsummer sun, more feverish. As well as the Tsar and the Prussian King, General Blücher was part of the mounted procession, and he was the next best thing to Wellington himself: there was a yell and a surge to get near him; and suddenly being part of the crowd was not exhilarating, but disturbing. Louisa felt herself carried along in the press, with her toes just drumming on the ground: she kept her arm firmly looped in Sophie's, but Valentine was borne away from them by a cross-current in the throng, and his head bobbed out of sight. There were screams, and even the horses of the bodyguard began to rear and plunge: Louisa saw a woman stumble and fall: the sensation of stifling powerlessness was dreadful. Dragging Sophie with her, she managed to fight her way to a break in the crowd near the trees, and burst free; and at that moment a tall, broad-chested gentleman in a military coat appeared before them.

'Miss Spedding,' he said, his glance just grazing over Louisa. 'Are you hurt? Your companion?'

'No – no, I thank you, Colonel Eversholt,' Sophie said, recovering after her first start. 'Only a little draggled. A shocking squeeze, is it not?'

'Shocking, dangerous and ill-planned. There is a great deal of rabble here beside the better sort. – Here they come again. Pray get behind me, or you will be swept up.'

The wild surging of people was so powerful and unpredictable, however, that at last Louisa and Sophie had to shrink against the trunk of a tree, whilst Colonel Eversholt stood with his arms braced back to protect them. The situation was too novel and alarming for Louisa to take much note of the introduction to a man of whom she had heard so much; but as the press of people began to disperse, she found a moment to take his measure. There was nothing in his impressive figure to suggest a man of five-and-forty; his large, strong-boned face was handsome too – but an uneasy face, furrowed and bleak, with a complexion that spoke of wine and long nights.

'You will pardon the proximity,' he said, as he stepped away. 'A necessary measure. You are unaccompanied?'

'No, no – my cousin is with us, but we became separated,' Sophie said. 'I hope he is not hurt. – Oh, wait, I see him – good heavens, he was carried almost to the gates. Thank you again, Colonel, for your assistance.'

Colonel Eversholt's unrestful gaze turned to Louisa. 'I do not have the honour.'

'Gracious, of course – this is Miss Carnell,' said Sophie, who appeared uncharacteristically nervous in his presence. 'My cousin – my very dear cousin – from Devonshire. Louisa, my dear, Colonel Eversholt. Who is the husband of Lady Harriet – whom of course you know.'

'Carnell?' The colonel repeated the name with a certain bright, hard interest: then bowed. 'Your servant, Miss Carnell. So, you are acquainted with my wife? The acquaintance was formed, perhaps, in Devonshire?' He had a peculiarly gentle, painstaking, almost tender way of speaking, suggestive of a man picking his way across hot coals. 'I am aware she spent the spring in the country.'

'Yes: Lady Harriet was our guest for a short time,' said Louisa, aware, with the acutest discomfort, that Valentine was making his way towards them.

'Then accept *my* thanks for your hospitality. I must do this, as it were, at one remove, but still I hope I know how to value polite attentions to my wife. I know, of course, she is returned to town, and have seen her; but such is my peculiar position, Miss Spedding, that I must ask you, her particular friend, how she does.'

'Oh, as to that, I saw her – it would be on Tuesday, or perhaps Wednesday, in Bond Street – at any rate, yes, I think she is well, Colonel Eversholt, quite well.'

'You think? Miss Spedding, I had expected more: I am only the deserted husband, but you are the favoured friend, who must be admitted to a far greater knowledge of her affairs than I.' He smiled a dull, seething smile. 'I press you unfairly, perhaps. For all I know, you too may be excluded from her intimacy: I hope not, for your sake. It is a very unpleasant thing, when it happens. One is made to feel quite the villain of the piece.' He turned as Valentine called out to them. 'You spoke of a cousin?'

'Yes – Mr Valentine Carnell of Pennacombe,' Sophie said. 'Louisa's brother, you know.'

'Ah, brother,' said Colonel Eversholt, softly. – Valentine was now before them, apologising for losing them, anxious for their safety, but his flow of words stopped as Sophie introduced their rescuer.

'*You* are Colonel Eversholt,' Valentine said, turning pale to his lips.

'I am, sir.' The colonel surveyed, or inspected, Valentine, with one cool sweep of his pale eyes. 'You speak as if it were a matter of surprise to you. Yet I do not think we have ever had anything to do with one another – have we?'

'No,' Valentine said, recovering himself a little. 'But I have the honour of her ladyship's acquaintance.'

'Oh, I know *that*,' Colonel Eversholt said dismissively, turning away from him. 'Miss Spedding, Miss Carnell – I shall not be needed now, though I would advise you to go home as soon as you may. The crowd may gather again. If you *should* see my wife, Miss Spedding, pray give her my compliments.' To Valentine he tendered a short bow. 'I am glad I was able to be of some assistance, even though it was not my place to do so. You should take care of your own, Mr Carnell, and not go a-wandering: that is my advice to you.'

He was gone, moving swiftly and softly for so large a man; leaving Valentine mute and white, and Louisa confronting a terrible suspicion – a suspicion that, she realised, she had had before her all the time, like an ominous crack in the ceiling that the eye convinces itself is a cobweb.

'To think it should be *him* who came to our rescue!' Sophie cried, as Valentine stirred at last, and went to fetch a hackney. 'Thank heaven you were with me, my dear: for if it had been me *toute seule,* he would have been very happy to see me quite trampled into the ground. Oh, yes: because Harriet has to do with me, and will have nothing to do with him; and he suspects everyone around her as increasing her enmity, and dividing him further from her. Well, now you have seen him for yourself, what do you think? Is he not monstrous?'

'I don't know,' Louisa said distractedly. 'He did do us a service.'

'Lord, what a thing to happen! The deserted husband, indeed! I can hardly wait to tell Harriet.'

For Sophie, characteristically, the encounter was merely to be seized on for its novelty and excitement. Louisa's own feelings were much more complicated. Monstrous – that was exactly what Colonel Eversholt was not: he was no monster or bogey, he was very real, and he was the lawful husband of Lady Harriet. She began to see the matter of the Eversholts' marriage from a new point of view: it was their affair only, and not to be meddled with, or taken up either as a noble cause or an enjoyable sensation.

But above all this stood her dreadful apprehension about Valentine. That is where he goes at night, she thought: he goes to Lady Harriet's house; and the colonel is aware of it. For the moment she could not allow the thought to develop further. It was sufficiently alarming, as the summation of all the chivalrous admiration Valentine had shown since Lady Harriet's first coming to Pennacombe. If he was simply infatuated, there was enough to trouble and disturb. Impropriety was not the point: having met Colonel Eversholt, and added the truculent impression he made on her to his dark reputation, she feared that Valentine was stepping from imprudence into danger.

But how was she to say anything of this to her brother? Loyalty – doubt – embarrassment – above all, adopting the censorious voice of their father: all impeded her. In the hackney home, observing Valentine's silence, and his still pale but quite composed, even proud expression, she ventured at last: 'It was awkward, being beholden to such a thoroughly rude man.'

Valentine gave a faint smile. 'Rude?' He shook his head. 'He is everything one supposed. It is almost satisfying.'

'Of course,' she went on, in a resolutely reasonable tone, 'one can never know the true facts of such a case.' But Valentine only smiled faintly again, and seemed gently to withdraw from her to a great distance.

She and her cousins were engaged the next day to go with the Tresilians to the Haymarket theatre; and several times before the curtain went up Louisa glanced at Mr Tresilian seated in the box beside her, with an urge to tell him of yesterday's encounter – without quite knowing what she expected him to say, or perhaps with an apprehensiveness about what he *would* say. Once the performance began, however, there was an end of all trouble: the piece was *Othello*, and for three hours she was lost to everything but the stirring compulsion of the tragedy. When the curtain fell, she found that she had seized and held Mr Tresilian's arm through the stupendous last dying moments of the jealous husband; and coming to herself, was quite prepared for him to be satirical. But no: his face revealed that he had been as rapt as she.

'Powerful – powerful stuff indeed,' he said, mopping his brow. 'I confess I did not expect it to come up to the Indian Jugglers as an entertainment; but really, I have been most agreeably surprised. Well, agreeable is not the word. There are no words.'

'"One that loved not wisely, but too well." That is very fine, is it not? I must say there is nothing in Byron to equal it. Only look at that woman in feathers, yawning her head off! How stupid people are.'

'I fear she has only come to be looked at, and finds the play a great nuisance, distracting people's attention.'

There was a great deal of movement in the theatre: – some were leaving now that the main piece was over, others, more fashionable, coming after a good dinner to take in the after-piece and the jigs. Louisa was surprised to see, in a box on the opposite side, Valentine among them. – Surprise was quickly succeeded by astonishment. A woman was with him: a woman who put back her veil to reveal the face of Lady Harriet Eversholt.

A glance was sufficient to reveal that Mr Tresilian had seen them too. 'Hullo,' he murmured. 'Your brother has conquered his aversion to the theatre, it seems.'

'I think – I think they must be with a larger party,' Louisa said.

'Ah, yes, I see them,' Mr Tresilian said grimly, his eyes fixed on the box, where Valentine and Lady Harriet were talking with lowered heads. 'Mr and Mrs Invisible, and all the young Invisibles. Charming family.'

Louisa was struck with a confusion of emotions; painful was the feeling of having her worst suspicions realised; but loyalty to Valentine, and the instinctive desire to defend him, were still pre-eminent. Luckily Kate was attending to Sophie, who was expressing her despair at the behaviour of the young man in the next box, and condemning him as the most infamous flirt, in between trying to catch his eye.

'Very public,' Mr Tresilian went on, shaking his head, 'and hence very provocative.'

'And that is exactly the point,' Louisa said eagerly. 'Valentine has this gallantry: he hates the mean-minded proprieties that would make an outcast of Lady Harriet, when she has done nothing wrong. He is all for openness and liberality. This is his way of proclaiming it.' At the same time she uttered an inward blessing that she had not told Mr Tresilian about the meeting with Colonel Eversholt after all.

'A very well-dressed outcast,' Mr Tresilian said. 'But I dare say you are right. Well, I am engaged to spend an evening at his club this week. You will not consider me mean-minded and proper, I hope, if I just mention to him that how this *appears* may be very different from how he conceives it. And there is not only his reputation to consider.'

'Very well: but as for me, I could never find anything to reproach in Valentine's conduct, Mr Tresilian – please have no uneasiness on that score.'

He was silent; and though she tried to turn her attention to the after-piece, she could not be easy. Her eyes kept returning to that box, and to Valentine and Lady Harriet so conspicuously together in it; and she was more relieved than sorry when they left early, Kate pleading a headache. Kate Tresilian was nothing if not observant, and Louisa suspected she had witnessed the spectacle too. If it were so, she longed to be able to mitigate the pain of it; but however she considered it, that lay out of her power. For it was out of Louisa's power even to quieten her own misgivings, or to suppress a suspicion that the curtain had gone up on quite a new act in their enterprise of living, and one that might take a turn more ominous than entertaining.

Chapter XIV

When Mr Tresilian had undertaken to speak to Valentine about the matter of Lady Harriet, loyalty had made her respond breezily: but inside, she seized thankfully on the one thing that seemed likely to quell her anxiety. The name of Mr Tresilian had long been synonymous in Louisa's mind with trust. When he said he would do a thing, he always did it, quietly and efficiently: she remembered an occasion at Pennacombe in her youth, when Valentine had lost a riding-crop, inlaid and engraved with silver, and was terrified to tell his father, whose gift it had been on his breeching. Mr Tresilian had said he would right the matter, against all Valentine's frantic assertions that it was impossible; and soon a perfect replica appeared, procured from Exeter, where Mr Tresilian had directed the craftsman in reproducing every detail; and he had guarded against the dangers of a parcel, which Sir Clement would have insisted be opened before his eyes, by carrying it in his coat-sleeve when he called, and discreetly placing it on the hall table.

Now Mr Tresilian had said he would consult with Valentine just as discreetly: he of all people could manage such a ticklish matter, and she did not doubt him. Or, at least, she chose not to doubt him; for her enjoyment of London was still so great that she was inclined to turn her mind away from anything that imperilled it; rather as the small cloud in the sky, on a day which our plans demand must be fair, is not to be regarded and will surely blow away.

An invitation for the Spedding household to dine with the Lynleys at Brook Street arrived, and quickened that enjoyment. – It was not something Louisa had ever expected to feel in such a prospect; but there had been a change. Her meeting with Francis Lynley had left a deep impression on her: she could not say whether she liked him, for her feeling lay at the bottom of a good deal of curiosity and perplexity, which was further entangled by her thorny relation with his brother; but she was very ready to see him again, and to compare the reality of that angular challenging face to the one that had been appearing repeatedly before her mind's eye.

Before the dinner engagement, Mr Tresilian spent his promised evening at Valentine's club; and calling at Hill Street the next morning, gave Louisa a brief account.

'I never knew fashionable dissipation could be so dull. There is a deal of fuss about sitting in the bow-window and being seen, which I could not understand; and it seems very modish to yawn continually. *There*, you may believe, I managed very well. But I found something that made up for all of this: the most delightful discovery. I have made the acquaintance of The Top. Do you know him, or it?'

'I have had the pleasure.'

'Is he not entrancing? I could study him for hours. It is not just the stupidity – it is the thoroughness with which it is kept up. To remember all that slang, and not deviate into normal language here and there: to *never* say anything remotely interesting or thoughtful, even by accidental lapse – this requires a special kind of talent. I can only look on in fascination. I think the high point of the evening was when he called me a "ninnyhammer" – but, no, comparisons are odious.' He shook his head in dreaming wonder; then with an altered expression added: 'As for Valentine, and what we spoke of, I am going carefully. He is a Carnell. It is no good telling him to take his hand out of the fire: he must be brought to believe that taking his hand out of the fire has been his settled intention all along.'

She ignored his hit against the Carnells: she was comforted by a picture of Valentine's evening entertainments so innocent of danger, and by Mr Tresilian's assurance that he would undertake another such expedition. She even allowed herself to wonder whether simply having Mr Tresilian's eye on him had brought Valentine to a sense of what was prudent, and made him withdraw from Lady Harriet's society. And, besides, the notion of *herself* as such a blind and wilful being, with all her long habits of caution and self-watchfulness, was so absurd that only someone of Mr Tresilian's whimsical temper could have fancied it.

Pearce Lynley, unsurprisingly, had taken a very good house in Brook Street; and, perhaps more surprisingly, had laid on a very good dinner, though there were only two other guests besides the Spedding party. Mr Lynley seemed bent on being agreeable, and was as nearly so as his inflexible manner would allow: it occurred to Louisa that this might have been a consequence of his being the host, and in his own household; and she even came close to the dizzying thought that his habitual stiffness when out in company might have been the result of awkwardness, or actual shyness. But she could not avoid the conclusion, drawing on what his brother had told her at their last meeting, that she herself was the reason for this: that even Mr Lynley's last angry words to her had revealed a feeling far removed from indifference; and it appeared an absolute confirmation of this that Mary Bowen joined them at dinner with her charge, instead of taking the usual solitary governess's tray in an upstairs room. There could, Louisa thought, be no other reason for this relaxation of strictness, and allowance of humanity, than to impress her, who had condemned his treatment of governesses so roundly; though Mr Lynley seemed to find the gesture alone sufficient, and studiously ignored Miss Bowen for most of the evening, even appearing to colour and hesitate whenever he was forced to speak to her, as if made uncomfortable by the evidence of his own unaccustomed benevolence.

All this was intriguing: but Louisa's first object was the resumption of her acquaintance with Francis Lynley. Whether his inclinations ran in the same direction, she was not at first sure: he appeared in lively spirits, and was universally civil, even listening to a long anecdote of Tom's, full of people he had never heard of, with nothing more ironical than a slight twist of his eyebrow. But when it was time to go in to dinner, Lieutenant Lynley was prompt to secure the place by her side; and once there to announce: 'There: now I am easy. I have done my duty, put on a respectable imitation of a normal human creature – and now, with you, I can be as black and savage as I like.'

'I am flattered – or I *think* I am, at any rate. Are you feeling black and savage about anything in particular? Or is it a general disaffection?'

'Oh, name anything you like. These crowned and ribboned boobies parading about the town – have you seen them? Tell me frankly what you thought.'

'Well, it was only from a distance; but I thought the King of Prussia looked exactly as a King of Prussia would – as if he lives in cold rooms full of busts. The Tsar, I thought, looked rather sad.'

'Ah!' he said, crookedly smiling. 'Absolute autocrat of a vast country – any amount of serfs to lash when he takes the fancy – and yet he is not happy. This must say something about us, though I hardly know what. Oh, I don't mind them, though it will be a great relief when they scuttle back to their palaces, and we can go back to hating all foreigners equally. No, the cause of my disaffection, like most, is purely selfish. Pearce and I have been disagreeing splendidly. He is anxious for me to take up some position in the world, and I am anxious lest I find myself doing anything of the kind.'

'Surely there must be something. You are free now of soldiering, which you have told me you did not like; and not to like something implies a preferred alternative.'

'Does it now? I wish I could be so sure. I have a dreadful fear that if I were manacled in a damp dungeon – add some poisonous toads to it, if you like – and a fairy were to appear, and effect my magical release, I should still be a little stumped as to *where* exactly she should whisk me.'

'This is discontent indeed: – such, I would venture, as can only be expressed by someone who is reasonably content after all. The truly miserable are silent.'

'Miss Carnell, you are rather terrifying: I mean, in your good sense. You remind me of a Portuguese doctor I knew when I was in the Peninsula – the only medical man I ever came across who was not a humbug. An officer of my regiment had been very sick with fever, and though the worst was past, nothing the army surgeons could do would restore his health. The Portuguese – round, fat, genial fellow, whiff of garlic, waxed moustache – took a good look at him, told him not to worry, and prescribed at least one bottle of Madeira a day and general good living. It worked admirably.'

'I am glad I remind you of someone so pleasant – though I can only hope the garlic and the moustache are not the chief triggers of association.'

'This will not do – you are cheering me up, and laughter spoils the indulgence of a black mood most abominably. I shall be frank: I *would* like some sort of position. If there was one that involved, say, taking up a comfortable post at

Charing Cross or the Strand, and simply watching everything that passed, and perhaps making a note of anything particularly interesting – sad – piquant – absurd – why, then I should consider myself perfectly and happily placed. But the positions Pearce means are those in which something is required of you; and that's where I turn to a man of jelly.'

At the other end of the table, a certain conscious look about Mr Lynley suggested he heard his name mentioned; but whether from pride, or in his new accommodating spirit, he did not glance their way.

'Surely,' Louisa said, 'you do not doubt you have abilities.'

'It's a curious thing: I would like nothing better than to show them – only I fear they would not pass muster with Pearce. That's why it is easier to stick to being a good-for-nothing fellow. He expects that: we know where we are. But if I *were* to try to be something more, I might disappoint him – and that is above all what I cannot contemplate. Absurd for a great fellow of four-and-twenty – but with Pearce I never feel that: I am forever a boy, looking up at him. And I *did* look up, you know, most adoringly.'

'It is not absurd at all. The influences of our childhood and youth cannot be underestimated, I believe: those are the experiences that shape us, far beyond their immediate power.'

'Do you mean there is no escaping them?'

'I think we must make the conscious decision to do so.'

'You speak feelingly. – I never knew your father, beyond our exchanging greetings here and there – or, rather, he barked at me, and I squeaked in return. But I understood he was something of a Tartar. Pearce was always full of his praises, but I read between the lines of those. So, Miss Carnell, have you escaped? An impertinent question, I know, but they are the only interesting ones.'

'I consider I am my own woman, now,' she said carefully. 'I think that can be said with no disrespect to anyone.'

'It should be said without fear or favour – it should be proclaimed. But you dismay me with this talk of decisions. It suggests effort, which I am always unwilling to make.'

'Well, what of your scheme of making a rich marriage? That will not be achieved without some application.'

'True,' he said, pushing away his plate with his most saturnine look. 'And there lies my obstacle. The whole business of love-making disgusts me. All its language and gesture is so miserably outworn: so tritely dramatic. I wish I could talk to my mythical bride as I do to you. Oh, you do not bridle, or look for compliments, or suppose there is something tremendous and apocalyptic about a man and a woman enjoying each other's society. And there, at the risk of sounding intolerably self-pitying, Pearce has the better of me again. I think he will find his golden dolly first. He appears very much taken with Miss Astbury, you know. He has called at Portman Square several times, and the other day was actually seen driving with her in the park – suitably chaperoned, of course: that aunt of hers who looks as though she has been kept in a trunk, or ought to be.'

'Mrs Murrow,' Louisa said, suppressing a smile. 'You are very unkind.'

'Oh, I can do a good deal worse than that. Now, as far as one can tell beneath Miss Astbury's excessively icy surface, she views him with a certain degree of favour likewise. But it is curious – I am not sure his heart is entirely in it.'

If this were a tribute to her continued power over Pearce Lynley, she was not sure how she felt about it – yet it was undeniably interesting. 'Well, I do not suppose his heart needs to be, in such a match. After all, your own project of marrying well surely does not require it.'

'Ah, I fear you have taken me too much at my word. I estimate that roughly half the things I say I do not mean – though I would be hard pressed myself to tell which half is which. No: if it were a love-match, it would be a very different matter.' For a moment he looked serious: then he shrugged with his little irritable laugh. 'Or so I conjecture. It is one of those fruitless but intriguing speculations, like the distance between the stars, or the annual number of lies told in Parliament.'

He was not an easy dinner companion – but one whose society very much absorbed her: the time passed too quickly, and she regretted having to leave the table to the gentlemen, and retire to the comparative insipidity of the drawing-room. There was, however, the chance to speak to Mary Bowen: Louisa had bought a volume of Wordsworth, and was getting on pretty well with it, though she was not convinced that a flower could produce *quite* such transcendent effects on the soul, no matter how hard you looked at it. But Miss Bowen seemed not in spirits:

she said she was glad Louisa was enjoying the book, and fell silent.

'Miss Lynley, I think, is in very good looks, and her address is particularly pleasing now,' Louisa went on, meaning a sincere compliment to Miss Bowen's tutelage; for Georgiana was conversing with Mrs Spedding in quite a normal fashion, and had not stamped her foot once.

'Oh – yes: one hopes so,' Miss Bowen said, coming out of abstraction. 'She is at a difficult age.'

'To be sure. Still, there must be a satisfaction . . .' Louisa faltered: Miss Bowen's look was so bleak.

'Satisfaction, did you say?' The surprising eyes flashed upon her, then turned away. 'I know nothing of that.'

Louisa hesitated. 'Are you – are you not happily placed here, Miss Bowen?'

For the merest moment Miss Bowen's reserve seemed on the point of yielding – then it was gone, her face resumed its distantly dutiful expression, and she said: 'Thank you, I am very happily placed,' in such tones as discouraged any further conversation.

Louisa pitied her: could only suspect that her real treatment in Mr Lynley's employ was far from the indulgence that her being included at dinner was designed to suggest. Soon, however, her thoughts were in a happier train. – Lieutenant Lynley was the first to rejoin them: he sat first beside Sophie, but very soon found an opportunity to move to the place beside Louisa.

'There – now I cannot be accused of monopolising you,

and have spoilt several gossipy letters. "Lieutenant Lynley was very particular in his attentions to Miss Carnell" – oh, scratch it out. – You look a little troubled. Will you confide in me? Though don't if the trouble is *very* tedious.'

'Oh, I was a little concerned for Miss Bowen: she seems rather hipped.'

'Poor creature: I begin to suspect that is her natural expression. I have tried to talk to her, but given it up. She is so very guarded – I am half afraid of her. I can never be comfortable with a companion who will not give *something* away, for then one can never gain an advantage over them.'

Louisa's attention was then claimed by Lieutenant Lynley, so fully that Mary Bowen was forgotten: until, soon after the tea was drunk, she looked up to find that Miss Bowen was gone. – Pearce Lynley was just closing the drawing-room door, with a tight-lipped and forbidding expression, which remained on his face some time after he had resumed his seat by Mrs Spedding. Something had occurred, it seemed: whether it had been some error of conduct on Miss Bowen's part, which had caused him to repent of his bold experiment in leniency, Louisa could not tell – but she thought it likely. As a reminder of the exacting arrogance of his nature, it was timely: for the image of his driving with Miss Astbury had imprinted itself on her mind with unexpected force; and if the glance he presently threw towards her and his brother were as displeased, even as jealous, as it appeared, then very well. – She thought Francis Lynley infinitely the superior; and though she quickly dismissed

Sophie's whispered remark in the carriage as they drove home – 'My dear, I do believe you are beginning to be in love with Lieutenant Lynley!' – it occurred to her that if she *were* to fall in love with him a little, it would be a very proper blow to Pearce Lynley's pride; and such as it would be a pleasure as well as a virtue to administer.

Chapter XV

The Tresilians being established in their new lodgings, it was incumbent that they call upon them – so pronounced Sophie, high priestess of the mysteries of calling. Tom accompanied her and Louisa to Lombard Street, not only out of civility but curiosity, for he declared with a faint shiver that he had never been so far east of town in his life; though as a novelty it must have disappointed, for the district appeared respectable, the people looked perfectly normal, and there was a sad scarcity of vulgarians sitting on piles of money or making bargains in the street while wearing excessively large top hats.

On the way Sophie rallied Louisa again about her fascination with Lieutenant Lynley.

'Oh, not that I blame you: I could easily be half in love with him myself,' she went on. 'There is something about him that compels – and though he can be very charming, there is an exciting sort of suspense about that because sometimes he will cut it quite off, and go into a dark mood and seem not to care a hang for you. But, then, for someone to be *too* changeable is not pleasant; and so he shall not dislodge my dear Mr Tresilian from the first place in my affections. Certainly there is not that sparkle in Mr Tresilian – but his blunt, dry way is just as engaging; and it is always to be relied upon. If there were an earthquake or a volcano, you know, I should expect to find Mr Tresilian quite unchanged.'

'Really, Sophie, you do talk a deal of gammon and humdudgeon,' said Tom, who had plainly been in The Top's company recently. 'First place in your affections indeed! There must be a round dozen of gentlemen squeezing into *that* place, and that's only to speak of this week. And it won't do, you know, to be adding Tresilian to your list of beaux in that way. He's a sober sort of fellow, not your drawing-room gadfly; and it is doing no justice to his character, or credit to your sense, to pretend otherwise.'

Fond as she was of Sophie, there was much in this with which Louisa felt ready to concur, though she did not suppose Sophie would take the slightest notice of it; but her cousin, instead of answering Tom in their usual tit-for-tat fashion, flushed and gazed out of the carriage window, before saying quietly: 'You know a great deal about waistcoats, Tom; but nothing of the thing that beats beneath them, commonly called a heart. Mr Tresilian is different, and *I* have heart enough to feel it.'

There was something new and significant in this, which threw Louisa into a state of perturbation she could hardly account for. All her previous feelings about the relation between Sophie and Mr Tresilian, ranging from curious speculation to mild disquiet, were overthrown by a great negative. – This must not be. There was everything that was wrong, there was nothing that was right, in such a prospect as seemed to be afforded, of Sophie's setting herself seriously at Mr Tresilian; and of his responding in kind, which was rendered probable by his evident fascination with her, and by that resemblance to his late wife, which Louisa's fancy had converted into a certainty. In this tumult she entered the tall, frowning house in which the Tresilians had the first floor – the very foreignness of the place to everything she connected with them increasing her ominous sense of a great mistake hovering; but once received into the rather pleasant rooms, observing Kate's gentle smile of welcome, Miss Rose's particular contentment in finding a draught to sit in, and Mr Tresilian being pleased at the visit, but not excessively pleased, her fears began to subside. Sophie soon commenced beguiling him – yet only, it seemed, in the usual way, and employing the same weapons she fired at any number of potential conquests; and Mr Tresilian seemed rather preoccupied than otherwise.

At length, when Sophie was looking over some new music that Kate had purchased, and both were trying to explain to Tom that the black notes were not the same as the black keys on the pianoforte, Mr Tresilian spoke to Louisa aside.

'I need to talk to you privately. Can you contrive to meet me? Say Berkeley Square at noon.'

'An assignation, Mr Tresilian? Very public – and hence very provocative,' she said, recalling his words in the theatre. But she failed to elicit a smile; neither did she feel as light-hearted as she sounded; and as they returned to Hill Street, she began to fear that no words could have been more ill-chosen.

It was a simple enough matter to slip out to Berkeley Square at the appointed time: everyone was allowed to come and go as they liked in the Spedding household, and the footman at the door wore a consciously tactful look, as one accustomed to a world of flirtations and little intrigues. At this Louisa felt some irritation. Must the human heart only skim across such insubstantial surfaces? The clouded brow, the mercurial speech of Francis Lynley, which were continually recurring to her mind, surely suggested otherwise.

Mr Tresilian, soon to be seen briskly walking towards her across the sun-bleached square, appeared to have regained some of his usual equanimity; but taking her arm he began without preamble: 'I hope you were not alarmed: I mean no great secrets – but still it was impossible to speak of it earlier. – I have been another jaunt with Valentine, which is why I look so deathly, and why this sunshine is an abomination.' He frowned: not so much at the sun, she thought, as at her. 'Did you know he has been going almost every night to Lady Harriet's faro-house?'

'I – I hardly know how to answer that question, Mr Tresilian.'

'A bafflingly complex one, I admit. Try narrowing it down to yes or no.'

'It is not something he has spoken to me about,' she said, recovering herself. 'Nor would I expect him to. How Valentine chooses to spend his time is, you know, quite his own affair.'

'I see. – You will not, then, want an account of the evening I spent with him there: night, rather. And morning, come to that.'

'You seem to think I should,' she said, greatly disliking her own brittle tone: but it was the thin ice on the deepest unease. 'But, come, as to his going almost every night, I cannot devise how you know *that*, from the evidence of a single occasion.'

'Because he is treated as quite a fixture there, and appears quietly proud of the fact. Certainly, once was enough for me: I never knew anything so wearisome. I had not even the entertainment of The Top to divert me. Apparently he goes there a good deal, but just now they tell me – what was it? Ah, yes, his pockets are to let. Oh, yes, they all talk like that: but they are poor things compared to The Top: they cannot keep up that meticulous, unvarying idiocy.'

'But, Mr Tresilian, if it was merely dull, I do not see the need for this—'

'It was dull for me, because I do not like throwing away money on the turn of a card. And that is all there is to faro: it is a game of pure chance. But they all talk solemnly of their luck running with them or against them, as if there were such a thing. Otherwise they are a mixed set: young gallants with half-broken voices, liverish old roués still in hair-powder. They gather about a great mahogany table, drinking rather indifferent wine, while this decayed little man, who looks like a notary laid low by fraud, deals the cards. And there is a great brute in rusty livery who goes about trimming the candles, and minding admittance at the door.' Mr Tresilian grunted. 'High life indeed!'

The picture was, she was compelled to admit, not a pretty one: though allowances must be made, she thought, for the sturdy prejudices of Mr Tresilian, who was after all a little of the puritan. 'And what of Lady Harriet? What does she do?'

'Plays the hostess: and I mean plays, for this is the great pretence she must carry off, in case the magistrates look in – that these are simply her friends, gathering for an evening of elegant society, which happens to include cards. So she tries to make conversation, and stop them quarrelling and swearing too many oaths; and this she must keep up till three and four in the morning, which is when the play is deepest. And it is plain that none of them, with one notable exception, holds her in the slightest respect, or considers her as anything but the convenient provider of a gaming haunt.'

'I pity her,' Louisa said, shaking her head.

'Yes: it is a great pity to see a woman with such advantages, and no lack of intelligence, finding no other resource than such barren stupidity,' he said, with more harshness than sympathy.

'You spoke of an exception. – You must mean Valentine.'

'Aye: he is quite the courtier to her,' Mr Tresilian said; and then fixed his grey eyes on the distance, as if contemplating a sea with an ominously heavy swell on it.

'Well, so he has always been. Perhaps it is unfortunate – in the eyes of the world, which is always quick to judgement. But I am sure there is a nobility in his feeling, which—'

'Yes, no doubt there is, but nobility has a hard time of it in that establishment, believe me. And I would be easier if he could contrive to play the knight-errant without squandering his money. Yes, he plays. He did not go at it like some of those fools, at least while I was there; but I heard one of them remark that he was devilish close-fisted tonight; and I calculate he must have lost near a hundred guineas before I could persuade him home.'

Louisa stopped dead. 'A *hundred*? But that is terribly deep play surely. I should not be able to sleep if I lost so much.'

'I should not be able to sleep for crying. But I dare say it is small beer in those sorts of circles, where wins and losses of thousands are gaily talked of. I don't like it – but if he is set upon throwing good gold away, I cannot prevent him.'

'I suppose, again, it is a way of rendering service to Lady Harriet,' Louisa said doubtfully: the strong sun was oppressive, and seemed to scatter her thoughts like rolling coins.

'Hm. You have not heard the worst of it. Very late there came a great knocking and commotion at Lady Harriet's door. The liveried brute tried to keep the interloper out, but he was brushed aside, and the next moment he was in the room. – Lady Harriet's husband: Colonel Eversholt. So I very soon collected, as he began announcing the fact very loudly – and adding, equally loudly, that he had every right to be under this roof, and we had none. I hardly know how to describe him to you: if I say impressive, I may give an idea that is too favourable.'

'I know: I have met him. – Go on, Mr Tresilian.'

'Have you? I hope when you made the acquaintance he was not so foxed as I saw him last night. Not incapable, though: not ungovernable, despite his being in such a passion. There was something mighty purposeful about him. He abused Lady Harriet broadly for blackening his name, and further lowering it by maintaining such a resort of vice as this: – still, he was insistent on the injury done to him as a deserted husband, and claimed that he had done everything to achieve a reconciliation: urged her to give up these flagrant courses and return to him. The brute was hovering, but as the colonel said quite coolly that he would shoot him if he advanced a step, he kept his distance. It was all very uncomfortable.'

'Uncomfortable!' said Louisa, aghast. 'I should think it a good deal more than that. But as for shooting – he is known, surely, as a great braggart, and then he was drunk . . . What did –' she stopped herself saying *Valentine* '– what did Lady Harriet do?'

'Bore it all very quietly: asked him to leave, which of course he would not; barely trembled, though no doubt she is used to him. She did choose to marry him, after all.'

It was not the first matrimonial choice to be an honest mistake, Louisa thought – but she would not say so to him; and her mind was occupied with an anxious surmise about what was to come next.

'Well, it was Valentine who stood up to him at last. – Oh, he was quite restrained: he is learning to carry his wine, and he was moderate in his expressions; said he was a guest in Lady Harriet's house, and as such considered her word was law, and if she had asked *him* to leave, he would have done so at once; urged the colonel to consider what was due to her as a lady and to himself as a gentleman. You wince.'

'The sun. He did not – he did not attempt anything rash?'

'He did not come to blows, or bare his breast to the colonel's pistol, if that is what you mean. But such is the man's reputation, and his evident temper, that any interference may be regarded as rash. Colonel Eversholt demanded to know his name, and what he meant by coming between him and his wife. That was when Valentine coloured up, and told him he was damned well not wanted there – and then I thought I had better try my four-penn'orth, as it was turning a little ugly. I spoke up very Devonshire, and made a great noise about wanting to win back my losses at the faro-table, not having long left in Lunnon, and how the colonel was spoiling the game: how I knew the law right enough, and if this house was let in the lady's name he had no rights there, and I'd fetch the Watch if he didn't leave us be. It diverted his attention, at least; but I don't know how it might have gone on, if Lady Harriet had not at last promised him faithfully she would see him tomorrow; and with that he left, still very bitter, and glaring like a cockerel at everyone. But especially at Valentine.'

'I don't know what to say,' breathed Louisa, feeling her

heart return to its accustomed place, after a short residence in her mouth. 'I was almost about to wish that Valentine were not so generous in his feelings – but that is surely a terrible thing to wish.'

'No, a sensible one. I told him so. I was afraid we might have a falling-out over it, but it had to be done. The fact is, if he sets himself up as Lady Harriet's protector, then he must expect people to see him as – yes, her *protector* in the other sense; and no amount of railing against the shallow proprieties of society, I told him, will alter it.'

'You do not believe he—' She stopped again: unable to move, or speak further, so acutely divided was she between shock and embarrassment; though the chief portion of embarrassment lay in the fact that she had secretly, and very deep down, wondered this herself.

'I do not believe,' he said in a low tone. 'And not only because of the vehemence of his protests when I said it. I simply consider he has too much sense and delicacy for that. But there, we did not quite fall out in the end: he was able to soothe himself at last by laughing at me, and saying I was a sad, blundering innocent. Rather like having your father back, in a way.'

'He does not mean it, you know,' Louisa said, with laughing pain.

'Your brother is almost as dear to me as – well, almost anyone,' said Mr Tresilian, urging her on towards Hill Street. 'Which is fortunate, as if I did not love him so well I could shake him. Well, there it is. I do not think I shall be invited to the faro-house again: which is no great distress to me.'

Louisa was already resolving inwardly that she must speak to Valentine herself; but his last words woke an alarm in her. 'Mr Tresilian, you will not quite give up on Valentine, will you?'

'Why, do you suppose he will not manage without my wise old saws?' he said, with a penetrating look. 'But, no, assuredly I will not. Though I cannot prevent him giving up on *me*.'

'That will not happen,' she said: she was determined that it would not; her own influence with Valentine must be exerted to prevent it. 'And thank you for telling me. Though I have not been easy in talking about him behind his back.'

'Nonsense. If that were the rule, there would never be any conversation at all.'

They were turning into Hill Street. Something he had said struck her, even through the cloud of her present perturbation. 'Mr Tresilian, when my father used to say those things to you: did you truly not mind?'

He studied the distance again, this time rather as if the swell on the sea had subsided to a surprising calm. 'I was always thinking of something else,' he said.

He would not come in; and in a moment she had reason to be grateful for that. – Valentine, most rarely for him, was home, so she could approach him alone.

No amount of discretion or care could render this easy; and the task was harder in that she did not wish to make

Mr Tresilian appear a tattle-tale. – But she had forgotten the intuitive understanding that had always joined her to her brother – perhaps because it had been less in evidence of late; she had barely begun to speak before he laid down his newspaper and reached out for her hand.

'You are going to read me a lecture. You have been talking to Tresilian. – No, no, I am not angry in the least; and I do not mean that about a lecture, because that's not in your nature. Or his, Lord bless him. But you are troubled. Come. Tell me where the trouble lies.'

'It lies perhaps in my remaining a cautious country sort of creature after all. I did not suppose you went out a-nights to Bible-readings; and Tom gambles, I know, because I have heard him talk about it – at least, something about his cursed luck with the bones, which I presume are dice, unless there is a much more sinister side to Tom than we ever guessed. – But, Valentine, gaming for high stakes alarms me.'

'So it would me, if I were differently situated, or if the stakes were really high, or if I were one of those unfortunates who simply cannot leave off. But I have, thank heaven, an ample independence; and as for what I have lost at the faro-table, it is nothing to what many young men lay out on fancy high-perch curricles and bloodstock. Or look at Tom's tailor-bills: I like to be well dressed, but a *few* good coats are enough. Sometimes, besides, I win: not so often as I lose, I know that, for that is the nature of gaming – but I make it up here and there. In novels and plays, I know, young men are always ruining themselves at the tables; but in real life one must be spectacularly foolish to do any such thing. – Truly, you must not be uneasy about it. Tresilian may be: but as he will be the first to admit, he does not like town or its ways, and as soon as he and Kate have had their fill of sights, they will happily quit it.'

'I shall try not to be uneasy,' she said, studying him: despite the hot weather, which had turned Mr Tresilian sailor-brown, his complexion wore the paleness of a man who lived by candlelight. No less handsome, however; and Kate was not the only young woman she had seen casting aching glances in his direction, though all were received with the same indifference. 'And perhaps if you, in the same spirit, were to try not to make me uneasy: if, now and then, you were to ask yourself, Would this make my country-cautious sister uneasy?, then—'

'I know what it is,' he said, smiling. 'I think neither you nor Tresilian would be quite so concerned if it were any other faro-bank than Lady Harriet's.'

'I have a good deal of affection for Lady Harriet, and I am sorry for her situation. But one cannot deny it is a difficult – a delicate situation. Valentine, I heard about Colonel Eversholt.'

His smile remained, but his cheekbones seemed to grow sharper. 'Tresilian is becoming a regular old gossip. Well, I dare say the morsel was too juicy to be resisted. Colonel Eversholt is, as I hope Tresilian conveyed to you, the most abominable man. If it were only violence and bluster – but there is manipulation too. I understood Lady Harriet a good deal better, simply from that one encounter. A last encounter, I hope.'

'Apparently she did promise to meet him.'

'Aye, so she did. It was undertaken to save her guests from more discomfort; but I know, from what she has told me, that her heart is now quite closed against him, beyond the possibility of reconciliation.'

'Yet they cannot remain otherwise than married,' she said gently and distinctly. 'I do not know much about these things, but surely divorce is only to be obtained by the very highest and wealthiest, and only then with the greatest trouble and injury to reputation. And even a formal separation does not free her—'

'My dear Louisa, you sound like a lawyer. Yes, no doubt these things are true; but they have very little to do with the natural feelings of the human heart. And it is those I am concerned with. Anything I can do to spare, to sweeten and to soothe those feelings in Lady Harriet, I will do. But you need not fear me in any danger. I have moved in the world a little, you know: I am no greenhorn. I am aware that the pleasure I take in Lady Harriet's society, is one that malicious tongues would convert to a baser meaning. Let them: it would be beyond their understanding in any case. This will sound monstrous egotistical, but she reminds me of myself.'

'I see there is a resemblance; but I do not think you could carry off bare shoulders as she does.'

'You laugh, but I know you are still uneasy. The fact is,

though she is obliged to maintain herself in a fashion that propriety deplores, and though her name is a dubious one to the Pearce Lynleys of the world, she is rather innocent than otherwise. She was long a dreamer, gazing at the world through the glass of wistful imagination: wishing to find a place in it, yet half doubting that it could ever be hers. The early influence that accustomed her to being lonely and disregarded was shaken off, perhaps, when she ran away to be married to that man – yet I don't know: I fancy it was only a sort of interruption, and inside she is still the same open, trusting creature whose neglect made such a rash choice almost inevitable. She is simply bewildered at what her life has become. I know what it is like to inhabit dreams – as you surely do; and we who have woken to a brighter, better reality at last may surely have a heart to feel for her, who stepped out into the broad sunlit prospects, only to find them turned into dark passages that lead nowhere.'

This was spoken with such a combination of warmth and delicacy – was so revealing of everything that was honourable, just and sympathetic in her brother's nature – that Louisa could not in conscience press him further without seeming to set a low value on those very qualities which, above all, she loved and esteemed in him. Some disquiet remained, especially from the glitter in his eyes when he mentioned Colonel Eversholt; but all had been said that *could* be said; and any disposition in her to renew the subject was lost in the surprise that greeted his next words.

'And after all, Miss Country-caution, what of you and

Francis Lynley?' He grinned at her look. 'There, I have caught you. No, no, I mean nothing of reproach, unless you were to find it in the fact that people are *talking*. And when do they ever do anything else? For my part I know little of him, but he seems well-bred enough, and notably human next to his brother. I surmise that to be a younger brother to Pearce Lynley must be a trial to any character, and the wonder is that he has not turned out a thorough scapegrace.'

'Lieutenant Lynley is no sort of scapegrace,' Louisa said promptly, 'and he would be very ready to prove it, if he were ever to be accorded any measure of trust or confidence.'

'You are partial,' Valentine said, smiling. 'No, no, I don't mind it in the least. We are partial creatures, you and I, Louisa; and I for one am glad of it. To be sure, the more you incline to *him*, the more you put Pearce Lynley's nose out of joint – but I do not suspect the operation of any such feeling.'

'Valentine, I do not incline to Lieutenant Lynley. – That is, I find much that is interesting in him, alongside much that is difficult and perplexing; though that is hardly to be wondered at, given his situation. But that is all: my heart is entirely secure, thank you; and as for my feeling for Pearce Lynley, I simply have none of any kind – none.'

All this was spoken with the greatest calmness: – yet Louisa discovered such a confusion of emotion within her that she was even glad to have their colloquy ended by the arrival home of Mrs Spedding, accompanied by her friend Mrs

Murrow: who saluted them in typical fashion by remarking that they both looked as if they were sickening for something, and she only hoped she wouldn't catch it.

While Valentine applied himself to the stony task of conversing with the visitor, Louisa tried to tell herself that she had done her best with him; but she could not escape a feeling that, rather than persuading, she had been persuaded.

Chapter XVI

Louisa's anxieties about Valentine's association with Lady Harriet and her faro-house were far from allayed by his tender assurances. The sensation remained of a strange distance between them, across which she gestured in vain; neither could she find perfect repose in Mr Tresilian's renewed undertaking to watch over him. Instead she found herself relying on the unsteady, even feverish comfort of distraction – which in London, this exceptional summer, was plentiful. The celebrations were coming to a head, with fireworks, regattas and military reviews among the public spectacles; and having made a large acquaintance in a society turned frenziedly sociable, Louisa found never a day, or part of a day, without its engagements.

In all this novelty and enjoyment, however, a keynote was struck, without which it would have been merely diverting noise. – Francis Lynley was the one she sought out, whenever they were mutually engaged. In his company and conversation she found an attraction that was not merely incidental: that could not be interrupted or discontinued without an itching wish to have it resumed; eagerly she looked out for him in the evening crush, or listened for his halting footstep on the stair in the mornings at Hill Street. There was everything in his temper and situation to engage her sympathies – she would not say her affections; and to Sophie's repeated teasings about her being *in love* she could present only a tolerant smile.

Her acquaintance with Francis Lynley was, besides, as frustrating as it was pleasing. Where he could be easy and vivacious, he could likewise be withdrawn and bitter; and in the latter mood, was not above saying that she would presently grow tired of vexing his brother by being attentive to him, and would then drop him.

'This is to paint me a very superficial creature,' she answered, with real mortification.

'Is it? Then I have paid you a compliment. To be superficial is the best thing in the world, surely. The superficial are always certain of endearing themselves wherever they go: no one is much inclined to worry about depths and, indeed, would rather prefer that you do not show any; and then the superficial are not likely to suffer great trouble or injury, for nothing goes very hard with them. No, no, shallowness is the thing: I would recommend it to everybody; if I ever had a child, I would urge its tutors – "Surface, please, cultivate the surface!"'

'But surely where there are no depths, there are also no heights.'

He laughed crossly. 'You reproach me very properly for my ill-humour by giving my nonsense serious attention, instead of walking away and talking to someone with a modicum of politeness.'

'If it were only nonsense, I should not mind,' said Louisa, still serious. 'But I cannot be easy if I have given even the faintest impression that I am using you as a – as a weapon against your brother. Between him and me there is, I hope, a perfect understanding that my father's hopes were founded on his own inclination, not mine: that is done with; and I should hate to think I have been coquetting over it.' She hated the thought so much, indeed, that she banished it quickly from her mind; and was glad when Lieutenant Lynley made one of his sudden leaps into animation.

'Now you have found me out exactly. It is just like when I used to beat my nurse's leg with a stick – oh, I assuredly did, that was the species of little beast I was as a boy – and tell her she was in a very bad temper today: meaning, of course, that I was. I talk of your vexing Pearce, because that is what *I* am doing lately. I cannot help myself.' He spread out his arms in wry appeal. 'It would be better if he were more overbearing; but damn it, there is a new kind of patience in his taking me in hand, which quite discomfits me. Some influence must be at work, to make him like this – capable of showing a little more feeling than a marble grate: a very little, at any rate. Perhaps I am merely coming in for the best of him.' He lowered his voice and drew closer, and she observed how very dark his eyes were – almost no distinction between iris and pupil. 'There was a great to-do yesterday, with Mary Bowen wanting to give her notice.

Whether he had found fault with her once too often, I don't know: she is quite a downright creature; but somehow he persuaded her to reconsider, probably calculating that he would never find someone so well able to manage Georgiana, and that it was worth a little sacrifice of pride to keep her. Ah, what an amiable picture of our domestic life I am giving!'

Louisa could not help wondering whether that influence of which he spoke was Pearce Lynley's continuing attachment to her. Certainly she was conscious of his addressing her with a persistent amiability, though it plainly cost him some exertion, and there was never any peril of his relaxing into pleasantness; and she could not but feel that if he was seeking to compete with Francis, even in a general way, he was presenting only a sort of varnish, which was very bland compared with the restless play of mind, the volatile spirits of his brother. But she was, as Valentine said, partial: – just how partial was revealed in her own surprise that Mr Tresilian did not much care for Lieutenant Lynley.

They met at Hill Street and elsewhere, and conversed with an apparent good understanding; but Mr Tresilian, when pressed, only said: 'Oh, he is well enough. In truth I almost prefer his brother, stiff-neck though he is. At least you know where you are with him.'

Louisa was used to relying on the independence of Mr Tresilian's judgement; and she was dismayed to suppose that he had fallen into a lazily conventional way of thinking, and had accepted the received idea of Francis Lynley as the troublesome and unreliable younger brother, who had planted those sad grooves between Mr Lynley's brows.

'Lieutenant Lynley, you know, has been much maligned,' she told him.

'Has he? I don't hear of it. He has an honourable wound from the Peninsula, and is respected for it; he is received in good society: everyone speaks well of him, and the ladies positively quiver when he is by.'

She felt a little scornful at the notion of the quivering ladies – certainly at her being numbered amongst them. 'It is a good opinion that has been hard earned; and I think he would willingly exchange it all to have his brother for once approve him, and allow that the indiscretions of the past may be outlived.'

'Oh, as to that, he is a grown man,' Mr Tresilian said, with a shrug, 'and grown men should grow up.'

It was like Mr Tresilian to be blunt – but not to be unfeeling. Louisa could only account for it, after some reflection, by a speculation that he was jealous. Francis Lynley had after all lived in a daring and precarious fashion; whereas James Tresilian, after the brief adventure of his marriage, seemed to have contracted an aversion to the slightest risk. He was often muttering about the extravagant speculations going on in the funds now that Bonaparte was gone, and prophesying bubbles bursting; and though she was willing to believe he might be right, it seemed to her a pity that he should also be such a cautious investor in experience, content with small returns of pleasure, and an annuity of inexcitement.

Such was the state of her feeling when the Spedding household received an invitation to a ball at the Portman Square residence of Miss Astbury: a ball of exceptional magnificence, as she learned from Mrs Murrow, for several of the visiting notables from the Continent were positively engaged for. – Even the Golden Miss Astbury could not manage a tsar, but at least one German princeling and a general would lend their august presence to the evening, and make themselves available to be stared at.

'Not that I can understand why all these foreigners are here,' mourned Mrs Murrow.

'Well, my dear, they are our allies, so we are celebrating defeating that dreadful Boney,' said Mrs Spedding, brightly.

'Why, what do we want to do that for?'

'It is the custom to celebrate victories, ma'am,' Louisa put in. 'Somehow celebrating defeats does not carry the same enjoyment.'

Mrs Murrow shook her head. 'I don't know: I never heard the like of it. We never had such things when I was young. They had much better go home. The next thing you know, we shall have Red Indians here; and if I were to see a Red Indian walking down the street towards me, I hardly know what I should do, I am sure: I think I should fall down dead on the spot.'

The picture thus called up was as agreeable as it was unlikely; but not even Mrs Murrow's fatuity could detract from the prospective pleasure of such an occasion. The Lynleys were invited, as Louisa soon discovered from Francis when he called – Pearce remaining quite a favourite, as he drily remarked, with the glacial Miss Astbury; and the Tresilians too, Mrs Spedding's good nature having secured them an introduction at Portman Square – though Louisa suspected Sophie had been the chief instigator.

'I mean to make him dance with me, as we did at Pennacombe,' she confided to Louisa. 'Then we shall see something.'

Louisa did not believe they would see anything – or, rather, did not wish to believe it. The thought of Mr Tresilian being caught in Sophie's gossamer web still disturbed her more than she could account for: – he was after all, to use his own words, a grown man. But she suspected that in many regards grown men, and women, did not grow up – that the fresh susceptibility of youth still sent its green shoots through the hard stones of experience. But she felt herself powerless, and contradictory: who was she to take Mr Tresilian aside, and warn him against such an entanglement? And was she not the same woman who was deploring his excessive habit of caution?

She could only trust that something would save him: – his own good sense: some apprehension of wrong paths, and right paths – something.

When the evening of the Portman Square ball arrived, sultry and airless, she experienced an intense relief and pleasure in being seated next to Valentine in the Spedding carriage. Here also she found grounds for hope that a right judgement would prevail. Instead of devoting the evening to his usual pursuits – which, though he gave nothing away, she took to be his continued, fascinated attendance on Lady Harriet – he had yielded to her careful persuasions: which were based on the simple truth that she would enjoy herself much more if he were there. This, indeed, was much nearer to what she had fancied when they had begun their enterprise of living; and on arriving at the house in Portman Square, which was brightly lit in every window, bedecked with flags and banners, and besieged by carriages, she felt that very little was wanting for her complete felicity, at least for the evening, which was as far as she cared to look. That want was quickly supplied: a glance across the great reception-room assured her that Francis Lynley was there, and they were soon joined by the Tresilians, in good spirits – Kate especially. She wore a new white gown that spoke as eloquently for her taste as her neatness of figure; but as ever it was the animation of amusement that brought her beauty to the surface. Among the guests was a German noble, to whom Lady Carr had introduced her, and who bore the redoubtable name of Count Pfaffenhoffen.

'I could keep my countenance a little more if he were not so grave and solemn,' Kate said. 'A Pfaffenhoffen ought at least to be a little jolly. – But it is very childish of me: I'm sure the name Tresilian sounds just as absurd to him.'

'A mercy Mrs Murrow did not have to make the introduction,' Valentine said. 'She would never have recovered from it.'

'The German language does have its beauties,' Kate went

on, 'but I fear it often sounds abrupt to our ears. That lovely name Cinderella, which is very pretty in French and Italian, as Cendrillon and Cenerentola, comes out in German as Aschenputtel.'

'Enough to make the prince repent of his choice.' Valentine laughed. 'But I had no idea you knew German, Miss Tresilian.'

'Oh, studying music you pick it up almost unawares,' Kate said, making a creditable attempt not to blush.

'It is not my place perhaps to remark on the subject,' intoned Miss Rose, who had responded to the brilliancy of the occasion by wearing a large cameo of someone long dead, 'but it was always my poor understanding that the moral of the fable consisted in the prince disregarding the superficial, and valuing those qualities in the heroine that had been overlooked. I may be wrong: I am sure I am.'

'I knew a fellow at Oxford who had the most ridiculous name,' said Tom, beginning his great rumble of laughter. 'One simply could not hear it without laughing out loud – it was so uncommonly odd. What was it now? Well, I cannot for the life of me remember it, but I can assure you it was the funniest thing.'

'Your assurance of the fact is all I need, Mr Spedding,' said Mr Tresilian. 'My sides are fairly splitting already.'

The rooms were very soon even more crowded than on Louisa's first visit there; but what had been irritating was now stimulating. She was known: no longer conscious of herself as an awkward outsider: eager to drink in faces and talk, to mark the impressive and be amused by the absurd;

and if she found a part of her pleasure in being admired, whisperingly commended, and sought after, she hoped that made her human rather than sinfully vain.

Before the dancing began, she made her way over to Lieutenant Lynley, aware that his lameness would render him unable to participate in it. – She did not mind for herself, but she minded for him. At the first sound of the music, however, he only glanced up, and said: 'Ah, now comes my salvation. I shall have the great pleasure of not having the pleasure. Oh, if you like I could make a great Byronish fuss about it, and look stricken and doomed and outcast, because I am shut out for ever from a quadrille. I have even thought of lumbering about the floor in spite of my recalcitrant foot, and disrupting the set unconscionably: – that might be amusing. But the unromantic truth is I never cared excessively for dancing. It is rather as if you were to be told you could never again drink lemonade in your life: you would have to work hard to fancy it a deprivation.'

It was spoken in his most rapid and careless way: still Louisa suspected, once the dancing began, that the exclusion would be felt; and she would willingly have stayed by his side for the first set, if it had not occurred to her that this would be precisely calling attention to it. She saw across the room that his brother had long been in conversation with Miss Astbury, and was now offering his hand: Miss Astbury very civilly declined, however – the German princeling was hovering, and on such an occasion precedence must be observed; even though he was a painfully young man with large ears, and such a chestful of medals that he must have begun winning them in his cradle. The next thing she knew, Pearce Lynley was before her, inviting her to dance, and she was accepting. – She hardly knew why: it was part perhaps of a general disposition to be pleased, reinforced by the happy sight of Valentine leading out Kate Tresilian. That Mr Tresilian was partnering Sophie was less surprising, as Sophie had earlier been inviting the invitation by fondly hanging on Miss Rose's arm, to that lady's stony astonishment, and sighing that with one or two exceptions the place was full of young puppies and nobodies whom she would rather die than dance with.

Mr Lynley, as befitted a man both athletic and self-controlled, danced well: that improvement in his manner which she had noted, though it was far from making him effusive, was still present; and she wondered, as an idle fancy, what she would have made of him if this had been their first introduction.

'Miss Astbury is having heavy work with her partner,' she remarked. 'He looks as if he would be more comfortable on the parade-ground.'

He smiled slightly. 'Fortunately she has more than enough grace and elegance to compensate.'

'She is much admired. By some, I conceive, for her fortune; but by others for her qualities. My acquaintance with her is so little developed I cannot judge; but you, I collect, have come to know her better, Mr Lynley.'

'I have taken great pleasure in the acquaintance. Miss

Astbury has sense, talents, and a steadiness of temper that must command the admiration of all but the most trifling minds.'

'And she is thoroughly moral,' Louisa said, recalling Miss Astbury's censures on Byron.

'I could not approve anyone, man or woman, who is not,' said Mr Lynley, with something of his old distant look. 'However, if you would place me among her idolaters, I must disappoint you. I would not speak disrespectfully of the lady who is, despite her aunts, really our hostess: I would only say that the sum is less than the many parts: the impression she makes is strong, but not deep or lasting.'

Louisa was surprised at this; and wondered if Mr Lynley had received a more significant rebuff from Miss Astbury than the loss of the first dance for him to be finding imperfections in her.

'Still, she would be a great catch, for any man who could win her,' she said.

'Indeed. And all the more important that he should not be dazzled. A man must know truly what he wants, or suffer to have it revealed to him too late.'

'I am glad to hear you admit at least the possibility of a man not entirely knowing what he wants,' said Louisa, studying him, 'and would be even more glad to know that this understanding was extended to your brother.'

He looked coldly at that: but the dance separated them before he could reply; and when they rejoined, he had retreated into silence, which she expected to be lasting. On the dance ending, however, he did not lead her back to her seat but, with a gentle pressure, detained her.

'There is perhaps more understanding between Francis and me, Miss Carnell, than you are inclined to give credit for. I have in the past, as head of the family and guardian of my grandmother's interests, found more to deplore than to applaud in his general conduct. But natural affections persist alongside our sterner judgement: we still love where we cannot wholly approve. This, I am sure, you are well placed to comprehend.'

Louisa had no doubt that Mr Lynley had heard the tattle surrounding Valentine and Lady Harriet; but she wished she could hear this confirmation of it without a blush. 'Certainly: and well spoken, indeed, Mr Lynley. I only think it a pity that you do not show this natural affection which you claim to feel.'

'I show it in the best way I know, by seeking to direct him in the most propitious courses.'

She sighed. 'And then you are surprised when he does not wish to be directed. Really, Mr Lynley, I—'

'Miss Carnell.' He startled her by seizing her hand: he was not a seizing man; but there was much that was altered about him, not entirely to her comfort. 'I know in the past I have tended to speak to you, on serious matters, in a way that may have appeared sharp – peremptory. As if I do not, did not know how to value feeling. Please believe that – though I hope I always did – I am learning to value it better, and more generously. If you will believe this, then allow me simply in that spirit to allude to my continued solicitude for you – without reference to the past; and to say, out of that solicitude, that I cannot view your growing intimacy with my brother – its rapidity, its heedlessness – without the strongest misgivings.'

Was this all? He had begun speaking – yes, feelingly, she would have said; but the warning against his brother seemed merely part of his old high-handedness.

'Very well, Mr Lynley: tell me why.'

He appeared – surprisingly again – to be struggling to express himself. 'I do not think,' he said at last, 'that Francis has a disposition for happiness – either to enjoy it, or communicate it.'

'If that is so, then the answer is surely to be looked for in the influences operating on his life to produce such a disposition.' And she would have added that if it were so, there was more in it to interest than to repel. – But Louisa was silenced by a new apprehension of intensity: in Mr Lynley's urgent gaze, and the force with which he retained her hand. Much was revealed. The blow she had inflicted on him had been felt, she could now believe, in his heart as well as his pride. It had made him more open and spontaneous – but his feeling had also been unhappily distorted into the pettiness of jealousy. He must vilify and denigrate his own brother, rather than see her merely on familiar terms with him: must prejudice her against him, rather than allow her to make up her own mind about Francis Lynley's character. So, he was directing her still: more subtly – but with just as little regard for her judgement. Her view of him was both enlarged and diminished; and in this confusion she sought only to escape from him.

'Mr Lynley, you had better let me go. You must consider – you of all people – the propriety of appearances.'

'I do not care for that,' he said, astonishing her again, 'if I could only know that you have at least listened—'

'Listened? Certainly. The habit of a lifetime is not to be so easily broken.'

She disengaged her hand, and walked away. They were certainly conspicuous on that empty floor, as the flurry of speculative glances confirmed. Her first impulse was to find Valentine – her heart was particularly inclined towards him now – but he was not to be seen. Part of her urged against seeking out Lieutenant Lynley straight away; but when her eye fell on him seated alone, she felt more strongly the absurdity of his brother's admonitions. To hear him talk, she was dangerously besotted: yet she found she was able to approach Francis Lynley with perfect composure, with no heart-flutterings or leapings – no pangs – no untoward eagerness, or fear that she would be tongue-tied in his presence. Yes, she was partial; and she felt that she had met no other man quite like him: but if this was love, it was a very much more rational business than she had supposed. It was refreshing, she found, to float free of these received ideas. And when Lady Carr materialised in front of her, and began introducing two very stupid-looking, doll-eyed females to Lieutenant Lynley, she was really very little vexed at the unwarranted interruption, and was able to take a seat quite calmly, and refuse several gentlemen the next dance with only a touch of peevishness.

The sight of The Top lounging towards her was above all unwelcome; but he showed no inclination to dance, and indeed in his tightness of starch was probably unable to.

'Here we are again, Miss Carnell, and hang me if I know why, for I never saw a flatter set!' he cried, leaving his customary pause for laughter; but as she did not feel impelled to fill it, he went on, staring about the room: 'Well, she has netted a few of the *ton*, but that roasts no eggs for me: I have been having some conversation with the Golden Miss Astbury, and it's as I thought: she is *not* all the crack. Her grandfather's fortune was begun with warehouses, you know; and for all her airs, she positively smells of the shop! If she thinks she can gammon me, she is fair and far off!' And with some more graceful remarks about his hostess's ancestry, which she was disinclined to answer, he lounged away in a cloud of pomade and exclamation-marks.

Sophie appeared at her side, lamp-eyed, fanning herself vigorously, and, nodding in the direction of Mr Tresilian, whispered: 'I shall get that man to an avowal yet, my dear – trust me.'

Louisa rather doubted it, at least tonight, for Mr Tresilian appeared thoroughly abstracted; but she was sufficiently alarmed to ask her cousin: 'And, Sophie, what then?'

'Oh, my dear, you look too far ahead. After all, never tell me *you* haven't discovered the sheer delight of the chase now. And though I am very far from a bluestocking, I do observe that it is the only time we women stand in any sort of advantage to men: it is our one authority. For once married – well, look at poor Harriet, with no more rights than her abominable husband's goods and chattels. Not that he has any.'

This was a new view of the matter; still, Louisa would rather have seen Mr Tresilian, with his general uprightness and honesty, exempted from the game. – But she had no more thought to bestow on this, as a parting in the crowd revealed Lieutenant Lynley, standing apart and looking very dull.

'Ah!' he said, brightening a little at the sight of her; but the shadows did not entirely lift. 'Those women have talked my head off. Everything, they tell me, is agreeable, delightful and enchanting. There was very little to be said once I had agreed to those dubious propositions, but they went on and said it all again. Come and be silent with me, and stare disdainfully at the world.'

'Must I be entirely silent? I would wish to say something to lift your spirits.'

'There I must beg you to refrain. A good proper dose of low spirits is something to be indulged and luxuriated in, like a cold. Have you never known the true pleasure of a cold? I cannot doubt it. Not a heavy cold, or a persistent cold: no, one that you know will be gone in a few days, and in the meantime you may sniffle and cosset yourself by the fire, and reply to solicitous enquiries, with a sigh, that you are a little better – not much; and you will try to eat a bit of that something choice they offer you, though you are afraid you will not be able to taste it. There – be truthful – have I not described to you the highest human felicity?'

'I don't know about the *highest*,' she said, smiling, 'but I am glad you have lifted your own spirits by talking of it.'

'No, no. You have done that. It is just your presence that restores me: there is my sovereign remedy. A great responsibility for you, I admit – to be always had recourse to, like a bottle of smelling-salts.' The liveliness in his face sank a little. 'In truth, I have been condemning myself for a very hypocrite. I was so blithe about my incapacity for dancing – but watching *you* dance has altered that.'

'I hope – I hope not the fact that I danced with your brother—'

'Not that. Lord, you make quite a handsome couple. But I saw how beautifully you do it; and it has even set me to cursing the Frenchman who fired that shot, though I have never felt any animosity to him before, and indeed, for all I know, it might have been one of our own.'

She hardly knew what to say; but then, as the music struck up again, an impulse seized her, and she brushed away the feeble little caution that trailed in its wake. 'Do you recollect the steps of the Boulanger? The figures, the position of the hands? Then trust me. We shall dance it, you and I; and what that French or English bullet prevents, I shall supply: I shall do the going down the set, the leaping and turning, for both of us.'

With an expression of some bemusement, he consented. They took up a position a little away from the set, near the musicians; and the doubt left his look as she showed how they could contrive: while he stood, she danced round him, taking and crossing his hands at the right moments, and merely facing him, on her toes and smiling, at those parts of the dance where they would have been separated. Soon his delight was as keen as hers; and if part of his relish lay in the fact that, as he remarked to her, they were being most scandalously stared at, she was not immune to that aspect of the pleasure herself.

'This is the best mode of dancing of all,' he said, as they drew close, 'for it means I never have to surrender my partner.'

They performed the proper bow and curtsy as the dance ended, and he led her to a seat – passing on the way Mrs Murrow, who could only gape and make inarticulate sounds, as if surprise had robbed her of the last vestiges of intellect. Here, however, Louisa felt the first check on her spirits, as she saw that Kate Tresilian had been sitting out, and with a more downcast look than even the presence of Miss Rose at her side could account for. It was unlike Mr Tresilian to leave her if she were unengaged: Louisa looked about for him, and at last discerned him in the vestibule, beyond the double doors – with him, the slighter figure of Valentine. They appeared in heated discussion – even argument.

By the time she reached the vestibule, Valentine was nowhere in sight; and Mr Tresilian was pacing about, high-shouldered, his hands stuffed in his pockets, and his uncropped hair in a very disordered state.

'Mr Tresilian? Whatever is the matter?'

His pale eyes came to rest on hers, uncomfortably, for just a moment, before he resumed his pacing.

'I have got at cross with your brother.'

'Where is he?'

'Gone. That is what our little disagreement was about. I saw him slipping out, and pursued him. I demanded to know why he could not for once spend a whole evening in our company, he replied that he did not have to answer to me for his movements, and so on. It was as unedifying as most quarrels are.'

'It is a pity,' Louisa said hesitantly, trying to read his expression, 'but perhaps, you know, he had another engagement—'

'Nonsense. Who goes to a ball when they have another engagement? My disappointment was Kate's. He appeared to be in thorough enjoyment of her society – had as good as asked her for the next set – and then made himself scarce without a word. It was not well done. Oh, I know what is drawing him away; and I was so vexed with him that I came out with it. I asked him if he were going to Lady Harriet's house. He did not need to answer: his look was enough. Then I wanted to know how much, just in round figures, he has lately thrown away at her faro-table. He informed me it was none of my business: which I dare say is true.' Mr Tresilian pulled up before a bust, representing a gentleman dressed in the novel combination of a full-bottomed wig and a toga, and glowered at it. 'But that is not the worst of his folly, in associating with that woman: as he well knows.' He turned to Louisa. 'As you well know also.'

She avoided his eyes. 'I do not like to think of you quarrelling over this – you who have been the firmest of friends. And I'm sure Valentine meant no harm—'

'A pity it has to come to a quarrel. But someone must make the young rip see sense. I always thought *you* not deficient in that quality.'

'Mr Tresilian, please don't reproach me. I have no influence over Valentine – nor would I seek it: that is quite understood between us. Just as he in turn would never seek to regulate my conduct—'

'Aye, I have seen that, and more's the pity,' he said harshly. 'This prodigious game you are playing with the Lynley brothers: first one must dangle, then t'other. I dare say it is very enjoyable for you: the consciousness of power always is. But the sensation is not so agreeable for those on the receiving end; and the spectacle is not pretty. You would do well to remember what became of Bonaparte, before you start enjoying your power too much.'

Louisa stared at him: stared away: was for some burning moments beyond speech. It was as shocking as if a trusted dog had turned wolfish. – There was nothing, of course, in what he said: absolutely nothing. It was his disappointment for Kate making him unreasonable; and something else perhaps – something she had seen all too much of.

'Thank you for the reminder, Mr Tresilian. But I cannot

consent to *you* directing and controlling my life: there was enough of that from my father.'

'Your father is dead,' he pronounced, his tone and look not at all softened. 'I do wonder how long you can keep pretending he is alive, so you can defy him.'

She turned on her heel and left him. She thought she heard him call something out to her, but whether it were reproof or remorse she did not want to hear it; and she plunged back into the ballroom, where the noise and movement, the stir and chatter, could perform their blessed task of shutting out thought.

Chapter XVII

The Spedding party left the Portman Square ball at a late hour; but Louisa's pleasure in the occasion was over long before then. In vain did she apply herself to the business of gaiety. Dancing, conversation, supper – none would answer: all was spoiled. Only in the company of Francis Lynley could she find a little solace – a little, because she could not approach him without a searing consciousness of Mr Tresilian's assertions: horrible and unjust as they were, they affected her, and she could not bring sufficient composure to Lieutenant Lynley's society properly to appreciate it. Happily he at least was the man she thought him: he respected her right to be distracted and subdued, and did not demand to know what was wrong, or make heavy attempts to cajole her into a different temper. Here, at last, was a gentleman who could speak to her without wishing to lay down the law to her; she wished others would follow his example.

The Tresilians left the ball early. One awkwardness was thus removed – or, rather, postponed: for another meeting with Mr Tresilian there must surely be, unless he decided to wash his hands of London and take the first coach to

Devonshire, and she did not know how she would face it. Even as she lay in bed that night, running the scene over in her memory, she was composing some very pointed and spirited replies to him; but there was no altering the fact that, misguided and unfair as his censures were, their coming from *him* had a peculiar power to grieve and agitate her.

She was eager to see Valentine, and hear what he had to say of his altercation with Mr Tresilian – and to find in him, perhaps, the understanding ally that he had always been to her through the troublous years at Pennacombe. But he had come home very late, and was very late rising; and thus to her distress was added the unwelcome suspicion that Mr Tresilian had been right in this at least – that the spell of Lady Harriet's house was far from broken. Breakfast was over, and she had gone up to her room to put on her bonnet and pelisse preparatory to a morning's engagement with Mrs Spedding, when she at last heard his bedroom door open.

Only a few minutes elapsed, and then there was a great clatter on the stair. – Valentine flung open her door.

'Good God, Valentine, what is it?' Her eyes dropped from his white pinched face to the letter he clutched in his hand.

Tremblingly he held it out. 'You had better read it.'

She took the letter, while her brother sank into a chair and put his head in his hands.

To Valentine Carnell, Esq.

Sir.

It is with the greatest reluctance, and even disgust, that I bring myself to address you; and on such a subject as a gentleman can hardly touch upon without the deepest mortification and resentment. – These, however, I must subdue, under the stricter necessity of notifying you of my knowledge, and my intentions. I have struggled to disregard the flagrancy with which you have lately advertised your unlawful intimacy with my wife, with the intention only of sparing her the obloquy that any greater attention must bring. I can struggle no more: the insult is no longer to be borne. I have sufficient proofs of that intimacy to make a recourse to the law not merely possible but incumbent on me as a man of honour. Be hereby advised, sir, that I intend to bring against you, as soon as the law-terms allow, at Common Pleas or King's Bench, a suit for criminal conversation with my wife, Lady Harriet Eversholt, and to obtain damages thereby commensurate with the infringement of my marital rights, the injury to my name and reputation, and the suffering inflicted on me by your disgraceful conduct.

I remain, &c

HENRY EVERSHOLT

For some time after reading this letter Louisa stood in doubtful wonder whether she were not dreaming: even glanced at the bed, as if she might see herself lying there; and then, assured of the letter's reality, glanced over it again and, with a last clinging of hope, tried to tell herself that she did not understand it – that it did not at all mean what she took it to mean, that it was an absurdity, and any moment Valentine would raise his head and laugh with her.

It would not do. The lesser legal details she did not comprehend, the outlines were all too clear. – This was, surely, ruinous.

But there was Valentine first. Alarm, speculation, preparation for whatever trouble lay ahead must give way to the first duty of her heart: to support her brother, and give him the assurance that his cause was entirely hers. She knelt down, and let her silence and embrace convey all.

At last he kissed her hand, and thanked her, and tried to show her a sanguine face; though the marks of distress were too evident.

'You comprehend Colonel Eversholt's meaning, I think,' he said, rising and taking up the letter again.

'He means to sue you for—'

'Trespass, I think is the strict legal definition,' Valentine said, with a grating laugh. 'Trespass on his property, meaning his wife. Dear God. A crim-con suit. I should not have believed it even of him – to see his wife dragged before the publicity of the courts, held up as an adulteress, to satisfy his pride and vindictiveness. Well, we shall see. We shall see.'

'Valentine – what he says of these – these sufficient proofs . . .'

He threw her a wild look. 'Louisa, you do not believe his accusation – the essence of his accusation – to be true?'

She hesitated. 'I am ready to hear, and believe, anything you wish to tell me, Valentine.'

He flushed crimson, and each had the greatest difficulty in looking at the other. 'My esteem – yes, my affection for

Lady Harriet is great, and it is warm. I do not deny that there may have existed a disposition – a temptation even – on both sides. But every impulse of respect and honour has operated against it.'

Louisa believed, or chose to believe: it did not much matter, she felt, beside the pressing question of what was to happen. 'Perhaps,' she said hopefully, 'this is merely an empty threat, more of his bluster: and if you were to undertake not to see Lady Harriet any more, for example . . .' But on recollecting her encounter with Colonel Eversholt, she could not even convince herself; there was, she suspected, as much steel as bluster in him: and Valentine was already shaking his head.

'No, no. He means to go through with it. As to these proofs – well, no doubt there are always servants or hirelings ready to be bribed and say whatever he wants the court to hear. I have read of such things in crim-con cases in the newspapers.' His brow contracted. 'Dear God, to think of Lady Harriet paraded – publicly humiliated in that way. Well: if he insists on it, then let it be. *I* shall defend her reputation – clear her of the slightest stain of dishonour. I must see her at once—'

'Valentine, no. – Surely that would be ill-advised just now – even playing into his hands. You had much better keep away, until – until we have taken advice.'

His look was stormy, as if for a moment he doubted her allegiance; but then it subsided, and he nodded, flinging himself down miserably, and said: 'I suppose so. But I hardly know where to begin.'

Louisa thought of their aunt Spedding, and their cousins: amiable, sympathetic and well-meaning – yet for any difficulty beyond a question of etiquette, or the right length of a sleeve, scarcely to be depended upon. There was only one answer.

'We must ask Mr Tresilian. He will know what to do; and we can rely completely on his confidence.'

Valentine chewed his lip. 'I doubt he will welcome an approach from me. We had something of a falling-out last night.'

'I know: so did I. But he will put that aside for something as important as this.'

'Hm. He will gloat.'

Louisa's own feelings about Mr Tresilian were still decidedly mixed – but she did not think gloating part of his character; and the matter was too urgent for finessing. She despatched a servant with a note to Mr Tresilian's lodging, entreating him to call at Hill Street as soon as possible; and then made her excuses to Mrs Spedding and Sophie. – This was easy: Mrs Spedding only smiled and asked how she liked the new trimming to her hat; and Sophie chuckled slyly, and said that she hoped Louisa would not be dull, though to be sure someone might call – someone like Lieutenant Lynley – who might help pass the time.

The name brought back the memory of their unconventional dance. Louisa could not help but sigh at it, and wish that the carefree and exhilarated spirit of that moment might return; but that, she was afraid, could not be soon expected:

and when Mr Tresilian arrived and, after the briefest of salutations, took in his hand the letter Valentine wordlessly extended, the growing gravity of his expression seemed to confirm it.

'How pompous,' he said at last, tossing the letter down. 'And what a wretched villain he is.'

'At last we agree on something,' Valentine said, very near to sullenly.

'You do know what this means, don't you?' Mr Tresilian said, gazing levelly at them each in turn. He looked a little worn, as if he had not slept well.

'It means he is prepared to expose Lady Harriet to all the notoriety of a crim-con suit,' Valentine said hotly. 'Expose her to a shame absolutely unwarranted. And it *is* unwarranted, Tresilian, before you read me another lecture—'

'I don't much care if it is or not – and neither, I suspect, does he. Colonel Eversholt is out for what he can get, Valentine. You are a man of fortune, and he sees a way of taking advantage of that. Have you heard the kind of damages the courts are awarding for crim-con lately? Ten thousand pounds is a fair rate, it seems. I remember one award not so long ago of twenty-five thousand. I do not know the state of your financial affairs and, of course,' he set his jaw, 'they are not my business. Perhaps you may realise such sums. But I would estimate that, even at the best, it would put you hock-deep in debt for the rest of your life.'

Valentine was very still. 'That is assuming the court finds against me,' he said huskily.

'Yes. Well, you like faro, Valentine, and litigation is an equally chancy bet. Then, of course, there are the costs, if you choose to contest the suit—'

'Naturally I will contest it. If I do not, it is tantamount to admitting guilt – above all, Lady Harriet's guilt. That I shall never allow – never.'

'But what of Colonel Eversholt?' Louisa said. 'Will not bringing such a suit involve him in costs? From what Sophie tells me, he is continually distressed for funds himself.'

'That's a consideration,' said Mr Tresilian, thoughtfully. 'It is an expensive business for the plaintiff. It may mean, perhaps, that the threat is not as serious as it appears. On the other hand, he may intend to go to his last penny to pursue it – as there are such rich rewards if he wins.'

'I still think I should go and see Lady Harriet at once – acquaint her with this outrage,' Valentine muttered.

Mr Tresilian drew a deep breath, and seemed to be holding back some strong expressions. 'My dear Valentine, she will know. And there is nothing to be gained, and much to be lost, by such indiscretion now. – Understandable, and entirely to your honour though it is.'

There was a sort of reconciliation in these words, a healing of the division of last night, which found an answer in Valentine's softened expression. Louisa was satisfied to see it; and could dispense with any such gesture to herself, especially as she was secure in her own case of being irreproachably in the right.

'I know nothing of Colonel Eversholt, beyond what I saw

of him that night at Jermyn Street,' Mr Tresilian went on. 'Is he a man likely to make these threats idly? Is he of a character to retract, or temporise?'

'He is monstrous,' Valentine muttered.

'The monstrosity we may take as read,' Mr Tresilian said drily, and looked to Louisa.

'I have met him only once. I would call him volatile – but not light-minded. Sophie might be able to tell you more.'

'No, no,' said Mr Tresilian, quickly. 'It is best if your cousins, and your aunt, know nothing of this for the present. Of course, if it does come to a court case, they must know; and by the same token you will have to stay in town, whether here or elsewhere.'

'I have no desire to leave London,' Valentine said. 'If I did, it would be – well, it would be slinking away with my tail between my legs.' From defiance he sank sharply and visibly into misery. 'Great God, I never imagined any of this. How can it be? I have done nothing wrong. Unless following the natural impulses of the heart is wrong. Well, no doubt it is. Father would certainly have told me so.'

Louisa could not help stealing a glance at Mr Tresilian, hearing this echo of his words last night; but his face was impassive.

'There is no profit in dwelling on how you got in this position,' he said. 'The fact is, you are in it; and we must consider every means that may get you out of it. The first thing is to speak to a lawyer – without prejudice, informally, just to see how the land lies. I know a good man in the

City. Helped me out of a devilish difficulty with the bills of lading for the *Cornelius*. To be sure, maritime law is more his speciality; but he's a canny fellow, and absolutely to be trusted. Come. We'll go now.'

Valentine, after a little protesting that he could not think straight, submitted; and Mr Tresilian bore him swiftly away. Louisa would willingly have gone with them, but there was surely nothing she could contribute; and it seemed that just now Mr Tresilian's briskness might be of greater benefit to Valentine than her sympathy.

Left alone, however, and relieved of the responsibility of supporting Valentine's spirits, she was at liberty to think, and to imagine: to picture the probable consequences of this unhappy predicament, in all their most vivid and terrible colours. The scandal, embarrassment and pain of a public suit, reported in all the newspapers and the subject of every malicious tongue – the blow to Valentine's reputation, regardless of the outcome, and how stingingly he would feel it – the worst result of an award of large damages, and the struggles it would put him through – debt, distress, insolvency, Pennacombe mortgaged or sold – the firm ground on which they had stood crumbling beneath them: all passed swiftly before her, until she was almost maddened by the contemplation of it, and her inability to do anything to change it. It was the injustice that afflicted her above all. – Whatever the secret truth of the matter, whatever Valentine had done or had not done, she could not conceive of its meriting *this* degree of punishment. Her thoughts turned towards Lady

Harriet – not angrily, but pointedly. She was doubtless an unhappy woman, and it was not altogether surprising that Valentine's charm and gallantry had operated on her to greater effect than her discretion would have advised; still, she must have known that there was some danger – must have heard a voice of caution, if she had not heeded it.

In a moment Louisa was decided. – She would go and see Lady Harriet: not to complain or upbraid, but to hear what she had to say, and discover whether there were anything in it that might help them to a solution. It was, besides, doing something: anything was better than this helpless suspense; and she was so eager for activity that she walked to Jermyn Street, taking a wrong turning on the way, and arriving very hot and thirsty.

Lady Harriet's house was not difficult to find: it was tall, squeezed, soot-blackened and very forlorn in its tottering grandeur. A yawning maid admitted her, and a large ugly man, whom she took to be the brute of Mr Tresilian's account, put his head out of a little room like a counting-house to bestow a stare on her. At last she was bidden to walk up. These, then, were the dusty stairs that gentlemen ascended to the enticements of the faro-bank; and coming to the open doors of a large saloon, she presumed this was where the business was enacted. She saw a great table, and a half-broken chandelier that gave the effect of a mouth with missing teeth, and a good many of the kind of ornate mirrors that seem designed only to become fly-blown. Probably it all looked better at night: it certainly could not look less prepossessing by day; and she found a moment to be thankful that Francis Lynley had never been drawn in by such dismal temptations as these.

Lady Harriet, however, received her in an altogether brighter room: a small parlour, which, though faded, bore evidence of her own touch. Hastily she moved some books and fashion-papers so that Louisa might sit down; then, seating herself, she held up a white hand.

'Miss Carnell – one word first. I know why you have come. Let me say that I would have given anything – anything – for this not to have occurred. And that once said, I give it over entirely to you. Whatever you wish to say, whatever reproach you wish to lay upon me, I am content to hear. You cannot think worse of me than I do.'

'Lady Harriet, I do not come to reproach you – at least— I hardly know where to begin. I felt that I *must* see you, because of the dreadful communication Valentine has received from Colonel Eversholt. You do know the substance of it?'

'Certainly,' Lady Harriet said, with a ghostly smile. 'I have received just such a communication. My husband seeks to pursue a crim con suit against Mr Carnell. He tells me that he is simultaneously notifying the gentleman, as he gracefully puts it. Was the letter very insulting?'

'It was . . . not pleasant. It could hardly be so – but then it is not the letter, you must understand, it is everything that it promises, or threatens. I am not experienced in these matters, but I am well able to understand that such an action is most serious in its consequences – even calamitous.'

Lady Harriet nodded. She went to a side-table and poured two glasses of canary wine; then asked quietly, with lowered lashes: 'How has your brother taken it?'

'He is greatly distressed,' Louisa said, 'angry, indignant. – But all chiefly on your behalf.'

Lady Harriet nodded again, biting her lip; then drew a deep breath and brought over the glass of wine. 'And you do not come here to reproach me! You are more generous than I fear I could be in such a situation. But then – if you will allow me to say so – you are very like your brother, in all ways.'

'All I seek to do is help Valentine. I cannot conceive that reproaches could do that – even if they were deserved,' Louisa said carefully.

'Oh, but they are.' Lady Harriet drank her wine quickly. 'The fault is entirely mine. I should never have encouraged Valentine – Mr Carnell, I should say – even to that degree of innocent friendship which appears so damning in my husband's eyes. I was often telling him that we ought not to be on such familiar terms – that we should not be so much together – but I know I did not tell him so with sufficient force. Because my heart gave my tongue the lie. I valued his company: I felt alive again. I even felt, yes, a woman. You saw, I dare say, the room where I keep my faro-bank? Delightful, is it not? Imagine it night after night filled with dull gamers: the heaviness, the low wit and rancour and greed. Instead, there is Mr Carnell – lively and sympathetic, quite the paladin indeed; and coming there because he sought my society, not the sordid commodity I supplied.'

'All the same, he has played at faro here,' Louisa said gently, 'and lost by it.'

Lady Harriet shrugged. 'It is as I said: I expect, and accept, every reproach. I may as well say that I urged him not to lay heavy stakes. But of course I should have urged him not to come at all . . . You said he is angry.'

'Yes. Not with you: he is above all angry that your character will be defamed.'

Lady Harriet laughed shortly. 'Believe me, I care nothing for that. Whatever ill name my husband cares to pin upon me, let it be. But for the others involved – there I do care, greatly. There is not only Mr Carnell. Your own name will be tainted by association with such a scandal.'

'Because I am Valentine Carnell's sister?' said Louisa, her heart swelling. 'Why, I can imagine no circumstance in which that would ever be anything but the greatest pride to me.'

Lady Harriet shook her head. 'You *are* like him. Good and true . . . But I should be glad to know, Louisa, that you are in a position whereby you will lose nothing – nothing immediately precious to you, in esteem or affection – if it should come to a public suit, with all the gossip, the notoriety, the stigma that such must bring.'

'Be assured of that,' Louisa said, with Francis Lynley's crooked, sardonic smile before her mind's eye. 'But you say *if* it should come. Lady Harriet, do you have any hope that it may not? Any intimation that your husband does not intend all that he says in this letter?'

'Hope – perhaps: but I have lived on hope with Colonel Eversholt these past few years, and am like to die fasting. It was hope that kept me by him when every sensible consideration spoke against it: hope that he would – not reform or improve, but simply be again the man I married.'

'You speak as if you still have some feeling for him,' Louisa said, observing her inward look. 'If it is so, then could you not use your persuasions with him, Lady Harriet? If approached by you, urged by you, might he not see reason?'

'That is exactly what he does not see, when he is near me,' Lady Harriet said, with a rueful smile, and a shiver. 'And I dare say that goes for both of us. If we had ever been in a way to be rational with one another, then none of this . . . But I will try. He may refuse to see me: and if he is indeed set on this legal process, then he would be correct not to.'

Louisa hesitated. 'I wonder . . . if Colonel Eversholt were to hear it from your own lips that there had been – no impropriety—'

'As *you* wish to hear it from my own lips, I think, Miss Carnell?' Lady Harriet said, her dark eyes glittering.

For a moment Louisa could not meet them. 'Doubtless it is a thing we should not talk of,' she murmured.

'Oh, it will all be talked off, in great and humiliating detail, come the court case,' Lady Harriet said, going again to the decanter. She paused, weighing the glass in her hand.

'I will approach him, yes, Miss Carnell, you have my promise. Anything I can do to avert this . . . But the difficulty is, my husband will tend to see any approach from me as a move towards reconciliation. And that there can never be. Not now – now I have had my eyes opened to what the word *gentleman* truly means. I can never consent to have them blinded again.'

Her assurance that she would try was given again before Louisa, refusing more wine, took her leave: she seemed in earnest, pressed Louisa's hand tenderly, and thanked her for her understanding. – It was something, but not enough to satisfy Louisa, who felt that Lady Harriet was still as wistfully wrapped up in the ideal of their situation as Valentine: a beautiful ideal, no doubt, but not one that the world would handle gently. Fatigued but restless, she returned to Hill Street, impatient for the return of Valentine and Mr Tresilian, and anxious lest the Speddings return first, for there would be an end of the possibility of their talking confidentially.

There was luck: Valentine and Mr Tresilian were first, and could give her an account of their meeting with the lawyer – or, rather, Mr Tresilian could, for Valentine, after the first affectionate and even desperate squeeze of Louisa's hand, retreated into a withdrawn and brooding temper.

'He is going privately to consult with a friend, another lawyer, more experienced in these matters,' Mr Tresilian told her, 'just laying it out as a hypothetical case – no names. But in the meantime he suggests that a letter in reply to

Colonel Eversholt's would be expedient. Letters count for a great deal in such a case. A letter simply stating innocence of the charge – nothing humble, of course, nothing supplicating,' he added hurriedly, glancing at Valentine standing rigid and high-shouldered at the window. 'And adding that the respondent is prepared to meet the colonel, without prejudice, to discuss the matter, at the address of some neutral party. Nothing more than that. – I think it our best first course, as soon as it can be managed.'

The look he gave Louisa was not lost on her; and as soon as he was gone, with promises to wait upon them tomorrow, with any new advice he could gather, she gently urged Valentine to the writing of such a letter. 'So I will,' was his firm reply, and he actually sat down and began it: but the arrival home of Mrs Spedding and their cousins enforced an interruption he seemed not greatly to regret. After dinner, Louisa persuaded him to his room, and to a second attempt at the communication: stood by, while trying not to stand by, as he wrote it; but very soon he threw down his pen, declared that he could not settle his mind to it, and announced his intention of going out.

'I must – I shall go mad lingering here, and gnawing over everything. It will do me no good, nor this intolerable business in hand,' he said, and at Louisa's look, or the look he chose to see, he added: 'I want only air and a change of scene. I do not mean *there*. If you will simply allow me to go to the club with Tom, it is all I engage for.'

She guessed from his asperity that he was mentally

addressing Mr Tresilian rather than her; and quietly acceded. Still, she could not sleep until she had heard him come in – at a reasonable hour, which suggested he had kept his promise – and even after that, lay long awake. She feared that the worst part of this for Valentine was his separation from Lady Harriet: that even now he was not seeing the matter straight, in all its gravity and momentousness.

Mr Tresilian was back the next morning and, after presenting only the briefest compliments to the Speddings, bore Valentine off again. There was the lawyer to see; and letters to be written, not only to the colonel but to Valentine's banker and the steward at Pennacombe, so that the state of his finances could be assessed. Mr Tresilian was all blunt briskness, as he had need to be, so despondent was Valentine's mood; but he found a moment in the hall before leaving to address Louisa.

'And what of you? You bear up well, I hope.'

'Certainly. I have to.'

He nodded his understanding. 'Well, things may yet be retrieved. But it is a sad interruption for you.'

He did not say of what; and she presumed he referred to his accusation about her 'game' with the Lynley brothers. Well, it was to be hoped he would find time to reflect on that. How mean, how petty those strictures appeared, now something so truly destructive was upon them! But, then, he had not seemed himself that night; and she wondered if the entanglement with Sophie had been preying on his spirits. She would have warned him against it – but *she* was not so eager as others to take on the gratifying role of dispenser of advice.

In the meantime she had conceived a scheme of her own that might be instrumental in Valentine's salvation. It was entirely her own – not to be mentioned to anyone. There would be – from Mr Tresilian surely, and Valentine probably – heavy objections. But men, she considered, did not understand everything: they knew all about the best roads to take, but never thought of the path across the fields. What she had in mind could not, she felt, harm their cause: it might even be the deciding factor: let events reveal. It meant she must cry off again from spending the morning with her aunt and Sophie – whose eyes glinted when she was told.

'My dear, town has made you a delightfully mysterious creature! Well, let me just mention that we intend calling on the Lynleys today; and if you like, I can apologise for your strange absence, at least to *one* of the gentlemen – I shall not say both.'

'I fear no misunderstanding in that quarter,' she answered calmly.

Louisa perfectly recollected the address at the head of Colonel Eversholt's letter; and once the Speddings were gone, she dressed with particular care, then took a hackney there.

Chapter XVIII

Silver's Hotel, off the Strand, proved to be a very masculine establishment: sporting and military in character – leathery and horsy; the yard filled with curricles and gigs, and bow-legged men smacking their palms with riding-crops and talking about rigs and turn-outs. There were more of the same in the public rooms, along with half-pay officers lounging and smoking and drowsing over newspapers, and young bucks after the pattern of The Top, working hard to perfect the cold, vacant smirk that would establish them at the pinnacle of fashion. Louisa found that, apart from the barmaid in the tap-room, she was the only woman there; and when she gave her name to the waiter, and asked if Colonel Eversholt would see her, she received a vast stare, and the most dubious nod ever accorded. He returned to tell her the gentleman was out; and stared harder when she said she would wait in the coffee-room, and asked him to notify her when the colonel returned.

She was prepared to wait, however long it took; but she was not quite prepared for the interest she excited. The waiter came back every quarter-hour or so, simply to stare at her again; and every lounger and strutter took her in at his leisure – which was the one thing they all seemed to have an abundance of, though lacking any notion of how to make use of it. At last she took up one of the newspapers: it had nothing in it she would have called news; instead abundant reports of famous guns, close-run battle royals, estimable gamecocks, fillies and hacks, all so dull and bewildering that she might as well have essayed reading Latin. It struck her, however, as she sat on through the vinous fug and the loud, hard talk, that the spheres of the male and the female were much more profoundly separate than was commonly realised; and it seemed less surprising that so many marriages turned out unhappily, when the two creatures involved came from such different worlds.

The morning had almost worn away, and with it her resolution, when at last the waiter appeared with Colonel Eversholt at his side.

'Miss Carnell. I am told you wish to see me.'

'Yes. Thank you, Colonel Eversholt.'

The waiter would have upheld his privilege of standing and staring: but a look from the colonel sent him scurrying away.

'You come alone?' Colonel Eversholt said. His manner, his expression betrayed nothing but a neutral politeness; but Louisa already believed him more given to self-command than his reputation indicated – and felt it made him more, not less, formidable.

'Yes, sir – and on a matter of some urgency, which is why

I have waited on you here. As the matter is also of some delicacy, I would be glad if we were able to speak confidentially.'

'Certainly. That can hardly be done here: I have a set of rooms upstairs, but you may doubt the propriety of attending me there. Speaking for myself, I can only say that I am a man of honour: that in itself should obviate any scruple. If, however, you had brought your maid—'

'I have no maid, Colonel, and I rest absolutely secure in your honour.'

He bowed: the little pursing of his lips as he led the way suggested that he was rather susceptible to compliment, but she cautioned herself against overdoing it.

His sitting-room was everything she expected of a hotel lodging – well-appointed in a faintly shabby way; and she noted how very little impress of himself he had placed on it. He was after all, she thought, a man without a fixed home. But her eye fell quickly on a miniature portrait propped on the mantelshelf. – It was of Lady Harriet. He followed her gaze, and frowned; and for a moment she felt herself a great intruder and meddler, before she recovered her purpose.

'Colonel Eversholt, you are probably aware of what has brought me here,' she began, trying to keep her voice level and calm. 'My brother and I have no secrets from one another; and given the – the purpose you have avowed to him in your letter, there can be no question of secrecy. If you hold to that purpose, then in time it will be rather a matter of the greatest and most pitiless publicity.'

'That is the case: yes. And it might have been better if

your brother had thought of it before he subjected *me* to the humiliating publicity attendant on his consorting with my wife.' Colonel Eversholt went from restraint to vehemence with startling suddenness: indeed, he seemed even to have surprised himself, for he coughed and smoothed back his thick wings of hair with a slightly unsteady hand. For the first time she detected a faint smell of liquor. 'But I must say, Miss Carnell, I wonder at your hardihood, in coming here to talk of such things. The mention of them is extremely repugnant to my feelings – and must be still more so to a young woman situated as you are. But let me guess: your brother has sent you to try what youth and beauty may do in extenuation of his mortal offence.'

'My brother knows nothing of my coming here, Colonel. I may as well say, as you will hear it soon enough, that he certainly intends contesting any such suit as you threaten to bring, on grounds of his, and the lady's, complete innocence.'

'Indeed? I wish him well of that.' The colonel did not sit: he stood large and braced by the fireplace, his eyes on the ashes, as if seeing there an emblem of his situation. 'There is, my dear madam, plentiful evidence to the contrary, much though it grieves me to offend your innocence by saying so. I fear your brother may have misled you: a deception that I fear must be added to the catalogue of his trespasses.'

'As I said, sir, Valentine and I have no secrets from one another. I know well that he has been a frequent habitué of Lady Harriet's faro-bank: that he has been seen with her in public. I myself saw them together at the theatre – and thought it very ill-advised. But if you were to understand, sir, a little more of Valentine's history, his character, then I hope you would begin to see that a quite different interpretation may be placed on this evidence. I do not deny,' she hurried on, as his chin went sharply up, 'that his conduct has been indiscreet and imprudent – that it has indeed laid him open to such imputations. But I am all the more able to believe his earnest protestations of innocence, from having viewed the progress of his acquaintance with Lady Harriet since her stay at Pennacombe – and having viewed him from a youth in which such an acquaintance was entirely outside his scope.'

'Come, now, Miss Carnell. If you would seek to persuade, you had better not try to delude. Whatever might be my private feelings about Mr Carnell, I know he is a gentleman of good family, with an estate of five thousand a year. This does not place him out of Lady Harriet's circle – as far as *acquaintance* goes.'

He had made sure, she noted, of assessing Valentine's fortune. 'Certainly – under the usual circumstances. But my brother and I shared an exceptionally sheltered upbringing, Colonel, under the tutelage of a father with strong, even eccentric views about the liberty, or lack of it, to be extended to young people; and the greatest mistrust of society. Until his death last year we had known nothing grander than the odd country assembly: we had never visited a watering-place, let alone London; we had never even received company at Pennacombe.'

'Indeed. It is all the more regrettable that your father's jealous care should produce, in his son at least, such unhappy results,' Colonel Eversholt said, in his softest, most implacable tones.

'It was a care that – not to speak ill of my father – was I fear likely to produce some distortion. But I do not mean in the direction of excess. I feel that I can say this to you, Colonel, because I know a little of the history of your and Lady Harriet's marriage.'

She half expected an eruption: but he only inclined his head. It reminded her, curiously, of being in the drawing-room of the rectory at Pennacombe, where Dr Sayles's large and temperamental hound would lie by the hearth, unperturbed by loud noises or sudden movements, but twitching and growling at the most trifling gesture or quiet remark.

'From what I understand,' she went on, feeling uncommonly dry-mouthed, 'there was much that was unfortunate in the disposition of Lady Harriet's family – an alternation between neglect and vindictiveness; and when she married the gentleman, the perfectly eligible gentleman of her choice, both she and he were to suffer quite unnaturally.'

'You are well informed,' he said: then shrugged. 'To be sure, it was common knowledge. We were shockingly robbed of our expectations.'

'And this is what I mean by the distortion of early influences. You and Lady Harriet married, I am sure, in good faith and for love, and could not conceive how any other construction could be laid upon it. What the world sees, and what we see, may be entirely different. So it is with Valentine. Colonel Eversholt, I truly believe that what Valentine feels for Lady Harriet, as it has always been since she first came to Pennacombe, is admiration: admiration in the purest sense, like a courtier to a queen. He had never known anyone like her, and was dazzled, and remains so, I think – to such an extent that he is blind to the appearances of propriety, and shocked to find that anyone can view his relation with her in any other light than that of chivalry.'

Colonel Eversholt gazed soberly at her for several seconds; then burst into a shout of laughter. 'Oh, dear me. Oh, Miss Carnell, forgive me, but I really cannot help myself.' The laughter stopped abruptly, though a sort of smile remained. 'Your upbringing, at least, must have been positively cloistered if you can believe such a transparent fiction about the nature of your brother's *admiration*. No, I am afraid he has been trading on your trusting good nature, madam: and so more shame to him.'

Louisa hesitated for a moment before the plunge. 'Colonel Eversholt, I have of course only heard one side of the story concerning your marriage. But I do believe you still love Lady Harriet.' She mentally added the qualification *after your fashion*.

He flushed. 'I do not care for the turn this conversation is taking. I should be sorry to have to use the term *impudence* to a lady whom I have hitherto found it easy to respect.'

'And I am sorry to press you in this way – but there is so much at stake for us, as you surely know, that I must dispense with formalities. They are after all not much observed, I think, in the debtor's prison. I cannot conceive how you would wish to see – how you could bear to see Lady Harriet placed under all the humiliating scrutiny of a crim-con suit.'

'Plainly you cannot conceive it, Miss Carnell, because you accord nothing to my sense of honour. I do not choose to make a parade of it, but the injury to my sense of honour is great: indeed it is intolerable.'

Ten thousand pounds, however, would make it tolerable, she thought; but she must be careful not to allow these thoughts to show on her face: he was no fool. 'I hope I am not insensible to such a feeling, sir. And I would not have addressed you thus, if I had not believed you susceptible to just those kind of finer feelings – honour, delicacy, and perhaps the peculiar chivalry that has inspired my brother to his unfortunate association with Lady Harriet.'

'I am very far from convinced that this finer feeling exists on his part,' the colonel said, throwing her a shrewd look. 'But let us suppose that it does: why, then, the chivalry? It is traditionally extended to women in distress. Is it thus that he sees my wife? Does he consider *her* the wronged and deserted one? Does he, in fact, take her part against me?'

'If so, then – then it is in the same idealistic spirit, I am sure,' Louisa said desperately, 'and of course no one is in a position to judge the rights and wrongs of such a situation except the parties themselves. But, Colonel, Valentine has – as I have – so very little experience of these things, and of the way the world moves, that his errors are rather to be expected than wondered at.' She found a moment to wonder, indeed, what Valentine would make of this countrified innocent she was painting him: she doubted he would like it at all – but with luck he would never know. 'And I believe that he will absolutely undertake to forgo the society of Lady Harriet, permanently, if by that road an understanding may be reached.'

He smiled greyly. 'Do you really believe that, or do you wish to believe it? Oh, Miss Carnell, you must not misunderstand me. I am far from welcoming the noisome attention, the scandal, the ignorant notice that must be taken of both my wife and myself by a recourse to law: it is entirely loathsome to me. But there is no other resort, it seems to me, for a man in my position.'

'But if I may venture to suggest – there is another: that of believing my whole-hearted assurance that my brother is guilty of nothing more than ill-judgement. A belief that once accepted offers you a further comfort: that of knowing Lady Harriet to be entirely innocent also.'

'Ah, a comfort: when half the town believes otherwise.' Frowning, Colonel Eversholt drew out his watch. 'Your pardon, Miss Carnell, I have an engagement; and it is besides too repulsive to my feelings further to talk of these things.' Suddenly he offered her what seemed a genuine smile. 'I will say, however, that I do not think I could have endured it even thus far, with anyone else. Your brother is more fortunate in his advocate than his conduct deserves. But I make no undertakings, madam, other than to assure you I will think on what you have said. Nothing in it presently inclines me to any other course than injured nature demands; but you have my word that I will not dismiss it from my mind.'

With this, as he opened the door and stood waiting, Louisa had to be content: but she was far from thinking it the worst result that could have been achieved. His pride and pomposity she must allow for: the greed and cupidity that Mr Tresilian attributed to him was unlikely to be easily conquered. But she was not hopeless of successfully appealing to his feeling for Lady Harriet: she had observed that he did not once allow his eyes to rest on her portrait, which seemed to her as revealing as if he had sighed over it. And if alongside that she had introduced a little doubt that his suit would be successful, then some breach had been made in what she had feared was an impassable wall; and she even dared to think it possible, though not probable, that his simple humanity might be reached through the same opening.

Much depended on Lady Harriet: on her fulfilling her promise to meet him, and adding her entreaties hard upon the heels of Louisa's. Add to these Valentine's letter – if he could be prevailed upon to write it – and the sum might be sufficient to draw Colonel Eversholt back from the brink. She was not sanguine, but she allowed herself at least to entertain the more promising proposition. The alternative, after all, could only be thought of with anguish, as fruitless as it was dispiriting.

Colonel Eversholt, punctilious but unspeaking, escorted her downstairs, and then with a bow left her. She found the waiter, who seemed to have missed her, and who made up for lost time by staring at her harder than ever, while she vainly requested him to send for a hackney.

'Let me do that,' said a voice at her ear, and Francis Lynley took her arm. 'I am no great genius, heaven knows, but I have not entirely lost the use of my wits like this fellow.'

'Oh! Lieutenant Lynley – I did not expect to see you here.'

He looked amused. 'I fancy my presence at Silver's is a little more likely than yours.' His glance followed the broad back of Colonel Eversholt.

'If you would be so good as to get me a hackney, thank you: and – it is very difficult, but if you could pretend you had *not* seen me, I would be very much obliged.'

'Oh, I am exceptionally good at forgetting things,' he said easily, as they went out to the yard. 'And I may as well be direct, and say I have heard the tales about your brother and Lady H. – Faro's Daughter, as they call her: a great nuisance to you, I collect. It is all the talk of the town, meaning it will be all forgotten in a sennight.'

She sent up a fervent prayer that it would; and was grateful again for Francis Lynley's constitutional aversion to leaping to judgement. At the same time she felt a selfish pang that this unhappy business was detaining her from his company.

'You have enabled me to get away from those dull fellows, besides,' he went on. 'They are from my regiment, so we feel obliged to clap each other's shoulders, and pretend we remember more about each other than we do. On that subject, or near it, there is to be an Exhibition of Grand Historical Transparencies, no less, at the Pantheon next week. Pictures of the principal battles of the late war, you know – I dare say they will be hysterically fanciful. No one cowering behind walls and wishing it would all stop. I am engaged to take Georgiana to it on Monday. Will you come with us? We shall be properly chaperoned, you see. Georgiana is the very last person in the world to stand any nonsense.'

'I should like it, indeed – if—'

'If you are not otherwise engaged, of course. And if society does not lose its ridiculous fascination with the war by then, which would be quite sensible. At least the Allied sovereigns are going home soon, to resume their peaceful task of tyrannising their subjects. Well: I shall *hope* to see you then. It should be amusing, though not up to our dance at the Astbury ball – I do not think anything can come up to that.'

He hailed a hackney, and handed her into it – his parting look curious, but full of his own peculiar regard. All thoughts of the ball, though they came back vividly enough, were to be banished: they excited too great and too pressing a confusion of feeling for her peace, when every effort of self must be bent on one end; and she might have said the same for Lieutenant Lynley himself.

At Hill Street she found, alas, no such fixity of purpose in Valentine in the succeeding days. At times he was lively and defiant, and spoke of the clearing of innocent names in grand terms; more often he was subdued, his voice hollow, his face ashen. Louisa did her best to rouse and cheer him; but his temper had always had a tendency to the heights or the depths, whenever it was tried; and this trial was so exceptional that she must accept the impotency even of her persuasions. Mr

Tresilian exerted himself likewise, but with limited success. Where there were things to be done – more legal consultations, a first essay at obtaining a defence counsel – he managed to brisk Valentine into doing them: but the letter he had urged remained long unwritten, and when at last Valentine completed it, there was so little of accommodation in it that Mr Tresilian sighed and said it had better not be sent. As grim, tight, tense day succeeded day, with the sun blazing unrelentingly on London – that high summer which is equal parts glare and wilting – even Mr Tresilian seemed to despair of lifting Valentine's spirit: he pursued much of the business, where possible, by himself, and sometimes seemed to take a pleasure in talking nonsense with Sophie, as a relief from the brooding shadow that consumed the rest of his time.

Once, pricked by a new thought, Louisa caught him at the door as he was leaving after dinner.

'I have fifteen thousand pounds,' she said.

'I know it.'

'If Valentine has need, it is his.'

Mr Tresilian started a little: then said quietly. 'It would sadly hurt your marriage prospects.'

'I have no fears on that score.'

He seemed to be studying her: but the brassy evening light was directly behind him, and his expression hard to discern. 'Your independence, then.'

'I could not contemplate my independence if Valentine lost his.'

Suddenly Mr Tresilian pressed her hand: his own was

agreeably cool in the stickiness. 'I do not believe it will come to that,' he said, and was gone.

If he doubted she was in earnest, she found no such doubts when she questioned her own heart. The enterprise of living that had begun the day they disposed of the fire-screen was a joint venture, which neither partner was to abandon: the bond that had joined them since infancy was not to be severed by such circumstances as these. She was not so unrealistic as to suppose either of them would adjust easily to poverty – but she was prepared for the struggle; and she continued some days in a state of firm, sober preparation. Sometimes still her mind was swept with anxiety and fear: then the ordinary business of living, of dressing and eating, seemed both precious and absurd; and to undertake an excursion of pleasure, even so mild as the visit to the Transparencies she was invited to make with Francis and Georgiana Lynley, appeared irresponsibly frivolous. But no: she sent him a note confirming that she would go: to do otherwise, she felt, would be to declare defeat and surrender – and the time for that was not yet. The thought of Francis Lynley – unshockable, wry, unconventional – was besides a light against this new darkness. When the appointed day came, she was impatient for two o'clock, the time of their meeting – but impatience was entirely displaced by astonishment at the events of the morning.

Pearce Lynley called at Hill Street. With him – actually on his arm – was the governess, Mary Bowen.

Chapter XIX

Mrs Spedding was too well-bred, and too careful of the ageing effects of facial expressions, to betray her surprise; but Sophie was all agog: and Louisa, looking from Mr Lynley to Miss Bowen, and finding nothing changed in them, and yet everything changed, was half convinced she was asleep, and that any moment some reliable dream-turn, like the entrance through the window of the King or the discovery that she was clad only in her nightdress, would fully assure her of the fact.

'Mrs Spedding, I have of course had the honour of introducing Miss Bowen to you before,' Mr Lynley said, when they were seated. 'But the introduction has not been made as I should wish it to be made. You have known Miss Bowen as my sister's governess.' He smiled – a little nervously, to be sure, but a smile nonetheless; and then turned the smile in the direction of his companion. 'I shall be very glad for you to know her on quite other terms – as my intended bride.'

Mrs Spedding, after the first speechless moment, supplied all the congratulation that courtesy required, and that her good nature was very ready to offer: Sophie exclaimed it was the most delightfully romantic thing she ever heard; and Louisa was left at last with the consciousness that she was the only one who had not spoken. Mr Lynley's gaze turned to her, but she could not quite meet it, though she must accept now that she was not about to sprout wings, or manifest any such comforting evidence of her being sound asleep.

'Mr Lynley, this is most – tremendous news,' she got out: swiftly she concluded that she might have chosen a better adjective, but none would come to mind.

'Mary and I appreciate that it may, to general appearance, seem sudden,' Mr Lynley went on, with some – not all – of his usual composure: his colour was too high, his eyes too bright for that. 'So we have taken it upon ourselves to call on our close acquaintance to convey it, before the formal announcement. Such are the peculiar circumstances – well, I will leave it to your candour to infer them. We have till lately stood in a very different relation, of course. That that relation was superseded by something else – by my growing esteem for Miss Bowen's qualities, and the ripening of that esteem into affection, and the strongest attachment – you may see: but our respective situations threw in its way various difficulties – difficulties under which she laboured the most severely, until I took courage, by frankness, by unvarnished declaration, to end them.'

The look he bestowed on Mary Bowen was a glowing one; and she, with a glance no less feeling but speaking plainly and directly as ever, said: 'You will understand, situated as I was, that I did not dare to hope. I scarcely even dared to feel. But when Mr Lynley asked me, I had no doubt of my answer, any more than of my own name.'

'Well, I am sure it is the most charming news, indeed,' cried Mrs Spedding. 'Nothing gives me greater pleasure to see young people engaged to be married; and I only hope you will set an example to my two. But where is it to be? In town, or in Devonshire? Of course I should wait for the formal announcement to know all this, but I am a monstrous curious creature.'

'In town, we think,' Mr Lynley answered. 'Though Devonshire, of course, shall be our home. There is one of the many pleasures I anticipate – presenting Hythe Place to its new mistress.'

And mighty lucky she would be considered to land it, Louisa thought: such at least would be the tart remark on many a tongue, when it was known that Pearce Lynley had married his sister's governess. She would be presented as a little schemer who had used every wile to trap him – but, no, not for long. A very short acquaintance with Mary Bowen must reveal her to be no minx; and that the attachment was a real one was evident in their every glance – evident, moreover, in the very fact that Pearce Lynley had overcome all his loftiness and pride to win a woman whose position was so much beneath it. Louisa was still adrift on a tide of astonishment, but not without grasping at some spars, some hand-holds of understanding, as she regarded the couple. She recalled his including Miss Bowen at dinner – to impress *her*, she had thought in her ignorance: recalled the odd moments of tense awkwardness between them, which she had ascribed to Mr Lynley's unyielding temper, but which now appeared as the probable result of two people falling in love and not daring to recognise it. Francis Lynley's account of Miss Bowen's giving notice, and his brother's persuading her to stay, must be traced to the same cause; and then there was that new warmth and impulsiveness in Mr Lynley's manner – which, once more, she had attributed to his continuing attachment to her. Here was a great deal to take in: she kept it at a distance for now, conscious that some of it wore a perplexing, chastening aspect; and what she could not above all contemplate without unease was speaking with Pearce Lynley alone. But she knew he wanted to: several times his eyes turned to her, with a serious urgency; and when opportunity came, with Sophie, who loved weddings almost as much as proposals, eagerly showing Miss Bowen a fashion-paper with the latest bridal modes, he took it at once, seating himself close by Louisa, and addressing her in a confidential voice.

'Miss Carnell, I do not flatter myself that you have any more or less reason to feel the surprise at this news, which must be general among my acquaintance. But I do consider you as having a particular right to know more of the circumstances.'

'Right, Mr Lynley? Dear me, I do not think I have any right,' she said, in what was meant to be a serenely pleasant tone, but which sounded to her own ears like the squawk of a captain's parrot.

'You are very good – but it is after all not so very long ago that I was paying you my addresses: though it does seem a long time, somehow,' he added, with a fond glance at Mary Bowen, looking unimpressibly through patterns of lace. 'Paying you what I was pleased to call my addresses, at any rate. You put me properly right on that score, though I was unconscionably slow to see it. Indeed, Miss Carnell, in the happiness which I have attained, I have a great deal to thank you for.'

'Thank me? Really, Mr Lynley, I cannot see how,' she said, relieved to find her voice, if not exactly level, no longer avian.

'No? You surely recall taking me to task over my high-handed way with governesses. I thought you merely sentimental and indulgent at the time; and I think it is one of those subjects on which we would never wholly agree – but something of it must certainly have lingered, for when Miss Bowen came along I took a little more trouble to apprise myself of her circumstances, and to consider her as a human creature, and not merely in the light of an employee. – But it is more than that. You taught me how to feel – or, rather, how to understand what I felt. Your father had designed us for each other; and it was only with time that I came to realise that in going along with those designs, I had not consulted my own feelings any more than I had consulted yours. I simply did not know what I wanted: but I assumed I did.'

'I see,' Louisa said, in great confusion: it was curious, to say the least, to have someone tell you in such warm, tender and generous fashion that they had never loved you.

'Now *she* knows what she wants,' he said, with another fond glance at Miss Bowen. 'There is such an admirable firmness and honesty. I remember when she first came to us, and I took issue with some little matter relating to Georgiana's lessons. No ground was given: her clear-sighted mind fixed on the truth, and set it before me. So I – I admitted myself in the wrong.'

'I had the highest esteem for Miss Bowen's mental powers, but I did not suppose them capable of miracles,' said Louisa, with more lightness than she felt.

'You have earned the right to satirise me, and I am reassured that you still feel able to do so. Mary, of course, is of a more serious turn of mind; it is where we strongly agree. The influence of her upbringing is naturally to be felt there.'

'Has she family living?' Louisa asked, from a curiosity that she was instantly sure must sound like malice.

'Her mother: she lives in Wiltshire, on a small annuity presented to her by the late marquis, her father's employer. It is to be hoped the distance will not be an object to her coming to us at Hythe, whenever she wishes.' He looked keenly at her. 'I well know there will be voices exclaiming at the inequality of the match: but Mary's connections, if not high, are respectable; and I hope I may count myself able to set a value on character, and not merely on rank and place.'

She did not doubt it: there was everything to suggest he had chosen freely, happily, and even wisely; and viewing the matter objectively, as she was striving to, there was surely cause for rejoicing that Pearce Lynley, too, had broken free of his bounds, and begun his own enterprise of living. 'I congratulate you, and wish you very well, Mr Lynley,' she said evenly. 'And though I still cannot think I merit your confidence, I thank you for it.'

'Thank *you*,' he said earnestly; and then, after a slight hesitation: 'Indeed I am so happy, that I would wish to undo even the minor occasions of unhappiness. – When we spoke at the Astbury ball, I was intemperate in my expressions about my brother. Please forgive, and forget them. Francis has created in me the habit of anxiety – I will say no more than that; but I was wrong to imply that you are not in perfect command of your own feelings, and able to form your own judgement.'

Pearce Lynley apologising to her: here was a fitting conclusion to a morning of wonders, Louisa thought, as the happy pair took their leave; but such a flippant formulation did not accord with her real feeling – whatever that was. She wanted time and space to examine it, and could hardly endure the conversation of Sophie, which was all of veils and honeymoons; and was glad at last to set out for the Pantheon alone, Mrs Spedding having offered her the use of her carriage.

Even here her thoughts were scattered: it was too close for the hood, but without it the stabbing of the sun, this damnable sun, was painful. She supposed she was not the first woman to feel a certain piqued deprivation at the loss of a suitor she had never cared for: nor, probably, the first to be sensible of a little mortification that the force of her charms could be so quickly got over, and so easily replaced. But she might have borne these reflections more philosophically, if they had not come so wretchedly entangled with Mr Tresilian's accusations at the Astbury ball. Power, he had said – a relish for power had animated her in her relations with Pearce and Francis Lynley. Well, her power over Pearce Lynley, if such it had been, was now decidedly overthrown; and according to Mr Tresilian, she should now be having a temper-fit to rival a thwarted Bonaparte. No: she felt nothing of the kind, or at least the degree. Probably the great shadow of disaster hanging over her and Valentine was sufficient to place it in the proper perspective. And, indeed, in thinking of that she found, at the centre of her feeling, a kind of wistful envy of Pearce Lynley. He had cast off early influence, and followed the promptings of the heart against the pull of caution and prudence – yet not to ruinous effect. It showed that it was possible, revealed a harmony of thought and feeling that aroused in her a vague but powerful longing, and a wish that it might not be, for her and Valentine, too late.

Hazy as these ideas were, she felt she might be able to communicate them to Francis Lynley. But when at last she saw him among the moving throng in the vast domed hall of the Pantheon, she found a disappointment in his heavy and cheerless looks that was not much assuaged by his conversation.

'So, I do not doubt you have heard the news, for Pearce

said he was to call on you, and what Pearce says he will do he will do.' He offered a meaningless smile. 'Quite a shock, is it not? I have been kicking myself for not marking the signs of it earlier – but, truth to tell, the notion of Pearce doing anything uncommon or interesting is so very fantastical that I never even began to entertain it.'

'I was never more surprised in my life,' Louisa said. 'But there, his choice is made; and altogether, in temper and disposition, I fancy they are not unsuited.'

'You have that right. And here's poor Georgiana, who must see her governess turn into her sister-in-law: deuced odd for you, Georgy.'

'It will be odd at first, but I do not much mind it,' Georgiana said, 'for I like Miss Bowen a good deal, as I might not like a stranger marrying into the family.'

'Lord. When *you* take the rational and sensible view, then there is no hope for any of us,' Lieutenant Lynley said mordantly. 'Well, here are the Transparencies: not quite as silly as one could wish, but they will do.'

The great mural-size paintings, lit from behind, were certainly colourful in every sense: Lord Nelson seemed to have taken his famous vanity to the extreme of wearing rouge; but what Louisa chiefly wondered at, as she passed along the scenes, was how it had ever taken so long to win the war – for the French seemed always to be on the ground being bayoneted, an operation the British seemed to find so easy that they winked and smoked clay-pipes while they were doing it. Lieutenant Lynley laughed at them, but half-heartedly; and was soon recurring to the theme of his brother's engagement.

'Really he is a marvel: one can only admire. I am trying to imagine the trouble, the brouhaha, the wailing and gnashing of teeth if *I* were to announce I was going to marry the governess – but no, imagination fails, it is beyond all scope. Yet how Pearce carries it off! How he bears all before him! Believe me, I was entirely sincere in my congratulations, if only for that.'

'Does it really displease you, then?' Louisa asked. 'You do not like Miss Bowen?'

'Oh, she is well enough. She scares me: but, then, I always expected that a bride chosen by Pearce would scare me. As *you* well know, from our first meeting,' he said, with a fleeting smile. 'But the fagging thing is, I must find myself a new berth somewhere, at some time soon. Not that I am unwelcome, no, no: Pearce has explicitly said that I must always consider their home my own. Which is handsome: he can be handsome. And I am being the opposite – ugly, ungracious, call it what you will – when I say, to you at least, that I cannot bear the thought of sharing in that sober felicity. One or other of them, I fear, will always be correcting me: if not my conduct, then my grammar.'

'Well – it looks as if you will have to seek that rich wife after all,' Louisa said, with a little laugh, which was the very opposite of her feeling. 'I wonder what, exactly, her fortune would have to amount to, to make her eligible as a candidate?'

'You should know me better now than to take me at my liverish word,' he said, almost scowling. 'I think there can be nothing worse than being locked in a loveless marriage.'

'But love in a cottage, they say, fares ill.'

'They say a great many things. What do *you* think?'

'I – I do not pretend to be indifferent to the comforts of life,' she said, suppressing a shiver that was quite at odds with the stuffy heat, 'but if one did lack them – or lose them – I believe compensations, great compensations, are still possible.'

'Oh, everything is possible. As my sainted brother has just proved. Forgive me, I am good for nothing today. Shall we go? Georgiana, you too must be heartily sick of me, and I mean to take you for ices at Grillon's to make it up to you, or so you won't complain of me when we get home.'

Louisa was sorry, but not sorry: he was not in his best spirits, and her own were hardly lively. Only as he was handing her into Mrs Spedding's carriage did he speak again.

'By the by, the talk is that your brother does not consort with Faro's Daughter any more. The fearsome colonel warned him off, one supposes.'

For a moment she could not answer: the subject weighed upon her heart with all its terrible oppression; and though she could not break confidence, she longed to be able to speak of it a little to him – to relieve the burden for a moment.

'Well, as you remarked before,' she said, 'it is one of those tattling things that is talked of and forgotten. Though if it were not—'

'Like Pearce Lynley and his governess bride,' he said gloomily, 'except there is no forgetting *that*: for some of us, it will go on and on. What a thousand pities it is that Pearce did not succeed in marrying you!'

Disconcerted, Louisa asked: 'Why would that have been better?'

'Oh! I don't know,' he said, in his most inconsequential manner; and chuckled. 'Not that I am wishing you on him – God forbid.'

'If he had,' she said, searching his face, 'he might have repented of his choice.'

'How so? Would you have led him a merry dance?'

She hesitated. 'You spoke of Valentine and the – the rumours attaching to him. Such associations, you know, would surely not have been gratifying to your brother. Though of course you do not mind them.'

'Of course,' he answered. 'But once married to Pearce, be assured, you would have been eternally safe from reproach: the dazzle of his righteous armour would have banished all scandal and trouble; great heavens, you would have been safe!' And laughing, half turning, he waved her languidly off.

Safe: from the awkward dissatisfaction of their meeting, and through the troubled commotion of her mind, this word rang like a deep bell. She sat numbly staring for some moments: then, when the carriage began to move, called out to the driver. 'No – not home yet, please. I want to – I want to go and see the Law Courts.'

'The which, miss?'

'Where the great cases are tried.'

'Oh, there'll be nothing in session there just now, miss. Not the right time.'

'It doesn't signify – I just want to see them.'

He shrugged, supposing her, perhaps, being a little countrified about the sights, and set off. It was a long, slow business, with a great snarl of wheeled traffic at Charing Cross, and another hard by Whitehall, where a brewer's dray had come to grief; but Louisa's mind was so occupied with a kind of purposeful act of imagining that she scarcely noticed. At last she raised her head to see vast, venerable roofs darkening the summer sky: on one side Westminster Abbey, with the Parliament-house ahead: darkest and most solemn of all, the building to which the driver pointed with his whip.

'Westminster Hall, miss,' he said, mopping his brow. 'Like I said, there's nothing doing just now. I fancy some cases come on at the Guildhall too – but I doubt you'll want to fag all the way over there besides,' he added hopefully.

No, this would do very well: here was sufficient dingy loftiness, and gloomy grandeur, to impress her mind: she could picture the arched and echoing interior, could even summon the musty smell of dreadful authority. In Devonshire the petty sessions and assizes had seemed commonplace bucolic affairs, like market-days, and her father used to grumble about the amount of drinking and idle gathering they engendered. Here, all was different: there appeared something terribly appropriate in the way this ancient bastion of the law stood flanked by the greatest edifices of government and religion. Here was power that there was no evading: here no allowances would be made, and the voice that spoke of good intentions and the heart's innocence must be rendered a pitiful whisper.

'Now, when the sessions are on, that's different,' the driver said, seeming to find disappointment in her frozen silence. 'We'd be carriages wheel to wheel then. Why, there's no show like it.'

She nodded: she had already pictured the spectacle – the crowded galleries, the gleaming rail of the witness-box, the silks and wigs; and she had placed Valentine and herself in the midst of it.

'Thank you for bringing me,' she said. 'Let us go home now.'

The vision was confronted; and she quailed at it sufficiently to make redundant the other sight she had readied herself to go and see – the debtor's prison. But her task now was to balance it against the other vision that she had been entertaining ever since Francis Lynley's parting words. The image of safety: experimentally and treacherously, she had allowed herself to picture her life now if, by some means, she had forestalled Mary Bowen, and brought herself to accept Pearce Lynley.

Mrs Lynley, mistress of Hythe Place, wife to one of the most respectable landowners in the kingdom, would be beyond the reach of trouble: her fortunes would be so solidly established that even if her brother should involve himself in scandal and ruin she could remain serenely untouched, if she chose. And there would not be voices lacking to say she should so choose: everything rational and sensible pointed to it.

The picture did not attract for more than a moment: swiftly its feeble glow was extinguished by the strength of her true feeling, her loyalty to Valentine, her complete belief that nothing could excuse such a cold, worldly match; still, she was disgusted with herself for the indulgence of that moment, and was glad that it was gone. Yes, even the shadow of Westminster Hall was a healthier place in which to move. But the resonance of that word *safe* was not quite ended. She thought there could be beauty in it, not mere prudence – if it encompassed warmth and truth of affection, the union of minds and hearts. There – there was something to be reached for; and hastily wiping her itching eyes as the carriage brought her back to Hill Street and to Valentine, she was grateful to have been given a glimpse of it, even if it seemed unlikely to be realised in the doubtful future that awaited them.

Chapter XX

At Hill Street Louisa found no news; and it was with renewed heaviness of heart that she realised some child-like part of her had been hoping for it – that she might somehow find Valentine and Mr Tresilian turning to her with lifted brows, inviting her smiling to a seat, and explaining that some accommodation – she hardly knew what – had been reached. Instead there was Valentine mute and pale, hands in pockets, dully shaking his head at her look; and the Speddings still full of the comfortable novelty of Mr Lynley's surprising engagement.

In the course of the long evening she found herself reviewing her own clandestine attempts at a solution to their predicament – and reviewing them, for the first time, with misgivings. Both Lady Harriet and Colonel Eversholt, in their different ways, had lent an ear to her persuasions, and so she had convinced herself that they might do good, or at least no harm; but now a dubious voice spoke up, and demanded to know how she could be sure that what she had done was not mere dangerous meddling. There was, after all, so much that was unknown to her in their situation: with Colonel

Eversholt she had only a very limited acquaintance; and it occurred to her on looking back that Lady Harriet, despite her having been a guest at Pennacombe, had never stepped across that threshold which makes a person truly known; and that even in their last interview she had felt herself somehow at one remove from Lady Harriet's thoughts and feelings, as if they were being expressed on a stage. If further evidence were needed, that she was not wholly easy with her own intervention, it surely lay in the fact that she had kept it secret – not so much from Valentine, who was too tenderly involved to judge it dispassionately, but from Mr Tresilian.

The suspicion thus roused that she might not have helped their situation, and even that she might have made it worse, was a bleak one with which to end the evening: the image of Mr Tresilian frowning over it completed the gloom with which she retired to bed, and which she had little expectation could be lifted by the coming of the brightest morning.

Bright it was: but it was with the lowest spirits, which she saw reflected in Valentine's hollow looks, that Louisa came down to breakfast. – Yet it was not, at least, to be a blank day. There was news. Just after breakfast the maid brought in the post; and Valentine's face as he saw the handwriting on the cover of the letter was enough to reveal to Louisa who it was from. Muttering an excuse to Mrs Spedding he started upstairs, and as soon as she decently could Louisa, struggling to conceal her agitation, followed him.

She found him sitting in his room, blinking like a man just woken abruptly from sleep, the letter on the floor before him.

'Look,' was all he could say.

Louisa took up the letter: at first the trembling in her hand made it dance before her eyes.

To Valentine Carnell, Esq.

Sir,

I tender you this communication, in the earnest hope and expectation that it will be the last I am ever required to make. After scrupulous consideration, and weighing the demands of honour against the claims of clemency and forbearance, both imperative upon the conduct of a gentleman, I have come to a decision regarding the recourse to a suit at law, namely that of criminal conversation, to which I alluded in my last, as the only hope of redressing the injury to my reputation inflicted by your apparent intimacy with my wife. My decision, founded on the grounds mentioned above, is not to proceed with the suit. – This is not to be interpreted as any vindication of your conduct: but so excessive is the publicity attaching to all parties in such a suit in these times that a gentleman can hardly contemplate it with equanimity; and taken all in all, I prefer to rest, sir, upon the private satisfaction of your assurance that all intercourse with Lady Harriet has ended, and that this estrangement will remain complete and lasting. This is the final word I expect to pen, on a subject extremely distressing to the feelings, and which I shall be very happy to consider for ever closed.

I remain yours &c

HENRY EVERSHOLT.

Louisa's first reaction was that it could not be: that such a longed-for turn of events, such a liberation from the oppression of doom under which they had been living, must be the result of a mistake – of wishful thinking, of a dream; and she had to re-read the letter several times before she could be convinced of the blissful truth. Only then could she shout her delight and embrace Valentine, who held her stiffly, as if he still doubted that he was awake.

'I have not misread it, Louisa – have I? He is giving the crim-con suit over?'

'That is what he says. There it is, in writing. Oh! Valentine, is it not beyond anything? I am so happy for you – such relief – I feel my legs are going to give way, or else begin dancing. Oh – keep that letter safe. We must send to Mr Tresilian – he will want it filed with the lawyer, or something. He will be delighted too – who could not be? Who would ever have supposed that Colonel Eversholt could bestow such happiness?'

Valentine's smile was unsteady. 'What can have made him change, do you suppose?'

She had her ideas about that; but they were to be saved for her own private satisfaction. 'I hardly know. Perhaps his friends have warned him against it, doubting its success. Probably he has been doing as you have – taking legal advice; and there he may well have heard unpromising things, especially about the costs he may be liable to. Perhaps he has simply seen sense. For my part I don't much care – as long as you are safe.'

She hugged him again. He still seemed half stunned; but he agreed that Mr Tresilian, who had laboured so hard on their behalf, should be told the glad news at once. They took a hackney to Lombard Street, and sent up a note for him to come out to them, mindful of preserving secrecy from Kate and Miss Rose; but he came hurrying out to tell them the ladies were gone shopping, and to invite them in.

'You say good news,' he said breathlessly. 'Am I wrong to hope—?'

'No, you are not wrong,' Louisa said, and checked herself in the strong, unforeseen impulse to embrace him too: that would never do.

In his parlour Mr Tresilian read the letter attentively, while Louisa could hardly keep still, and Valentine gazed mutely out of the window, as if seeing the world for the first time.

'Well,' Mr Tresilian said at last, blowing out a great breath. 'Thank heaven. Something has made him see sense.'

'Exactly what I said,' cried Louisa. 'The costs, perhaps, the risk – even the damage to his own reputation.'

'Certainly I do not think it is his better nature,' Mr Tresilian said. 'As you say, prudence may at last have been the motive.' His eye fell on Valentine. 'Mind, there is nothing to prevent him threatening such an action again: it would make him look a fool, but he could do it – if these conditions are not met.'

'Ah, yes,' Valentine said, his voice muffled by the glass, 'those conditions.'

'Which, of course, are conditions your own good sense

has already recommended to you,' Mr Tresilian went on. 'We have known from the beginning that that *must* be the case.'

'To be sure.' Valentine turned. 'It is a victory – and, like most victories, has a little hollow taste about it. No, no,' he added quickly, at Mr Tresilian's look, 'I am thankful, most heartily thankful, believe me. I am sensible that I have been saved from a dreadful prospect – all the more dreadful in that I did nothing wrong to deserve it.'

Mr Tresilian's face remained thoughtful; but after a moment he shrugged and went to the decanter, saying lightly: 'Well, I dare say none of us gets what we deserve, for good or ill. I shall not prate of learning lessons: let us instead simply celebrate your delivery. It is rather early, but we can pretend the sun is over the yard-arm.'

'Now I know you are happy,' Louisa said, joining him, 'because you are using nautical expressions.'

'Oh, stow it and drink your grog,' he said, handing her a glass.

'Truly, though – I understand your caution, but – there is nothing to fear now, is there?'

Mr Tresilian raised his glass gently to hers, with one of his rare, bright smiles. 'There is nothing to fear.'

In such an elevation of spirits as now seized her, nothing could come amiss. After Mr Tresilian had talked of informing their lawyer of the news, and Valentine, drinking deep, had said little, Kate and Miss Rose returned. Louisa had never been so glad to see Kate's gentle face: Miss Rose, she thought, was a well-meaning woman in her way; and she looked over and admired their purchases with an enthusiasm that set Kate glancing a little anxiously at the decanter.

On their return to Hill Street, she remained exultant; but she took some time before nuncheon to be alone, and indulge in a little prayer of thankfulness. – Whether after all it was her own persuasions, joined perhaps with those she had implored Lady Harriet to make, which had operated on Colonel Eversholt to this most felicitous result, she could not tell; and she would not tempt Fate by any crowing satisfaction. Other influences there must have been, including those she had suggested to Valentine and Mr Tresilian; but she had noted that phrase in the letter – *your apparent intimacy* – with its suggestion of an interpretation of Valentine's conduct that could only have come from her; and so, just perhaps, hers had been the grain that tipped the balance. To joy and relief was added the warm hope that she had not failed her brother; and that she was much more equipped to deal with the great world than anyone, from her father to Mr Lynley, had ever given her the credit of believing.

A shadow – a slight shadow – remained. Valentine began to resemble himself a little more, during the course of the next couple of days: he talked freely, paid attention to his dress, and took an interest in those small matters of life that had been swallowed up in the threat to his future. He had promised faithfully to abjure the society of Lady Harriet: he remained fully sensible that there was no alternative, and that his association with her had brought him close to ruin, and Louisa was certain the promise was kept. But sometimes he gave way to downcast looks, to sighs, and to speculations on how Lady Harriet was faring: he would ask Sophie if she had seen her friend about, and what were her looks; and altogether revealed that he was not in a way to forgetting her. It made Louisa a little impatient – but impatience did not crowd out understanding; and she was above all concerned that Mr Tresilian should not be hard on him. These little lamentations Mr Tresilian heard with a barely concealed disgust; and once he growled that if he heard that woman's name once more, he would imitate Miss Rose's example and drop himself off a cliff.

'He is not unthankful, believe me,' Louisa urged him at last. 'He knows the great reprieve he has had – knows I am sure that his involvement with her was ill-judged. But the feelings are not so easily or so soon to be commanded. They are like – well, they are like trailing plants, profuse and untidy.'

'Pruning-scissors are the answer to that,' Mr Tresilian said, with a grim mime. Louisa smiled; but Mr Tresilian was unsoftened: and she began to feel that the caution, the silent watchfulness that he continued to exercise after the first burst of relief was excessive. There seemed about him a new reserve – a deepening of abstraction: several times, when calling, he appeared on the brink of saying something, either to Valentine, or to herself, which he then relented of, and buried in his breast. Louisa felt it was a little hard that the heart should always be on sentry-go; and when she mentioned that the Speddings had an invitation to a masquerade ball next week, and she hoped to go too, his response made her a little irritable in return.

'Are you now? I should have thought— Well, never mind.'

'What should you have thought, Mr Tresilian? Surely there are no perils here. This is nothing to do with – that other matter. That is all settled—'

'Yes, let us hope so. Indeed, I wish everyone would see it so, and draw the appropriate conclusions.'

She hesitated. 'But you said – did you not – that there was nothing further to be feared from that quarter – from the colonel?'

'I do not fear anything but the consequences of unbridled folly. Those have been averted once. No one in his right senses steers back into a storm,' he said coolly, walking away.

She wondered if he meant a reproach to her, for taking up engagements so soon after the dizzying reversals of menace and release; but other than adopting a hair-shirt and throwing ashes on herself, she did not know what he expected her to do. She was every moment grateful for the removal of that terrible threat; and in that spirit was inclined to value every pleasure, and relish every experience. Caution: it was Mr Tresilian's strength but also, she felt, his weakness – deriving perhaps from his early marriage. She wondered, too, if he were a little out of sorts from being no longer useful.

Yet his words did not go unheeded. The precariousness of their security had certainly been revealed to them by this late imbroglio: and whilst their escape was a matter for celebration, it must surely prompt reflection also. A reminder, and an occasion for a soberer mood, came in the shape of a caller at Hill Street, an earnest gentleman much involved with an association for the relief of debtors. Afterwards Tom and Sophie groaned that he was the most shocking bore; but the memory of Westminster Hall, and the sensation of being dwarfed in its shadow, were sufficiently strong for Louisa to send him a banker's draft in donation, and to make the equally important transaction of counting her blessings.

As for the masquerade, she remained in two minds. She wondered if Lieutenant Lynley were going: then interrogated herself as to why that should make a difference. If Valentine wished to go, she thought, that might decide it; for she wished them to be together as much as possible, as they had been before the episode of the Eversholts. But they, alas, remained his one theme. She tried to divert his thoughts to other channels; but she feared that while his head told him that he must consider the welfare of Lady Harriet as nothing to do with him, his heart said otherwise; and that the unhappiness of infatuation would considerably outlast the elation of his escape.

Though Valentine continued to solicit intelligence of Lady Harriet from Sophie, it was with little result; for Sophie, while temperamentally inclined to divulge any information that came her way, admitted that though she was not absolutely *dropped* as a friend, she heard little of her nowadays, and saw less. She was all the more eager, then, to share a piece of news that must excite interest; and fairly burst upon Louisa and Valentine with it, as they sat by the open drawing-room windows trying to catch a little breeze in the stifling noon.

'What a pair you look! But *I* have something that will revive you. And is it not curious, by the by, that I never suffer from the heat? Tom says it is because I am such a wisp of a thing, and that if we have a summer storm I must be careful not to perish in it, like a mayfly. Well, and what do you suppose is the news? Will it be believed that poor Lady Harriet is actually reconciled with the colonel?'

Valentine started up. 'Reconciled – what do you mean? That is surely impossible. You mean they have come to some accommodation – some agreement to a legal separation—'

'As for the *accommodation*, that is most definitely under one roof,' said Sophie, with her most impish look. 'I have it on the strongest authority – an intimate of both Lady Harriet and the colonel, from his time at the Palace. They are properly reconciled, and vow to place past misunderstandings behind them, and live henceforth peaceably as man and wife; and as they have both been in indifferent health, they have left broiling London behind them, and taken a house at Hampstead – a very pretty house, it seems, right on the salubrious heights. Well! you know me – the last thing I am is credulous: I must be fully satisfied of proofs before I catch at a tale; and so I went to Jermyn Street, very hardily, and rang the bell. And it is assuredly so: the faro-house is all shut up, except for a servant to mind it; but Harriet had left me a sweet little note – though very short – wishing me well, and saying that she and her husband were gone into a country retirement, and did not anticipate an early return to town. Is it not amazing? I shall not refer to knocking me down with a feather, for Tom would no doubt say *that* is easily enough achieved at any time. How lucky you are, Louisa, not to have a brother who is forever saying disobliging things about you.'

Louisa had remarked with alarm the rapid changes in Valentine's expression throughout this narration; and felt that she had better say something, for Sophie was cheerfully awaiting a response. Sophie could hardly have been quite unaware of Valentine's inclination towards her friend; but she lived so thoroughly in a world of flirtation, of takings and likings, all conducted at the most superficial level, that she had placed it there most comfortably, and did not suspect she touched any dangerous depths.

'You are sure there is no misunderstanding?' Louisa said, trying to sound easy and unconcerned. 'After all, there is such a deal of gossip about the Eversholts generally, and things can become so garbled—'

'Just as *I* thought, until I had her note,' Sophie said, 'but that leaves no doubt of it. I have been puzzling over it exceedingly; and can only conclude that it is as it appears – love has overcome all that division can do. For, you know, I never felt that Harriet's heart was quite closed against him, despite all his iniquities: I fear we women are sad geese in that way.'

'But what can have caused the change?' Louisa murmured, as Valentine snapped to his feet and began pacing the room.

'It may be that the colonel has promised a thorough reformation – as he has done before, to be sure,' said Sophie. 'Only this time he has carried conviction. Perhaps he has come to a proper appreciation of what he has lost; after all, there are many men who would consider that in Harriet they possessed the dearest treasure. And perhaps he really *does* intend a change for the better. I should like to think that it can happen, you know – that the worst rogue can be reformed. We mortals should all like to be given the benefit of the doubt. I sound quite holy today, don't I? I did pass St Martin's church on my way home, and very nearly went in, or thought about it anyhow, which may account for it.'

Valentine left the room; and Louisa, concealing her own agitation, stayed talking with Sophie as long as she was able, gleaning nothing more than these bare facts of the Eversholts' taking a house at Hampstead, together with a general opinion that Lady Harriet's faro-bank must have been exceptionally profitable for them to afford it – before at last seeking her brother alone.

She found him, to her perturbation, seated at the writing-desk: the pen was mended, but the sheet of paper before him was as blank and white as his expression. She put her hand on his shoulder. 'Town tattle,' she said quickly. 'No one knows better than us how to disregard it—'

'No.' He patted her hand, with a brief tender smile. 'Bless you, Louisa, you do it very well, but you know that's not true. They are certainly gone together; and the question I must answer, or go mad, is why.'

'It is a question— Oh, Valentine, after all that has happened, it is a question that should not concern you.'

'It is a question I must answer or go stark mad, so there we are,' he said, avoiding her eyes. 'For God's sake, she left that man – she exposed herself to all the indignity and difficulty of the unsupported wife, because she could not bear his treatment of her, of which, from our late intimacy, our late friendship, I know more than you may suppose. What could make her return to him now? It is incredible – intolerable.'

'Whatever her reasons – and I do not deny that I greatly wonder at it myself – still it is not for us to enquire into them. Above all, not for you, Valentine.'

He shook his head, and scored deep lines across the letter-paper. 'I had thought you would understand me, Louisa. You always did before.'

There was a wound in this, which she would have been more able to feel if anxiety had not taken the first place – anxiety that he would do something rash, which might overturn all that had been achieved. Her thoughts flew to Mr Tresilian: – but he, she was afraid, would not be forbearing, and she must trust to her gentler persuasions.

'You knew her, certainly, very well, and had a keen sympathy for all her distresses,' she said. 'But we must consider – we cannot, and should not know all the circumstances, surrounding so private a thing as a marriage; and between man and wife there may be many complexities of feeling, which it is beyond us to penetrate.'

'I speak of simplicities of feeling. The simple disbelief and abhorrence this must arouse in all but the most jaded and cynical heart. She could not do it of her own free will, Louisa. There must have been some form of coercion – some overwhelming pressure: I cannot conceive what, but I do not doubt that that man would consider nothing beneath him, no lie or trick or subterfuge, in the pursuit of his will.' Valentine tore the page across and sprang to his feet. 'I must know – I cannot rest until I know the truth of it. It is no manner of use writing: he will be sure to supervise her correspondence.'

'What are you going to do?'

'Ride out to Hampstead, of course. Seek an interview.'

'Valentine, this is madness. Have you forgotten the terrible threat that was but lately hanging over you? Do you not see that if you go after them now they are reconciled, and seek to thrust yourself upon them, you will be reawakening those worst suspicions in the colonel's mind, with still greater force? I beg you, Valentine, consider your future: consider us.'

Her appeal was not wholly without its effect; his lips quivered – but still he shook his head, and persisted: 'It cannot be as it appears. Sophie must have it wrong. It may well be that they are both at Hampstead: many people are repairing there for the air just now. They may even have ended up in the same large house-party, by unlucky management. Aye, now that seems more likely. Let me only ride out there – I undertake to speak to neither of them, only to ask around, to discover the true facts – and I shall be contented.'

Louisa doubted that; and she thought his whole plan folly – but seeing that he would not be diverted from it, and that he might pursue it independently of her once her back was turned, she proposed a compromise. If he really insisted on going to Hampstead, she must go with him: hers would be the enquiries, and she would take one of Mrs Spedding's cards with her, for greater disguise. Beyond that she could not look: she deeply regretted indulging him even this far, but saw no help for it.

As for her own feeling about the Eversholts, she would very willingly have never thought about them again; but being brought to it, her suspicion was that her own intervention, however indirectly, had brought them together. She had urged Lady Harriet to a meeting, in which the innocence of her relations with Valentine was to be canvassed: she had impressed that same innocence on Colonel Eversholt, perhaps with something like success: feelings must have been discussed between them, misunderstandings perhaps cleared away, and a new start possibly appeared to them in the aftermath. Such had never been her intention: all her aim had been to save Valentine; and if this reconciliation had been an additional consequence, then very well. – She saw in it no matter for praise or blame, or responsibility: they were, as Mr Tresilian would say, a grown man and woman.

Louisa was no rider; and once Valentine, with some reluctance, had acceded to her going with him, he proposed the hire of a post-chaise, and hurried her to the livery-stables at Red Lion Yard. The chaise was procured with fortunate despatch: but every delay was agony to him; he could barely keep still while the horses were put into the traces, and once on the road he urged the driver to such a speed as was quite impossible while they were yet in the city streets, and would only sit back once they were past the Camden Town turnpike and struck the open highway.

'We should have asked Sophie for more particulars,' he said suddenly, with a stricken look. 'We only know of this handsome house on the heights – nothing more.'

'We are sure to discover something,' Louisa said. 'Hampstead is a sort of spa, and visitors like the Eversholts will be noticed.'

'That's so. I remember Tom saying he took a cure there, and preferred it to Bath. There will surely be a visitors' book, or something of that kind.'

The air was certainly clear and clean after the heat of the city, and at any other time Louisa would have found it wonderfully refreshing: but the oppression of her spirits was not to be blown away by breezes; and nor could they be lifted by the pleasant sight of the heathery slopes, green woods and water-flashes presented by their approach to Hampstead. The resort was plainly well populated: there were many strollers, invalids in chairs, children bowling hoops – but the two he sought, as Valentine's frantic glance revealed, were not to be seen. Fortunately their coachman knew Hampstead well, and without asking put up at the yard of the Green Man, by Well Walk; and as this appeared a principal inn and hotel of the place, Louisa thought her simplest course was to make enquiries there.

'No, Valentine, I had better do it. Please, stay in the chaise. I shall not be long.'

She was not: nothing could have been easier, she found, than gaining intelligence of distinguished visitors to Hampstead. The housekeeper of the inn, of whom she first made enquiry, was not sure about the colonel, though she could swear to at least one major; but the landlord, bustling her aside, was able quickly to assure Louisa that Colonel and Lady Harriet Eversholt were certainly in residence – had taken Norlees House, above Whitestone Pond, and had been good enough to patronise the Green Man for its stabling; and a gentleman passing through civilly chimed in, to the effect that he knew them well, or rather by sight: that they had tried the waters, and twice been seen in the Great Room.

It was not, then, to be doubted. Louisa hardly knew how to tell Valentine, for fear of his reaction; but at last, rejoining him in the chaise, she chose simply to relay the information, and watch his face.

His lips thinned: but all he said, after a short struggle, was: 'Let us go and look at this Norlees House.'

'You will not present yourself there, Valentine,' she said. 'I will not endure it.'

'No: I only want to see it,' he said, quite mildly. So their coachman sought directions, and presently brought them up a winding road to pull up before the wicket-gate of an elegant white house, more villa than mansion; and with its prettily flowering gardens, espaliers and snug arbours, more lovers' bower than either.

Valentine gazed: said at last, 'I see,' and rapped on the roof, to Louisa's breathless relief, to tell him to drive on.

On the return journey, he was wholly silent until they again reached the Camden Town turnpike, where the groan of the gate seemed to rouse him from the deepest thought. He blinked around him, and said distinctly: 'Well, I know how it is, now. It is altogether sadder than I could have supposed.'

Louisa, taking this for an admission that he had recognised the truth of the Eversholts' reconciliation, and was resigned to it, reached for his hand; but ignoring that, and sitting up with energy, he went on: 'She has done it to save *me*. It is magnificent, and dreadful. Apprised of her husband's intentions for a law-suit that might ruin me, she has sacrificed herself: she has overcome very natural aversion, every consciousness of the wrongs done her, and delivered herself once more to him, so that that blow should not fall on me. Dear God, I can hardly bear to think of it: though if anything can make it tolerable, it is the knowledge that she is all and more than I thought her – a heroine, indeed, in tender selflessness. What pain and humiliation it must have cost her! And how little he deserves her, who can win back his wife by such vicious means! – for I am almost sure that was his intention all along. But she has spared me by not sparing herself. It was a curse that she ever saw me – but no, no, I will not say that: I will never say that.'

Valentine's eyes were feverishly alight: there was no doubting that this explanation he had arrived at, while it disgusted him, also moved him beyond measure. – His bafflement was overcome: Colonel Eversholt was reliably devilish again, and Lady Harriet restored to the angelic. But Louisa was desperately uneasy: she still thought her own estimate of the case more probable; and without disparaging Lady Harriet, she could not conceive of such a worldly woman committing an act of pure self-abnegation. She was afraid that Valentine was deluding himself, and in such high-flown terms as suggested his attachment to Lady Harriet was perilously intact. Wanting to say all this, she found that her tongue would say nothing: fear of some further rashness if she opposed him, perhaps, disabled it; but she suspected, from his uplifted look, that he had just now no ears to hear, and must hope that a more rational mood might possess him, as Hampstead was left further behind.

On arriving at Hill Street, they found Mr Tresilian waiting alone in the drawing-room. He never took any notice of the prescribed hours for calling, turning up whenever he wanted to; and had come when the Speddings were dressing for dinner. He laid down his newspaper with a smile when they entered – but a glance at their faces must have shown him that all was not well.

'Ah, you are looking cheerful, Tresilian,' Valentine remarked. 'Obviously you have not heard the news.' He went to the side-table, poured himself a full glass of wine, drank it, and poured another.

'Not news of a kind to be found in the *Chronicle*, I take it,' Mr Tresilian said, watching him.

'Lady Harriet and Colonel Eversholt are – are no longer separated,' Valentine said. 'They are once more living together as man and wife. In a delightful house in Hampstead, no less. We have just seen it.'

'You have done what?' cried Mr Tresilian; but Louisa, with a calming gesture, interposed.

'From a distance, that is all. We had the news first from Sophie – and it was a little unclear as to detail so we took a ride out there, in order to discover the truth.'

'Yes: the truth. It does not seem greatly to surprise you, Tresilian,' Valentine said. 'Had you already heard of it?'

Mr Tresilian shrugged. 'It was in the wind.'

'And what do you say to it?'

'Nothing. It is no business of mine what they do. It was unfortunately your business, for a time, when the colonel made those threats – but that is over now, as you well know. Let them go their ways, Valentine.'

'The curious thing is, I know you are not unfeeling,' Valentine said, drinking down his second glass of wine, 'and yet you will persist in portraying yourself so. Consider, for a moment, what has happened. Lady Harriet has returned to a husband who has treated her shamefully: returned to a life that must involve her in misery and abasement. That in itself is surely enough to move the hardest heart. But does it not occur to you what her motive must have been?'

'You think she has done it for you,' Mr Tresilian said, with a weary look. 'Is that it? No, no. Leave go of that, Valentine. Very fine I know, but a fiddlestick nonetheless.'

'I begin to wonder if I was wrong to take you into my confidence,' Valentine said bitterly. 'It seems to me we might have mismanaged the whole affair, if *she* had not taken it into her own hands, and effected my rescue at such cost to herself—'

'Valentine, you do not know all,' Louisa burst out, unable to bear it any longer. 'I had never meant you to know this – nor you, Mr Tresilian. But after that first letter came, I – I tried to do something on your behalf, by going privately to see Lady Harriet. Colonel Eversholt also. I did not mean anything underhand, and all I undertook was to plead your cause – and your innocence. I did ask Lady Harriet to approach her husband, simply to urge that innocence, in the hope that face to face he might accept it. And when I saw Colonel Eversholt, I simply spoke what I believed – what I knew to be the truth: that his accusations were groundless; that there was nothing, except perhaps a little heedlessness, to be reproached in your conduct; and begged him to reconsider. I did not think it could do any harm – and I do not know what success I had. But it is there, I suspect, that explanations are to be found: there, perhaps, the path to their reconciliation was opened. I do not know – and I must agree with Mr Tresilian, it is not for us to enquire.'

'Well, I must say you are remarkably cool about it all,' Valentine said, in a pinched voice. 'You have kept this secret from me so well, Louisa, that I must beg leave to wonder whether this is *all* the truth. You persuaded Lady Harriet to meeting her husband: are you quite sure you did not press her further, to do her wifely duty, to throw herself on his mercy? Did you have more of a hand in this than you recognise?'

'Before you abuse your sister,' said Mr Tresilian, in a soft but carrying voice, 'you had better hold your tongue and listen to me. I shall not say this more than once: it was never intended to be told; but plainly you are still so damnably set on your folly that nothing else will shake you from it. – Valentine, you have been taken in. This shabby little plot was hatched between Lady Harriet and Colonel Eversholt, both, to extort money – the money they are always so deplorably short of. I do not know, I cannot tell, at what point they decided you were a fitting mark for the scheme: at some time after you came to town, at any rate, and your attachment to her was made plain. They certainly were separated, as they have been more than once in their rackety marriage; but they were reunited a good while ago.'

'What do you mean?' cried Valentine, turning crimson.

'Just what I say. When Colonel Eversholt threatened a crim-con suit, I made my own enquiries. Cronies, creditors, servants. The brute who kept her faro-house was very happy to talk for gold, and it was plain that Lady Harriet and her husband were often together there; sometimes he would even be sleeping upstairs, while you were laying stakes at her faro-table.'

'But of course this is a fiction,' Valentine said, with a bemused look, 'and I cannot understand why you are making it up.'

'Ask around yourself, then. You will soon be disabused. His creditors had Jermyn Street as his address. Amongst them was a coachmaker at Long Acre, who perfectly remembered Colonel and Lady Harriet Eversholt coming to his workshop three weeks ago, to look over a curricle he was building for them – and to assure him, by the by, that his bill would soon be paid in full.'

Louisa could hardly bring herself to look at Valentine. But Mr Tresilian went on remorselessly.

'It was the sort of evidence that might well discredit his suit, I thought: it might even convince a court that the whole thing was undertaken, as of course it was, as a piece of sheer swindling blackmail. But that still meant a court case, with the shaming publicity we wished to avoid, if possible.' Mr Tresilian's eye lit on Louisa for a moment. 'I thought it would be possible. I understood what they wanted; and so I went to see Colonel Eversholt, presented what I knew, and invited him to settle on terms. He was evasive, he shifted his ground – he is no fool; but at last he realised he had better take what was offered. It was not all he, or rather they, had hoped for from a crim-con suit, but it was a fair result. I did wonder how long it would be before they set up house together again: not long at all, as it turns out. I would expect them to be in society again by the winter – perhaps to fall conveniently out in mid-season. Oh, yes, I would take my oath they have done this before.'

In the whirl of emotions that flung her mind about during Mr Tresilian's account – in the astonishment, the indignation, the anger at herself for her own blindness – Louisa found the strongest was pity: pity for Valentine, caught up through the most ardent and idealised feelings in a scheme so sordid, so humiliating, and so destructive of all he believed. She could not wonder that her brother stood with his arm half raised, as if to ward off the blow of self-knowledge that must come.

'So: as I said, this was never meant to be told, and I am no more happy in telling it than you are in hearing it,' said Mr Tresilian, grimly. 'But my hand was forced; for otherwise you would be descending on Castle Hampstead to rescue your lady from the giant's clutches, and we should be back where we started.'

Valentine's hand went to his wine-glass; but it was as if he lacked even the strength to lift it.

'As for your part,' Mr Tresilian said to Louisa, in a gentler voice, 'it was undertaken in good faith, I am sure, and I'm sorry you were put to the trouble; but you see it can have made no difference, when they were in perfect communication with each other, and all had been arranged between them.'

The sting of knowing she had been made a fool of was little to bear: there were greater things at stake. 'Mr Tresilian, you spoke of settling on terms,' Louisa said. 'What exactly did you mean?'

'Why, paying them off. That was what they had always wanted, in court or out. It was the only way. As they had been careless, the fellow could not bargain too hard. He held out for five thousand: he got three; and I collect he was well satisfied with that, from the promptness with which he wrote you of withdrawing his suit.'

'*You* paid him?' Louisa cried. 'You paid Colonel Eversholt three thousand pounds to—'

'To good effect,' Mr Tresilian rapped out. 'Paid *them*, one should properly say: for the pair are nicely sharing their spoils, as is evidenced by their Hampstead retreat.'

'No,' Valentine said. The wine-glass slipped from his shaking hand and shattered on the floor. 'No, I cannot hear any more of this. You must have taken leave of your senses. Good God, Tresilian, such an unwarrantable interference in my affairs! It is treating me like a child – it is treating me as my father would have treated me, and he had at least the excuse of blood for his overbearing conduct. To go behind my back in this fashion – and with so little delicacy – for in handing over that money, you were as good as saying that Lady Harriet *was* guilty—'

'You blind fool, do you still not see that they *wanted* the appearance of guilt? Or else where was the profit? But of course I knew you would think in that way – of her honour and reputation and all the rest of it – which is why I undertook the business. Now it's done, and there's an end. You fell prey, Valentine, to a pair of plausible adventurers. It is not the first time the crim-con laws have been taken advantage of to such an end. Thank your stars you did not come off worse.'

'Just now, Tresilian, I am not in a way to think of any worse result than this,' Valentine said, in a dull, mechanical voice. He dropped to his knees and began picking up the shards of broken glass.

'Valentine, leave that,' Louisa said, 'you will cut yourself.'

'Already have,' Valentine said, holding up a bloodied finger. 'Not to be trusted, you see: not with anything.' He rose stiffly. 'Of course the sum will be paid back, Tresilian, immediately.'

'As you wish, or not,' Mr Tresilian said, with a shrug. 'Set your finances straight first.'

'That is the last piece of advice I expect ever to hear from you,' Valentine said, bestowing on his old friend the bitterest and coldest look; and with a little patter of blood-drops, walked out of the room and the house.

'Well, well,' Mr Tresilian said, taking out his handkerchief to mop his brow: she thought it momentarily stole to his eyes also. 'That was not what I wanted, believe me. But no matter, he is clear and free; and so all will be well in time. Now you had better dismiss me also, I should think.'

'Why?'

'Because you are loyal to him in all things,' he said gruffly. 'Admirably so. But I had to speak up, when he began turning on you. I could not stand by and see that.'

'Couldn't you?' she said – conscious of being able to answer only very stupidly; but so many responses had been demanded of her, in this bewildering day, that she felt she could scarcely summon an appropriate reaction if the house went on fire.

'All I have done—' Mr Tresilian began again: but just then he heard Tom's foot on the stair; and muttering about being unequal to company, he made his goodbyes, and hurried away.

Chapter XXI

Louisa waited up for Valentine that night, and had long to wait; and when he finally came in, he was rather the worse for wine, and in the company of The Top: who, as far as she could discern through the thickets of slang, had undertaken to see him home safely. She thanked him; but he was still inclined to linger about, chaffing Valentine and uttering his short, empty laugh, and she found his presence the greatest irritant to nerves already sorely tried by the events of the day. She got rid of him at last by assuring him, with some slang invented on the spot, that Valentine would do perfectly well: 'Don't fradge yourself, sir: he is only a little niddle-noddled.'

'To be sure he is!' cried The Top, readily; but he took his leave looking faintly disconcerted, as if entertaining the terrible suspicion that he might not be bang up to the mark, a sure card, and the pinkest bloom of the *ton* after all.

Valentine wanted only to go to bed, and was perhaps in no condition for discussion; but when she mentioned Mr Tresilian, the bleariness left his eyes, and his voice was hard and precise. 'Don't speak of it, Louisa. I have said all there is to say. I shall pay him back; and then there is an end of all communication between us. You must do as you please; but for my part, the breach is complete.'

The morning saw no alteration in him. Any allusion to the subject was met with the same curt response, and the same refusal to pursue it. He went out riding with Tom, and Louisa was left to dwell on the matter alone: to try to make sense of all that had happened, and set in some sort of order her painful perplexity of feeling.

In one respect, the mist of bewilderment had already lifted, and revealed something very clear and sharp. – With the Eversholts, she knew very well how she felt. There was nothing of extenuation, nothing of regret – except the regret that they had ever set eyes on them. Calling them to mind, she experienced only anger and contempt. That she had ever given Lady Harriet the hospitality of their roof was a bitter reflection for her. She did not suspect that her guest had then begun any such plans as had lately borne their corrupt fruit: that must have waited on town, and the quickening of Valentine's fascination; but there must have been in Lady Harriet a disposition to look out for her chances, to use stealthy and subtle means towards her end, which was as detestable as the most flamboyant villainy. That Sophie had never detected the duplicity of her friend's character was unsurprising, given the Spedding tendency to think well of everyone, and to wish to be liked in turn; but it was a pity, Louisa thought now, that that universal goodwill was not tempered by a little firmness of judgement. As for Colonel

Eversholt, the evident smallness of the man scarcely even merited the strength of disdain. All in all, she concluded the couple were well suited – and she only hoped that in the future troubles of their marriage, the real would come to outnumber the invented, and that they would know for themselves all the distress and anxiety that they had been so willing to inflict.

She ardently wished, however, that Valentine could begin to see them in such a light; but he was so devotedly attached to the image of Lady Harriet that he had created that there must be a great tearing and wrenching of self before it could be destroyed. There, she thought, was the true source of his implacable feeling towards Mr Tresilian – for he was the one who had dethroned her, in his brief and crushing narration yesterday. He had presented Valentine with the evidence of his folly, and so Valentine had violently dashed it away: all the more violently, as his pride was touched on every point. It was no wonder that he had invoked the name of his father, in deploring the interference, the high-handedness of Mr Tresilian's paying off the Eversholts. There, the first impulse of her heart had been to agree: had she not accused Mr Tresilian of playing the father to her when he had condemned her conduct with the Lynleys? It was overbearing – belittling: a tacit declaration that one was not fit to handle one's own affairs.

And yet the reflection that followed that first impulse could not allow Mr Tresilian's action to be painted in such simple colours. – If it was interference, it was also generosity

– stupendous generosity. Mr Tresilian was a prosperous man, certainly; but few prosperous men could willingly part with a sum as large as three thousand pounds to relieve the difficulties of a friend – difficulties that, in a part of her heart she could never show Valentine, she must admit to be in some degree self-inflicted. And it was an action he had intended should be secret – never to be rewarded with gratitude or acknowledgement: only the heat of argument, only Valentine's obstinacy had brought it out. Why had he done it? Mr Tresilian was not demonstrative: his friendship for Valentine, which she knew to be deep, ran perhaps deeper than his surface revealed – but still the magnitude of the gesture confounded her.

There was, of course, Kate. It was no use denying that Kate Tresilian had been quietly and fixedly in love with Valentine for a long time; and it might be that Mr Tresilian, believing in Valentine's worth, believing that time would remove those dazzling and excessive sensations that his entry into society had produced, had acted with a view to that longer future, when a steadier character might waken more fully to Kate's qualities, and return her affections. But this was still a good deal to stake on an uncertain train of events; and there seemed in it a ponderous calculation that did not accord with what she knew of Mr Tresilian's character.

No: all was dubiety and confusion; and more than once on that heavy day did she come close to wishing they had never come to London. The supreme thankfulness that they had been preserved from ruin reigned still, but its power was diminished by these unhappy consequences: Valentine unable to reconcile himself to the truth of his association with Lady Harriet, and the painful estrangement from Mr Tresilian. And she could only think of them, wearily: she could not unburden herself with speech. Valentine, when he was home, remained darkly absent, and would not speak to her except on trifling matters; and even if she had been able to confide in her aunt or her cousins, she could not have expected understanding there. Louisa realised, as evening dragged to a close, that the person she had most been accustomed to turn to, when she needed to talk rather than chat or converse, was Mr Tresilian: the very person from whom she was now cut off. Certainly Valentine had said she might do as she liked, in regard to him – but such an awkwardness between the families was not easily overcome. Mr Tresilian plainly supposed that he was not welcome, either to brother or sister, as he did not call that day: nor did the next morning bring him – to a disappointment that Louisa could hardly credit in her own breast; for she hardly knew how she would address him.

Distraction came, in what seemed at first the most promising manner. – They were invited to dine at the Lynleys'. There, surely, in the sharp playfulness, the ripple and prickle of Francis Lynley's company, she would find a relief for overstrung feelings. It was true that there was first the embarrassment of Valentine's declining to go with them, and her anxiety about how he would comport himself in the meantime; and once arrived at Brook Street, she must confront another perplexity. – Pearce Lynley was all cordiality in his welcome, all attentiveness in his hospitality, and all glowing pride in being able to receive as an honoured guest his future bride – for as a matter of propriety, Mary Bowen had removed to another lodging until they should be married. Certainly Mr Lynley would never be an easy host: there remained too much correctness and seriousness in his manner; and she did not suspect there would be an abundance of laughter in the household of the future Mr and Mrs Lynley. Still, Louisa must confront the fact that she had misjudged him. There was more flexibility, more humanity than she had supposed – or than she had wished to suppose. For she saw that he had borne the insuperable handicap of being approved by her father: and no degree of charm and amiability, she realised, could have overcome that. It was a chastening reflection. In perseveringly resisting influence, she had been influenced. – When, she wondered, could one escape it, and begin thinking for oneself?

'Never,' was Lieutenant Lynley's reply, when she put this question to him, in more general terms, at dinner. 'Abandon all hope of that. We are fixed from the cradle.'

'Thank you. You have recommended me to a course of despair.'

'I am glad to have performed the service, and would do it for all the world if I could,' he said, and applied himself to his wine. He looked at his most dark and saturnine; and the few further remarks she elicited from him confirmed that he was in the lowest of spirits, and still wholly preoccupied with the matter of his brother's marriage, which he spoke of in the same withering terms as he had employed at the Pantheon. Louisa was disappointed: it seemed to her, in her own dejected mood, that there was surely self-indulgence in this; and she told herself, given this unsteadiness of temper, this captious yielding to the emotions of the moment, that it was very fortunate she was not in love with him. She was unequal to the task of lifting both his spirits and her own; and resigned his entertainment to Sophie, who was seated on his other side, and who was always quite content to go on being fascinating without any visible result.

The next day began no more propitiously, with Valentine absent from breakfast after another late night, and the Tresilians' manservant bringing over a book that Louisa had lent to Kate. In other circumstances she might have taken no notice of this; but now it was impossible not to see it as a signal of their lasting estrangement: and all it needed now, Louisa thought, as she returned the volume to its place on the shelf in her room, was a call from Mrs Murrow to seal the morning's gloom. Prompt upon that came the knock at the door, followed by Mrs Murrow's complaining voice in the hall; and Louisa had to consult her reflection in her mirror to make sure that she was not absolutely grimacing, before she joined the company downstairs.

'Well, and here's the other one!' was Mrs Murrow's greeting: so unaccommodating even for her, and accompanied by such a baleful stare, that Louisa suspected something out of the common was amiss. 'He didn't make *you* privy to it, I dare say. Or perhaps he did, which makes it even worse.'

'There, my dear friend, I have told you not to agitate yourself over it,' said Mrs Spedding, all smiling placidity. 'And as for Louisa, I do not think she *does* know what we have been talking of, and she must be quite mystified.'

'Oh, let me tell it, Mama, for it is the most delicious thing,' cried Sophie. 'Louisa, will you believe that Valentine has actually made a proposal of marriage to Parthenope Astbury? Is it not capital? Is it not beyond anything marvellous?'

Louisa, supposing some kind of joke, looked from her cousin to her aunt, and then to Mrs Murrow: who seemed to find a world of gloomy satisfaction in her expression, for she resumed: 'Ah, indeed, you might well look so shocked, Miss. It has quite set us all by the ears. My sister has been obliged to take a posset and lie down this morning, for she is not strong: though she is a good deal stronger than me, I must say – and how *I* have borne up I cannot think.'

'You poor thing, I am exceedingly sorry for your trouble,' said Mrs Spedding, 'but it is nothing so very exceptional, you know: Lord, there will be more proposals than that for your dear niece, I'll be bound, before she is settled.'

'So there will: I can hardly bear to think of it,' sighed Mrs Murrow; and then, directing the full force of her sourness at Louisa: 'But proposals, it is to be hoped, for which there has been some preparation – some due attentions paid, some evidence given of a proper attachment: that was how it was in *my* day.'

'It was certainly very sudden – but that is all *we* know, my dear,' Mrs Spedding said. 'It is not as if Miss Astbury and my nephew are quite unacquainted: why, when I had my little musical party, with the lady who performed so brilliantly on the trombone—'

'Harp, Mama,' put in Sophie.

'Was it a harp, dear? I have a strong recollection it was a trombone – but I am sure you are right. Well, on *that* occasion I recall Valentine and Miss Astbury talking together for a good while: and I am sure there must have been others. Louisa, perhaps,' Mrs Spedding said, twinkling, 'could tell us a tale or two if she chose.'

Louisa was still so astonished by this intelligence that she could hardly frame a reply. 'I beg your pardon, Mrs Spedding, I— Do you mean, had I any knowledge of Valentine's intentions? I did not, certainly. But perhaps I am not understanding this aright. You mean that Valentine actually made a proposal in form, to Miss Astbury?'

'Last evening – at Mrs Challender's rout,' said Sophie, eagerly. 'He was very proper, and asked Lady Carr's leave to pay his addresses – and mighty surprised she was, for she had never an inkling that he thought anything of Miss Astbury, and no more did I, nor Tom, and plainly neither did you. Is it not the most famous thing? I can hardly wait to quiz him about it!'

'It was— I collect the proposal was refused,' Louisa said faintly.

'You may be sure of *that*,' said Mrs Murrow. 'And pretty

summarily, you may be sure. My niece, thank heaven, is not the sort of goose to say yes to the first man who asks her: leave alone when it is done with such precipitancy – such a want of decorum. How she is contriving to support her spirits, I cannot think.'

'But, my dear friend, you told me Miss Astbury was in fine fettle, and hardly discomposed by it at all,' smiled Mrs Spedding.

'So she is: but *how* she is, I cannot think; and I am most grievously overset by it all.'

'Well, but you feel things so keenly, my dear,' Mrs Spedding said, patting her hand. 'I do not think we need to look further than your sweet niece's exceptional beauty, and the impressionable heart of my nephew's ardent youth. I can remember being young very well – and some people have been kind enough to say, I hardly seem past the first bloom of youth myself; and these things happen. I hope Miss Astbury, if she cannot be flattered, is at least not put out; and I hope Valentine is not too badly disappointed. I dare say everyone involved will be able to laugh about it, before very long.'

Louisa was grateful for her aunt's emollient character; but she feared it would be long indeed before such an unaccountable incident could be a subject of amusement, at least in her own case. If all had been well with Valentine, this rash proposal to a woman for whom he had shown little admiration would have been thoroughly disconcerting; and knowing his current state of mind, she could not think of it without the deepest perturbation and bafflement. Was it perhaps the wild throw of the disillusioned lover, trying to show he was unwounded and heart-free? But the lover of Lady Harriet he could never be, and no such demonstrations could be expected to have any effect on her. Nor could she imagine him deciding to abandon his romantic temperament, and turning with a shrug to the path of worldliness. – This haste, this suddenness: this indifference to the possibility of appearing abject or absurd: none if it was like him, and all of it alarmed her.

Fortunately the arrival of another caller enforced a change of subject, and furnished a distraction for Mrs Murrow's mind, if such it could be called, in that the caller bore the outlandish name of Mr Smithson, which she must have repeated to her several times before she could overcome her incredulous distaste at it. Still, it seemed to Louisa an intolerable time before the departure of the visitors freed her at last to run upstairs and knock at Valentine's door.

He was up, and dressed, his hair combed: he was sitting by the window, handsome and graceful as ever – but so pale. Even his hands had a papery look.

'I have just seen the Murrow leave,' he said, quite gently, 'so I suppose you know about it.'

'Yes. And I am so very glad the answer was a negative, Valentine. I could not have endured such an icy sister-in-law.' It was the only way she knew how to begin.

'I suppose they are all clacking about it.'

'It would be surprising if they did not. But, then, you

have been clacked about, as you so elegantly put it, a good deal lately. And it will all presently die down, if—'

'If I choose to let it.' He gave an ashen smile. 'We always did understand each other, didn't we? I fear in this, however, I have quite passed your understanding.'

'Certainly I could not believe you in love with Miss Astbury. So I suppose something else was in your mind last evening. Beyond that I cannot go.'

'She took it rather well, in truth. Considering that it was very near a piece of impudence. But I thought – as far as I was thinking anything at all – that it was worth a try: that it was no more rash, for example, than throwing down a stake at a gaming-table.' A little raw colour appeared on his cheekbones. 'Or a faro-bank.'

'But surely no better as a cure for unhappiness.'

'Unhappiness? Well, I suppose that is a sort of term for it. – Louisa, I think you will despise me. Be assured I do so myself, more than you can conceive. I must have money. My bank-balance is horribly inclined to the wrong side of the ledger. Where did it go? You can guess, I am sure.'

With forced calmness she said: 'Lady Harriet's faro-bank. But, Valentine, can it be so much? I thought you did not play deep.'

'That is how one begins: but then small stakes begin to appear very contemptible, and one seeks higher excitements . . . I did not, thank heaven, become quite addicted to it. No, my addiction –' with a flinching look '– lay elsewhere in that house. But, still, the damage was done. I have lost so much that I cannot see any way to get myself clear: that is, to meet my obligations. And so, I thought: try it. Do as others do: have a fling at a rich marriage: what is there to lose? The spirit of mercenary coldness is everywhere, it is universal. Nothing else is expected. Oh, it was ridiculous, to be sure. But I had nothing to fear from a refusal.'

'Valentine, I do not despise you. I am only anxious for you. You say you cannot meet your obligations: do you mean you have large debts?'

'Large, no. If I were to slink home to Devonshire at once, and live quietly and prudently at Pennacombe for the next year, then I should be in no great difficulty. But there is an exception. I can hardly call it a debt: it is more an absolute, unbreakable obligation. And the money for that I cannot realise.'

'Do you mean – do you mean Mr Tresilian? The three thousand pounds?'

She saw him wince at the name. 'That is the sum. Somehow I must get it, soon – it is imperative, Louisa, and if I do not—'

'But, Valentine, consider: this is James Tresilian. I know you are – much at odds with him just now; but in justice, think of the man you know. He will never press you to repay it: he gave it freely, and wished you never to know of it: whatever else you think of him, you cannot suppose this.'

'Justice – aye, you are right to speak of justice,' Valentine said, jumping to his feet and pacing the room. 'Oh, Louisa, Tresilian was right – shamingly right – and the injustice is mine. It is an injustice I can scarcely bear to think of – and that is why I must, must repay him. It cannot restore me to his regard, but it is all I can do to atone. – There. You are thinking, Here is Valentine being capricious again. First he is all obstinacy, now he is all repentance. No, no, you would do well to think it. I know it is how I must appear: it is how I appear to myself, God help me. I should have been fair to him before now: but, of course, I know best, I must have the evidence before my eyes. Well: I have been properly rewarded. I have seen them, Louisa.' With visible exertion he turned to her, and nakedly met her eyes. 'I went out to Hampstead again, yesterday. God knows with what intention. Well, yes, probably to confront them: to hear it from Lady Harriet's lips that it had all been a cruel charade, and – no. I didn't want that, I wanted her to say it was not so, she was blameless, forced to it by her husband: Valentine, forgive me. Something like that. Curious how our folly increases – how we gallop as we near the cliff-edge. Well, it did not come to that. I was most quietly, neatly disabused. It needed no confrontations. While I was gathering my courage, and my fine speeches, to go up to Norlees House, I wandered into the pleasure-garden by Well Walk; and there, among quite a numerous company, were Lady Harriet and the colonel. I was able to observe them very easily, very well. They were looking over the play at the bowling-green: arm in arm: smiling and laughing, and admiring a lucky hit; but above all, most absorbed in each other. At length they strolled on to the tea-house, where there were some seats in the shade, and he handed her to one, and they kissed. And then I came away.'

'Oh, Valentine, I am indeed sorry. Sorry that you should have to see it in that way. – And yet I hope you understand me when I say that I am not sorry also. I am even glad – if it means I can have my brother back.'

'Instead of the foolish, self-deluding coxcomb, eh?' he said, a little savage; but he allowed her to take his hand in hers.

'No: he was always Valentine. Even in his feeling for Lady Harriet – which has brought him to such pain that I dearly hope it may be soon overcome. Not quickly, not overnight: no one could expect that.'

'I fancy Tresilian does – or wishes it,' Valentine said, grimacing. 'But, then, his eyes were opened long before mine. And there was I, convinced that in my feeling for Lady Harriet— Well, I thought, *Here* is something that does not belong to the world. It cannot be ticketed or consigned to the appropriate place. Very well, I confess I was a good way to being in love with her. But it was a love that I knew could not be fulfilled, and in that, you know, there was the most curious kind of beauty . . . And all the time it did belong to the world – in the most grubby, sordid fashion imaginable.'

'I think we all belong to the world, in the end, no matter how we try to rise above it.'

'Is it so? I still wish it were not. But I trust your word. You have been much more sensible than I, in our enterprise of living, Louisa. I admire you. You have not been careless of your heart – left it exposed to the dangers of betrayal and predation. You have always known what you are about.'

She shook her head, faintly smiling. She only hoped it was true: – certainly she could not imagine being confronted with such a terrible revelation of her own blindness as Valentine had been.

'Great heaven, what must Tresilian think of me?' he said fiercely, prowling about again. 'Don't answer it. – You will speak for him, of course, say that his regard is unchanged. Perhaps it is – but surely deep down he must despise me. I think in truth that was why I was so severe on him. Because I could hardly bear to think of losing *his* good opinion, almost above anyone's.' He raised his eyes to her, looking very young. 'The only thing worse would be to lose yours.'

'That will not be. I recall the old Valentine too well: indeed, I think I see him before me now. I fancy the other Valentine's last act was that rather – hasty approach to Miss Astbury. Whatever would you have done if she had accepted?'

'Lord knows. – Well, no: I would have thought, Very well, now I can pay Tresilian back. After that would come the lifetime of unhappiness of a mercenary marriage. At that mad moment I would have accepted the bargain.'

'This debt means so very much to you. Valentine, as I said before, my money is yours. Take it, and pay Mr Tresilian at once, if it will make you easy.'

'No, no. This is letting my folly rebound on you. It would reduce your independence and choice: and were they not the very things we set out to enjoy, when we threw away the fire-screen, that day at Pennacombe? How long ago that seems, and how little it has turned out as we expected . . . ! No, Louisa, bless you but no. I cannot pay Tresilian the debt. But what I can do is approach him: ask him if he will consider an arrangement, a term, perhaps over five years, in which it may be repaid.'

'And be reconciled with him? Oh, Valentine, *that* indeed is what I most wish. It must feel strange, strange and wrong, to be at odds with him: even I feel it: already I miss him most peculiarly, or miss the thought that he will be always there.'

'Well, I don't know. It will not be easy: I confess I am a little stiff-necked – and he may not wish a reconciliation. – But I shall make the attempt. I shall go and see him. That at least will be the action of a sensible man instead of a Bedlamite. And if things can be settled, then – Louisa, do you think we should prepare ourselves to go home?'

She was startled, and for a moment could not speak. The word *home* could not help but touch her heart, especially when uttered by Valentine now, in all the attaching honesty, the frankness and rightness of feeling that she had wished to see restored. Yet a void opened up at the thought of leaving London: a sensation of something missing or unfinished that she could not account for.

'Oh, I know it may seem that I am hurrying to quit the scene of my disgrace,' Valentine said, with a conscious laugh. 'The same thought has occurred to me – but then I tell myself not to give a jot what people think. I do not mean going back to Devonshire in haste, but addressing ourselves to the reality: we never supposed we would be staying with the Speddings for ever; and if I am to retrench, and begin repairing my damaged credit, then it had better be begun soon.'

'Yes. Yes, to be sure we cannot outstay our welcome,' Louisa said. 'And it will be delightful to see Pennacombe again . . . But of course, as you say, we should not make haste. There are all the preparations to be made – and the proper leave-takings.'

Valentine agreed: still she felt him to be more urgent in his desire to begin the preparations than herself; and with the same promptness, he undertook to go at once and call on Mr Tresilian, to make the proposal he had suggested.

'I may come back with a flea in my ear,' he said at the door. 'If so, we must think again.'

She did not think it likely: nor could she suppose for a moment that Mr Tresilian would press for the money; but if by some chance he did, or if Valentine still could not rest under the burden, she meant fully to repay it from her own fortune. It was at her disposal; and she would have given a great deal more for the re-establishment of Valentine's peace, which must include her own – and all of which, she now saw, was more dependent on that amity, openness and warmth that had always existed between them and the Tresilians than she could ever have guessed.

After an hour Valentine returned. He had not been able to see Mr Tresilian for he had gone down to Gravesend to see an old friend in the maritime line, and to look over a brig that was to be sold, and might not be back until tomorrow – though his return *then* was certain, for he had promised to take Kate and Miss Rose to a grand *fête* that was to be held in Hyde Park, to mark the departure of the Allied Sovereigns.

'So Kate told me,' Valentine said, 'and I have no reason to disbelieve her. There was nothing in her reception of me to suggest Tresilian had said anything – anything of that wretched business, or spoken against me to her. That is a great relief.'

This was, in all ways, hopeful: but a clearer view of how matters stood between them must await the morrow; and in the meantime Valentine, still with a shade of melancholy about him, but with an energy that bespoke the return of his spirits, and a more sensible appreciation of his situation – of the good fortune that exceeded the ill – began those preparations of which he had spoken. He wrote to the steward at Pennacombe, enquiring as to the state of the Devonshire roads, and advising him to make the house ready for the family's present return. – Louisa's thoughts insisted on recurring to the Lynley household. With Pearce Lynley she felt she had come to as fair an accommodation as could be expected: she felt that, when they were all back in Devonshire, she would be able to meet him with composure and civility – even, perhaps, with the cordiality of friendship. With Francis, she was conscious of feelings at once more lively and more dubious. There had been something so dissatisfying about their late meetings. She had known he was prone to that hollow, negative mood – she did not reprove it: but to see him continually sunk in it left her feeling . . . not slighted, but somehow undervalued. With her, he had always been animated and generous: she had, she thought, enabled him to be himself; and it seemed perverse in him to be rejecting her influence. If she could only see him again before their departure, and try to restore it: – she hoped she was not being self-conceited in believing that it would be to his benefit.

This was, of course, unless he was deliberately withholding himself from her, in apprehension of where his inclination might lead: unless he was setting a guard on his heart, for fear that it was close to being taken. Absurd, Louisa thought: but, still, it would be better to *know* it was absurd, by demonstration and evidence. Willingly would she have called at Brook Street to seek it – but Sophie and Mrs Spedding, plainly used to her crying off, had gone out without troubling to ask her to accompany them, Tom was involved in the grave and awful business of being barbered, and Valentine was preoccupied. She would not slip out alone: not because of the impropriety but because she simply felt there had been enough hole-in-the-corner doings of late. Let all be openness, directness and truth, she thought – including between Francis Lynley and herself – and she would be content.

Such was the state of her thoughts when she closed her eyes that night: and such when she opened them, to discover that a letter had been pushed under her bedroom door.

Chapter XXII

Louisa's first troubled conjecture – that Valentine had taken some new step which he only dared confide to her in writing – was quickly disposed of. The hand on the envelope was Sophie's. Calmer now, she opened the letter in the expectation of some choice gossip that her cousin could not await breakfast to tell her.

My dear, dear Louisa [it began], *I write in the utmost haste – and have a thousand things to think of – but cannot entirely fix my mind on any of them, until I have taken a moment to acquaint you, my dearest cousin, with what has most happily befallen me. – Louisa, I am running away this night to be married. Is it not prodigious?*

Having read so far, Louisa was seized with such a violent trembling that the letter blurred before her eyes. 'No, no – it can't be—' she burst out aloud: swiftly her mind conjured the image, and recoiled from it. Gone to Gravesend for the night? – Ah, no: Mr Tresilian had gone with Sophie: she had completed her conquest, and he had plunged himself into that terrible error, of which her heart had been misgiving her so long, but which only now presented itself in the full force of alarm, regret and reprehension. With the greatest difficulty did she restrain her shaking hand, sufficient to continue reading the letter.

I can hardly convey how excited and transported I am – I declare I am almost dizzy – and black and blue from the continual pinching of myself to be sure I am awake; but so it is, my dear cousin, and so I know you will find it, when the time comes for you to find an equal happiness. I know you, of all sweet people, will understand why we are going away to marry. Mama is the most indulgent creature alive: still she might fret and worry, as the attachment is so recently formed (as if that could ever count for anything! as if love cares for the calendar!) – and though our families are now well acquainted, the match may *be felt as not the most desirable that could be had. And so rather than put her to the trouble of weighing it and talking of it, we think it best to do it this way. It is presenting her with a* fait accompli *– as I always did when I made the list of dinner-guests for her, and she would look at it and say, 'Yes, those are the very people I wished to invite' – God bless her a thousand times. I have besides a mighty impatient eager spirit – I wonder if you have noticed? – and it is so very thrilling to think of slipping away, and returning as a married woman. Yes, I am romantic – and you I know do not disapprove it. Nor do I fear that you will fault my choice, or fail to wish me happiness. You have been on familiar terms with him yourself: – you will*

recall my teasing you about him, indeed: but you were always so very firm, so quietly collected, in denying any special feeling in that quarter, that I have no anxiety on that score – and feel sure you will be able to meet Francis and me, when we are Mr and Mrs Lynley, with gladness and pleasure – and will be able to call him cousin with all the kindly affection you have ever shown to me – your loving – half-distracted
SOPHIE
P.S. I have written Mama separately. Tom too. He will call me a blockhead.

For some minutes – for a time of which she had no conception – Louisa sat on the edge of her bed, still holding the letter. She did not tremble now. Alarm and dread had given way to a dull, stony astonishment, which did not agitate but deadened her, until she felt it almost physically impossible to move from this spot.

Francis Lynley, and Sophie. There was no struggle to put the pieces of this puzzle together: they came easily to the hand. Sophie admired him – perhaps not more than several other gentlemen; but it would have taken very little return on his part to strengthen her feeling, and plainly that return had been made. Sophie had a comfortable fortune; and so, his object of a rich marriage had been achieved.

It was an object he had talked of laughingly, at first: then, lately, when she had alluded to it, he had disdained it with all apparent seriousness. So, either one of two things must be the truth: either he had attached himself to Sophie because of her money, or he had fallen headlong in love with her. Perhaps some middle ground might be admitted – that he had been drawn by her undeniable personal attractions, and then drawn still closer by her wealth. But what weighed most heavily, in Louisa's mind, was this scheme of running away to be married. Sophie willingly responded to the excitement of it, but Louisa doubted she had originated it. To run away and be married was to forestall objection and prevention: it was to make sure of her.

Well, then, it was so. And if there were anything to dismay or disturb in this event, it must only be that general, mild apprehension felt on behalf of a couple beginning their life on a hasty footing, and with a less than sincere attachment. Sophie was of age, and knew the world: this was no seduction of an innocent heiress. Whatever happened besides, they would not be poor; and Louisa suspected that Sophie's temperament was of that kind most resistant to unhappiness, in which no amount of pains prevent the seeking out of compensatory pleasures.

And after all, as Sophie said in the letter, Louisa had no claim on Francis Lynley, explicit or unacknowledged. She was not in love with him: she had said so; and, as this news most emphatically showed, Francis Lynley was not at all in love with her.

The strange paralysis of limb, will and feeling – if not of thought – persisted; but at last the sounds of voices and commotion downstairs made her force herself upright. She dressed as quickly as she could, and went down to the very temperate, Spedding-like uproar that Sophie's elopement had created.

In the breakfast-room Tom and Mrs Spedding had been comparing their letters, and quizzing the servants; and on Louisa's arrival it must all be gone through again – though to little result. Sophie had left similarly affectionate notes for her mother and brother, with the same announcement: she was going off to marry Lieutenant Lynley. Where or when could not be devised; but it was certain that she, and a fair quantity of her luggage, was gone, and that no one in the household, above or below stairs, had heard her go. A nocturnal escape, for someone of Sophie's sleepless habits and light tread, was not difficult to achieve: a carriage waiting round the corner must be presumed, and indeed the housekeeper had located a stable-boy across the way who could swear to having seen it: though on second thoughts it might have been, he added, with more imagination than helpfulness, a coal-dray, a watchman, or a very large dog.

'Oh, my dear nephew, what a sorry pickle you find us in!' cried Mrs Spedding, when Valentine joined them. 'What a set we are! You will not believe the romantic surprise Sophie has sprung upon us. Really, these children will be the death of me!'

She looked, however, more flustered than truly distressed; and once Valentine had been apprised of the facts, and had expressed his concern for Mrs Spedding's trouble, he sensibly took on the responsibility of ordering breakfast to be laid. Tom, meanwhile, kept on shaking his head, picking up his letter, reading out the words 'Dear Tom', then laying it down and shaking his head again; and at last said, with blushing heaviness: 'Well, the thing above all to be hoped is that this is what it appears to be. That is, they *are* to be married. If Lieutenant Lynley's intentions are not strictly honourable, then – then I shall have some pretty hard words to say to him, trust me. Not that I suspect anything of the kind, you know – for he is a capital fellow: never knew a better. I only wish I had smoked it before: but Sophie's a devilish sly one.'

'That is to be hoped indeed,' Valentine said, 'but pray, Aunt, do not give yourself any unnecessary anxiety. There is surely nothing known of Lieutenant Lynley's character that would suggest a base design. I have never heard anything – and I am sure Louisa has not.'

The episode of the girl at his grandmother's house, in his youth, was naturally in her mind; it evinced the same impulsiveness, the same susceptibility to the urge of the moment: – but still she believed that calculation had driven him, more than passion, in this undertaking. He had everything to gain from marrying Sophie: much to lose, in credit and reputation, from betraying her. 'I have not,' she said. 'But the thing we need to be certain of is where they have gone. Sophie being of age, there is no need for Gretna Green; but unless they have had the foresight to have the banns called in a local church, which seems unlikely, they must surely procure a licence, whether in London or elsewhere.'

'Dear, dear – what a naughty creature she is, putting us

to such trouble!' sighed Mrs Spedding. 'And what she will do for new clothes, I can't think! And then where are they to live? I do not mean they will not be welcome here, to be sure. I have nothing to say against Lieutenant Lynley: he is rather charming, and perfectly well-bred – and as my poor girl is plainly head over heels with him, I am the last person in the world to stand in the way of her happiness. But I do not suppose he is a man of fortune. He is a younger son, after all; and he is stood down from the army. But, then, the Lynleys are a very good family: and intimately known to you, my dears, my Devonshire connections – and so there is much to be said for the match; and I think we must simply forgive Sophie for this confusion she has thrown upon us, and hope for the best.'

Thus Mrs Spedding reasoned herself into tolerable comfort: too fond of her daughter to be indifferent to her welfare, but too averse to unpleasantness even to imagine a threat to it. The discussion went on, rather inconsequentially, though Valentine tried to bring it to some sort of order; and Louisa found that drab petrifaction coming over her again. She felt, in so far as she felt anything, that she wanted to pull the covers over her head and go to sleep for a long time, and then wake to something different: but what the something different might be she could not conceive.

Valentine was just suggesting that they should make some communication to Mr Lynley at Brook Street, when his name was announced. He came in all composure, succinctness and purpose: it was what was wanted, Louisa thought, and she was in some sort glad to see him; though in another she had the greatest difficulty in meeting his eye.

'Mrs Spedding. I must omit formalities. The letters I see before you, and the disorder I observed in the hall, convince me that you know all.'

'Quite so, sir; and I hope you will forgive the disorder, and forgive likewise that my reception of you is not all I could wish,' said Mrs Spedding, glancing doubtfully at her coiffure in the pier-glass. 'We are all in a taking, and I hardly know what is to be done.'

'First, ma'am, let me offer my apologies for the trouble and distress you have been put to. I knew nothing of my brother's intention in this: nor perhaps was I in a position to prevent it; still, I feel a responsibility, as head of the family, and have not stayed a moment longer than was necessary, in putting enquiries in train, before coming to you. Let me state what I know: then we may compare. I last saw Francis yesterday evening, when he complained after dinner of a headache, and retired early. I awoke this morning to the news that his bed had not been slept in, and found a letter addressed to me: short, and containing little besides the information that he had contracted a secret engagement to Miss Spedding, and that they were gone away to be married.'

'Oh, my dear sir, this exactly corresponds with our own case,' cried Mrs Spedding, as if at the discovery of some curious and pleasant coincidence. 'Though Sophie writes me very affectionately – and assures me of the great warmth of her attachment to your brother: which, believe me, I am not at all in doubt of.'

'I see. It is, of course, my hope that – regrettable as the circumstances are – my brother's attachment is of an equal firmness, now that they have acted upon this resolution. It is not that I have any particular reason to doubt it –' his eye seemed about to alight on Louisa's at that '– but I cannot tell: he is not accustomed to speak to me of such things. I have, perhaps, been too little receptive in the past for him to feel that such a confidence would be welcomed. Nevertheless, if I may say this without infringing delicacy, you must feel an anxiety lest the rashness of this act is not the worst of it: lest the intention of marriage be unfulfilled. It has given me the most acute concern; but there is that in his letter in which I find a ground for cautious hopefulness. He alludes to my own coming nuptials, and – to use his own words – promises to beat me for once, and be the first to introduce his bride to our grandmother. I believe I may have mentioned her: Mrs Poulter, a widow of large fortune, residing in Nottinghamshire. Francis has always been the favourite with her –' he coloured, and in that flush, and in the involuntary phrase, Louisa saw much '– that is, a favourite with her – used to her indulgence, and secure in her approval. If they marry, it must be by licence. Mrs Poulter is related to the bishop of the see; and so may be of great assistance to them. Even in other ways. I do not think that my grandmother could receive Francis and his bride without wishing to do something generous for them. So I conclude that everything – both convenience and interest – will take him, take them, to Nottinghamshire.'

'Well, I must say that puts rather a different complexion on it, Mr Lynley,' said Mrs Spedding, dimpling, 'and though my anxieties have not been great, simply because I could not believe evil of anyone bearing your name, still anxieties there were. – And I dare say, from what you have told me, that they might well be married from your grandmother's house: which is a pretty sort of compliment to her. And if she *were* to do something for them, to be sure that would be very agreeable. Sophie has an ample fortune – but I'm sure you will forgive the natural tenderness of the parent, Mr Lynley, when I wonder whether your brother brings anything comparable to the match.'

'Francis has nothing,' Mr Lynley said crisply. 'He had a portion from Mrs Poulter, but that, I assume, is gone. But you may be assured, ma'am, that he will not marry solely on the fortune of Miss Spedding. I have a strong presentiment, as I said, that Mrs Poulter will wish to settle something on him; but I am quite prepared to make up the deficiency myself, without conditions. The happiness, the security of your daughter requires no less.'

Here, indeed, was Mr Lynley acting handsomely: Mrs Spedding plainly felt it, and was all smiles, civility, and relief – seemed indeed in a way to considering Sophie's elopement a thing not to be regretted at all, but to be rejoiced in.

'However,' he went on, 'if you have any disquiet, Mrs

Spedding – any presentiment that my brother's conduct may not be all that the solicitude of a mother could wish – then I shall undertake their pursuit at once. Enquiries have yielded nothing yet, but they may do: and there is my suspicion of Nottinghamshire as their destination to proceed on. I can certainly try to catch up with them, to dissuade them – to stop them, if you wish it. I should say,' he added, and this time he did meet Louisa's eyes, 'that I do not consider myself in a position to control my brother's affairs. But if you wish me to make the attempt, I am ready at once.'

Mrs Spedding hesitated – but not long: as everyone must agree, both parties were of age, and there could be no question of compulsion, if such a pursuit were undertaken. It might even be making them see as criminal what was only thoughtless and headstrong, and driving them to excesses of defiance that had never been their intention. – They must await the result; but Mr Lynley hit upon the happy notion of sending a trusted family servant post-haste up to Nottinghamshire, there to report back by letter immediately what he found at Mrs Poulter's house. This he undertook to commission at once; Tom and Valentine, meanwhile, put their heads together over their knowledge of coaching-inns and livery-stables in the vicinity, in case the hire of a post-chaise for Nottinghamshire might be discovered by enquiry; and Mr Lynley seized the moment to address Louisa apart.

'I have been forced to be brief,' he said, 'and to concentrate on practical matters. But I wished to say to you that I am sorry: deeply sorry, if you have been hurt by my brother's conduct.'

'I . . . hurt, Mr Lynley? Indeed I cannot conceive how. – I am concerned for my aunt, of course: but for myself I do very well, thank you.'

'Here is a turn-about!' Mr Lynley said, eyeing her closely, and with something of a rueful smile, on features she had never considered susceptible to it. 'I talk of my feelings: and you cannot express yours.' He said no more; but he took and pressed her hand with a gentleness that suggested his silence came more from tact than triumph; and some minutes after, having made sure they were unobserved, drew forth a letter from his pocket.

'What is this?'

'He left it for you. If there is anything useful in it, of course you will make it known. Otherwise – well, it is yours.'

He took his leave shortly afterwards; and as soon as an opportunity arose, with Valentine and Tom still deep in coach-roads, and Mrs Spedding in the niceties of a trousseau, she escaped upstairs to tear open the letter from Francis Lynley.

Note, rather. It was very short: though even before she had reached the end of it, Louisa felt that she had done with letters for ever, and never wished to read another word inscribed by human hand.

My dear Miss Carnell –
Sophie says she will be writing you – so you will know all.
Still I cannot refrain from addressing you – in private as 'twere.
Because in you I know I will find comprehension. While
everyone else is clucking, you will be smiling. Now, mark me, I

think very well of Sophie: I mean us to be happy, as far as that means anything. But still – you know the shifts we must be put to in this world. We must do what we can to maintain ourselves. Look at you, at Silver's Hotel: the fellows told me what an unconscionable time you were upstairs with Colonel E. – but then your brother was in that scrape with Lady H., and so you did what had to be done. I admire you for it. We shall remain very good friends, I am sure.

F.L.

Chapter XXIII

It was long – yet it was not long – before Louisa recovered from the blow administered to her by Francis Lynley's note. There was a world of indignation, mortification and disgust to be got through: very horrible it was; but if there had been more substance, there would have been more struggle. The man who could believe this of her, and could say it to her, was not to be rewarded with the attention that even a furious attack on her would merit. – That could be answered: this could only be dismissed. She soon tore the note across, and let it lie on the floor.

Only then began, however, the true anguish. Pearce Lynley had spoken of her not expressing her feelings: the real difficulty lay in defining them. Yet in spite of the stinging and misting and ineffectual wiping of her eyes, Louisa could see very clearly that this was an evasion.

From the moment of finishing Sophie's letter, her feelings had been plain. Vanity: vanity profoundly wounded; and even the cheerful insult she found in Francis Lynley's note had only probed at the same flinching spot. Not so long ago she had been in the piquant position, as she thought, of being an object of regard and fascination for both the Lynley brothers: if she had not known then, she knew now how beguiling she had found this. – The present reversal was complete. Pearce Lynley was to marry a woman with whom, despite her ineligibility, he was much in love: Francis Lynley to marry a woman with whom, she suspected, he was not very much in love, for the sake of her fortune. If her affections had been at all engaged to him, then she must here acknowledge a lucky escape: – here was his true character revealed.

And so, a nonsense to feel herself alone, and no one else alone! It was as much a delusion as Valentine had suffered over Lady Harriet. And perhaps after all she was judging too hastily. Francis Lynley had been the victim of early influences, which had directed him towards this duplicitous course: it could not excuse, but it could explain. With such a prickly consolation, with such an acid balm, did Louisa try to soothe her spirits; and succeeded only in driving them to a greater agitation. In place of the earlier numbness, she was now in thrall to a restlessness so acute that it was torture to sit still. Worse, there was no one to whom she could unburden herself. Valentine had been too absorbed in his own unhappy adventure of the heart to pay much heed to the progress of hers. But on forcing herself at last to return downstairs, she found that remaining here, even in silence, was unendurable – where nothing was to be talked of but Lieutenant Lynley and Sophie. Her one wish was to be out of the house; and at last she was presented with an opportunity.

Mrs Spedding suddenly bethought herself of Mrs Murrow, who would be expecting to see her today. Of course there must be a suspension of her usual engagements; but her dear friend really must, she said, be informed of the reason, or else she would think the worse – as if Mrs Murrow ever thought anything else. If Mrs Spedding wished to pen a little note, Louisa suggested, she would be happy to take it over to Portman Square herself. Her aunt gladly complied; the note was soon written, and the carriage was offered, but Louisa said she would rather walk. Exercise, fierce exercise, only would do; and before leaving, she told Valentine aside that she intended to take a turn about the park on her way back, to clear her head.

Released, she set out, and was at Portman Square almost before she knew it. The footman to whom she handed the note told her the family were at home, but she quickly declined to step in. Mrs Murrow, like a toothache, was a thing in any case to be avoided; but it was Miss Astbury whom she specially did not wish to face today. Indeed, Louisa wanted to see no one: returning, she flinched from the faces she passed in the busy, glaring streets, as if they had been so many burning torches thrust at her. She must shut it all out; exclude everything but the vigorous stride of her legs, and the corresponding activity of her pounding mind.

She had torn up that infernal note from Francis Lynley, but it soon reassembled itself in her thoughts. Could he really have believed that of her? – that she had resorted, with Colonel Eversholt, to the ultimate persuasion? If so, it said much for the tenor of his mind. Either it was fixed in finding the worst, the most discreditable in every situation; or else Francis Lynley, under the raffish scepticism, was actually a prig. Swiftly, and with blinding vividness, did it all pass before her: – her relation with Francis Lynley; begun with a disposition on her part to think well of him, and ill of his brother: pursued with this disposition always uppermost, so that every evidence was twisted to suit it. It might well be that in the beginning he had assessed her as a possible candidate for the advantageous marriage that was to secure him from dependence either on his brother or on his own exertions; but at last, he had found her wanting – in fortune, perhaps, and in reputation. He had certainly known of Valentine's involvement with Lady Harriet – might well have heard of his financial losses, and judged the connection to be imprudent; and then seeing her at Silver's Hotel, had needed nothing more to convince him that Sophie Spedding, who had never been associated with anything more scandalous than flirtation, would better suit his plan. Yes, it made perfect sense; and it was not the least part of the great revision of assumptions being forced upon her to realise that Francis Lynley had consulted his interests, where his brother had consulted his heart.

And Mr Lynley had even warned her against him – spoken of his not being formed for happiness; but, of course, his voice was like her father's, and not to be listened to. With flaming cheeks she recalled the scene of the Astbury ball, and the dance she had so proudly, defiantly, performed with

Francis Lynley. That dance formed a more apt figure for their relation than she had known: her dancing prettily around him, he happy to admire her – but no chance, no possibility that they would ever dance together.

But she was far from fixing all the blame on him. The greater portion must be hers. If she had not supposed herself in love with him, or liable to be so, she should not have thrust herself into such intimacy. It was an intimacy which had bred the assumption that she must always be first in his regard; and its inevitable result, the wounding of her vanity, and this painful revelation of the thoughtless, coquettish part she had played.

Well, no doubt as the news of the elopement spread, she would find herself – having made no secret of her partiality – smirked at and whispered about. But no one could consider her more of a fool than she thought herself. Valentine, if mistakenly, had loved. She had only delighted in power – as Mr Tresilian had said. What *he* would think was a further twist of anguish – though a moment's reflection convinced her that he was the last person in the world to crow over such an unhappy vindication. It was not in his nature: – and he might, besides, be a prey to similar sensations when he discovered that Sophie had made a secret contract, if he was as inclined to her as Louisa suspected. Fortunate for him, though, his perpetual caution, which had held him back from any declaration: she was wrong ever to have deplored it.

Reaching Hyde Park, she found some relief in the open spaces, the more generous air. – Still there were people, strolling, on horseback, in carriages, smiling and chattering: exhibiting all that ordinary indifference, that everyday disposition to be not displeased with life, which strikes like a calculated insult on the mind conscious only of its own suffering. Preparations, besides, were under way for the gala this evening: wooden stands were being put up, with a deal of hammering and sawing: ropes and lanterns were being strung between the innocent trees. It would look very well at night, no doubt, but by day it had a tawdry appearance; and even the grass, already punished by the exceptional gatherings of this exceptional summer, resembled a species of green dust, and gave off no freshness. Valentine had spoken of going home: now she seized on the idea. She summoned the peace of Pennacombe – the stone walls, the rooks calling in the avenue, the familiar groan of the staircase, the wind that sometimes reached them, salt-laced, from the sea at Teignmouth. It did something – but fell short, like a wish for the simplicities of childhood.

Quickly she turned aside; someone was moving towards her across the turf, and she did not wish to see anyone she knew. Then she felt her arm lightly touched, looked round, and saw it was Mr Tresilian: and that was different.

'Valentine said I might find you here,' he said. 'Lord, you look exhausted.'

'Not at all,' she said; but she realised how fatigued she was, and was glad to take his arm. 'Valentine – then you have seen him?'

'Briefly. I called at Hill Street, and found – well, a certain degree of disturbance, as you must know. Your aunt was good enough to tell me what has happened, enjoining me to the strictest confidence – as if it will not be all over town in a day. But Valentine and I managed a few words.' He smiled faintly. 'And we shook hands.'

'Oh, thank heaven.' Here, if anywhere, was some comfort. 'I have been so grieved . . . But are you truly reconciled?'

'For my part, I never wished to be anything else. But I did fear that his hostility would not be quickly overcome. I am glad; though he did mutter something about talking more of it, which I do not quite understand.'

'He means the debt, Mr Tresilian. It is his settled intention to repay it, as soon as possible – it is our intention, indeed. We cannot rest easy until then.'

'Oh, the money, you mean,' he said indifferently. 'No, he seemed more himself – and that was my chief concern.'

'He is,' said Louisa. 'At least, he now recognises the truth. He saw them together, at Hampstead. No, he did not speak to them. He merely saw – and it was all that was needed.'

'Brutal,' sighed Mr Tresilian, after a moment, 'but perhaps the best way – the only way. Well, let them go to blazes together. I do not suppose Valentine will forget quickly, but the pain will go, at last. – My other concern—' He stopped, and looked searchingly into her face. 'Tell me to go and boil my head if you like. But when I heard about young Lynley and Miss Spedding – my thoughts turned at once to what you must be feeling. And so I had to seek you out. Ah – I'm sorry,' he said, as she was silent, 'I had better go and perform that unlikely culinary operation.'

'No, no, I don't mind, I – I only wonder why you should be so concerned. I was greatly surprised, to be sure, and I hope that all turns out well – but it is nothing of any great consequence to *me*.'

'Really? I should be glad to know it. Yet I do not think you would be walking here alone, and fagging yourself half to death, if it affected you so little. I must imperil my head again – and say that I rather suspected you were in love with him.'

'What absurd things you do say,' spluttered Louisa, in great confusion. 'There was never anything in my acquaintance with Lieutenant Lynley to suggest – to suggest—'

'There was a good deal to suggest, to the observant eye.'

'Well, then, as you are so uncivil as to keep badgering me about it,' she said, fighting a ridiculous urge to cry, 'I shall have to say that I was certainly not in love with Francis Lynley, as far as I am aware.'

'Ah. As far as you are aware.'

'Yes, and don't be so provoking, Mr Tresilian. I should certainly hope to *know* if I were in love with someone.'

'I suppose so,' he said softly. 'I do not mean to intrude. I only wish to be assured that you are not hurt.'

There was a gentleness in this that brought the tears even closer; but she was able to suppress them by looking up at his own grave, thoughtful face, and turning her mind to what he must be feeling. 'You have my assurance. And as we are being candid, Mr Tresilian,' she said, 'I must confess to feeling a similar anxiety for you.'

'For *me*?' he said, his whole scalp lifting in surprise.

'I thought – I wondered if you were a little attached to Sophie. Even,' she added, attempting a smile, 'without quite knowing it.'

'Lord. What curious creatures we are, in our assumptions. Well, I confess I was not delighted when I heard the news; I feel she might do a great deal better than *him*. But as for any attachment to Miss Spedding . . .' He shook his head.

'Call it a certain fascination, then. That I am sure was obvious – to the observant eye, as you put it. Indeed, I—' It seemed a time to put aside caution: she made the leap. 'I had a presentiment – if you will forgive me – that she put you in mind of your late wife.'

His glance was keen – but she saw he was not offended. 'You are perceptive,' he said, after a moment. 'There is a resemblance, and it came often to mind. But a difference also. Sophie is naturally gay-spirited, which is why I do not much fear for her, even married to such an unsatisfactory dog as he is like to be. But Maria's was not a happy nature, in truth.'

'Her name was Maria,' said Louisa, wonderingly.

'Why the amazement? You surely did not suppose it to be Frederick.'

She smiled, and felt the strangeness of it on her face, as if it were an entirely new sensation. 'It is just that I do not recall ever knowing her first name. Somehow it makes her more real. I beg your pardon – this is impertinent.'

'Not really. I do not speak of her overmuch. Because—' He paused, took off his hat, made his hair more untidy than before, and continued in a firm voice: 'Well, that is the past. It is the one thing we cannot change.'

'But I remember you saying once, at Pennacombe, that you did not regret it,' she said hesitantly.

'Oh, I do not. Much to the annoyance, no doubt, of my well-wishers.'

'Yes. People are so very pleased to see us fall down that they can barely conceal their disappointment when we get up unhurt. But how cruel my father used to be to you on the subject! I always wondered how you could bear it.'

'I would not have done, if it had been anyone else. But if I had ever answered him back, he might well have banished me from Pennacombe – such, as you well know, was his temper; and that was the one thing I always sought to avoid.'

'Because then you would lose Valentine's friendship – and the ability to look out for him. Yes, I do see it.'

'Not only that,' he said; and then, with an air of turning the subject: 'So, you have been settling for yourself that I was in love with Sophie Spedding.'

'It was only a suspicion that you might be. And it was not conceived in idle curiosity, believe me. More than once of late I – I thought to speak to you of it; even to speak a word of caution. There has been much, in recent events,' she said, colouring, 'to make me know the value of caution.'

'Good – though I hope it will not make you turn to psalms and needlework.'

'No – but Valentine and I have talked of going back to Devonshire. I do not think he will be . . . tempted again by such enticements as the faro-house: still, to be away from the scene, to be in a place where we may be quiet and – well, not lavish in our living, seems eminently sensible.'

'He has lost a good deal of money, I take it.'

'I should not speak of it without his consent, but – it cannot signify, as he wishes most earnestly for your friendship to be renewed, in all its old confidence, and would have no secrets from you. He is rather high and dry, as The Top would say.'

'I thought he must be. Well, as long as he does not put himself in the hands of money-lenders, he will surely get clear, if he does as you say, and tends his garden a while.'

'But, Mr Tresilian, the sum you paid Colonel Eversholt – the great gesture you made – this is what we cannot get over. That is why you must have our assurance that it will be paid, if not immediately. There is Valentine's pride, too: you must consider that.'

'I do: I did, when I made the transaction. But that is not all that lay in the balance.' Mr Tresilian stopped walking, and for a moment seemed absorbed in the study of a crushed dandelion on the gravel at his feet. 'I have the greatest regard and affection for Valentine, believe me. But from the moment Colonel Eversholt threatened his action – all along – I have had a further aim, a further care. Whatever trouble and scandal came must affect not only Valentine, but you. Your name, your liberty, your happiness were at stake; for I knew that you would share every pain of your brother's, even take the greater part upon yourself.' He raised his eyes to hers. 'It was done— Louisa, it was done for you.'

The sun – the sun must be making her so stupid, because she found herself hardly able to understand him. Yet the sky was clouding over: it could not be the sun. 'I thought – no, I thought perhaps you were thinking of Kate, when you—'

'For once I was not. I was thinking of you – as I always think of you, every waking moment. You were not meant to know of it; but it would secure you from all those dangers I saw threatening your content, and that was enough. Or I thought it was enough. But now I cannot help myself. The thought of you being made unhappy over that whelp Lynley was the last spur to – to this. What I have long wanted to say—'

'Will you make room there, sir?' grumbled a fat gentleman wishing to get by.

'Sir, I am trying to declare myself to a lady, and I am exceedingly ill at it, and I would be obliged if you would clear away,' cried Mr Tresilian, in a seaman's voice: the gentleman scuttled.

'Mr Tresilian, you are surely jesting,' Louisa said, with a dizzy feeling about her head, or heart – she could hardly identify her own anatomy. 'I know we are accustomed to speak jokingly, but this—'

'This is something else entirely: yes. I love you, and I must be serious about it: I have loved you for a long time, with a love I thought steadfast and unchangeable; but I was wrong:

it has grown greater and deeper. It is everything I base my life upon.'

She half turned from him: it seemed her mind simply could not accommodate any more surprises, and certainly not such a profound, life-changing one as this; but she turned again, and the terrible pressure of confused feeling found a little angry vent. 'You say it was done for me. That bargain. But you could not surely conceive I was to be bought – that I would accept your – your love out of gratitude for what you had done.'

'You were never meant to know of it,' he said, with a grimly sorrowful look. 'And I know you are not to be bought. But I would do it again – three, or thirty thousand pounds, or everything I possess, yes. Because I would do anything for you.'

The gaze he fixed on her – tender, powerful, and sad – was too much: with a broken word of apology she turned and hurried away from him.

She had been unjust, she knew, in that last remark; but still she struggled to see the situation in any true, clear light. James Tresilian in love with her! – long in love with her, he had said. How could it be so, when she had never any suspicion of it? And why was this so different – so different from her feeling when Pearce Lynley had presented his arrogant suit at Pennacombe, entirely different, too, from any emotion she had experienced in her relation with Francis Lynley? She plunged on, leaving the path, darting between the trees: once again desperate only to be moving, dreading to be still.

All their history passed before her: there was nothing in it to puzzle or agitate; always Mr Tresilian had been there, sturdy, humorous, unimpressible, firm in friendship and solid in sense: always, she saw now, his had been the watchful care, the unobtrusive advice on which she and Valentine had relied. And always he had loved her. Not Sophie – how wide of the mark she had been there was a consideration that might have amused her, if she had not been at such an intolerable pitch of feeling. But she found she was glad of it: Sophie could not have deserved the kind of devotion that it was plainly in his nature to feel – that he felt for her.

Her exertions outdid her will: she was forced to stop, to lean against the trunk of a tree and fetch her breath. It was hard on him, to run away like that, but she could no longer meet those intensely blue eyes without— Well, without what? Impatiently she turned on herself: why must she answer all these infernal questions? And there was another question. And where was he now? Where was Mr Tresilian? Perhaps this day was not real at all. Perhaps she slept still and dreamed: could she remember waking? But, yes, she remembered all too well, there had been Sophie's letter pushed under her door. She looked down at her hands: they were trembling violently, almost as violently as when she had opened that letter. – When she had thought, for an appalling moment, that the one who had committed himself to Sophie was Mr Tresilian.

And there, at last, she saw herself revealed. How wretched, how unbearable she had found that thought! – out of solicitude for him, she had supposed. But solicitude could not have made her tremble like that; and it was not solicitude that was making her tremble like this. There was nothing else for it but to recognise it, with a sensation like a great shout within her, as love.

Where was he? Here. He had pursued her, and was now walking more slowly across the grass towards her, with a shadowed look.

'Oh, Mr Tresilian,' Louisa cried: almost tearful; but, no, she found she was smiling. That was Mr Tresilian: the feeling of smiling. 'Oh, James, you never said.'

He checked himself; gazed: then, with a trembling to equal her own, reached for her hand. 'You know me,' he said. 'Never over-hasty. Why did I never say? Doubt, I suppose: doubt that someone as beautiful and enchanting as you could ever feel for someone like me.'

'You should not speak so. Not the first part, that was very nice – but about yourself.'

'A bad habit. But that was what I started, blunderingly, to say before: how little your father's asperities bothered me. He could say anything he liked about me, as long as I could be there to see you. And so I got into the way of simply being in love with you: finding enough in your smiles, your talk, your very existence to content me. And then you wanted to try your enterprise of living. I did not want to stand in the way of that: though, as you know, I could not long rest without coming to London after you.'

'And I thought it was Sophie.'

'When will we have done with Sophie? Away with her

on a broomstick. It is Louisa, Louisa only, that must be our theme. Why did I not say? Caution. The influence of my marriage, perhaps, after all, cautioning me against venturing my heart; but that was a wrong idea. Influences can always be shaken off. Caution, detestable caution: it has long been my pride, and like most things we are proud of, I have used it too much.'

'I have always considered myself cautious too,' she said, smiling, 'though from the figure I have cut in London, you might well doubt it.'

'No, no; I have admired: when you have walked into a reception-room, and turned every head, I have admired: when the men gathered round you pressing for a dance, I have – well, in truth I have gnashed my teeth somewhat. But in all your loyalty to Valentine, in all that good and generous feeling you never failed to show even when sorely tried, I have admired. – Do you recall that day at Pennacombe when Kate's kitten ran up the tree, and you climbed up to get it?'

'I do. And I rather hurt myself jumping down, though I would not admit it.'

'Hm, I thought you did. Well, there was a lack of caution, if you like: but how I loved it; and how I wished, cautious wretch that I was, that I could catch you in my arms as you came down.'

Louisa looked from his glowing face to the branches above them.

'I could climb into this one, if you like.'

'Let us omit the tree,' he said, and took her in his arms.